THE FURIES

THE FURIES

Two Charlie Parker Novels

John Connolly

EMILY BESTLER BOOKS
—
ATRIA
NEW YORK   LONDON   TORONTO   SYDNEY   NEW DELHI

EMILY BESTLER BOOKS

ATRIA

An Imprint of Simon & Schuster, Inc.
1230 Avenue of the Americas
New York, NY 10020

First Emily Bestler Books/Atria Books hardcover edition September 2022

EMILY BESTLER BOOKS / ATRIA BOOKS and colophon are trademarks of Simon & Schuster, Inc.

For information about special discounts for bulk purchases, please contact Simon & Schuster Special Sales at 1-866-506-1949 or business@simonandschuster.com.

The Simon & Schuster Speakers Bureau can bring authors to your live event. For more information or to book an event, contact the Simon & Schuster Speakers Bureau at 1-866-248-3049 or visit our website at www.simonspeakers.com.

Manufactured in Spain

1   3   5   7   9   10   8   6   4   2

Library of Congress Cataloging-in-Publication Data
Names: Connolly, John, 1968– author.
Title: The furies : two Charlie Parker novels / John Connolly.
Description: First Emily Bestler Books/Atria Books hardcover edition. | New York : Emily Bestler Books/Atria, 2022. | Series: Charlie Parker ; 20 |
Identifiers: LCCN 2022008117 (print) | LCCN 2022008118 (ebook) | ISBN 9781982177003 (hardcover) | ISBN 9781982177027 (ebook)
Subjects: LCGFT: Detective and mystery fiction. | Novels.
Classification: LCC PR6053.O48645 F87 2022 (print) | LCC PR6053.O48645 (ebook) | DDC 823/.914—dc23/eng/20220224
LC record available at https://lccn.loc.gov/2022008117
LC ebook record available at https://lccn.loc.gov/2022008118

ISBN 978-1-9821-7700-3
ISBN 978-1-9821-7702-7 (ebook)

For Jennie, beloved Fury

Furies (Greek Erinyes): in Greco-Roman mythology, the underworld goddesses of vengeance.

THE SISTERS STRANGE

1

A word is worth one coin, silence is worth two.

—Chaim Potok, *The Chosen*

I

Like Noah and his ark, the town of Athens, in Bradford County, Pennsylvania, seemed destined forever to be associated with floods. In 1916, a new steel bridge built across the Susquehanna River was destroyed by flooding. The only human casualty was a local farmer, Abraham Hiltz, who had been on his way to warn his neighbor of the rising waters when he was hit by a train that tossed his body one hundred feet from the tracks, as a bull might brush aside a matador. But the waters were to blame for his death, whatever anyone might have said to the contrary, since old Abraham wouldn't have found himself in such a rush if it hadn't been for the river becoming a torrent.

Ever since, the locals had kept a wary eye on the Susquehanna, and sometimes their worst fears were realized. In September 2011, most of the town had ended up underwater when Tropical Storm Lee caused the river to burst its banks, and it was accepted that the Susquehanna would flood again in the future. But what was a small town of some 3,200 people to do, situated as it was between the Susquehanna and Chemung rivers? It wasn't as though the Historic District could be put on the beds of trucks and moved to higher ground; and anyway, folks liked Athens where it was, and just the way it was. Once a person started running from nature, well, he was unlikely ever to stop, because wherever one went, nature would be waiting. One might as well have tried running from oneself.

Like most small communities, the inhabitants of Athens looked out for one another, although the price to be paid for this was a certain loss of privacy. A person could mind his own business if he chose, but that didn't equate to a shortage of people eager to help him mind it, should the opportunity arise, or being curious about what kind of business it was that he was so keen to hide from view in the first place. Still, some managed to keep their interests concealed, and old Edwin Ellerkamp was among them. He lived in a rangy house to the north of town, a rambling stone place called The Elms, which had been in his family since the mid-1800s. The Ellerkamps made their money on the railroads, before losing most of it in the stock market crash of 1929, and never quite succeeded in finding it again, although Edwin and his older brother, Horace, had managed to restore the Ellerkamp fortunes somewhat through hard work and wise investments. It meant that the Ellerkamps weren't rich by Manhattan standards, or even by Scranton standards, but they were doing fine for themselves compared to the rest of Athens, or even the rest of the Valley, the name given to four contiguous communities in the states of Pennsylvania and New York, of which Athens was one. Edwin and Horace, the last of their line, were able to continue living in The Elms, pay their bills on time, and employ a local woman named Ida Biener to cook and clean for them. This left Edwin and Horace with more time to read, watch daytime soap operas, and collect old coins. The Ellerkamps paid Ida well, too, which ensured her silence and discretion—or a degree of both acceptable to all parties concerned, by Athens standards.

When Horace passed away, not long after the flood of 2011, Ida kept on working for Edwin until her knees began to give out, by which point she had paved the way for her daughter Marie to take her place. The daughter was a virtual facsimile of the mother, right down to the lock on her mouth, because there were far worse ways—and far harder—to make a living in Athens than by cooking and cleaning for an old man who kept his hands to himself and didn't leave too much of a mess after going to the bathroom. Sometimes Marie's own husband didn't seem to know where he was pointing that thing. Why he couldn't just sit when he peed, like a sensible human being, she'd never been able to establish. Lord knows, he took every other opportunity to sit when it was offered, so there appeared to be no comprehensible reason why he couldn't have extended that policy to peeing, too.

Marie had now been working for Edwin Ellerkamp for nigh on a year, and yes, he might have been a bit odd, but who didn't reach eighty without developing a few eccentricities? There was his coin obsession, for a start, and the collection of books on numismatics, history, and obscure religious beliefs that he and his late brother had accumulated over the years, which rivaled in size the holdings of the local Spalding Memorial Library. His dietary requirements were very specific, too, because Edwin was intent on beating the house odds and becoming the first man to live forever, or near enough to it. Nothing unhealthy passed his lips, and he took so many pills each day that it was a wonder there was any room left in his stomach for real food. To his credit, he remained sprightly, and Marie had to concede that his brain was sharper than hers, but his days struck her as joyless, which might have explained why Edwin Ellerkamp was such a grim old man.

No, he was worse than that, Marie had decided: he was poisonous. Her mother had suggested as much to her before she began working for him, even if Marie now felt that Ida had been understating the case. It wasn't anything Edwin did, or said; it was more a negative energy he gave off, one that had tainted the whole house. It lurked in the corners, and shadowed her from room to room in the manner of a malign black cat. On occasion, when she inadvertently disturbed Edwin during his examination of a coin or perusal of a book, she caught an inkling of something in his eyes beyond mere annoyance, like the brief flash of a sharp blade before its owner thinks better of using it and sheaths it once again. And although he bathed regularly, dressed in clean clothes every day, and used some old man's scent each morning, Edwin carried about him a whiff of vinegar.

But a job was a job, and this one paid twice as much as she might have expected to receive elsewhere, and for half the work. Despite these boons, Marie remained glad to leave The Elms at the end of her working day, and sometimes it would take an hour or two for its residual gloom to lift from her. Marie's mother had worked for the Ellerkamps for twenty-five years, even if exposure to them or The Elms hadn't affected her as deeply or immediately as it was agitating her daughter. But then, Ida Biener always did have a way of shutting herself off from unpleasantness, or else she couldn't have remained married to her husband for thirty years, Charles "Chahlee" Biener being a lush, a bigot, and a shitbag of the first order. When he finally passed away, the only reason anyone came to the funeral home, Marie herself included, was to ensure he was actually dead.

Marie was therefore aware of the reality of men more deficient than Edwin Ellerkamp, even as the specifics of why he made her so uneasy continued to elude her, as did the reason for her conviction that he harbored ill will, or even active malevolence, toward the world or some unnamed part of it.

Ever and again, one just knew.

———

MARIE'S DUTIES REQUIRED HER to work from 9 a.m. to 1 p.m. three days a week, 3 to 6 p.m. two days, and from 9 to 11 a.m. on Saturdays, when she prepared Edwin's meals for the weekend and ran any last errands he required. Edwin preferred to have his food freshly cooked each day, and had offered Marie extra money also to work Sunday mornings, but apart from being a good Christian, Marie wanted—needed—at least one day a week away from The Elms. Edwin persisted in muttering some about it, and had even hinted that Ida might care to fill in for her on Sundays, but Marie wasn't about to let him have his way, and her mother's knees weren't going to get better if she returned to domestic labor—or not without being replaced, and Ida Biener wasn't in the market for that kind of surgery, either financially or psychologically.

In addition, Marie noticed that her mother's mood *had* improved since she'd left Edwin Ellerkamp's employ, and Marie had no desire to cause a regression in a woman who was, by nature, prone to melancholy. The alteration in her mother's demeanor also caused Marie to worry about what degree working at The Elms might be altering *her*, like a body slowly being contaminated by constant exposure to harmful radiation. She would give Edwin Ellerkamp only a few more years, she assured herself, before seeking gainful employment elsewhere. By then her children would be older and wouldn't require her to be around so much. And who knew? In a couple of years Edwin, for all his pills, breathing exercises, and nutritional fancies, could well be rotting in the grave. The Elms, and whatever wealth he had accrued in life, including that coin collection, would have to be disposed of, and there was a chance that Ida and Marie might be remembered in his will. They had done more than anyone else to ease the passage of the years, and for all his oddness and underlying distastefulness, Edwin was not entirely without gratitude: Marie had received a generous bonus the previous Christmas, and more often than not Edwin remembered to thank her when she left for the day.

But Marie had to concede that, on this particular cold, damp afternoon in late January, she was in no mood for any of Edwin's nonsense. Her eczema was flaring up, and she had slept fitfully. At least Edwin had never objected to the extra cost of the skin-friendly laundry detergents and cleaning products she purchased for her duties, and had even advised her to try using turmeric, both in supplement form and as a topical cream, which helped with the discomfort. Nevertheless, she didn't think she'd be scrubbing with quite her usual vigor that day, and she wasn't likely to be whistling while she worked, either.

The house was quiet as she let herself in through the front door, Edwin having entrusted her with a key a couple of weeks after she took over from her mother, once he was assured of her probity. Silence was unusual, though; whichever room he occupied, Edwin liked to listen to

WRTI, the classical music station out of Philadelphia, and Marie had, through osmosis, become something of an aficionada, to the extent that she could now identify a range of classical pieces from the first couple of bars. Contrarily, she had failed to reach an accommodation with opera, and wished Edwin would let what was left of his hair down once in a while and listen to music that was a bit more contemporary, stuff with a beat that didn't come from a timpani section, and lyrics sung in a language other than Italian or German.

"Mr. Ellerkamp?" she called. "You awake in there?"

She would have been surprised were he not, Edwin Ellerkamp rarely sleeping beyond 8 a.m., despite, as far as she was aware, never going to bed before one or two in the morning, or so he claimed—and why would he lie? What he did with all this time she could not say, but a significant portion of it, from her observations, must have involved reading about old coins, examining old coins, and finding ways to buy and sell old coins. Many of said coins, which he stored in mahogany cabinets and glass-fronted display cases, couldn't even be held in the hand, because they were kept in sealed individual containers for protection. Marie understood the reasoning, but considered it a shame that they could only be looked at, not handled. She was a tactile person, and everything she loved—her husband, her children, her dog, the little knickknacks on her own shelves—was imprinted with her touch. She couldn't see the point in having something and not being able to caress it with her fingers or her lips.

While coins constituted the main part of Edwin's collection, he also liked ancient crosses, religious icons, and pre-Columbian pottery, some of which Marie found marginally more interesting than coins. But as with most aspects of Edwin's life, Marie did not speak about the contents of the house with others, and even her husband was not aware of the extent of the old man's obsession. If word got out about it, Marie wouldn't have put it past some Valley lowlife to break into The Elms, and even hurt Edwin into the bargain. Marie did not wish to be party to any such theft or suffering.

The most valuable items were kept in a wall safe behind the bookshelves. A section of the shelving was hinged, with a release catch built into one of the supports; apply some foot pressure to the support, and the shelf clicked free. She'd seen Edwin open it once, but she hadn't stayed to observe further for fear he might grow concerned that she was spying on him. If he were to be robbed, she didn't want to give Edwin or the police any grounds for suspecting her of complicity.

Marie closed the front door behind her and listened. Edwin Ellerkamp had still not answered. She sniffed the air. Familiarity with The Elms had attuned her not only to its rhythms but also to its scents, and instantly the air smelled wrong to her, like a toilet that hadn't been flushed fully, its contents allowed to sit for too long. Now she followed the stink with a rising feeling of dread, because she'd encountered a version of it before, back when she had been the one to discover her father's body on the kitchen floor. Her mother had been away, visiting her sister in Lambertville, New Jersey, and Marie had spent the previous night at her best friend Evelyn's. Charlie Biener had died in his pajamas, probably after getting up during the night to hunt for milk—or more likely a beer—in the refrigerator. The massive stroke that felled him also caused him to soil himself, and forever after Marie would associate that odor with death. It was one of the reasons she kept her own bathroom so clean, even if her husband complained that he smelled of lavender for the day should he remain in there for too long.

The stink was coming from the living room, its door slightly ajar.

"Edwin?" she said, worry causing her to lapse into informality.

She pushed the door open, and her coat fell from her hand.

"Oh my God," she said. "Oh my God, oh my God, oh my God . . ."

II

The Great Lost Bear was crowded in the way that only the best bars could sometimes be, as though the gods of drinking and socializing had chosen this of all nights to smile upon it. There was space to move, space to sit, space to speak without being overheard, space to order a drink at the bar, and a mood of good humor prevailed. Even Dave Evans—who habitually tried to be gone before the evening rush descended on this venue that he'd owned for so long—had stayed late, because sometimes the Bear just felt like the place to be.

Beyond the Bear's walls, Portland was changing. Cities were always in the process of transformation, but I didn't like the new Portland as greatly as the old. I wasn't so foolish as to try to deny that it was partly a function of age, a desire to hold on to as much of the best of the past as possible because I knew how much had already been lost. Ultimately, we are all descendants of Lot's wife, unable to resist the urge to gaze back at what we'd been forced to leave behind, but in this case it wasn't the advancing years alone that were contributing to my mood. I saw locals reacting unhappily as more hotels rose along the waterfront, and they read about the opening of restaurants in which they couldn't afford to eat. Cruise ships docked, disgorging blasé passengers who bought T-shirts, nautical souvenirs, and a couple of beers and a lobster roll in some tourist-trap eatery, but who weren't in the market for forty-dollar steaks. Yet someone was eating in those places; it just wasn't me or anyone I knew. It felt at times as though the city was being sold out from under us, and when the process was complete we might, if fortunate, be permitted to press our noses against the glass in order to observe how the other half lived.

But then I could also remember when Portland was less prosperous, and people toiled to make a living amid the decrepit wharfs on Commercial Street and the empty lots off Congress. The poor had always struggled, and would continue to struggle, but now they had to hold down two jobs just to stay afloat, and in bad times they drowned. Some of these thoughts I shared with Dave Evans as we sat in the Bear that night, but it was nothing he hadn't heard before, and from smarter men.

"Strange Maine," said Dave Evans, who was drinking a porter so bitter that some antecedent of it had probably once been offered to Christ on the cross.

"The store, or the whole state?"

"The store. That's the marker, the canary in the coal mine. When that goes, we can raise a cross above the city that was and lock the cemetery gates."

Strange Maine stood at 578 Congress. It sold vinyl records, cassettes, CDs, VHS tapes, DVDs, and used Stephen King books alongside ancient consoles and board games so obscure that even their creators had forgotten them. It had been around since 2003, but felt like a throwback to a more distant era. I had no idea how it stayed in business although I was grateful that it did. Each time I passed, I tried to leave some money in the register. My daughter Sam, who already loved vinyl records, along with virtually any cultural artifact older than she was, thought it one of the coolest places on earth—or in Portland, at least.

"You know how ancient we sound?" I said.

"You started it," said Dave.

"Well, there's a lot about this city that I've begun to miss."

Which was when Raum Buker came into view, and I realized there were some things about the city that I hadn't missed at all.

———

THERE ARE MEN WHO are born into this world blighted, men who are blighted by the world, and men who are intent upon blighting themselves and the world along with them. Raum Buker somehow contrived to be all three in one person, like a toxic, inverted deity. He came from somewhere deep in the County, as Mainers termed Aroostook, the largest region in the state: 7,000 square miles, with 70,000 people to share them, a great many of whom were content not to be able to see their neighbors, and even happier not to see strangers. Raum's father, Sumner, had worked as a cleaner at Loring Air Force Base, where the B-52 Stratofortress bombers were once based, but lost his job for lighting up a cigarette next to a fuel dump. Since Loring's tanks stored nearly ten million gallons of aviation fuel alongside more than 5,000 tons of ordnance, the resulting explosion would have left a crater that could be viewed from space.

Once he'd been shown the door from Loring, Sumner Buker decided that he was temperamentally ill-suited to the strictures of regular employment, and his time would be better spent engaging in low-level criminality, drinking, sleeping with women who were not his wife, and smoking anywhere he damn well pleased. To these lifestyle choices he committed himself with commendable zeal. Sumner hadn't made many wise decisions during his time on earth, but he did choose the perfect woman to be his life partner. Vina Buker also liked drinking and smoking, slept with men who were not her husband, and was once arrested while trying to fill a panel van with canned food and toiletries from the Hannaford in Caribou, at which she happened to be employed. Sumner and Vina took turns occupying cells at the Aroostook County Jail in Houlton, which meant that one of them was always home to neglect their only child, Raum. Inevitably the boy was conveyed into foster care, and shortly thereafter his father fulfilled an enduring ambition by dying in a fire caused by an unattended cigarette, taking his wife with him.

Raum was a sickly youth, but with more brains than both his parents put together, even if that wasn't likely to earn him a mention in the record books. He was placed with a good family down in Millinocket, where he proceeded to do everything in his power to make his foster parents despair of him. This set a pattern for the future, as Raum was shifted from foster home to foster home, each tougher than the last, until finally he ended up in an institution. By then he'd earned a reputation for hitting back hard, but in juvie he learned how to strike first, because he wasn't so sickly anymore. It would be unfair to say that he developed a taste for violence; he was no sadist—that would come later—and was shrewd enough to learn to control his temper, but when he had to use aggression, he did so without hesitation or remorse. He took his knocks in turn, and one particularly brutal altercation with a guard left Raum with bleeding on the brain that came close to killing him. One month after Raum's release, someone entered the guard's property and severed the brakes on his wife's car, resulting in a collision that would leave her walking with the aid of a cane for the rest of her life. Raum didn't forget hurts. It was possible that he even manufactured cause to take offense, just to give himself something at which to lash out.

So it could be said, with some justification, that Raum Buker didn't have the best of starts, but that was true of many who didn't subsequently decide to make the world regret the steady hand of the doctor who had delivered them. Raum became his own worst enemy by election, and resolved by extension to become the worst enemy of a lot of other people, too.

In adulthood Raum was physically imposing, and might even, in dim light, have been regarded as handsome. He was also profoundly dishonest and sexually incontinent, with a malice that, at its worst, was both deep and cruelly imaginative: he had once used a hand plane on a carpenter who owed him money, shaving the skin and upper layers of flesh from the man's buttocks and thighs. The debt was less than a thousand dollars; a man left in pain for the rest of his life, over a three-figure sum. Gradually, like fecal matter flowing down a drain, gravity brought Raum to Portland. He kept company with men whom others avoided, and women who were too foolish, desperate, or worn down by abuse to make better life choices.

Then a curious rumor began to circulate. Raum Buker, according to semi-reliable witnesses, was involved with two sisters, the Stranges. The older Strange, Dolors, lived in South Portland and owned a coffee shop. (Her parents hadn't been much for spelling, and intended to name her Dolores. Regardless, she was destined to end up with a moniker meaning "sorrows," which might have impacted on the subsequent patterns of her existence.)

The younger Strange, Ambar—that defective spelling gene raising its head once again—lived over in Westbrook, where she worked as a dental assistant. Both were unmarried, and by popular agreement Dolors was likely to remain so. She was a forbidding woman at first sight, mouth pinched tight as a miser's purse. Ambar was prettier, but was regarded as lacking her sister's acumen. I was familiar with them only by sight and reputation, and was content to let that be the way of things. Still, the news that the Sisters Strange, as they were known, might be sleeping with Raum Buker was met with a degree of incredulity combined with some small sense of relief, since it meant that only three people instead of six would be made unhappy by the ensuing carnal arrangements.

One story, which might or might not have been true, was that the Sisters Strange were, appropriately enough, estranged, and had not spoken in years. Raum had begun sleeping with Dolors before also— possibly by accident, but probably by design—taking Ambar to his bed. He then continued to alternate between the pair for a number of years, sometimes consorting with one or the other, but often juggling both at the same time. Either each sister was unaware of the other's presence in Raum's life, which was unlikely, or they chose to tolerate the peculiarity of the relationship rather than deprive themselves of their share of Raum's attentions, a circumstance beyond the comprehension of mortal men. This is not to say that these complex liaisons were juggled without conflict, for the police were summoned on more than one occasion to deal with domestic disturbances in Westbrook, South Portland, and at Raum's apartment in Portland's East End. But then, no relationship is ever perfect.

Raum had served time in a variety of houses of correction; like a lot of sharp men and women, he wasn't as sharp as he thought. He eventually ended up doing four years in Maine State for a class C felony assault, elevated from a class D misdemeanor because he had prior convictions for aggravated criminal trespass, criminal threatening, and terrorizing. Upon his release, Raum completed eighteen months of parole before vanishing from the state. Mourning at his departure was confined to those owed money by him, and even they were prepared to swallow their losses in return for his absence. The Sisters Strange were not canvassed for their views. As far as anyone could tell, the siblings continued to lead separate lives, connected only by blood and their respective unions with a man who remained unloved by all but them.

Was there another side to Raum Buker? No man is completely bad, and I'd heard tales of small kindnesses, often rendered by him to those who had fallen further and deeper than the rest: ex-junkies, old whores, aging criminal recidivists. When Raum had money, he shared it with them. If someone was giving them bother, Raum, if he was so disposed, gave bother in return. It might have been that, in these lost souls, Raum saw some glimpse of his own future, and sought to build up goodwill in the karmic bank; yet there was no consistency to his interventions, no apparent logic to the objects of his largesse. In the end, his actions may have been a mystery even to himself.

Now Raum had returned to Portland from his years in the wilderness, and all that could be said for sure was that scant good could come of it.

III

M urders were rare in Athens, Pennsylvania. In fact, serious transgressions were unusual in the town, where the crime rate was less than half the national average, and theft, assault, and property offenses took up most of the Athens PD's time and resources. With that in mind, Beth Ann Robbin, the town's chief of police, sought the assistance of the State Police Bureau of Criminal Investigation just as soon as she glimpsed the state of Edwin Ellerkamp's body, because she knew when she was out of her league. Now Beth Ann and a pair of state police detectives, all suited and booted, were watching as the crime scene investigators prepared for the removal of the remains. The three officers had gone over the room together—looking, examining— before returning to the doorway to permit the body to be taken out.

Edwin remained uncovered on the couch by the fireplace, which meant that Beth Ann's gaze kept being drawn back to his engorged mouth and throat. Some of the coins had spilled onto his chest during his final struggles, but the majority were still inside him. She'd never come across such coinage before, the edges uneven, the markings in some cases barely visible, so old were they. A few were about the size of her thumbnail, and the rest only marginally larger. She pondered how many might have been required to choke the victim to death. It resembled, she reflected blackly, one of those fund-raising drives that the Elks

Lodge came up with at Christmas, where you paid a dollar to guess the number of nickels in a jar. Correctly guess the number of weird coins lodged in old Edwin Ellerkamp and you can take them home with you, once they've been disinfected—oh, and his killer has been found. I mean, let's not get ahead of ourselves here. Beth Ann gave an involuntary snort, and was surprised to feel a tear spurt from the corner of her right eye. Christ, an old man who kept to himself, forced to eat coins until he choked and died . . .

"Valerian," said the more senior of the detectives, whose name was Peter Condell. "I knew it would come to me."

Beth Ann was surprised that Condell hadn't taken retirement by now, because he had his twenty-five, and more. He could have sailed into the sunset with 75 percent of his highest year's salary, which is what Beth Ann would have done in his shoes. Instead, here he was, in a living room that smelled of death, staring at a corpse that was bleeding money from its mouth. Beth Ann wouldn't have said that Condell looked happy, exactly—that would have made him some form of psychopath—but she suspected he wouldn't have wanted to be anywhere else, or doing anything else, at that precise moment. Condell was born to be police.

"Like the herb?" said the other detective. Shirley Gardner was a young Black woman with the kind of perfect skin Beth Ann would have killed for. She was wearing a nicely cut blue trouser suit and comfortable, but polished, flat shoes. Next to her, Condell resembled an unmade bed that had been slept in by bums.

"Like the Roman emperor," Condell said. He didn't sigh or roll his eyes. He corrected Gardner matter-of-factly, and she took no umbrage. She clearly wanted to learn, and Condell had a lot to teach, not only about police work. "A Persian king is reputed to have killed him by feeding him molten gold, although other accounts suggest he flayed Valerian alive."

"Why?" said Beth Ann.

"Why did he kill him," said Condell, "or why might he have forced him to swallow molten gold?"

"Both."

"Well, he died because he lost a battle and was captured, if I remember right. As for the story of the gold, assuming it's true, Valerian tried to buy his freedom, and the king took offense. Whatever the reason, it was a punishment." Condell pointed a finger at Edwin Ellerkamp. "Just like this."

"Not a robbery gone wrong?" said Beth Ann. That had been her first instinct, and she never liked second-guessing herself. When dealing with the local population, her first instinct was usually right, although she was prepared to accept that it might be a bad habit to indulge in more esoteric instances.

"Whoever killed this man didn't come here to steal from him," said Condell. He gestured to the safe and its open door. The contents were disturbed, as though a search had been conducted, but it remained full. "Or if they did, they had a specific object in mind. I don't know a great deal about coins, but his safe contains at least five or six Liberty Head twenty-dollar gold pieces, all from the nineteenth century, and that's not the only gold in there. As for the rest, some of them look very, very old. If they were worth keeping locked away, then they're of value, and if they're of value, they're worth stealing. So why break into a man's house, force him to open his safe—unless it was already open—and then leave gold lying in plain sight after killing him?"

They had spoken with Marie Biener, the woman who discovered the body, but she didn't know enough about Ellerkamp's collection to be able to tell them what, if anything, might be missing from it. Condell and Gardner hadn't yet ruled her out as a possible accomplice, but Beth Ann was certain that they would soon enough. She was familiar with the family, and had been just a couple of years ahead of Marie in high school. The father might have been a louse, but Marie and the rest of the Bieners were good people.

"So it was retribution?" said Gardner.

"Wouldn't you say?" said Condell. "There are simpler ways to kill a man than this."

They heard movement from behind, and turned to see a gurney being maneuvered into the hallway, ready at last to move the body to the Bradford County Medical Examiner's office in Troy. By the following day they'd know just how many coins it had taken to kill Edwin Ellerkamp, but there remained the opportunity to open a discreet book on it. Then again, if anyone ever found out, Beth Ann wouldn't have to worry about the timing of her retirement, because she, and all involved, would be out of a job.

"I don't like to jump to conclusions," said Gardner to Condell. "You taught me that."

They stepped aside to let the ME's staff through, and watched as one of them began bagging the victim's hands and bare feet so that any matter lodged on the skin or under the nails would not be lost. An evidence technician stepped in to store individually the loose coins on the victim's chest and around his lips. After a brief consultation, it was decided to bag the head as well, but not before a cervical collar was put in place to stop it from moving during transportation to Troy, thereby minimizing any disturbance or damage to the contents of the mouth.

"Yeah," said Condell, "jumping to conclusions is bad. But," he added, "I'll bet you a brown bag lunch this is about coins."

"Thank God we have your expertise to guide us," said Beth Ann.

"That's what I'm here for," said Condell. "By the way, care to have a friendly wager on how many coins they find inside him? A dollar a guess."

CHAPTER

IV

Raum Buker stood by the host station and surveyed the crowd in the Great Lost Bear. His glance passed over me before returning, alighting on my face like a bug on a window. We had history, Raum and I. Toward the end of his parole period, during which he'd worked at a local warehouse in order to fulfill one of the conditions of his release, he'd begun falling back into bad habits and worse fellowship. He and a pair of buddies decided to put pressure on older store owners in Portland and South Portland to hire them as assistants or security guards, even if the stores had no need of them. Not that Raum and his boys would have shown up for work anyway, this being the most basic of protection rackets, the type that probably dated back to cavemen, although it was hard to tell whether the likely absence of Raum and his pals represented a worsening of the deal or an improvement on it.

It was Raum's mistake to target a woman named Meda Michaud, who ran a little bakehouse and deli off Western Avenue and played weekly bingo with Mrs. Fulci, beloved mother of the Fulci brothers. The Fulcis were overmuscled and undermedicated ex-cons with hearts, if not of gold, then of premium nickel silver. They were also devoted to their mother, and by extension to anyone their mother liked. Trying to strong-arm Meda Michaud was, in the eyes of the Fulcis, scarcely

less appalling than harassing Mrs. Fulci herself, and they were thus of
a mind to separate Raum Buker's limbs from his torso before feeding
them to his associates until they choked.

But the Fulcis were also familiar with Raum's reputation, which
meant that any confrontation they initiated was destined to escalate.
If the Fulcis killed Raum or simply left him maimed, neither outcome
being beyond the bounds of possibility, they'd have ended up in prison,
although the citizens of the state would have sent muffin baskets at
Christmas as tokens of gratitude. On the other hand, if they didn't put
Raum down, there was a good chance he'd come after the Fulcis or
those close to them, once his broken bones had healed. Even if it took
years, Raum would have found a way to avenge the outrage.

Ultimately, Louis, Angel, and I offered to keep the Fulcis company, and also do most of the explaining to Raum, the Fulcis being
doers rather than talkers. We caught up with Raum and his friends at a
Nason's Corner dump called Sly's, formerly part of the business empire
of Daddy Helms. In my adolescence, Daddy Helms had once hurt and
humiliated me for vandalizing a stained-glass window in one of his
bars. After all these years, the memory of that act of deliberate destruction still shamed me, but I'd been a foolish, angry young man back
then, and a foolish, angry older man for a good deal longer. Daddy
Helms taught me the error of my ways, although he'd done so by causing my friend Clarence Johns to betray me. Clarence had been with me
on the night we took care of Daddy Helms's window, and Daddy's men
had found him first. To save himself, Clarence had implicated me, and I
took the punishment for both of us: stripped naked on a deserted beach
before being covered with fire ants. Even now, I could still recall the
pain and indignity, and had not yet decided which was worse.

I never did find out if Clarence knew what Daddy Helms had
planned for me that night. We didn't talk after, and Clarence was now
with his Maker. But had our roles been reversed, I wouldn't have for-
saken Clarence—not out of any great sense of honor or loyalty, but

because I had too much rage inside me to give Daddy Helms that kind of satisfaction. And there was also this: I used to welcome suffering, and any injury I endured only fed my animosity. By then my father had taken his own life, and cancer had stolen my mother from me. Even Daddy Helms's stained-glass window—an attempt by a man afflicted by ugliness to add some beauty to his world—was an affront to me. If you go seeking ways to bring down hurt upon yourself, life will oblige you, because it has hurt in store for you anyway, but it will happily welcome any assistance you're in the mood to offer. Better, then, not to oblige it any more than necessary. I'd like to have said this was a lesson hard-learned, but that would suggest my education was in the past, whereas it was still ongoing.

Daddy Helms was long dead, his fat rendering in the fires of hell, but Sly's was a fitting monument to him, being dark, dirty, and filled with vermin, both animal and human. The barstools were fixed to the floor with heavy hex bolts, and the booths were covered in the kind of vinyl that didn't hold stains, although the owners had opted for red just to be on the safe side. The neon sign in the window promised HOT FOOD & COLD BEER, but the only source of sustenance was a decrepit pizza oven that smelled of burning insects if one got too close. Legend had it that someone once ate at Sly's, but if so, the body had never been found.

Raum and his boys were standing at the bar just inside the door, which saved us having to get the soles of our shoes all sticky and soiled. We invited the three of them to step outside for a conversation, because politeness costs nothing. When they declined, and much less politely, the Fulcis dragged Raum's buddies out by the hair and ears, while Raum followed under his own steam to preserve his dignity and the symmetry of his features. Nobody intervened, and no one made a move to call the police, who would probably have laughed at the idea that they might be tempted to intervene in a minor dispute at Sly's. Because we wanted to keep it friendly, we let Raum light a cigarette, although Louis knocked it from his mouth before he could take the first drag because there were limits to our tolerance. We then explained the Meda Michaud situation to him, and advised him to re-examine extortion as a source of income. Raum wasn't minded to listen at first, but he paid more attention when Louis put a gun in his mouth. Some people's hearing can be funny that way.

Raum might have contemplated defying the Fulcis, and he might even have contemplated defying me, but he wasn't stupid enough to go up against all five of us, or not with Louis involved. Louis stood out in Portland for all kinds of reasons: tall, Black, well dressed, and gay— not that anyone was asking, or objecting, where the last was concerned. Louis had also done things that Raum Buker hadn't, including, but not limited to, some killing. Raum was suddenly in the presence of an apex predator, and that frightened him. He still didn't like being told what to do, but we didn't care. To guard against any second thoughts he might have entertained after we were gone, we encouraged the Fulcis to haul his buddies around some more by the hair and ears before dumping them in the Fore River to cool off. It marked the end of Raum's fledgling protection racket, and he left the state soon after. I didn't know where he'd gone, and had never asked. As with an ongoing ache that suddenly vanishes, all that's required of one is to be grateful.

But now here was Raum, making the Bear look bad, and nobody wanted that.

"You need a stricter door policy," I told Dave.

"I think we may need to brick up the door entirely," he said.

Which was when the Fulcis, who'd been playing Jenga at a table of their own, spotted Raum.

CHAPTER

V

Certain big men can move very fast when they're riled, which makes them doubly dangerous at close quarters. They possess an innate grace, as though the ghost of a dancer has taken up residence in their bones. Watching them fight is like witnessing a violent ballet, with all the swans lying unconscious when the curtain finally descends.

The Fulci brothers were not those men. Instead they resembled old locomotive engines, in that it took them a while to build up a head of steam, but once they did, it was unwise to get in their way.

The first sign of impending disaster was the sound of Jenga tiles scattering on the Bear's floor, followed by at least one table and any number of chairs. By the time Dave and I were on our feet, Paulie Fulci was already closing in fast on Raum Buker, his brother pounding along not far behind. In retrospect, Dave and I were fortunate that the Fulcis were still accelerating when we reached them, and not yet at full tilt, because we were just able to apply the brakes before they could lay hands on their quarry. Raum saw them coming, and looked like he was seconds away from climbing over the bar to escape, which wouldn't have saved him since the Fulcis would probably just have plowed right through it. I improved my grip on Tony, Dave got another arm around Paulie, and a couple of bartenders displayed a foolhardy level of bravery by positioning themselves between Raum and the Fulcis, like occidental versions of that guy who stood in front of the Chinese tanks in Tiananmen Square.

"The fuck is he doing here?" said Paulie.

The question didn't strike me as being directed at anyone in particular, although it could have been meant for God Himself, an accusation of divine error for failing to erase Raum Buker from the annals. The Fulcis were great believers in God, although God remained conspicuously silent on the subject of the Fulcis' allegiance to Him. As one would.

"Yeah," his brother chimed in, although Tony's inquiry was clearly aimed at Raum, not God, because his version also contained the words "you senior-abusing motherfucker."

A space had cleared around Raum. None of the other customers wanted to be caught up in whatever was unfolding, and no one who knew him was willing to stand alongside him. Men like Raum don't have friends, only associates, and the latter won't take a side unless there's something in it for them—something, that is, other than a beating.

But Raum, being an asshole, didn't know when to keep quiet, or didn't feel the obligation now that he thought the Fulcis were under some semblance of control. He was already shooting his mouth off, and I saw that he'd bought himself some new teeth. They were big and white, and made him look like an advertisement for Chiclets. If he'd known how tenuous was my hold on Paulie Fulci, he'd have been a lot less loquacious. For an instant I was tempted to let Paulie run free, but I didn't want to be responsible for collateral damage to a bartender.

"He's not worth a night in a cell," I told the Fulcis.

"Come on, then," said Raum, "come on," making come-hither gestures with his hands. "You fat fucks," he added, for good measure.

"No, he is worth it," said Tony.

I looked at Raum in his dark, shiny suit, with his backcombed hair and his installment-plan teeth, and thought that Tony might be right, but common sense prevailed.

"Raum," I said, "you need to stop talking. Now."

And miracle of miracles, he did.

VI

Marie Biener sat at her kitchen table, a cup of decaf coffee going cold before her. She'd already spoken with Beth Ann Robbin back at the Ellerkamp house, but Marie wasn't surprised to find herself talking some more about her former employer, this time in the additional company of two detectives from the state police. Unfortunately, she couldn't tell them any more than she'd already shared with Beth Ann. If Edwin Ellerkamp had any enemies, she didn't know of them. If he'd become involved in some dispute over coins, he'd never mentioned it to her, and she hadn't overheard anything that might have led her to believe that his life could be in danger.

"He wanted to live forever, you know," she said. "That didn't turn out so well." This sounded more callous than she'd intended, so she shrugged an apology.

"Did you like working for him?" Gardner asked.

"The money was good, and so were the hours. I suppose he was pretty easygoing, all things considered. He was fussy about his food, but that's about it."

Which was, Gardner noticed, not answering the question.

"But did you like working for him?" she repeated. "Did you like him?"

Marie looked at Beth Ann, who could almost read her thoughts. As it happened, Marie saved Beth Ann from any further psychic-level displays of empathy by speaking them aloud.

"If I said I didn't, would it make me a suspect?" she said.

"You're not a suspect, Marie," said Beth Ann, which was the truth as far as she was concerned, whatever reservations Condell or Gardner might have entertained.

"We think he was killed between midnight and six," said Condell. "If you want to, you could tell us where you were during those hours."

"I was in bed," said Marie. "With my husband. And the alarm system was on. We had it installed after that spate of burglaries a year or two back, and now Ray activates it as a matter of course before he turns in. I don't mind, especially not with the kids to worry about. To leave, someone would have to deactivate the system, and there would be a record of it. It's easy to check. I can show you the code."

Condell made a note.

"We have to ask these things," said Gardner.

"I understand," said Marie. "And in answer to your earlier question, I didn't particularly like Edwin. I worked for him because he paid well and on time, and his house was ten minutes from mine, but we weren't friendly, and we rarely spoke more than a few words to each other. Edwin wasn't friends with or close to anyone, as far as I could tell, but that didn't bother him. He liked his own company, and he had his coins."

"What about the alarm system at his house?" said Condell. "Did he have a routine?"

"I don't know," said Marie. "He was always awake before I got there so I never had cause to use it, but I remember him telling me once that he turned it on in the evenings, once he decided that he didn't need to go out again, not even for a breath of night air in his yard."

"The alarm had been deactivated," said Beth Ann. "It happened just before midnight, according to the record on the system."

"Maybe he heard something outside and went to check."

"That might be it," said Condell. "Did you know that he kept a licensed firearm in the house?"

"Yes, he stored it in his bedroom. I saw it once or twice, a little revolver."

"We found it in the kitchen, beside the sink."

"Then he definitely must have brought it downstairs with him, because I've only ever seen it beside his bed."

They asked Marie a few more questions, and she answered them as best she could, but it didn't appear as though they were going to leave very much wiser than when they'd arrived.

"I have one more favor to ask," said Condell.

"Sure," said Marie.

"Would you be willing to take a detailed look around the house with us, just to see if anything strikes you as out of place or absent?"

"Of course. Now?"

"No, the crime scene investigators are still doing their thing. But in the morning?"

"Just tell me when."

"Ten?"

"Ten is good."

"Okay, then."

The three visitors stood to leave. Marie could hear the kids watching TV in the living room with her husband. She had a Bolognese sauce on the stove, ready to go, and just needed to boil the spaghetti. They'd be eating later than usual, but never mind; it had been an unusual day.

She walked the officers to the door, and opened it to the dark.

"Was Edwin a religious man?" said Beth Ann. "I ask only because you and your mom probably knew him better than anyone. If a service has to be arranged, it would be helpful to know the denomination. Did I say something funny?"

Marie was smiling.

"Denomination," she said. "Like money. Denominations were his denomination, mostly. That was why I was smiling."

"Mostly?" said Condell. He, too, was smiling, but Beth Ann noticed that he was watching Marie closely, and she was impressed at how little got by him.

"Once, when he was in a talkative mood—for him—he showed me a bunch of old coins. They were Viking currency that had been found in England. He said that, over time, he'd started to share some of their beliefs. He liked the idea of a world filled with gods and demons, all of them active in the affairs of men, instead of just one god who preferred to stay hidden."

"Was he joking?" said Gardner.

"Edwin didn't joke."

"I don't think we can arrange a Viking funeral," said Beth Ann. "We may just go with humanist."

VII

It took us a while to get the Fulcis to dial down their tempers from boiling to merely simmering, by which time Raum had ordered himself a beer and found a safer spot over by the restrooms. It was a mystery why he'd come to the Bear in the first place, unless it was to meet someone. It had never been one of his regular haunts, even less so since the Fulcis had thrown his two lackeys into the Fore before advising him that, if he failed to mend his ways, he, too, would find his way into the river, in his case with an engine block attached to his ankles to speed him on his way. It was almost as though he'd made the trip to the Bear just to bait the Fulcis at their favorite bar, which bespoke a degree of confidence in himself to which he had no right.

"You ought not to have let him in here," said Paulie to Dave.

Tony was helping Paulie into his jacket, because Paulie was more sensitive and impetuous than his brother, and therefore did not wish to remain within striking distance of Raum, which was certainly for the best.

"I didn't roll out the red carpet, Paulie," said Dave. "He was on the premises before I even noticed him."

"Yeah, well, you ought to have, you know, anticipated such an eventuality."

"I'm not psychic," said Dave, while obviously chewing over who might have taught Paulie a word like "eventuality."

"Then find someone who is," said Paulie, "and put him on the fucking door."

Tony patted his brother on the back. Only in Paulie's company could Tony have come across as sane and reasonable. He had a shorter fuse than Paulie, which was no small boast, but lately displayed more frequent signs of rationality.

"This place is important to us," said Tony. "It's like our second home."

Dave winced at that, but let it pass. In his heart of hearts, Dave dearly wished the Fulcis had found another bar to call a second home, or any home at all. They might have added color to the Bear, but it was principally a purplish shade of red from Dave's high blood pressure.

We watched the Fulcis leave. One of the floor staff was picking up Jenga tiles and broken glass, while a second tried to figure out if the table could be salvaged.

"I might have a word with Raum," I said.

"I'll send him on his way when you're done," said Dave.

"I'll take care of it."

"You don't have to do that. I can look after my own bar."

"Call it a favor," I said, "to you and the Fulcis."

Dave nodded. We had always gotten along well, Dave and I, and always would.

I headed over to where Raum was sitting. Now that he'd removed his jacket, I could see he'd muscled up while he was away. He'd also added to his small collection of prison tattoos. None of them was any good, except for an intricate pentacle, a pentagram surrounded by a circle, dotted with runic symbols. That one, on the underside of his left forearm, was raw and red.

"You got a minute, Raum?"

He was holding a bottled domestic beer, and not a good one. It was a drink he could have ordered at any dive in town, but instead he'd come all the way to the Bear, one of the best microbrew bars in the country, which kept domestics only for people who didn't know any better, or had given up experimenting the day they got married.

"Sure," he said. "Pull up a chair, take a load off."

"I'll stand."

"Good. I was just being pleasant."

He yawned, showing off his bright new teeth. When last I'd seen him, his mouth had resembled the ruins of Dresden. This was a changed Raum Buker, although I couldn't say that I liked this variant any more than the previous one.

"When did you get back into town?" I said.

"A few days ago."

"Been anywhere interesting these last few years?"

"Around."

"Prison around?"

"Not a subject for discussion."

But his right hand went almost unconsciously to the pentacle tattoo, where he added to the scratch marks. While he worried at it, his ravening eye caught a young woman leaving the restroom. She didn't look flattered by the attention, and no one could have blamed her. I kicked the sole of his boot, which brought his attention back to me. He wasn't pleased at being kicked, but didn't do anything about it beyond scowling. If Raum ever took a run at me, he'd do it from behind.

"You planning on staying in Portland?" I asked.

"Why, you need a date? All my time inside, I never did a guy, and I'm not about to start with you."

"You haven't answered my question."

"Because I haven't decided yet."

"Let me help you," I said. "That's twice I've saved you from being stomped by the Fulcis. There won't be a third time."

"Big man. You still letting those animals do your dirty work?"

"No, I take care of my own."

"What about those two New York swishes, you give up hanging on their coattails yet?" He peered over my shoulder. "I don't see them around and"—he sniffed ostentatiously—"I don't smell cheap perfume."

"You strike me as an altered character, Raum," I said, "but not an improved one."

It wasn't the tattoos alone, or the teeth, or the musculature. At first I thought he might be juiced, because he was radiating a strange energy, but his eyes didn't have that telltale brightness. In fact, for all his bluster, they betrayed uncertainty, like a man who suddenly discovers that the ground beneath his feet is not as stable as he once recalled.

"Time changes us all," he said.

"Prison has made a philosopher of you. But what I meant was that I don't recall you being so brave back when you were trying to roll old ladies, and Louis was forced to stick a gun in your mouth to make you stop."

"I remember," said Raum. "I've filed it away for future reference."

"I'll be sure to make Louis aware of that. You know, you got drool on his nice, clean barrel. Next time, he'll bring an old gun to check the quality of your bridgework. In the meantime, don't come back to the Bear. It's not your kind of place—unless you came here to see someone, in which case it's not their kind of place, either."

Raum set down the bottle, still half-full. He stood and rolled his shoulders, a prizefighter waiting for the bell.

"No, I got no one to meet, not here, and I was leaving anyway. Like you say, it's not my kind of place." He waggled a finger at me. "But it may be that you and I will knock heads somewhere that *is* my kind of place, somewhere nice and dark, when there's no one around to fight your battles for you."

"Just you and me, Raum?" I said. "Sure, I'll take those odds."

He grinned, and somewhere a puppy died.

"Oh, no," he said. "I learned a lot these last few years. When we meet, you'll be alone, but I'll have *my* friends with me."

"You don't have any friends," I said, "except the imaginary kind, and they're no good in a fight."

"We'll see, when the time comes."

I was done with him. He'd stopped being interesting the day he was born.

"You take care, Raum," I said. "I'd hate to see nothing happen to you."

————

I RETURNED TO SCARBOROUGH in driving rain. A truck had jackknifed on Route 1 and the traffic was all backed up, so I listened to *1st Wave* on Sirius while I watched the police light show. *1st Wave* finished on a Smiths song, but I couldn't listen to the Smiths in the same way anymore, not since Morrissey had turned into one of the people he used to despise, so I turned off the radio and drove the rest of the way in silence.

Later, with only shadows for company, I regretted permitting Raum Buker to get under my skin so quickly. He was an evolutionary blip, but no more than that. The jails were full of men like him—and the cemeteries, too, nature ultimately finding a way to cull the anomalies from the herd. Yet experience had taught me not to ignore sensations of unease. When I'd done so in the past, I'd been wrong. When I'd paid attention, it had left me better prepared for what was to come. So I drew a circle of my own around Raum, isolating the pentagram of his form, and listened for trouble's song.

VIII

B eth Ann Robbin was waiting outside the Ellerkamp house with Condell when Marie arrived the next morning, the detective named Gardner presumably being otherwise occupied. It hadn't escaped Marie's notice that before leaving the previous night, and just as he appeared to be on the verge of vacating her doorstep, Condell had asked to check the system record on her alarm panel, because, as he put it, "if we don't do it now, someone may ask later why we didn't." Marie presumed that confirmation of her presence in bed, and at her husband's side, meant she was definitely no longer a suspect, which was a relief. Then again, it bothered her somewhat that all the time Condell had been sitting at her kitchen table, he might have been viewing her as someone potentially capable of feeding coins to an old man until he choked to death.

An Athens PD patrol car was stationed in the driveway, the cop at the wheel reading a newspaper. Marie had watched the local TV reports about the murder the previous night, and again before leaving the house, but none of them had mentioned the manner of Edwin Ellerkamp's demise. She supposed the police were trying to keep that quiet for as long as possible so as not to draw the crazies.

She followed the two officers into the house, and together they began a room-by-room check. Beth Ann told Marie that the crime scene technicians had worked through the night, so it was okay to touch stuff, although she was given gloves and plastic booties to wear as a precaution. They started upstairs and worked their way down, but as far as Marie could tell, the rooms looked much as they always had. Some of them she rarely entered, as they were not in use, Edwin preferring to limit his domain to his bedroom, the kitchen, the living room, and the dining room. The latter two spaces were connected by a pair of double doors that were never closed, and the dining table had long since been removed. The area had served as Edwin's library, study, and TV room, and was where he spent the preponderance of his time. It was left until last.

The first thing Marie noticed was that the open safe was now empty.

"We decided it wouldn't be wise to leave it as it was," said Condell, when she mentioned this. "We had an expert come in from the Philadelphia Mint to advise us, and just by looking she pointed out a bunch of stuff that ought to be under lock and key. Mr. Ellerkamp had a lot of very valuable coins. We could be talking about high six, even low seven figures."

Marie was shocked. She'd often wondered how much the collection might be worth, but her best guess had been at least 50 percent shy.

Condell had a file under his arm, and from it he produced a series of photographs of the room, taken before Edwin's body had been removed. That way, Marie could check any anomalies against the photos to determine if they were a result of police activity or something else. Marie went over the room slowly, trying to balance her memories of it against what she was seeing now, all the time with the awareness of what had happened there. The couch on which Edwin had died was gone, taken away for further analysis. Four round depressions on the carpet marked the position it had once occupied, and blood spots served as a reminder, were one required, of its owner's final torment.

Marie stood before the fireplace, where a gilt nineteenth-century mirror reflected the room back at her. It had always been a bitch to clean, requiring a ladder and a good sense of balance, but she was unlikely to have to worry about it anymore. She was turning away from it when a mark caught her eye.

"There," she said. "That's new."

She pointed at a blemish in the bottom-left corner of the mirror.

"I don't see anything," said Beth Ann.

"You need to look at it from an angle, close to the glass."

Beth Ann did, Condell beside her. They saw a series of smudges, as though greasy fingers had been rubbed across it, creating a stain that was about a foot square, although one that had passed unnoticed because of the manner of its execution.

"I cleaned that mirror the day before yesterday," said Marie, "and I left it spotless."

"It doesn't look random," said Beth Ann. "There's a pattern."

"Not just a pattern," said Condell. "I see traces of blood."

Condell held up his phone and used it to take a series of snaps. When he was done, he ran through them on the screen. The last, either through luck or skill, was nearly perfect.

"Now," said Condell, "just what the hell is that?"

IX

For a few days I saw and heard no more of Raum Buker, and experienced no great sense of regret. I finished up some routine jobs that paid the bills: the confirmation of a simple case of insurance fraud; the interviewing of potential witnesses for an upcoming trial; and the shadowing of a straying spouse as ammunition for an imminent divorce case. (Roby Logan, who'd been a PI in Bangor back in the sixties and seventies, once told me that the worst misfortune ever to have befallen the trade was the introduction of no-fault divorce in Maine back in '73. After that, he said, he could no longer afford a new car every year.) Nobody got so irate with me that they felt inclined to throw a punch—or worse, pull a gun.

Each night I'd take a hot bath, because lately I hurt more than I used to, and a bath helped. Afterward I'd look in the mirror, note my scars, and test how deep they went. Sometimes I'd think about how I'd come by them. I'd heard it claimed that the mind buries the memory of suffering in order for life to go on, but it's not true, or not from my experience. Some said the same about women and childbirth, but I knew plenty of women, my ex-partner Rachel included, for whom the pain of parturition remained fresh even years after the event. I could still recall the agony of the shotgun blasts that had almost taken my life—did take my life, if you talked to the doctors, because I died on that operating table and they brought me back not once, not twice, but three times. I still woke in the night to feel the pellets tearing through me, and then I died all over again.

On an icy early February morning, I took the long drive south to visit the graves of Susan, my wife, and Jennifer, my first daughter. I'd paid to have the marker cleaned, and the moss cleared from the carved letters. It made the stone look almost new, so that briefly I was a younger man again, seeing their passing confirmed for me by an artisan's hand. The bite of their loss had dulled, but it would never entirely dissipate, and that was as it should be. Someday, long after I was gone, their identities would be erased entirely by the elements, or the stone would fall and become overgrown by vegetation, and this, too, was in the way of things. They wouldn't be the first to be forgotten in this manner, not in that place. They lay in an old cemetery, and their names would be added to its secret list of the lost.

I would never join them in that plot, though. I had made a decision a long time ago not to rest there. It would have caused too much pain to the surviving members of Susan's family, and I was already responsible in their eyes for a sufficiency of misery. In the end, it wouldn't matter to me where I was laid, although I'd chosen to be buried next to my grandfather in Scarborough's Black Point Cemetery, if only to save anyone else the stress of making the decision on my behalf. I knew that I'd be seeing Jennifer again in the next life—Susan also, perhaps, but certainly Jennifer. I knew, because sometimes I still glimpsed her in this life, too. She haunted me, and I was grateful for her presence.

For the most part.

CHAPTER

Beth Ann Robbin was once again sitting in Marie's kitchen. The morning sunlight streamed through the drapes from a clear blue sky, but it contained no warmth, no warmth at all. Even with the radiator turned up full, Beth Ann felt the winter chill prowling, nipping.

Beside Marie sat her mother, Ida. Marie had told her about the mark on the mirror, and shown her an image of it forwarded from Condell's phone. She'd been requested to do so by Condell, if a few days after its discovery. Marie guessed that the police had drawn a blank, or the state detectives had briefly forgotten about her mother's long employment at The Elms. Beth Ann arrived to do the follow-up interview, although she had always regarded Ida Biener as a dull woman who wouldn't have noticed the Second Coming had Christ materialized in her own yard. But miracle of miracles, even the most obtuse of individuals still possessed the occasional capacity to retain and retrieve information.

"I've seen that before," Ida told Beth Ann. "The stick figure thing."

"Where?"

"On Mr. Ellerkamp's computer, not long before I retired. It was so odd-looking that it stayed with me. He had it blown right up so it filled the big screen, and he was talking about it to someone on the phone."

"Do you recall what he said, or who he was talking to?"

Ida shook her head.

"Not really," she said. "I never stuck my nose in his business. I knew he wouldn't like it."

"When you say 'not really' . . ."

"I might have heard a name, but I could as easily have misheard it, because I was already leaving him to his business. I could come back and clean later, and not disturb him. Funny the things that lodge in your mind. Ask me where I was last Tuesday, and I'd struggle to tell you, but a darn stick figure on a screen I can recall."

Her big, soft eyes stared back at Beth Ann. It was, Beth Ann thought, like being regarded over a fence by a particularly placid cow.

"And what," Beth Ann persisted, "was that name you heard?"

"Jeez, it was such a long time ago now. I'm kind of sorry I ever mentioned this, causing a fuss over nothing."

"It's not nothing, Ida," said Beth Ann. "And we need all the help we can get, however small it might seem to you."

Ida wrinkled her nose as she struggled to think.

"Kebbell, maybe?" she said. "Or Kibble? I have a cat, you see, so when I think of kibble, I think of her. Oh, it's in there somewhere. Concentrate, dummy." She seemed on the verge of slapping herself on the forehead when her face cleared. "Kepler," she said, with relief. "I'd swear it was Kepler. Kibble, Kepler. If it had been anything else, then *whoosh*, it would be gone by now."

Beth wrote all three words—Kebbell, Kibble, and Kepler—in her notebook. When she looked up again, Ida's face had clouded.

"You know," she said to Beth Ann, "I also think that image stayed in my head because it scared me. Now why would that be, do you reckon? I mean, it's just a stick figure, right? There's no reason for it to have frightened me, or Mr. Ellerkamp."

"Sure, just a stick figure," said Beth Ann, although she had to admit that something about it was unsettling. Then: "But you say Edwin Ellerkamp was also frightened by it?"

"I thought so then, but I might be doing that thing, you know, where you feel one way about something and think someone else must feel the same way about it, too?"

"Transference," said Marie.

"If you say so. You know more about that stuff than I do, what with your therapy and all."

Marie blushed deeply.

"Jesus, Mom," she said. "Broadcast it to the whole valley, why don't you?"

"It's only us and Beth Ann, and she won't tell."

Ida winked at Beth Ann, who shot Marie what she hoped would be interpreted as a reassuring glance. Marie cast her eyes to heaven.

"And you never saw this symbol again?" Beth Ann asked Ida.

"Never."

Beth Ann closed her notebook. It wasn't much, but it was a lead to share with Condell and Gardner. If this Kepler was a coin collector, someone in the numismatic community might know about him.

"Thank you for your help, Ida," she said.

"It was terrible, what happened to Mr. Ellerkamp," said Ida. "He was a good employer. Marie won't find another like him, even if he wasn't a Christian. I used to josh him that for all his coins, he wouldn't be able to buy his way into heaven when the time came. Didn't matter if he believed in God or not, he'd have to answer for the manner of his living just the same."

"And what did he have to say to that?"

Ida Biener's innate imperturbation was briefly disturbed, like standing water rippling from the impact of an imperfectly skimmed stone.

"He told me," she said, "that with the right coin, even gods could be bought." Ida crossed herself: a good Catholic making amends for blasphemy, even in reported speech. "But then," she concluded, "Mr. Ellerkamp was a very strange person, and if this Kepler was associating with him, he was a very strange person, too."

———

IN AN ONTARIO PROPERTY, an hour from the border with the United States, a laptop was open in an otherwise dark room, its glow casting a bluish light on the face of the man examining the screen. An email had come through— not to his principal account, the one he used to receive information on auctions and sales, but to the secondary address. Only a handful of people were privy to it, and they used it sparingly. Most preferred not to use it at all, because his reputation preceded him, but he had money, and didn't quibble over price. Meanwhile, when he sold, there could be no concerns about provenance, and if he made it clear that further information was required, it would be provided. If he found out that attempts had been made to conceal something from him, consequences would result.

He opened the message, which contained only a link to a website address ending in .onion, the address itself consisting of a random series of letters and numbers. Using a VPN to add a further layer of security, he accessed the Tor browser, which brought him to a site on the dark web. It was an auction listing, although the seller remained anonymous, or believed himself to be. But the man had learned that every seller had a signature, a series of tells that could be discovered in the online presentation of a listing, the formulation of the description, and the conditions of sale. Taken together, they were rarely definitive, but they did permit one to narrow one's scope if one were a concerned buyer anxious not to be ripped off, or if one were seeking restitution for a scam that had already occurred. But rip-offs were rare in the circles in which he moved, either online or real world; the danger lay with the law, not with those involved in the marketplace, and anyway, only rarely did he venture onto the dark web. He was old school—older, indeed, than anyone could have imagined.

He read the listing carefully before bringing up each of the images in turn, using a digital magnifier to examine them in detail. Finally, he checked for other items from the same source, but found nothing of similar value or rarity. When he was done, he closed the listing, and picked up a pair of worn dice from his desk. He shook them in his fist and threw a double six.

He had no intention of bidding for something that had been taken from him. He already had an idea of who the seller might be, not only from the language of the listing but also because just a handful of specialists possessed the knowledge and resources to dispose of such an item, so very uncommon was it. Nonetheless, he was frustrated. He had hoped to deal with this problem before anything went to market, and preferably without recourse to further violence. He had lost his temper with Ellerkamp, even if the theatricality of the old man's demise would serve as a warning to others. He was surprised the police had not publicly revealed more about the case, or that no mention had been made of the calling card left on the mirror, although this, he admitted, might have been an indulgence too far, even for him. Despite the official silence, rumors were already spreading about the death, which suited his purposes. It was important that prospective buyers should be made to understand the implications of involving themselves in his activities, and the best means of having his possessions returned to him was by first ensuring that there was no safe outlet for their disposal.

Again he threw the dice. Again, a double six.

Ellerkamp had died after revealing all he knew, but what he knew had not been enough. The collector had been surprised that the instigation of the theft had been traced back to him; almost as surprised, in fact, as he was to discover that the thieves had double-crossed him. It was at this point that his attacker had become truly enraged, feeding Ellerkamp coins until he suffocated before filling his mouth with whatever surplus it could accommodate, and more.

Afterward, the man from Ontario had been forced to put out feelers, to call in markers and favors. More than anything else, it troubled him that he had been required to venture beyond the safety and confines of his lair because of the avarice of venal individuals. He disliked drawing attention to himself, which was why he had long been a recluse. Hearsay was one thing, but it was better not to lend it substance by confirmation. He was also already growing weaker, and consequently was at his most vulnerable just when he was called upon to act in order to save himself.

Shake. Throw. Double six.

The listing would draw interested parties, some of whom might be as adept as he at identifying anonymous sellers. This immediate issue would have to be dealt with before the vendor made an attempt to dispose of objects to which he had no right of sale or ownership. The man from Ontario closed his eyes. He had to conserve his energy. Causing pain could be an exhausting business. But he feared sleep, feared it because, for the first time that he could recall, he might never wake from it again. This, he thought, was his punishment for worshiping a fickle god—worshiping it, and giving it a place in which to dwell.

No, not alone a place.

A body.

XI

Two weeks after my encounter with Raum Buker at the Great Lost Bear, I heard stories from South Portland that Dolors Strange might have returned to his bed. One day later, someone else told me that Raum had been seen eating steamed clams with Ambar Strange down in the Old Port. When I dropped by the restaurant to check if this was true, the kid who'd waited on their table couldn't say for sure if Raum's dining companion matched the description I gave of Ambar Strange, but he thought it did. He remembered Raum clearly, though, on account of his too-white teeth and the liberal tip he'd left—in cash. It sounded as though Raum had come into money.

Finally, and oddest of all, Raum was spotted candlepin bowling with both the Sisters Strange at 33 Elmwood in Westbrook. This time there could be no doubting the veracity of the sighting, because the three of them were present on the bar's security footage. They even gave the impression of having a good time together—or some approximation of it, given Dolors Strange's naturally lugubrious demeanor and the undeniable involvement of Raum in the proceedings.

I spoke of Raum Buker and the Sisters Strange with Angel and Louis when they traveled from New York to Portland for a few days of R & R. Angel and Louis had begun to spend more and more time in Maine since the former's illness. Their apartment by Eastern Promenade had big picture windows that looked out over Casco Bay, and the sight of the sea salved Angel's spirit. If Angel was happy, Louis was happy. Certain couples became like that as they grew older. It saved a lot of strife.

I'd known Angel and Louis for many years. How we met—well, that was another story, but they'd stood by me after Susan and Jennifer were taken from me, and they had continued to stand by me in the years that followed. I'd stood by them, too, and if there were those who speculated about why a former police detective turned PI kept company with two criminals—one of them, Angel, a thief, and the other, Louis, a harvester of men, the last of the Reapers—they knew better than to offer an opinion within earshot of any of us.

"Why are you so concerned about Buker?" said Angel over fried chicken in honey sauce at CBG on Congress. "After all, it's not like you're on the meter for him."

CBG had previously been Congress Bar and Grill, and before that, Norm's. But to confuse the issue in the arcane way of Portland drinking establishments, the old Norm's had formerly operated from premises across the street. That place was now called the Downtown Lounge, although older patrons still occasionally referred to it as Norm's, and did so even after the new Norm's had opened opposite. This was how people arranging to meet up in Portland sometimes missed each other entirely.

"I don't know," I replied. "But I swear, I hear him ticking before I go to sleep at night. He's like a bomb waiting to go off."

"He didn't look like much, last time I saw him," said Louis. "But then, he was struggling to speak with his mouth full."

"I think the taste of gun oil has persisted," I said. "He shared some unkind sentiments about you."

"Such as?"

"I'd blush to repeat them, but let's just say he's not down with the gay folk."

Louis considered the problem.

"Could be he needs to be reeducated," he said. "You know, encouraged to think differently. Positive reinforcement."

"Are you suggesting a carrot-and-stick approach?"

"No," said Louis, "just a stick."

"A stick shaped like a gun?"

"Maybe."

"Or we could all stay out of his way," said Angel, "and let events take their course."

Louis and I stared at him.

"Right, how stupid of me," said Angel. "What was I thinking?"

"He's done some more time since last you saw him," I said.

"Where?" said Louis.

"I asked around, and heard possibly Jersey. I haven't started digging yet to find out why, but I might start, if only because it's probably better to know. Also, if his abundance of confidence is anything to go by, he has money, or is about to make some. He always did have a mercenary streak. He's either pulled a job, or has one planned."

"So?" said Louis. "If he's already advertising his presence, and getting in people's faces, he'll end up back in jail or getting his lights punched out, or both. But unless you're hoping to rehabilitate him, or his score involves burgling your home, he's not your problem."

I didn't bother arguing, even though I disagreed. I couldn't help but feel that Raum had entered my orbit for a reason, and the decay of that orbit must inevitably result in a collision.

Louis asked after my daughter Sam. He mentioned that he and Angel were contemplating a road trip to Vermont, and hoped to stop by to see her. I considered offering to join them, but decided Sam—and more particularly Rachel, her mother—might enjoy time with Angel and Louis that was uncomplicated by my presence. I was getting along better with Rachel than I had in a long time, and even her father was demonstrating something resembling tolerance for my company. Rachel and I might no longer have been together, but we both loved our

daughter and maintained an affection for each other. Most of our difficulties were now in the past. Our separation was better for Sam, too,
and she seemed to understand.

But then, that child understood more than any child should.

Angel, Louis, and I parted company, they to walk back to Eastern
Promenade, and I to drive back to Scarborough. The night sky was
clear, and bright with stars. They were reflected in the waters of the salt
marshes, so it was as though the earth were a thin disk in the manner
conceived by the ancients, and the pools were holes in its crust through
which a man might plummet into the vacuum were he to take a careless step.

As I pulled into the drive, my headlights caught a form standing on
the lowest branch of the bare tamarack tree at the eastern edge of my
yard, which overlooked a small pond: a black-crowned night heron,
its pale underside like a mirror reflecting the moonlight; a nocturnal
hunter, emerging to feed when its competitors were asleep. I hadn't
glimpsed it before, and had mixed feelings about its presence. The other
marsh birds would soon start to breed, and their eggs and their young
would be vulnerable to the heron, especially the terns over by Pine
Point. But I wasn't about to trouble the bird. I might even have felt a
certain commonality with it.

———

EVENTS DID TAKE THEIR course, as events are wont to do. Raum Buker
was about to re-enter my life with a vengeance, but that wasn't even the
bad news. He might have been a troubled, troublesome man, but the
one who followed after him was infinitely worse.

CHAPTER

XII

Two days after my meal with Angel and Louis, I met Will Quinn at Two Lights in Cape Elizabeth. The Lobster Shack eatery above the rocks was closed up for winter, and the cold wind coming in from the sea meant that few people were around to notice us. Those locals who had chosen to walk by the lighthouse kept their heads down, which was even better. To help ward off the chill I'd brought along late-morning take-out coffee for both of us from the C Salt Gourmet Market, and a couple of pastries for soakage.

I didn't maintain an office, just as I didn't employ a secretary who secretly carried a torch for me, and with whom I could exchange lightly sexualized banter. I kept all my current records and case notes at home, and the older paperwork in storage. My cell phone functioned as an answering service, and I never took on more work than I could comfortably manage alone. I owned my home, had money in the bank, and a retainer from the Federal Bureau of Investigation—your tax dollars at work—offered me a degree of leeway that others in my profession might have envied, if they had known anything of it. The retainer, for what was nebulously described as "consultancy services," came with strings attached—every retainer did, just like every favor—but they were pretty elastic. Admittedly, I'd been forced to cut one or two of them in the past, but only as a last resort. SAC Edgar Ross, who was responsible for administering those funds from an office at Federal Plaza in New York, had been known to shout at me when I did this, but I liked to think it was because he cared too much. I *liked* to think this, but I knew it to be untrue. We take our consolations where we find them, and if we can't find any, we make some up.

When I had to engage privately with clients, I did so at their home or office. If that wasn't possible, I preferred to opt for quiet, neutral ground. Early morning at the Bear often worked, before it opened for business at 11:30, but I'd sat down for consultations in coffee shops, the back rooms of bookstores, even in one of the empty theaters at the Nickelodeon. Because of some of the cases in which I'd been involved, my face was better known than I'd have preferred. If you were seen talking to me, you or someone you knew was in difficulty. If you didn't care to advertise that fact, I fully understood.

But often I found it helped initially to meet clients in the open air, and talk while we walked. It was less formal and oppressive, and freed people to share whatever they needed to share. They didn't even have to look at me if they didn't want to. They could just unburden themselves, and I'd listen. In that sense, it wasn't all that different from the quiet of the confessional, apart from the promise of expiation—and the fees, although I'd waived enough of those to give my accountant nightmares.

Two Lights had been Will's suggestion. He was already waiting for me when I arrived, standing by the Lobster Shack, watching the waves crash on the rocks, like a figure from some nineteenth-century Romantic painting, assuming any of those artists had favored models wearing plaid work shirts. I knew Will from around town, and we'd exchange a nod or pleasantry when we met. He was a small, bearded man in his early fifties, unmarried, no kids. I'd always found him shy, even slightly naive, as though the casual cruelties of the world remained somehow baffling to him. He ran a lumber company in York: rough-sawn hemlock and kiln-dried pine, with a sideline in custom sawing, although you got fined if the blade hit iron. His clothing always bore a fine coating of sawdust, and he carried traces of it on his skin and hair. I think he liked it that way, and there were worse smells than timber with which a man might be associated.

I handed him his coffee and pastry, along with a stirrer and a couple of sugars in case he needed them. He added both sugars while we walked, and we chatted about the weather and the lumber business while feeding most of the pastries to the gulls. He asked after Rachel and Sam. I told him they were fine, and that Vermont was being largely gentle with them.

"Vermont's nice," said Will. "My mother lives with her second husband in the eastern part of North Dakota. First time I visited, I thought I'd never seen a place so flat. I asked a gas station attendant if there was anything worth seeing, so he pointed to a hill just about a mile from where we were, and told me I could always go stand on that. So I said to him, 'What will I see?' and he said, 'The same as you can see here, except without the hill.' I think there might have been a metaphor involved, but I couldn't be sure."

"So did you climb the hill?"

"Sure, because it was something to do. And it wasn't so much a hill as a mound. I'd have gotten a better view standing on a chair."

And with that, Will got around to his reason for asking to meet me.

"You know Raum Buker?" he said, and it gave me no satisfaction to realize that my belief in the intermingling of our destinies had been vindicated.

"Yes, I know Raum."

"Is he a friend of yours?"

"I haven't yet hit rock bottom, so no."

"That's what I assumed. I just wanted to be sure before this went any further." He sipped some more of his coffee. "I usually take it sweeter," he said.

"I could go back and get you more sugar, but I'd have to charge you for my time."

"I'll survive."

"I thought you'd take that attitude. What's your problem with Raum?"

"I've been seeing someone," said Will. "A woman," he added, just in case this needed clarification. "I like her a lot."

"Well," I said, "that's good," although I guessed it wasn't unreservedly, or else we wouldn't be having this conversation.

"It was, until Buker showed up," said Will, "because the woman is Dolors Strange."

I don't know why I was surprised to learn that Will Quinn and Dolors Strange might be an item. Perhaps it was because Will appeared an unlikely candidate to be sharing his affections with the same woman as Raum—and more pertinently, to have found those attentions welcomed. It was like learning that someone enjoyed simultaneously listening to death metal and Perry Como.

"How long has this been going on?" I asked.

"Me and Dolors? About four months. It started when she came by to pick up bark mulch for her yard."

Which, I supposed, passed for meeting cute in the lumber trade.

"Had you known her before then?"

"Never set eyes on her. I didn't even know she used to be with Buker until he showed up in town. I live a quiet life, likely too quiet. It could be I ought to get out more, but when I do get out, I often end up wishing I hadn't."

"Don't beat yourself up over it," I said. "Time spent not knowing Raum Buker is never wasted. But I have to ask: Why are you telling me this?"

"Because he's bad for her, and I think she's scared of him."

"Did Dolors admit this?"

"More or less, before she said that we ought not to see each other for a while."

It might have been the wind, but his eyes were tearing up. He wiped at them with the sleeve of his jacket.

"That breeze does take a shortcut, doesn't it?" I said.

"'When the wind is in the east, 'tis neither good for man nor beast,'" Will recited. "My mother used to say that. I can't bring to mind the rest, but the part about the east wind always stuck with me. Now that I come to think of it, I don't believe she ever told me more than those two lines. I love her dearly, but she could never see the doughnut, only the hole."

Nearby, a great black-backed gull stood on a rock and stabbed with its beak at the underbelly of a crab. The force of the impact sent the crab tumbling to the stones below. The gull followed. The sight did nothing to lighten the mood.

"Did Dolors say why she wanted you gone?" I said.

"Sure. Because of Raum."

He looked at me as though only an idiot would need that explained to him, and conceivably he'd been wrong to turn to me in his time of tribulation.

"What I mean is, was it because she wanted to get back together with him, or because she was worried about what might happen if he found you warming your feet by her fire?"

Will thought about this.

"I hope it's the second one, but neither option is very flattering to me, is it?"

"This isn't about flattery, and whatever you say stays between us."

He sighed.

"I thought she really liked me. I'd like to presume she still does. I'd even started to consider, you know—"

"Marriage?"

The word came out freighted with more incredulity than I'd intended, and Will couldn't help but pick up on it.

"She's a nice woman," he said reprovingly, "once you get to know her."

I apologized. "So you think she's trying to protect you."

"Still doesn't make me feel too good about myself. I'd like to go after

Buker with a tire iron, but what good would that do? I'm no fighter. I'd just end up like that damn crab."

The gull had retrieved its breakfast, and was chomping down hard on one of the legs while the rest of the crab dangled helplessly in the air. I hoped the crab was dead. It wasn't as though the world was running a deficit of misery. The gull adjusted its grip, tossed the crab in the air, and caught it again. I heard the shell snap. Half the crab's body dropped to the ground, putting the issue to rest.

"Not if you hit him from behind," I said.

"I couldn't do that either. With my luck, I'd miss."

I didn't mind speaking with Will Quinn, or providing a sympathetic ear for his problems, but I couldn't see how his difficulties concerned me.

"I'm a private investigator, Will, not a relationship counselor. There's a limit to what I can do for you here."

Will turned to face me.

"But this isn't only a relationship problem," he said. "It's also an occult one."

XIII

Detectives Condell and Gardner had hit a dead end with the Edwin Ellerkamp case. Whoever was responsible for his death was either very accomplished or very lucky, because they had retrieved no fingerprints or DNA from the scene, or none that should not have been there; the blood on the mirror was Ellerkamp's own, and had been applied by someone wearing gloves. The detectives had tried to trace calls made to, and received from, a pair of unidentified numbers on Ellerkamp's cell phone, but so far all that could be determined was that the numbers had been generated by an anonymizer app that rerouted calls to another device. Such apps were used by people selling goods on the Internet who preferred to keep a buffer between themselves and potential buyers, as well as those who were dating online or off.

Oh, and by criminals, because they really did value their privacy.

The next step would usually have been to obtain a warrant in order to force the creators of the app to reveal whatever details they might have possessed about the ultimate source or destination of those calls, except the app had been tracked to the dark net, which meant that a) any order, even if obtainable, would be unenforceable in practical terms; and b) the communications between Ellerkamp and the holder or holders of those numbers almost certainly involved some degree of illegality, because otherwise such levels of concealment would have been unnecessary.

Since the discovery of the body, Condell and Gardner had become more knowledgeable than either of them might have desired about the thriving market in illicitly acquired coins, whether stolen from collectors, stores, and museums, or dug up by treasure hunters and not reported to the relevant authorities. Increasingly, they were coming around to the view that Edwin Ellerkamp might have cheated someone in a coin transaction, or involved himself in the purchase of stolen property, and been killed for doing so. His collection was in the process of being catalogued and appraised, but at least some of the items appeared to have no paperwork to indicate their source or manner of acquisition. In addition, it continued to strike Condell as odd that so much of value had been left untouched in the house. What kind of individual would be so obsessed with coins as potentially to kill a man over them yet not steal his trove? Someone, Condell thought, with a peculiar sense of honor, if nothing else.

And then there was the matter of the marking on the mirror. As far as anyone could tell, it was a variation on the occult symbol for "bane," meaning something evil or destructive; that, or the killer couldn't even draw a stick figure properly. Condell would have liked to write it off as the latter, but increasingly he was leaning toward the former, which didn't please him one bit. Bad enough that an old man should have been forced to choke on what had been identified as Anglo-Saxon silver sceattas dating from the seventh and eighth centuries, with some Greek silver drachms from before the time of Christ thrown in for variety. The addition of an occult element only complicated proceedings further.

Thankfully they had managed to keep a lid on the precise manner of Ellerkamp's death for a few days, although it had since entered the public domain in the form of a couple of newspaper reports. Too many people knew of what had happened for it not to have leaked eventually, and the coin aspect had subsequently been confirmed by the police.

The presence of the symbol on the mirror, though, was being kept under wraps; for now, no benefit could accrue to the investigation from circulating it widely.

One other fact about Ellerkamp's murder was being kept on a need-to-know basis. In the course of the autopsy, coins were not the only items removed from his throat and stomach. The medical examiner had also retrieved a pair of old dice, their sides misspotted: the first die was marked only with ones, twos, and threes, the second with fours, fives, and sixes. The latter, Condell had learned, was known as a "high man," the former a "low man," and they might once have been used to bilk rubes in games of chance. Radiocarbon dating analysis had established that the dice had been made in the sixteenth century, and a process known as pRIA, or protein radioimmunoassay, had identified the substance used in their creation as human bone. Ellerkamp's housekeeper had never seen dice in her employer's collection, and could not recall him ever mentioning them, while none of the books on his shelves dealt with such artifacts. This did not rule out his possible ownership of them, but it was equally plausible that his killer had introduced them into Ellerkamp's body. It was another peculiarity to add to a growing list.

While murders might have been rare in Athens, they were more prevalent in the rest of the Commonwealth of Pennsylvania, along with wrongdoings of a less extreme but nonetheless vexatious stripe, so Gardner and Condell had more than enough criminality to occupy their working hours. Already they could feel the Ellerkamp case growing cold.

But that bane symbol: as Condell's mother would have said, it was coming between him and his sleep, because what kind of killer signed his name with a rune? If it was a signature, one possibility was a killer who either had taken lives before, or intended to take more, and wanted to make certain that his handiwork was correctly attributed. The second possibility was a killer who assumed that the fact of the rune's existence would eventually be made public, and would have meaning for specific individuals, in which case it was meant to be construed as a warning, or some form of confirmation. So far, though, searches of state and federal databases, including the FBI's National Crime Information Center, had drawn blanks. Oh, there was no shortage of runes, because anyone who had ever bought a copy of *Led Zeppelin IV*, or frequented a tattoo parlor, knew what a rune was, and some of those people had gone on to commit crimes, including a number in which runes had played a part. But the bane symbol featured in no crimes, solved or unsolved, with a connection to coins or antiques, and Condell was reluctant to broaden his parameters to include any bored kid who had ever defaced a wall because he'd listened to too much Norwegian black metal. Neither had bone dice produced any matches.

He considered again the story of Valerian, choking to death on molten gold. But Valerian had made the mistake of crossing a ruler. Who had Edwin Ellerkamp crossed? Some fierce, cold prince, some dark king? Condell pushed away the thought. This was no king, no prince. A sadist, yes, but no ordinary one, touched with confidence, even arrogance, for he had marked his work. Those who did that wanted to be caught, or had no fear of it. The fact that Ellerkamp's killer had left no evidence of his presence in the house beyond a body and a rune suggested the latter.

For the present, Condell and Gardner would continue their canvass of coin dealers and collectors—and in person, where possible, because Condell was skilled at picking up on a lie. Someone in that community knew why the rune had been left on a mirror in Ellerkamp's house, which meant they also had an idea of who might have put it there. Of course, the rune could have been designed to throw the police off the scent, but then why not make it easier for them to find? No, Condell was convinced that it had meaning, and he categorized its placement as an error on the part of the killer, even if it was an act that had been weighed and deemed necessary—perhaps, he speculated, by a roll of bone dice. A risk, therefore, but a risk worth taking.

Yet still Condell circled: Why? Why was it important? Why take that chance?

He decided he needed a nap, even though it was not yet noon. But what was a day off for, if not napping on a whim? His wife was at work, while his dogs were already asleep on the floor, and therefore in no position to pass judgment.

As is often the case, an answer to that last "why?" came to him as he explored the terrain between sleeping and waking.

A confirmation of identity.

A warning.

Condell opened his eyes.

The killer had not found what he was looking for at Edwin Ellerkamp's house.

XIV

R euben Hapgood rarely opened his premises before 10 a.m., and sometimes not even then. A note on the door invited customers to call a number if the store was closed—which it was from Sunday to Wednesday—but Reuben didn't always answer his phone either, and picked up messages only at his own convenience. The Internet had transformed his business, just as it had so many others, and now even the store itself might have been regarded as surplus to requirements, given that Reuben had essentially replaced it with a virtual shopfront through which he could display his stock to the world. Despite this, he had so far resisted moving fully online, hesitant to sever himself completely from tradition and family history.

Reuben had inherited his vocation—no, his obsession—from his father, who had opened the store on a back road outside Whitefield, New Hampshire, in 1946, shortly after returning from Europe minus the little finger of his left hand, thanks to a piece of German shrapnel that he later had encased in Lucite and put on display behind the counter. The Lucite block was still there, along with a photograph of Reuben's grandfather, Farley Hapgood, standing beside an array of coins bearing the mark of Athelstan, first king of England, the picture taken just a few years before Grandpa Farley emigrated from his homeland of Dorset to a new life in the United States. Farley had been an amateur archaeologist, participating in digs across Dorset, Hampshire, Somerset, and Wiltshire, the four modern counties that corresponded to the ancient kingdom of Wessex, and had discovered the Athelstan coins while conducting a solitary search of freshly plowed fields near Bridport. He had excavated two dozen in total, along with pieces of gold wire and a small, near-perfect gold brooch. Farley had set aside just three of the coins for himself, eventually passing them on to his eldest son, who in turn bequeathed them to his only child, Reuben. The latter, being less sentimental than either of his forebears, had duly sold two of the coins, but he wasn't so avaricious as to part with all of them. The last—bearing the words "Athelstan Rex" on one side surrounding an image of the king, and a cross on the reverse with the name of the maker and mint— Reuben had instructed to be buried with him, in the manner of an ancient warrior carrying some of his wealth into the next world.

Reuben had been married once, but that was long ago, and no children had resulted from the union. He and his ex-wife were no longer in touch, which said much for the depth of their original feelings for each other. No hostility remained between them—in fact, no residual unresolved emotions of any kind. They'd drifted into marriage, then drifted right back out again, like a couple briefly visiting an unsatisfactory Tunnel of Love at a funfair. He'd never bothered marrying again, although he enjoyed the enduring companionship of an obliging lady friend over in Guilford, Vermont, who prized her independence as much as Reuben did his, and would no more have consented to share a roof with him than to have invited rats to colonize her abode. His only surviving relatives, cousins of various removes, were distant and incommunicado. Reuben's will stipulated that, in the event of his death, his private collection and the contents of his store should be examined by experts from the Smithsonian, who would be permitted to add up to 50 percent of what they liked to their own hoard. The rest was to be sold at auction, and the proceeds shared equally among five named animal welfare charities, Reuben having always preferred the company of cats to people, except where the possibility of making money was concerned.

But Reuben hoped that the day of his passing might yet be remote, because he was only sixty and in good health. His principal vices were wine and fresh sourdough bread, which he felt were modest enough, and perhaps made up for the third, which revealed itself in a certain moral latitude when it came to the acquisition and sale of ancient coins and associated items. Reuben didn't steal, but he wasn't above permitting what had been stolen to pass through his hands. He could only hope that, when he died, nothing too illegal might remain on the premises, because he would prefer not to have his reputation for probity posthumously besmirched. Then again, any such items that were discovered would probably be acquired by the Smithsonian anyway, so no harm done—or not much. It wasn't as if those to whom he'd sold illegally acquired coins had melted them down, although he knew of one collector who'd had Greek and Roman coins set into his bathroom floor, which bothered Reuben somewhat. His customers had taken pleasure in their purchases and cherished them. Better that, in Reuben's view, than to have them consigned to some museum basement, as the prized items in his own collection were certainly destined to be.

The nature of his customer base was the other reason Reuben elected to maintain his physical store. Certain men—and collectors of coins were predominantly male—still preferred to conduct their transactions in person, and examine prospective acquisitions in a suitable environment, which for them meant being surrounded by coins. In that sense they resembled bibliophiles, and Reuben understood their desire because he shared it. Even when the shutters were down on the store, and the sign was turned to CLOSED, Reuben frequently remained inside, quietly studying, photographing, communicating, negotiating, with music playing low and one of the cats snoozing on a cushion beside him.

But it was now Thursday, and even by Reuben's tardy and eccentric standards, the store should have been open for at least an hour. The cats crossed the road with him, as they always did, then raced on ahead just in case a rodent or bird might be available for some fun. Reuben entered through the rear door, having first made sure that no suspicious characters were in the vicinity and no unfamiliar vehicles were parked nearby. One couldn't be too careful, because there was no shortage of junkies and lowlifes who thought a coin dealer represented an easy mark. For this reason Reuben carried a compact little Ruger with him when he walked to the store, and a foot-operated panic button beneath the counter connected directly to the Whitefield PD. Reuben had also elected not to economize when it came to the alarm system, and his own cottage stood directly across the road. If the alarm was activated—and so far any activations had been entirely accidental, thank the Lord—he would be able to see with his own eyes what was happening.

All of which meant that, upon arriving inside, the two cats at his ankles, Reuben was disconcerted to find a man seated in one of the armchairs in the back room. He was dressed in shades of brown, a worn trilby hat on his lap and a pistol that was much bigger than Reuben's in his right hand. The hand looked swollen, and the fingernails diseased, the ridges raised, the centers sufficiently concave each to have contained, without spilling, a single drop of water. His skin was flaking, and his eyes were rendered milky gray by a film over the iris and pupil, the left almost totally obscured, the right only partially so. If he wasn't already close to death, Reuben suspected, he soon would be.

"I know you have a gun," he said to Reuben, "because you'd be a fool not to. Now would be a good time to remove it slowly from your person and lay it on the floor."

Reuben slipped the Ruger from its belt holster and set it down. One of the cats sniffed at it curiously.

"Lock the door."

Reuben did as he was told. It took him three tries to get the key in place, his hands were shaking so much.

"Are you here to rob me?" he said.

"I'm no thief." The man sounded affronted.

"Then what do you want?"

"My name is Kepler," said the intruder, "and I think you may have something that belongs to me."

Will Quinn was a Christian man. He attended St. George's Episcopal every Sunday, and his company donated generously to local charities at Christmas. I wasn't sure what his experience of the arcane might have been, but I was prepared to bet good money that it was fairly narrow, and limited to late-night movies on cable.

"Have you seen Buker since he got back?" said Will.

"We had a moment at the Bear. I hadn't planned on arranging another reunion."

"Did you happen to get a look at the latest tattoo on his arm?"

"I saw it. It's a pentacle."

"I know what it is," said Will. "I looked it up on the Internet. It's an occult symbol. It's used in the invocation of spirits."

The best thing about the Internet was that it was easily accessible and available to most. The worst thing about the Internet, meanwhile, was that it was easily accessible and available to most. Technically, what Will had read was true, but on a more benign level the pentacle also symbolized the cycle of life and the connections among the five elements. I knew because I, too, had looked it up. I pointed this out to Will.

"You think Raum Buker got himself tattooed because he's in touch with the cycle of life?" Will responded. "You did say you'd met him, right?"

He had a point. Raum didn't strike me as a cycle-of-life type of guy, and the only time the word "benign" might ever be used in connection with him would be if he developed a tumor.

"Will, half the men who do time come out tattooed, and a few of the women, too. Have you any idea the number of contrariwise swastikas I've noticed on the backs of ex-cons? Most of them are too dumb even to get that much right. They only ever see it in the mirror, so they think it looks okay."

"This isn't a swastika," said Will, "and Buker's many things, but dumb isn't one of them. Even Dolors says he's different. I'm troubled for her safety."

So I was not alone in regarding Raum Buker as a transformed man.

"Different how?"

"Meaner, certainly, and odder. He's nervy, and he told her he has problems sleeping, or it might be she knows that for herself."

I saw his mouth form a cussword, but he bit it back. He wasn't the swearing type, even when tormented by a vision of the woman he loved in bed with another man.

"That's me being paranoid," he said, "and it's unfair to Dolors. Forget I said it. But Buker—"

He hesitated.

"Go on," I said.

"Dolors says he smells of burning."

———

WILL QUINN LEFT TWIN Lights not exactly happy, but a little less unhappy than when he'd arrived. Against my better judgment, I'd agreed to speak with Dolors Strange about Raum Buker. Will had insisted on paying me for my time, and I'd consented to bill him by the hour. In reality, I didn't expect to be charging him for more than however long it took me to drive to Dolors Strange's place of business, listen to her tell me to get lost, find somewhere else to buy coffee, and drive straight back home again.

Before Will left, I asked him about the relationship between Dolors and her sister, Ambar.

"It's solid now," he said. "Their mother died a year ago come March, and it made them realize that each of them was all the other had. It also helped that Buker wasn't around any longer. He ran with both of them for a while."

Will shook his head silently, although whether in wonder or disgust was unclear. It might have been a combination of both.

"And now that he's on the scene again?" I asked.

"I hear he'd like things to return to the way they were."

He looked embarrassed by what this implied. I could hardly blame him.

"How do the Sisters Strange feel about that?" I said.

"Dolors says she doesn't want him in her life again, not that way, and that I shouldn't worry about it. She says it's never going to happen."

"And Ambar?"

"According to Dolors," said Quinn, "Ambar is shakier."

"Then why were the two of them keeping company with Raum at a bowling alley over in Westbrook a few nights back?"

"I wasn't aware of that."

"The question stands."

Will just shrugged miserably.

"I really don't know."

XVI

R euben Hapgood was seated directly opposite the man who called himself Kepler. The cats were keeping their distance, which was unusual for them. They were attention seekers, and weren't above curling up in a customer's lap if he sat still for long enough, but the newcomer had triggered their survival instinct, which also went for Reuben himself. No one had ever pointed a gun at him before, but he was operating on the basis that anyone who bothered to introduce one into a conversation might be prepared to use it, too.

Reuben had heard of Kepler. He believed he might even have sold him coins on a few occasions: though the buyer had been anonymous, and the payment was made by money order, the box number to which the items were sent had rung bells for two of Reuben's associates. They'd warned Reuben to make sure that everything about the coins was in order, because Kepler had a reputation, although neither of the dealers could pinpoint its origins, or tell him anything about the buyer beyond the fact that he wasn't one to be underestimated.

"I saw an advertisement on the dark web," said Kepler. "I have reason to believe you might have placed it."

Reuben made the mistake of mulling over his reply, so that by the time he'd formulated it, the opportunity for dissembling had already passed.

"I occasionally use the dark web," said Reuben, "but I prefer not to."

"Except when you're selling items of dubious provenance, or anything that might attract the attention of the authorities."

"One has to be cautious. You know that. Even a false accusation can be time-consuming to deal with, and hard to disprove. You're a collector."

"But not a thief," said Kepler.

"Neither am I."

"You act on behalf of thieves."

"I act on behalf of sellers," said Reuben, "some of whom, uncommonly, I concede may be thieves," he concluded lamely.

By his right foot one of the cats meowed, as though chiding him for his evasiveness. Kepler frowned at it. The change in expression caused a sore to open by the right side of his nose. It leaked clear fluid that ran down his cheek. Kepler dabbed at it with a finger, and his nose wrinkled in disgust, like a man smelling his own imminent mortality.

"Only a thief," said Kepler, "would be in possession of a Two Emperor."

The Two Emperor being offered for sale on the dark web was among the rarest coins in the world, dating from the ninth century. On one side it depicted King Alfred of Wessex, also known as Alfred the Great, alongside King Ceolwulf II of Mercia, who had largely been erased from history. The other side featured Alfred alone. Just two such coins had ever appeared on the open market. The first had been found in 1840, the second more than a century later. A minimum bid of $50,000 had been placed on the coin being sold via the dark web, but the true value was in excess of $100,000.

"How can you be sure?" said Reuben.

"Two reasons," said Kepler, "with the first of which you're already familiar. Given the rarity of Two Emperors, any offered for sale could only have come from a treasure trove that had been discovered and not reported to the relevant authorities in Britain. It would, therefore, be stolen property by definition. In this particular case, though, it also happens to be *my* stolen property, because I am familiar with every mark on it. It's one of some two hundred coins that were taken from my personal collection not long ago."

"I suppose," said Reuben, "that it would be pointless to request proof of ownership."

"Would you like me to gut one of your cats?" said Kepler.

"No," said Reuben.

"Then we'll take my ownership as given, shall we?"

"That," said Reuben, "will be fine."

Kepler watched as a drop of fluid from his cut exploded on his trouser leg, there to join other stains, some of them fresh.

"Only an unscrupulous man would agree to sell that coin on another's behalf," he said. "Such a man, were he also clever and not too greedy, would have arranged a private sale, so that no one would even have been aware of his involvement beyond the buyer and seller. You, being quite clever but also quite greedy, set up a restricted-access auction site on the dark web, in the hope that the original owner would never come across it. You were in error."

"I didn't know the coin had been stolen from you," said Reuben, which was partly true. He'd been advised by the seller not to delve too deeply into questions of provenance, and had acquiesced, but he had his suspicions, like a handful of others in his line of business. They'd all read of the death of Edwin Ellerkamp, and stories were circulating.

"Would that have made any difference?" said Kepler.

"I might have been more circumspect," Reuben conceded.

Kepler managed something resembling a grin. It caused another sore to begin weeping, this one close to the left corner of his mouth. He retrieved a handkerchief from his pocket to dab at the seepage. Reuben wondered how old this man might be. Shortly after his father's entry into the trade, he had dealt with someone who went by the same name, and who had already enjoyed something of the same notoriety. When Reuben took over the store, he had gone back through the old files out of curiosity and noted his grandfather's dealings with a Kepler, the transactions involving coins of significant rarity. No first name, just a last. For a time, Reuben had assumed that numismatics was an interest that had been passed down the Kepler line, just like his own. Later, as he became privy to the rumors, he grew less certain. Yet how long could one man live? Not much longer, Reuben believed, if the fit of coughing that now overtook his visitor was anything to go by. But the gun never wavered, not that Reuben was even considering trying to rush Kepler. Reuben was not a coward, but neither was he a fool.

"If you don't mind my observing," he said, "you appear unwell."

Kepler removed the handkerchief from his mouth. Reuben saw blood on it, and more: fragments of blackish brown matter like semi-chewed tobacco. He could smell them, too, like bad meat cooked over sulfur.

"I'm dying," said Kepler. "But thankfully," he added, "it's not terminal."

XVII

As I drove from Twin Lights, I found myself wishing that Will Quinn had found someone else with whom to fall in love over mulch. I could judge Dolors Strange only by the company she kept, but a woman who consented to share her bed with Raum Buker was swimming in deeper, colder waters than a man like Will Quinn should ever have dared to explore. I think a part of Will might have wanted to save her—if not from Raum, then from herself. But by common consent Dolors was no fool, or not beyond the weaknesses of the human heart, so she couldn't have been blinkered when it came to her choice of lover. It might have been that, like some of those who lead straitened lives, she had elected to flirt with danger in order to bring excitement into her existence, and was, or had been, prepared to accept the consequences for the duration. Her younger sister, though, had been wilder in her youth, and that kind of wildness has a tendency toward dormancy rather than outright elimination.

It was time to play compare and contrast with the Sisters Strange.

XVIII

Reuben Hapgood led Kepler to the closet beside the store's little kitchenette and bathroom. When opened, the interior revealed only a rack with coat hangers and a couple of spare winter coats, but a catch behind the rail released the rear panel, exposing the Viking Security Safe. The Viking had been designed with gun storage in mind, but suited Reuben's purposes equally well. It was made from a tamper-resistant steel-and-chrome hybrid, and was both fireproof and waterproof. Access was via fingerprint recognition, but it also had a PIN code alternative.

"Open it," said Kepler.

Reuben used the PIN code, and didn't try to hide it. He could always change it later, assuming Kepler didn't shoot him. Also, he didn't like the idea of using fingerprint recognition in front of this man, just in case Kepler took it into his head to remove Reuben's index finger and retain it as some kind of backup. Reuben had heard of a dealer in Albuquerque who'd had his right hand removed by thieves. They'd broken into his home at night and performed the amputation on the kitchen table, although they'd had the decency to kill him first. When they were done, they'd gone to his place of business and used the hand to open the safe. Why they hadn't simply put the dealer in a car and forced him to cooperate, Reuben didn't know. He surmised that some people just liked inflicting harm on others.

Inside the safe were four shelves, on which Reuben stored his most valuable merchandise. From the upper shelf he took a black cloth bag and placed it on the table of the kitchenette.

"Show me," said Kepler.

Carefully, Reuben removed the rigid coin holders, or "slabs," from the bag. The slabs were sonically sealed to create a virtually airtight environment, with the coins themselves suspended within a second inner shell to prevent movement or vibration. The only way to remove the coins was to break the shell. When Reuben was finished, thirty slabs lay on the table. Kepler examined them without touching, but whatever he was looking for, he did not find. Even the sight of the Two Emperor barely gave him pause.

"Where are the rest?" he said.

"That's all I have," said Reuben. "It's everything he offered."

Kepler regarded him without speaking.

"I'm not lying," said Reuben. "I told you: had I known the coins were yours, I would never have agreed to handle them."

It wasn't much of a defense, Reuben thought, and hardly counted as a statement of moral probity, but it was all he had.

"I believe you," said Kepler.

Reuben released a ragged breath, which he hadn't even realized he'd been holding.

"Now give me his name," said Kepler.

Reuben hesitated.

"I don't want anyone to get hurt," he said.

"It's too late for that."

Reuben recalled what he had read about Edwin Ellerkamp's end, and understood that his own life was hanging by a thread. He almost asked Kepler if he'd killed Ellerkamp, the question waiting to be spat out, until he realized that the reply, if given, would damn him. He knew the answer anyway, or thought he did, but sometimes a person desired confirmation, and to hell with the consequences.

"I received the coins from Egon Towle," said Reuben, which was the truth.

But not the whole truth, and therefore nothing like the truth.

———

KEPLER WAVED THE GUN at Reuben, indicating that he should take one of the chairs. When Reuben sat, so, too, did Kepler, but heavily and wearily.

"I'm aware of Egon Towle," said Kepler. "I had always considered him to be an inconsequential man. It bothers me that I was mistaken."

"He loves coins," said Reuben, "and his knowledge of them is remarkable."

"His knowledge of other subjects, too," said Kepler, almost wonderingly. "How long he must have spent stalking me. Such care he must have taken so that I would not become aware of his attention, or hear the approach of his footsteps." He was silent again for a time, then: "But he couldn't have planned and carried out the theft alone."

"I only met Towle," said Reuben.

True, but once more to a degree.

"Where is he now?" said Kepler.

"In hiding, I should think. From you," Reuben added, even if this was obvious. But he was frightened, and a frightened man deplores silence.

"You must have a means of contacting him," said Kepler.

"An email address and a phone number."

"I want both."

"Do you mind if I take out my cell phone?" asked Reuben.

"Not at all."

Reuben retrieved his phone, pulled up Egon Towle's contact details, and displayed the screen to Kepler.

"Write it all down," said Kepler.

Reuben took a pen from his pocket and scribbled the number and email address on a receipt from his wallet.

"What did he say about the rest of my coins?" said Kepler, as he stored the paper away. "Did he plan to put them on the market?"

"I asked if there were more," said Reuben. "He said there might be."

"Is that all?" he said.

"Yes."

And here, at last, was the big lie, but Reuben had been practicing it, and it sounded flawless to his ear. He waited for Kepler to call him on it, but the moment passed and Kepler's attention moved on.

"I could shoot you for the inconvenience you've caused me," he told Reuben. "It wouldn't give me much satisfaction, but I admit it would give some."

"I'd rather you didn't," said Reuben.

"Of course you would. It would also be hypocritical of me. I've never stolen from another man, and I've never bought anything that I believed had been purloined from another collector. But I have acquired items that I knew to have been found on digs and not reported, including the Two Emperor. It came from the Leominster hoard."

"I thought as much," said Reuben.

The Leominster hoard, also from the ninth century, had been uncovered by two British metal detectorists in 2015, at a place called King's Hall Hill near Leominster in England's West Midlands. It included jewelry and hundreds of coins, all of which had probably been concealed by a Viking raider who hadn't lived long enough to retrieve his treasure. Instead of reporting the hoard, which was valued at up to $15 million, the finders had elected to sell it, and were jailed for their efforts. By then most of the contents had vanished, most likely on the black market, although this had never been established conclusively, and the culprits were loath to elaborate on their fate.

Carefully, reverently, Reuben picked up the Two Emperor coin.

"I never thought I'd see one of these," he said. "Had I been the one to find it, I would never have sold it."

"I was offered three, and there were more, I'm sure," said Kepler. "I bought one, because I needed only one. There were others who might have appreciated owning the rest."

He extended a hand, and Reuben reluctantly surrendered the coin to him.

"What is the most valuable piece in your inventory," said Kepler, "your life apart?"

Reuben didn't even have to think about the question.

"An 1875 Coronet Head gold five-dollar half eagle," he said. "Excellent condition."

"That's a two-hundred-thousand-dollar coin," said Kepler.

"I've had offers, but none above one-fifty."

"I'll buy it from you."

"What?"

"I said I'll buy it."

Reuben gaped.

"How much?" he said.

Kepler reached into his pocket and withdrew a single dollar bill.

"One dollar."

"You're joking."

"I'm really not. You will complete a proof of purchase, I will give you the dollar, and our business here will be concluded."

"I won't do it," said Reuben.

"Then I'll shoot you. You'll still have the coin, but you won't have your life."

"You'd cheat me, even though I've returned what was taken from you?"

"No one is cheating you. Money will change hands. The proof of purchase will be signed. And let me remind you, you have given me only some of what was stolen."

"I'm not responsible for the rest," said Reuben. "And two hundred thousand is a high price to pay for an error of judgment."

"I'm not penalizing you for your flawed judgment, but for lying to me. I think you knew those coins were mine from the moment Egon Towle came to you with them, and you had already been primed by him to acquire them. Towle wouldn't have risked larceny on this scale unless he had a scheme in place for the disposal of the goods. Admit it, Mr. Hapgood. I'm tired, and my patience is growing thin."

Reuben had been in business long enough to recognize the difference between a buyer's market and a seller's, and right now he was mired in a seller's nightmare.

"I told Egon I didn't want to know the source," he said, "but once he began providing a partial inventory, I knew it was you. After all, I sold you that 1856 Flying Eagle penny." He gestured at the table. "I remember the nick below the year."

"And now your lapse will cause you to incur a loss on one 1875 half eagle. Unless—"

From the pocket of his waistcoat, Kepler produced a pair of yellowed dice.

"A simple game of chance," said Kepler. "You throw one die, I throw the other. Highest wins. If you score high, I'll let you keep the coin. Score low, and you forfeit."

Dealers like Reuben Hapgood were all gamblers, of a stripe.

"I'll take that deal."

Kepler tossed one of the dice to Reuben, and briefly shook his own in his fist before throwing a five. Reuben also shook, and threw a two.

Reuben held up his hands. He was beaten.

"It's in the safe," he said.

"Then get it."

Reuben stood and approached the safe.

"And Mr. Hapgood?"

Reuben looked back.

"Don't touch that little pistol on the top shelf."

And Reuben thought: *Shit.*

XIX

R aum Buker locked the door of the storage unit, checked it was secure, and headed back to his car. Ambar had taken care of the rental fees for the unit while he'd been in prison, but he'd already paid back some of what he owed her. He might even pay back the rest, everything going well, as long as she didn't bitch at him too much. The unit contained most of his worldly goods, which didn't amount to a whole lot: some clothes, a few pieces of furniture, bits of paperwork, and various possessions from his childhood that had survived the fire in his parental home, and which he was too sentimental to get rid of. He could still smell the smoke on some of them. Given the particulate nature of scents, he supposed that microscopic fragments of his parents probably constituted an element, which was another reason to hold on to them. His mom and pop might have been stone-cold losers, but neither of them had ever raised a hand to him, and they'd brought him up as best they could. True, they hadn't been much for hugs, but neither was Raum.

One of his pockets jingled as he walked away from the lockup. It contained five quarters, three dimes, a couple of nickels, and a Roman gold aureus struck to commemorate Faustina the Elder, wife of the emperor Antoninus Pius, who was deified by the Roman Senate after her death in about A.D. 141. The coin was worth $3,000–4,000, but

Raum had agreed to accept $2,000 from an online dealer in return for a quick sale. He had promised Egon he wouldn't do anything with the coins until he received the all clear, but Egon was currently elsewhere, negotiating the dispersal of the first portion of the Kepler trove. Raum was in need of funds, and there were plenty more coins where this one came from. Admittedly, it would now be the third Raum had sold, but the dealer had promised discretion, and a man had to live, especially after years of incarceration.

Raum's arm was itching like crazy. It was always worse after he visited the unit, and he knew he wouldn't sleep well that night. It was Egon's fault, with his damn stories. He'd planted strange ideas in Raum's head, but if those ideas made them rich, then Raum could put up with them for a while longer—but not for too long, he hoped, because the nightmares were becoming very, very bad.

Even when he was awake.

In the front of the store, Reuben Hapgood completed the proof of purchase, and handed over the half eagle and accompanying paperwork to Kepler, who added both to the black cloth bag containing his recovered possessions, as well as the Springfield 911 pistol from the safe, the Ruger, and a second Ruger that Reuben kept under the main counter. Reuben had to concede that the man was meticulous. He had even deactivated the surveillance system, a fact of which Reuben became aware only when Kepler produced the hard drive and stamped it to pieces in front of him.

"Are we done?" said Reuben.

"I think so," said Kepler. "Unless you give me cause to return."

"I won't talk to the police, if that's what you mean," although Reuben had been considering doing exactly that once he'd cleared the store of any items with provenance open to dispute.

"What would you tell them?" said Kepler. "That you were forced at gunpoint to sell a valuable coin for a dollar? They might believe you, or they might not, assuming they could even find me. But I've been playing this game for a very long time, Mr. Hapgood, longer than you can even begin to imagine. I've monitored your sales, both open and clandestine. You operate in some very gray areas, and you've left a trail. If you were to cause difficulties for me, I would be forced to cause difficulties for you, all for a half eagle illegally obtained to begin with."

"How did—?" Reuben began to ask, before stopping because it wasn't worth proceeding any further. He'd bought the half eagle for $45,000 from a thief-turned-multiple-murderer who was now sitting in a cell at Walls Unit in Texas, waiting for the Supreme Court to turn down his final appeal so the state could proceed with his execution. Reuben had been hoping that the eminent justices might seal the deal sooner rather than later, just in case the condemned man decided to ease his way into the next life by confessing his sins in this one. Looking on the bright side, which wasn't very bright, this was now one less worry for Reuben.

Kepler produced two sets of cable ties from the pocket of his overcoat. Reuben looked at them in alarm.

"There's no call for those," he said.

"I've found that absence makes some hearts grow braver," said Kepler. "I'll secure your hands and feet, but otherwise you'll be free to move. I'm sure you can find a way to get to a blade, by which time I'll be well gone."

Reuben wasn't happy about this, but he knew there could have been worse conclusions. He put his hands behind his back, docile as a lamb, then lay on his belly so a tie could be applied to his ankles. The restraints were uncomfortable, but not so tight as to cut off his circulation. When he was done, Kepler helped him to a sitting position and squatted beside him.

"I'm not going to advise you against contacting Egon Towle and telling him about our conversation," said Kepler. "If you choose to admit that you've shared his details with me, that's your decision. It may even encourage him to see the error of his ways, and help him come to his senses before circumstances deteriorate any further. But any misfortune coming his way, he has brought upon himself—and you have strife of your own to manage, so your obligations to him are limited."

That part about "strife of your own" struck Reuben as an odd thing to say: undeniably true, obviously, both as a general existential observation and in reference to his current predicament, but odd nonetheless. He was, admittedly, bound hand and foot, and down a valuable coin, but he was alive, and likely to remain so for the time being.

"I'm sorry," he said.

"I know you are."

Kepler produced a roll of duct tape from the folds of his coat and commenced wrapping it around Reuben's head, covering his mouth. Reuben tried to protest, but Kepler was too fast for him.

"In case someone comes by," said Kepler, "because I really would prefer you to be silent until the time is right."

Then Kepler did a curious thing. Just before he left, he picked up both of Reuben's cats and carried them away with him.

The moon on the one hand, the dawn on the other:
The moon is my sister . . .

—Hilaire Belloc, "The Early Morning"

XXI

Dolors Strange's coffee shop was called, not surprisingly, Strange Brews. I'd never darkened its door because I hadn't wanted to drink coffee or eat a pastry prepared by someone with intimate physical knowledge of Raum Buker, not even if they'd scrubbed their hands with Lysol throughout the intervening years. Inside, as befitted its name, Strange Brews was decked out like a fortune-teller's tent, all red drapes and overstuffed cushions, with crystals, incenses, oils, candles, and New Age books for sale alongside muffins, cookies, and doughnuts. The walls were hung with the kind of paintings and drawings that passed for art among people who dreamed of someday owning their own unicorn.

The place was devoid of customers when I arrived, but that might have been a direct consequence of the music playing in the background, which sounded like it had been composed for an elf's funeral. Dolors Strange was working the register, assisted by a teenage girl with a high pain threshold for piercings. I sometimes wondered what I'd say if Sam decided that intensive body modification was the way to go. If she was committed to suffering, I could always suggest she join the Marines, or become a Browns fan.

Dolors Strange was in her midforties, but looked older. She had let her hair go gray, which suited her, with the result that the severity incongruous in her youth was now more appropriate to her years. No one would ever have called her beautiful, except possibly Will Quinn, but she was interesting-looking, perhaps even attractive in the austere way of certain graveyard statuary. She was checking the change drawer of the register, counting the coins with long, delicate fingers. Her nails were painted a reddish purple. The color matched the veins that stood out on the backs of her hands, as though deoxygenated blood was accumulating at her fingertips.

"Ms. Strange?" I said, reaching for my license. "I was hoping I could talk to you for a moment. My name is—"

"I know who you are," she said, barely glancing up at me. "I read the papers. I can even take a guess at your business here. What's he done now?"

"Who?"

"Raum. Why else would you want to speak with me? You can't be running so short of conversation that you're reduced to bothering strangers."

She dropped the final *r* on the last word, the way certain Mainers did. It turned the comment into a kind of bleak pun on her own name. The kid with the piercings scowled at me, or it might have been the weight of metal dragging her features inexorably down.

"Raum does come into it," I admitted.

"I'm not his keeper. You have an issue with him, go talk to him yourself." She finished counting and gave me her full attention for the first time. "Unless you only do that when you have toughs to back you up. I heard how you and your friends once stuck a gun in his mouth."

"The gun was a last resort," I said.

"Not in your case, if what I've heard is true."

"That stings," I said.

"I'm sure you'll get over it."

"Plus, it wasn't my gun. I'm very particular about where I put that."

"I'm sure."

She bagged some nickels and closed the register. Before she did, I spotted a few ones, and a couple of fives, but no larger bills. It caused me to wonder how well Strange Brews might be doing. It stood on an unprepossessing section of Main Street between two larger units— one empty, the other housing partly occupied office suites—and was set slightly too far back from the road, so that by the time drivers might have noticed it was there, they'd already have gone past it. Signs on the noticeboard indicated that Strange Brews hosted a monthly mindfulness group, and something called the Strange Knitters every second Tuesday, but I doubted there was much money in facilitating mindfulness, and it was hard to knit and drink coffee at the same time.

"Did Raum happen to mention that we met at the Bear not so long ago?" I said.

"He might have. He's got no love for you, Mr. Parker."

I caught the faintest hint of a smile, although it wasn't a nice one. In her head, I think she was picturing Raum acquainting me with some of that payback he had promised.

"If you're done with the register," I said, "perhaps we could speak a little more. In private."

"Yeah, I'm done with the register, but that goes for the discourse, too. If Raum hears you've been by, I'll be in a world of torment, but you'll be keeping me company."

"Some people are concerned that you're already in a world of torment, Ms. Strange."

She squinted at me, and her lips managed, against all odds, to grow even thinner. Gradually some of the tension eased from her, and I glimpsed something like resignation, or regret.

"I can guess who that might be," she said. "You tell Will he has no reason to fret. I can handle Raum."

And only the slightest tremor to her voice and hands gave away the untruth.

XXII

Reuben Hapgood had managed to get as far as the kitchenette, although not without falling over twice, it being harder to negotiate a room full of obstacles with one's arms and legs secured than might have been anticipated. Finally, after banging his head painfully against a chair arm, he had opted for an awkward shuffle on his knees. When he reached the kitchenette, he backed against a drawer, pulled it open, and got his hands on a paring knife. It wasn't very sharp, and he fumbled it a couple of times before managing to figure out the best way to hold it in order to saw at the bond on his wrists.

Reuben had decided that while the encounter with Kepler could have gone better, it could also have gone a great deal worse. Kepler didn't know that Reuben had paid hard cash for only three of the coins supplied by Egon Towle, and had effectively taken the rest on consignment, including the Two Emperor—not that Reuben would have encountered any difficulty selling the latter, but he didn't have enough cash on hand to pay even half of what Towle expected to make from the sale. In other words, counting the half eagle, and the three coins bought from Towle, he was down about $60,000, which was bad. On the other hand, he was still alive, which was good, and he had also managed to keep back from Kepler both his own involvement in the planning of the theft *and* the identity of Egon Towle's partner, Raum Buker. Reuben believed Buker might be capable of handling Kepler. What was more, Reuben knew that Buker had been entrusted with the lion's share of the haul, including—

Reuben paused in the twin acts of cutting and assessing. A storage box stood on the floor by the bar fridge in which he kept milk for the cats and a selection of candy bars for himself. The box was constructed of plain cardboard, about two feet in length and a foot in width and height, with a lid on top. It wasn't a type that Reuben ever used, and he couldn't recall ordering anything that might have arrived packed in it.

He recommenced his efforts and felt the cable tie give way beneath the edge of the knife. He removed the duct tape from his mouth, sacrificing some skin and hair along the way, and set about freeing his feet. Once this was done, he tossed the knife aside, walked to the box, and knelt beside it. Gently, he removed the lid. Inside the box were two containers of gasoline wrapped in detonation cord, and a timer affixed to a blasting cap. The face of the timer had been painted with Wite-Out to obscure the countdown. *Score low, and you forfeit.* Reuben, a little too late, now grasped the nature of that forfeiture.

He started for the back door, but Kepler had secured it behind him and taken the keys. The spare set was contained in a magnetic lockbox attached to the back of the safe. Reuben didn't want to go anywhere near that incendiary device again, but now he had no choice. Offering up his first prayer in many years to the God in whom he still mostly believed, Reuben ran for the safe. He was halfway there when he learned that God was otherwise occupied.

And Reuben Hapgood burned.

XXIII

I'd struck out badly with Dolors Strange; not that I'd anticipated a better outcome, but if we don't have misguided optimism, what do we have? The sensible move would have been to wipe my hands of the matter and advise Will Quinn to go back to hanging out in his lumberyard in the hope that love, having once found him there, might consider coming around for a second try.

On the other hand, all human beings contain within them a self-destructive urge. It typically manifests itself as addiction—food, drugs, alcohol, sex, gambling, and violence (because that, too, becomes addictive)—but even the most disciplined of us will sometimes hear the call of compulsion, and see for an instant the world through craving eyes. It's the voice that speaks in your head as you walk along a cliff edge, before offering a vision of your body tumbling to the rocks below. The more vulnerable you are, the more insistent it becomes. The only ones untroubled by it are the dead.

Thus, having failed with Dolors Strange, he knew it was natural also to court failure with her younger sister. The dentist's office at which Ambar Strange worked operated half days on Wednesdays, which I didn't discover until I dropped by. I should have taken that as an omen, but by then I was committed, so I continued to her home.

Ambar lived in a two-bedroom Cape cottage off Railway Avenue. The property was probably worth about $300,000. Real estate records showed that she had bought it for just over $200,000 back in 2015, so it had turned out to be a good investment. It was painted burnt ocher with a cream trim, and had a small, over-ornate portico enclosing the front door, lending it the aspect of a gingerbread house. All that was needed to complete the picture was a witch, but I had to settle for a would-be ogre.

Raum Buker emerged from the rear of the cottage as I pulled up to the curb, Ambar Strange following behind him, her hands buried deep in her pockets. She was six years younger and six inches shorter than Dolors, and carried just enough weight to soften the edges that showed so distinctly in her sister. Her hair was a vivid red, and tied in a ponytail that hung over her left shoulder. She was wearing a quilted vest with a sweater and jeans, and tan work boots that looked excessively ungainly on her small frame, and were too clean to have ever served any practical purpose. Her head was down, and she radiated low-level misery.

She and Raum spoke for a few minutes beside the front door. When he leaned over to kiss her, she turned her head so that he caught her cheek, not her mouth. He tried again, this time gripping her chin with his right hand, but she pulled away. Raum wasn't happy about this, and let her know it—loudly. With the window rolled down, I heard it all.

"Fuck you," said Raum. "You asked me to come over."

"For help," said Ambar, "not for that."

"It's busted glass. You want help, call a glazier."

He stomped back to his car. Raum Buker: gentleman caller, comforter of the afflicted. He was driving a red Chevy Monte Carlo in rough condition. If he'd paid more than five hundred dollars for it, he'd been robbed.

I hoped he'd paid more than five hundred.

Ambar Strange went back into her home through the front door and closed it behind her, which meant she didn't see what happened next. As he reached the car, Raum rolled up the sleeve of his jacket and began scratching at the pentacle tattoo on his arm. It might have been festering; I've never been tattooed, so I couldn't say for sure. But as I watched, Raum progressed from scratching to tearing, his nails gradually digging through the skin into the flesh beneath, and I could see the blood running down his wrist and palm before dripping from his fingers to the pavement. Despite the pain he must have been causing himself, his expression never varied, not once. His face was a mask of absolute desolation.

XXIV

I once listened to a talk given by a writer who believed some men were so morally corrupt that their depravity found a physical expression, their moral disfigurement manifesting itself as an alteration to feature or form. It was a variation on phrenology and physiognomy, the discredited pseudoscientific convictions that the shape of a skull or face might disclose essential traits of character. Were it true, the job of law enforcement would have been made significantly easier, and a lot of time and effort could have been saved by jailing all the ugly people. But evil—true evil, not the mundane human wickedness born of fear, envy, wrath, or greed—is adept at concealment, because it wishes to survive and persist. Only when it's ready, or is forced to do so, does it reveal itself. Not even evil is free from the rule of nature.

Certain parasitic wasps lay their eggs either on, or in, host creatures, frequently caterpillars. The injector, known as an endoparasitoid, attempts to introduce its eggs into the prey, which—if the effort is successful—will continue to mature, its development unhindered by the alien organisms it is carrying. But the wasp has to take precautions. The caterpillar instinctively recognizes the threat posed by the predator. It wriggles and jerks. It bites, or secretes poisons from its skin. It might even win, if it struggles hard enough. But often it doesn't struggle sufficiently.

Sometimes, it doesn't struggle at all.

When the wasp is done, and the eggs have been laid, it places a chemical marker on the host. The wasp has to avoid injecting the same host twice, nor does it want other wasps to target it. But even now the caterpillar has not yet entirely lost the battle against fatal infection. If its instinct and strength allow, it can seek to purge itself of the parasites by ingesting alkaloids from certain plants. Yet not every host will attempt to do this. Why is unclear.

The host that does not fight, does not purge, will succumb. The eggs grow by absorbing bodily fluids before the larvae eventually hatch and feed on the surrounding tissue from within, chewing their way out as the host dies. Until this moment of revelation, all that may be observed is a creature, internally blighted but outwardly unchanged, going about its business.

I now believe that something foul had infested Raum Buker, although even with the benefit of hindsight, and some imperfect knowledge of the events that followed, I can't be certain what it was. My guess is that his immunity to contamination—because only the very worst of us are born without some protection—had been compromised by flaws in his nature and upbringing, leaving him vulnerable to attack. I'd like to think he tried to fight it. I may be wrong. What I witnessed that day outside Ambar Strange's cottage could just have been a man driven to mutilate himself by an irritated wound, but I feel—I hope—it was more than that.

I think it was Raum trying to purge himself before it was too late.

Unlike her sister, Ambar Strange didn't immediately recognize me or display any particular resentment toward my presence on her doorstep. She might, though, have been anticipating greeting a chastened Raum Buker when she answered my knock, because she appeared simultaneously disappointed and mildly relieved, which is a difficult combination to pull off. Up close she looked tired, the kind of cumulative exhaustion that comes from the loss of more than a single night's sleep.

I showed her my PI license, and she scowled as she made the connection.

"You the guy who stuck a gun in Raum's mouth?" she said.

I was starting to wish that Louis had found another way to focus Raum's attention. The way he was going, he was likely to get himself a bad name in every dentist's waiting room and New Age coffee shop in New England.

"That was a colleague," I said.

"You didn't try to stop him?"

"He's difficult to dissuade once he has his heart fixed on something." She mulled over this.

"I guess Raum probably asked for it," she said at last. "I'm surprised it hasn't happened more often."

She was still holding my license. She peered at it again. I thought she might have been nearsighted, because I could see a depression at either side of her nose where spectacles had left their mark. The license was returned to me, and her thought processes moved on.

"So who hired you?" she said. "Because that's how you guys work, right? It's not like you're the police. Is this about Raum, or me?"

"Raum. As for who hired me, I'm working for someone who's worried about your sister."

"Will Quinn," she said, brightening. "I'm right, aren't I?"

"Yes, it's Will."

"He's sweet. Dolors could do a lot worse."

"Like Raum?"

Her smile faded.

"There's no need to be rude," she said. She took in the dead-end street, searching for his car. "And you wouldn't talk like that to his face."

"He's gone," I said. "I watched him drive away. And I've said worse to his face."

"He'll be back."

"You don't sound completely happy about that."

She shrugged. "Like your friend with the gun, Raum's also hard to dissuade once he's set on something."

"And what would that be?"

She gave me the cold eye.

"What do you think?"

It was difficult to know how to respond to the Stranges' singular sexual arrangements, past or present, without sounding prurient or prudish. Theirs was the kind of entanglement that made a man want to grab David Crosby by the scruff of the neck halfway through a rendition of "Triad," his ode to troilism, and shout, *See, David,* this *is why you can't go on as three.*

"Could we talk inside?" I said.

"Raum wouldn't like it."

"Raum doesn't have to know."

Ambar Strange folded her arms. It was cold, so she had reason to shiver, but in this case the weather didn't strike me as the cause.

"He'll know," she said, and her voice was very small.

I brought to mind again her sister, and the giveaway tremor. I saw Raum scratching at his tattoo until it bled. I counted three fearful people, but I couldn't say if they were all frightened of the same thing.

"Ms. Strange," I said, "what's he doing back in Portland?"

"He served his time. Why wouldn't he return here?"

Because I'm a trained investigator, I noticed she was avoiding the question.

"Do you know where he was incarcerated?"

Because it never hurt to be sure, and Ambar Strange could save me some digging. Also, facts were one thing, but personal testimony sometimes trumped them.

"East Jersey State Prison."

"Any idea why?"

"For getting caught."

"Funny. Other than that?"

"An accident. Ask him yourself."

"It's a pleasure to which I can look forward," I said. "But until that happy day, this is a big country, and Raum and Portland have never seen eye to eye. He could have gone to a lot of other places and attracted a great deal less attention. Did he return here because of you or your sister?"

Her face twitched, as though I'd touched on an old wound. The answer was given before she had time to stop herself.

"Neither," she said. "He's *waiting*," and she managed to load that word with a wicked amount of scorn.

"Waiting for what?"

She unfolded her arms and made a dismissive gesture with her right hand.

"Oh, just waiting. Raum always has some get-rich plan."

"Has he told you what the current one might be?"

"To stop being poor. When that happens, he'll make sure Dolors and I get our share. Nobody will get hurt, and it's nothing the police will care about."

She said all this the way someone might read the end of a familiar fairy tale in which they could never quite believe, yet from the rote recital of which they derived some passing comfort. I did my best to keep a straight face, but skepticism won out, and Ambar Strange witnessed me lose the fight.

"He swore by it," she said, "and I believe him. That's all I know. I mean, why am I even talking to you?"

"Why *are* you talking to me?"

"Because Raum deserves a break," she said. "He's done his time, but his reputation follows him, like a weight tied around his ankles. If people like you could just leave him alone, he might find a way to get settled. You're convinced he's rotten, but he's not. I know what he's done, the good and the bad, and I think one outweighs the other."

She didn't say which weighed heavier, though, and I suspect we might have differed on it anyway.

"I'm not entirely unsympathetic," I said, by way of compromise, and I wasn't. I knew how hard it could be for ex-cons to survive on the outside. The straight world, or what passed for it given the ubiquity of human frailty, was more hostile to those who had served time than it was to most constituencies.

"No?" said Ambar. "Forgive me if that sounds hollow to my ears."

"Do you know where Raum is staying?"

She reddened. "He *was* staying here."

"But not any longer?"

"No."

"Can I ask the reason for the move?"

"You can ask. You won't get an answer, though, not from me."

"Which brings us back to where Raum is currently laying his head."

"Cheap motel beds, when he can't find a couch to surf."

She started to go back inside. My window with her was closing.

"One last question," I said.

She banged her head gently against the doorframe in frustration.

"What is it?"

"What were you and Raum arguing about earlier?"

"You saw that?"

"Some of it. I heard it, too."

"A door pane at the back of the house got damaged last night. I was worried. I thought someone might have been trying to break in, but Raum told me it was probably just an animal."

"Why would he say that?"

"Because the screen door was all torn up, and the glass was scratched."

"Would you mind if I took a look?" I said.

"Yes, I would."

And with that, Ambar Strange closed the front door in my face.

XXVI

I'd enjoyed more productive working days, having learned virtually nothing from my encounters with the Sisters Strange. By now it should have been clear to me that their problems, and those of Raum Buker, whatever form or combination they might take, were really none of my concern. Neither sister gave signs of welcoming my interest, and Raum himself was unlikely to buck that trend. On the other hand, I'd made a vocation out of curiosity, and it was too late to seek alternative employment now.

But it wasn't solely a matter of personal or professional stubbornness. Raum had disorder following him like a dog in heat—Ambar was right about that much—and he'd brought it to the doors of the Sisters Strange. If he did have plans on the boil, they were likely to involve dishonest dealings, if only for want of many alternatives. The Stranges might have believed themselves capable of handling him, and under ordinary circumstances they would doubtless have been right: Raum was no match for two smart women, because most men aren't a match even for one. But you don't watch someone tear strips from his own skin, especially a man with Raum Buker's history, without becoming concerned for those around him. Everything about Raum felt off-kilter, and perhaps Will was right to fear that he might prove a danger to Dolors or Ambar. If I walked away, and something happened to either or both of the Sisters Strange, I'd have to live with my failure to act, and I already had enough guilt to sustain me for two lifetimes.

And there was Will himself to consider: I'd agreed to work for him, and that had to amount to more than two inconclusive conversations before turning tail. Will might have been a quiet, shy man, but he hadn't succeeded in a business like lumber without his share of strength and stubbornness. If he cared enough about Dolors Strange, he might feel impelled to act on her behalf if I gave up, and whatever his better qualities, they would be no match for Raum's worse ones.

Any further inquiries I might have wished to make, though, were curtailed by an urgent call from my lawyer, Moxie Castin, for whom I also did investigative work. At Moxie's request, I spent two days looking for a reluctant witness in a domestic manslaughter case, eventually tracking her to a camp up by Chamberlain Lake. By the time I'd convinced her to return to Portland to testify, the stakes in the game being played by Raum Buker and the Sisters Strange had been raised again, and a new player was making his presence known.

XXVII

In a motel room by South Portland's Maine Mall, Kepler sat before a screenshot of Raum Buker lying on a bed in lodgings that were even more nondescript, and definitely more down-at-the-heel, than Kepler's own. Buker, Kepler noted, had done little to impose his presence on the room: whatever possessions he might have brought with him were neatly stored away, and when he ate at the single small table, he opened a window to let out any odors and placed his trash in a sealed plastic bag to be disposed of at the first opportunity.

In some ways, though, the spruceness of Buker's lodgings mirrored Kepler's, although the latter's showed even fewer signs of human habitation, and some might well have disputed the use of the term "human" in connection with his occupancy. The bed was made, the bathroom had barely been used, the closets were empty, and an ancient leather bag, of the kind once favored by nineteenth-century medical practitioners with a drinking problem, contained all his traveling needs. He took the bag with him when he availed of housekeeping, which he did each day, setting it by his feet as he ate poached eggs and fried apples at the Cracker Barrel while waiting for his room to be cleaned, because hygiene was important to him.

Every morning he would toss the sheets and muss the pillows on the bed, even if it had not been slept in. He would dampen the towels and throw them in the tub, just to give the impression of use. If he rested at all, he did so during the day, and then only for an hour or two. Like certain mammals, Kepler was primarily nocturnal. He was now also in constant pain, and struggled particularly with maintaining a horizontal position for any extended period of time. He self-medicated with over-the-counter remedies—and where necessary, under-the-counter narcotics, too.

Floriana, the maid responsible for servicing his room, had noticed a distinctive but not unpleasant odor about it, which she tended to associate with her great-grandfather, her *bisabuelito* Adelardo, who had spent the entire span of his years in a grand mansion located in the Paseo Montejo neighborhood of Mérida, Yucatán. As he grew older and poorer, Adelardo had been forced to rent out more and more rooms in the mansion, until finally he was reduced to living in the attic, a tenant in what had once been his own home. But every morning Adelardo would shine his shoes, put on a shirt and tie, and promenade for hours around the Plaza de la Independencia before imbibing a single glass of tepeztate at El Cardenal. He might have been reduced to the status of a near pauper, but that was no reason to let standards slip.

On Sundays, Adelardo would apply his special scent, the one he poured only sparingly from an unmarked bottle, before hearing Mass at the cathedral. The cologne, the source of which remained a mystery to Adelardo's family, had a base of civet and rosewater, and it was a version of this same smell that Floriana detected in room 313. It caused her to feel an instinctive deference toward its occupant, Mr. Kepler, a regard only enhanced by the five dollars he left for her each morning, despite the fact that his room took barely any time to freshen, and frequently appeared to be as unblemished as she had left it the day before, if not more so. (Floriana had worked as a housekeeper for three decades, and never failed to be shocked by the many ways in which seemingly ordinary men and women were capable of defiling their habitations.)

It did not matter to Floriana that Mr. Kepler looked odd, or that she had never heard him speak. Neither was she concerned that, when viewed in proximity, his clothing was more distressed than it first appeared, for this also had been true of her *bisabuelito*. If they passed each other in the hallway, Mr. Kepler would silently raise his hat and smile, a curiously old-fashioned gesture in a world that increasingly viewed kindness and civility as signs of weakness, even as his lips parted to reveal spaced, decaying teeth, their enamel striated with fault lines of dark yellow.

Yet for all Mr. Kepler's many apparent, even undeniable, good qualities, Floriana did her best to avoid crossing his path, and tried not to look him in the eye when she did, because she couldn't help but flinch at the evidence of grave illness. Neither did she spend more time in his room than was absolutely necessary. She made sure to wear rubber gloves while moving through it, but still washed her hands with disinfectant when done.

Her sleep patterns had also become disturbed. Floriana worked two jobs—she stocked shelves at Shaw's four evenings a week, and all day Saturday—so exhaustion usually ensured immediate oblivion, but for the past four nights she had not rested well. She would wake in darkness, and feel the urge to check the latches on the door and windows of the apartment she shared with her husband and two adult children. She tried to fight it, but the longer she waited, the more alert and disquieted she became. She would get up as quietly as she could, make her rounds, and return to bed, only to wake a couple of hours later to commence the routine again.

Four nights without proper sleep.

Four mornings spent cleaning Mr. Kepler's room.

And sometimes, as she tested the locks, Floriana thought she could pick up the faintest hint of rosewater and civet, and she wondered if this was how incipient madness smelled.

XXVIII

The bell above the entrance to Strange Brews tinkled, but Dolors Strange didn't turn to see who might have come in, because Erin, her assistant, could take care of it. Right now Dolors was more concerned with why the cinnamon rolls she'd defrosted just the night before were speckled with mold. The only reason could be that they'd arrived that way from Becker & Co., the local bakery that supplied her, but Johanna Becker was reluctant to accept that this might be the case, and was trying to blame Dolors for storing them improperly. Since Dolors was counting every dime in order to keep her business running, determining responsibility for the mold was a matter of some financial import.

"Dolors," said Erin.

Dolors waved a hand at her to hush. She had Johanna on the ropes, and wasn't about to be distracted before she could land the crucial blow. Finally, after further back-and-forth, Johanna, with nothing resembling good grace, agreed to have a dozen freshly baked rolls delivered to Strange Brews within the hour, free of charge, to replace the original consignment, if only to get Dolors off the phone. Satisfied, Dolors turned to see what the next problem might be.

Her sister, Ambar, was standing at the counter. She was crying.

"You got a minute?" said Ambar. "Because I think we need to talk."

XXIX

Following a discussion with Will Quinn, in the course of which we each made our respective positions clear and came to an agreement about how best to proceed, I ate an early lunch at the Bayou Kitchen while I worked the phone.

As rumor suggested, and Ambar Strange had confirmed, Raum had been an inmate in Jersey at East Jersey State Prison under Title 2C of the New Jersey Code of Criminal Justice: five years for manslaughter, which was at the lower end of the sentencing scale. He had killed a man named Clayton Dempsey in Lindenwold during an argument over a parking space that then continued into a nearby bar. The disagreement escalated, Dempsey threatened Raum with a broken bottle, and Raum stabbed him to death with a knife used by the bartender to slice lemons.

A couple of witnesses subsequently recanted and claimed that Dempsey had broken the bottle accidentally, with no intention of actually using it as a weapon, but enough doubt was sown in the minds of the jury for Raum to have avoided a first-degree felony charge, and a sentence of ten to thirty years. The defense of reasonable provocation in the heat of passion was accepted, and Raum got sent down for five. Under New Jersey's mandatory minimum sentencing guidelines, he served fifty-one months in prison. East Jersey was the state's second-oldest facility, housing maximum-, medium-, and minimum-security prisoners. It wasn't an easy place to do time, and nobody would be rushing back for a second taste of its hospitality, but it wasn't as bad as New Jersey State Prison in Trenton, which was grim as all hell, with a reputation for inmate violence. If that pentacle tattoo represented the sum total of Raum Buker's scarring from almost five years in the New Jersey prison system, he could consider himself halfway fortunate.

I was curious to know what company Raum might have been keeping down there. A man who emerges from prison sporting a pair of Waffen-SS cracker bolts has been hanging around with white supremacists. Someone who comes out with a Pagans tattoo is likely to start shopping for a motorcycle. But a prisoner who returns to freedom bearing an occult symbol on his arm—well, he's fallen into some unusual society. Of course, it was entirely possible that a bored inmate with too much time on his hands, combined with exposure to the kind of books or DVDs that fundamentalist preachers liked to rail against during Sunday sermons, might take it into his head to get inked with pitchforks and horned devils, but Raum Buker didn't strike me as falling into that category. Raum thought before he acted, which made his wrongdoings so much more difficult to forgive.

I'd been dancing around the margins of Raum's life, but it wasn't yet the moment to confront him directly. There weren't many things worth learning from the company of lawyers, apart from the fact that it was best avoided, but among them was not asking questions to which one did not already have the answers. That didn't quite work for investigations, but a version of the same rule could still apply: Try discreetly to discover for yourself as many answers as possible before you begin asking any questions aloud. Before I again confronted Raum, I wanted to find out as much as I could about his reasons for returning to Portland. From the inquiries I'd made, I now knew where he was living.

I was about to pay an unsocial call to the Braycott Arms.

XXX

Dolors Strange waved to her sister as Ambar drove away from Strange Brews. Ambar always seemed so small, so vulnerable, but never more so than now. She had shown Dolors the bruises left by Raum Buker on her arm, as though his fingers had burned their imprint into her skin. He hadn't intended to do it, Ambar said, but whether he'd intended it or not was of no consequence: Raum had hurt Ambar, which meant he'd overstepped the mark.

Even while they were alienated from each other, Dolors had worried about Ambar. They had been close in childhood, drifted apart during adolescence, and actively clashed in adulthood, but Dolors had never ceased to feel protective of her younger sibling. Their mother had acted as a conduit for information, and made various efforts to encourage a reconciliation, but only her final illness, and ultimately her death, had succeeded in bridging the distance between the sisters. Dolors struggled to recall what it was that had caused their estrangement to begin with; under duress, she doubted she could have pointed to any single incident or exchange to justify years of mutual hostility. It was just that, for a while, their differences were too extreme, and their similarities too close, for them to be able to coexist comfortably in the same spaces.

Of course, there was also Raum. In the beginning the sisters had not even been aware that he was sleeping with both of them. It had amused him, Dolors now knew, to move from one to the other, sometimes in the space of the same night. Raum possessed an undeniable streak of sadism, and although he had never admitted it to either of them, Dolors thought that the idea of driving a final, insurmountable wedge between the Sisters Strange might have appealed to him. In that, at least, he had failed, because when they did finally learn of the arrangement, they had confronted him together, and he had laughed in their faces. Dolors had vowed to have nothing more to do with him, but Ambar—well, for her it was more difficult. Raum had buried his hooks deep in Ambar, because she did not have her sister's protective carapace. When Ambar told Dolors that she was sleeping with him again following his return to Portland, Dolors could only stare at her in bafflement. No envy intruded (because that would have implied desire), only a renewed awareness on Dolors's part that some of her sister's ways, like those of God Himself, were beyond all understanding.

Dolors had difficulty remembering what it was about Raum Buker that she had initially found so attractive, beyond the fact that it was nice to be wanted by a man, even one such as he. In Ambar he had satisfied some deeper need—for company, for protection—but she was struggling with the version of him that had emerged from incarceration. Now he had left his mark on her, and a man who did that once would do so again, if permitted. A good sister would have advised Ambar to walk away, even to go to the police. Occasionally, though, as in fairy tales, what was required was not to be good, but to be clever.

So Ambar would stay with Raum, and Dolors would observe.

Observe, and prepare.

XXXI

The Braycott Arms was situated just off Park Avenue, and had once operated as a railroad hotel, back when Union Station was located on St. John Street. Union Station was torn down in 1961 to be replaced with a strip mall that nobody had ever liked, when the future looked, smelled, and sounded like an automobile. Even by the standards of grand nineteenth-century railroad architecture, the old station had been something special, designed to resemble a medieval French château, with a high clock tower and pink granite walls. People wept openly when that tower fell, or so my grandfather told me.

Nobody would have wept if the Braycott Arms fell, particularly if it took some of its tenants with it. Back in the day, the Braycott had catered to a lower order of traveler than the nearby Inn at St. John, which had since reinvented itself as a boutique hotel. By contrast, the Braycott's current owners had a reputation for tolerating antisocial behavior to the point of active facilitation, and had they conducted background checks before renting, virtually every unit in the place would have remained empty. It wasn't somewhere to call home, just somewhere from which to call home. The parole service tried to discourage recently released prisoners from taking a bed there, but sometimes the ex-cons didn't have a great deal of choice, the majority of landlords being understandably reluctant to welcome malefactors into their buildings. As a result, the Braycott frequently held more people with criminal records than the Cumberland County Jail.

The longtime manager was a guy named Bobby Wadlin, who lived in a single-bedroom apartment just inside the front door, and broke a sweat by standing still. He spent most of his day behind a scarred plexiglass screen with a slot for accepting money and dispensing mail and keys, and had never been known to take a vacation. During disputes over rent or damage, he would reluctantly take it upon himself to act as a moderating influence on the faceless owners, like Simon of Cyrene being pressed into assisting Christ with the cross. Since Wadlin *was* one of the owners, along with his two brothers and a sister-in-law who wanted nothing more to do with the Braycott than cash the rent checks, negotiations didn't take very long, and usually ended unsatisfactorily for the tenants involved.

Wadlin, true to form, was seated behind his screen when I arrived, watching an old western in black and white on a portable TV hooked up to a DVD player. Wadlin was always watching old westerns in black and white. Even if they were made in color, he'd alter the setting on the TV so he could view them in monochrome. There was probably some psychological insight to be gleaned from this, but life was short. In any event, it wouldn't have made me like him any more than I already did, and I didn't like him much at all. Despite the cold, he was wearing a short-sleeved shirt and a blind man's tie, the garishness of the latter's colors an attempt to compensate for the utter grayness of the rest of his existence.

"Bobby," I said.

Wadlin kept his eyes fixed on the screen.

"I'm watching my show," he said.

"Raum Buker."

"What about him?"

"Is he in?"

Wadlin tore his gaze from the TV for long enough to check the key hooks. Residents were not permitted to take keys with them when they left the premises, not even for a short time, just in case one fell into the wrong hands and was used to gain entry to the Braycott in order to surreptitiously disinfect it.

"Out," said Wadlin.

"I'd like to take a look at his room."

"Our guests expect privacy and security."

I put a twenty in the slot. I figured Will Quinn was good for it, even if it was unlikely to be receipted. Wadlin, meanwhile, was financially comfortable enough to be offended by the size of the bribe if he chose, but he didn't so choose. Doing something for nothing was against his principles, or what passed for them in the absence of any actual principles. He also knew that if he didn't help me, I'd find a way to make life difficult for him in the future, because this wasn't the first time I'd had business at the Braycott, and it wouldn't be the last.

Wadlin produced a spare key from a drawer, leaving the main one on its hook should Raum Buker return.

"Don't be up there too long," said Wadlin.

"I'll try not to disturb the dirt."

"I'll warn the roaches you're on your way," he said, returning to his western. "It might help us get rid of them."

XXXII

The medium- and long-term rental units at the Braycott Arms were larger than those of the average motel but smaller than a modest apartment. There was one elevator, which mostly worked, and one washer-dryer, which mostly didn't. The paintwork was battered, the floorboards were scuffed, and the ceilings had more cracks than a medieval artwork, but everything was at least superficially clean, as long as one's standards weren't excessively high. The halls and stairways smelled of cooking, and I could hear music playing and televisions blaring. Tourists had been known to stay at the Braycott, but only when too desperate or ill-informed to do otherwise, and they rarely made it to a second night, or not without barricading their doors. The only regular visitors were parole officers and police.

Raum Buker occupied a corner unit on the third floor. I passed one person on the way up, and he was too busy conducting a cell phone conversation about pot to even notice me. He stank like a grow house, too, which came with the territory. Ever since Maine legalized recreational marijuana, the sickly sweet scent had become ubiquitous. You could get a contact high just from taking an Uber. If you stayed in the ride for too long, you had to fight the urge to order brownies and listen to "Dark Star" on heavy rotation.

Someone was shouting in the room next to Raum's, carrying on a one-sided argument with an unseen other that I suspected didn't involve a phone, a relentless stream of invective and obscenity punctuated by occasional sobbing. The soliloquy just added to the constant backdrop of noise at the Braycott Arms. It reminded me of prison; doubtless it reminded some of the residents of prison, too, which might have been one of the reasons they elected to stay there. I'd known ex-cons who were unable to sleep properly for months after their release because they couldn't cope with the silence, just as others couldn't deal with open spaces. There were lots of reasons why former prisoners ended up back behind bars, but probably the most disturbing of all was that it was easier than being free.

I knocked on Raum's door. The main key might have been sitting on the hook in Wadlin's office, but that didn't necessarily mean the room was unoccupied. The list of those who'd been shot for making that mistake was worryingly long. Only when I was sure that the unit was empty did I try the lock. Each of the Braycott's doors had a peephole, so I couldn't know if I was being observed from nearby, but I was banking on the likelihood that its tenants preferred to mind their own business in the expectation that others would extend them the same courtesy.

Raum's lodgings held the odors of bleach and damp towels. The door opened directly into a bedroom, the bathroom to the left, with two windows on the opposite main wall, the color scheme tending toward sour cream and rancid butter. It was furnished with a double bed, a table and chair, a vinyl couch, a microwave oven, and, in one corner, a stovetop. A refrigerator stood on one side of the stovetop, with a closet on the other. A cheap flat-screen TV was bolted to the wall in front of the bed, with the remote anchored to the nightstand by a short length of heavy cable. The room was devoid of pictures or superfluous decoration, but a stain occupied the wall above the couch, as though a previous tenant had blown their own or someone else's brains out, leaving the residue to dry into the paintwork.

Raum's occupancy hadn't altered the place substantially. A few items of clothing hung in the closet, and his socks, underwear, and T-shirts were stored beneath in separate drawers. A pair of boots and a pair of sneakers were arranged on a sheet of plastic by the door. A shelf above the stove held coffee, sugar, cereal, popcorn, an open bag of potato chips secured with a clothespin, and a loaf of cheap white bread. The refrigerator contained milk and unsalted sweet cream butter. I checked under the neatly made bed and pulled out a suitcase. It wasn't locked, and revealed nothing of note when opened. I put it back where I'd found it. The only personal touch was a photograph in a chipped wooden frame, which leaned against the wall beside the kettle. It showed a much younger Raum standing between what must have been his parents, each of them clasping one of his hands. All three were wearing swimsuits, and sunlight had faded the image's original colors to a uniform pale brown. I opened up the frame by releasing the clasps at the back, but it contained only the picture. A date was written on the back: *May '83*, in what looked like a woman's script. I reassembled the frame and restored the picture to its place.

The organization of the room wasn't a surprise, not from someone who'd done time. Prisoners learned how to use space, and the Braycott Arms didn't exactly invite a man to spread out and make himself at home. Yet even by those standards, the unit was very much a temporary refuge. It wouldn't have taken Raum more than five minutes to pack up and depart, leaving no obvious sign that he had ever moved through the Braycott's environs. I wondered if he had another hideaway somewhere, perhaps up in the County, because whatever was contained here couldn't possibly have represented all his possessions. Spending twenty dollars of Will Quinn's money on a bribe had, it seemed, bought me absolutely nothing.

I gave the bathroom a second look as I prepared to leave. A cup, a plate, and some silverware were drying on a towel by the sink. The medicine cabinet was already open, and held only antacid and ibuprofen, along with some sleep remedies that suggested Raum, as reported, was having difficulty getting a night's rest. The only incongruous element was a sprinkling of black dust between the faucets of the sink. I hadn't noticed it anywhere but there.

Without thinking, I reached up and closed the cabinet door. My face stared back at me from the mirror, but something was superimposed on it, a drawing on the glass in what looked like soot:

And I thought that I might not have been the first person to intrude on Raum Buker's privacy that day.

XXXIII

Kepler's cell phone pinged as he was walking through the motel lobby to his car, but the desk clerk waylaid him to advise on some necessary maintenance that would require a heating technician to gain access to his room, and by the time Kepler got to his vehicle a good three minutes had gone by. He read the alert, and opened the associated app. Kepler couldn't help but smile in anticipation: Raum Buker was about to find the message left for him in his room.

Then Kepler's smile faded, because whoever was in that unit, it was not Raum Buker.

XXXIV

It didn't strike me as wise to dawdle at the Braycott, so I took a photo of the mark on the mirror before using the peephole to make sure the hallway was clear. The view was foggy, which bothered me for a reason I couldn't immediately pinpoint, because the lens, when I checked it, was clean. I tried to retrieve a memory of something I'd read, but it wouldn't come, and forcing it wouldn't help. No one seemed to be around, so I made sure the door was locked behind me and headed for daylight.

Hearing footsteps, I paused at the stairwell. Raum Buker was one flight below, and ascending rapidly. Bobby Wadlin could have called up to let me know that Raum was on his way, but that wouldn't have been his style. If Raum decided to kick up a fuss about someone trespassing, Wadlin could simply have claimed that the key was stolen while his back was turned, and let Raum try to figure out the logistics once he'd calmed down.

The elevator was on one of the other levels, which meant it wasn't an option, so I moved quietly to the fourth floor and listened. I heard Raum go down the hall, followed by the sound of his door opening and closing. I was curious as to how he'd react to the sight of that symbol on his bathroom mirror. It was possible he'd put it there himself, but it wasn't likely given the tidiness of the rest of the space. I could have hung around outside his room in the hope of eavesdropping on his response—a phone call, with luck—but that wouldn't have been the brightest of moves in a building full of criminals, some of whom certainly had something to hide, and a couple of whom might even have had a bone to pick with me. I hoped it was a reflection on the nature of my profession, because the other option was more depressing to contemplate. Regardless, I'd probably made more enemies than friends in life, even if they were the kind of enemies a man should be proud to have.

With lurking out of the question, I returned to the lobby. Bobby Wadlin was still watching his cowboy show.

"I see Raum came back," I said.

"That's because he lives here," said Wadlin. "A guest ought to be able to return to his room without hindrance, as long as he pays his rent." He cocked an eyebrow at me. "You and him exchange pleasantries?"

"I decided to take a rain check."

"It could be you're not as dumb as they say."

I wasn't sure how to answer that, so I let it pass.

"Has anyone else been in that room today?" I said.

"Nope, just Buker, because you weren't there either, right?"

On the screen, someone was stealing Brian Keith's horse in *The Westerner*. Since Keith was under the gun, he didn't have a whole lot of say in the matter, and was reduced to throwing his hat at the ground while his dog watched. I knew he'd get his horse back in the end, though, because this was early Sam Peckinpah. Had it been later Peckinpah, Keith would have ended up dead, his dog and horse along with him. I asked myself how many times Bobby Wadlin might have watched this episode. Both too often, I decided, and not often enough.

"What about housekeeping?" I said, even as I listened for any indication of Raum descending from his quarters, which would require me to cut short the conversation.

Wadlin paused his show. If he was going to watch it, he'd wait until he could do so in peace.

"That's extra," he said. "Buker takes care of his own cleaning. He's not alone in that, but he keeps his room tidy, which is more than can be said for some. We check all the units regularly, just in case they start to stink. One time, we had a woman kept a dead cat in a bag. I had housekeeping get rid of it, and told the woman we didn't hold with people keeping animals in the rooms, dead or alive. You know what she said?"

"I couldn't possibly imagine."

"She said it wasn't an animal, it was a pet, and we shouldn't ought to have interfered with it without her say-so. Next day, housekeeping went back to the room, and there was another dead cat in a bag. I have no idea where it came from, and I didn't ask. I just sent her on her way— with the cat. I'd like to say that was the oddest thing I've witnessed here, but I'd be lying."

I decided that if I ever sank so low as to be faced with the prospect of living at the Braycott, I'd shoot myself. Then again, I didn't doubt that some of the current occupants had once made the same promise to themselves. The Braycott wasn't the bottom, but if you looked down from inside it, you could see the bottom looming.

"Any strangers come into the building today?" I asked.

Wadlin pointed to a sign on the plexiglass shield. It read NO VISITERS AFTER 5PM.

"It's not five yet," I said. "And 'visitors' is spelled wrong."

"Well, I'm only paid to notice visitors after five. And if you want to open a classroom, go someplace else."

"I'll do that. I wouldn't want to compete with the running of your charm school."

A security camera was trained on the lobby.

"Does that thing record?" I said.

"Wouldn't be much use if it didn't."

"What about the one on the back door?"

I knew from previous visits that there was also a camera at the rear of the Braycott.

"That's out of action. A rat ate through the wiring. Still works as a deterrent, though, because the tenants haven't been told."

"Any chance you could let me look over the recording from the one that does work?"

"None," he said.

"You're a piece of work, Bobby."

"That's what my momma always told me."

"Probably just before she tried to drown you."

Bobby Wadlin tossed a gummy bear into his mouth, hit the remote to restart *The Westerner*, and nodded solemnly.

"She had," he said, "very firm hands."

CHAPTER

XXXV

I didn't immediately drive away from the Braycott Arms. Even had I done so, its smell would have remained with me, so I put the windows down and waited for Raum Buker's next move. Eventually he would notice the symbol on his bathroom mirror, and he'd know what it meant, otherwise the point of leaving it in the first place would be rendered moot. I wanted to be around to see what he might do next.

To pass the time, I googled runes, paganism, occultism, and a whole lot of other search terms guaranteed to raise eyebrows if my phone was ever seized as evidence. It didn't take long to find what I was looking for. The symbol on the mirror was a pagan signifier for "bane," or "deadly." Either someone had an odd sense of humor, or Raum had just been given another reason to regret getting that tattoo on his arm.

His Chevy was parked in the Braycott's lot, the only place outside a junkyard that might have made it look good. If a fire was burning nearby, I wouldn't have been surprised to see a couple of the cars at the Braycott start up spontaneously in order to immolate themselves on it. Fifteen minutes went by, then thirty, without Raum emerging, but I didn't want to re-enter the Braycott if it could be avoided. Apart from my having to deal with Bobby Wadlin again, it would mean confronting Raum in a confined space, and while he was rattled. I didn't know if he had a gun, but the odds were in favor of it. Men like Raum operated on instinct, and their first response to a threat, however nebulous, was to secure a weapon. The law might have prohibited anyone who, like Raum, had been convicted of a crime punishable by a year or more in jail from owning a firearm, but criminals were notoriously shaky when it came to issues of jurisprudence.

I made a call to Chris Attwood, who was now a regional correctional manager for the Maine Department of Corrections. Attwood was based in an office over on Park Avenue, not far from where I was currently parked. We'd first crossed paths after one of his charges, a man named Jerome Burnel, approached me for help. Burnel should never have been put behind bars to begin with, and I'd succeeded in clearing his name, although that vindication came too late because by then he was already dead. The case had stayed with Attwood, though. It had stayed with me, too: my daughter Sam had almost died as a result of my involvement.

"Mr. Parker," said Attwood, "as I live and breathe."

"I didn't think anyone still said 'as I live and breathe,' " I replied, "not unless they smelled of lavender and Morgan Freeman was doing all the driving."

"The DoC likes to maintain certain social niceties. We're hoping it rubs off on our clients."

"Your optimism is a credit to you, but I have one former client in mind who might puncture that particular balloon: Raum Buker."

"I heard he was casting a shadow again," said Attwood. "The tide goes out, but it always comes back in. What's he done?"

"Officially, nothing more than be an irritant, but that's an existential state where Raum is concerned. Unofficially, I think he's brought bad luck with him, and that can be contagious."

"Buker wasn't one of mine. Jo Niles was his PO when he was on our books. She's taking care of workplace inspections today, but I can ask her to give you a call."

"If she could also save me some digging, I'm good for a bottle of wine."

"I'll pass that offer along. What do you need from her?"

"Raum recently cashed out on five years for manslaughter in East Jersey State Prison," I said. "That much is public record. I want to know who his cellmates were, if he had any, and what friendships he might have struck up while he was inside."

I waited while Attwood made some notes.

"Care to give me the angle?"

"Arcane. Raum has got himself an occult tattoo, and that wasn't his style before he went down."

A noticeable pause followed.

"With you," said Attwood, "it figures."

But he wasn't being dismissive, and he didn't laugh. After what had befallen Jerome Burnel, he knew better.

As I killed the call, Raum Buker emerged from the Braycott Arms. I got out of the car, and he stopped when I called his name, but didn't look surprised to see me. Bobby Wadlin could have opted to hedge his bets by letting Raum know I'd been inquiring after him, while stopping short of admitting his role in supplying a key to the room. Then again, the Sisters Strange might also have been in touch to let Raum know of my conversations with them, alerting him to my interest. If only one of them had contacted him, my money was on Ambar.

"I hope they gave you a room with a view," I said.

"The views cost extra," he replied. "Like the towels. What do you want?"

He didn't sound hostile, just resigned, and I knew that Wadlin hadn't mentioned my visit.

"To talk."

He peered over my shoulder as though expecting to glimpse the Fulci brothers approaching rapidly in a cloud of dust, like rhinos rampaging across the Serengeti. Only when he was convinced that the coast was clear did he return his gaze to me. Much of the cockiness he'd displayed at the Great Lost Bear was gone, but it was not fear alone that had replaced it, although fear was certainly a component. There was an eerie calm to him, the sort that descends on individuals after the worst has come.

"Why were you bothering Ambar?" he said.

So there it was. I made a mental note to buy a Powerball ticket that week.

"Did she say I was bothering her?"

"She said you'd been around. In your case, that amounts to the same thing."

Which was, I had to admit, a good line.

"Some people are worried for the Sisters Strange," I said.

"Because of me?"

"Because of you."

"They have no right to be," said Raum. "I've never hit a woman."

It wasn't the first time a man had said those words to me, often with the same odd tone of pride, even self-satisfaction. What I took from it was that they'd considered striking a woman, but had ultimately resisted the temptation, which made them great guys.

"That may be true," I said, "but you've done some hurting nonetheless. That carpenter you tore up with a planer doesn't move so well anymore, and five years in East Jersey says you put a man in the ground."

"Well, you'd know all about bodies. You ought to have shares in a cemetery."

"We can keep scoring points off each other," I said, "or we can have a useful conversation."

He glanced at his watch.

"So speak," he said. "I can listen to you now if it means never having to listen to you again, but make it fast."

"Tell me about the pentacle tattoo."

Whatever he'd expected me to say, that wasn't it.

"What about it?"

"Where did you get it, and why?"

"I have a few tattoos."

"Not many like that, I'll bet."

I saw him poised to scratch the brand at the mention of it. He caught himself, and stopped, but his fingers still itched to get at it.

"I saw it in a book," he said. "I thought it looked interesting, different. I'm sorry I bothered. I think it's infected."

"That I can believe. What are you frightened of, Raum?"

"Not you and your friends, that's for sure," he said, and the old Raum, the blowhard Raum, raised his head for a moment before sinking into silence. The new Raum's heart wasn't in it, and evinced only embarrassment at the bravado of his alter ego.

"Look," he said, "I don't want any more conflict with you or the Fulcis. I shouldn't have gone to the Bear that night, and time will tell if I should even have come back to Portland, but I'm here, and I have business to conclude."

"What kind of business?"

"None of yours, but once I'm done, you won't see me again. I'll stay out of the way of Dolors and Ambar. You could say they've cooled on me some. As for you and me, we got no quarrel, not unless you want to make one."

And then the strangest thing happened. The only way I can describe it is that Raum Buker's face contorted into a grin, but the grin wasn't his; and a presence peered from behind his eyes that had no right to be in his head, like an intruder peering out from the windows of a familiar house.

"Is that what you want, Mr. Parker?" said Raum, and his voice held a dissonant countermelody, like plainsong in a ragged key. "Because I'd advise against it."

While he was speaking, his right hand surrendered to the urge to claw at his left arm, which began to bleed again. I pointed at his hand, from which redness was dripping.

"You should get that looked at," I said, and left him to his pain.

XXXVI

That evening I dropped by Will Quinn's home to update him on what we in the investigative trade like to term "progress," usually when we're billing someone and haven't made a great deal of it. I didn't hold much back, because there wasn't a lot worth holding back, and I had no obligations to anyone involved but Will. The only detail I kept to myself, for the present, was the odd change to Raum Buker's voice and expression at the end of my encounter with him. I didn't want Will to get the impression that I jumped at shadows, even if I could have given him chapter and verse on why I'd had cause to do so in the past.

"So you think that mark on the mirror might be a warning?" he asked.

We were sitting in his kitchen. He'd done all the joinery and cabinet-work in the house himself, and it was a hymn to exposed wood. He was a fine craftsman, but the place could have done with a few rugs and a bit of color to liven it up. It was like spending time in a casket without the plush.

"I think it's more that someone wanted Raum to know his room had been searched," I said. "There's no other reason for entering a man's lodgings when he isn't there and leaving a calling card."

"But why?"

"To light a fire under him. Either whoever searched it didn't find what they were looking for, and thought a scare might spur him into doing something that would reveal its whereabouts, or they were reminding him of an obligation. I'll admit it's theatrical, but it was also effective. Raum didn't look happy when we parted, and it wasn't alone because of me."

"You didn't follow him to see where he went?"

TV shows and movies have made everyone an armchair expert on forensics and the mechanisms of detection. If viewers applied the same principle to medical dramas, half the population would be offering helpful advice to surgeons while they operated, or cutting out the middleman and performing their own amputations at home.

"That approach might have been too obvious," I said, "even for me. And so far, Raum hasn't done anything wrong, other than interfere with your love life."

Will grew wistful, then morose, as though I'd just reminded him of what he was missing while being forced to keep his distance from Dolors Strange.

"Do you think Buker meant it when he told you he was done with Dolors and her sister?" said Will.

"Going on past experience," I said, "Raum might have been sincere at that moment because he wanted me out of his face, but if circumstances change, or he gets in a fix, he'll be back—if not to Dolors, then to Ambar. I might be wrong, but Ambar strikes me as more vulnerable than her sister, and her feelings toward Raum may be more ambivalent."

Will examined his hands. They were those of a workingman, pitted and scarred. He probably couldn't recall a day that hadn't ended without fresh cuts to his skin, or didn't involve digging out splinters. He'd been alone for a long time, and might even have given up on ever meeting someone until Dolors Strange came into his life. Now he'd invested his future in her, but it was being threatened by her past.

"What would you do," he said at last, "if I were you?"

It wasn't how the question was usually posed—"if you were me" was more typical—but I understood the reason. Will was asking what I, as a private investigator, would do if I found myself in love with a woman like Dolors Strange, and at odds with a man like Raum Buker as a consequence.

"I'd be honest with Dolors," I said. "I'd tell her how I felt, and that I wasn't about to stand by and leave her alone to deal with whatever was coming down the pike—because, Will, my presentiment is that something *is* coming. You'll just have to trust me on that. Depending on how bad it is, and how deeply Raum has screwed up, it may buffet the Sisters Strange, or it could strike them with force, but they're in its path because of their history with him."

"And then?" he said.

"I'd try to find out exactly what Raum has done," I said. "I'd go looking for the source of that tattoo, which might take a degree of effort."

He worked through the implications. He was a practical man.

"I can look after the Dolors part, but not the rest," he said. "Can I hire you to try?"

I took in his face, his scars, and his too-male house. I took in his past, his present, and a series of futures, in only one of which was his sorrow excised.

"You already have," I said.

XXXVII

I returned to the Braycott Arms the following morning. Bobby Wadlin was still behind his plexiglass shield, and still watching cowboy oaters, but in all the times I'd been at the Braycott, I'd rarely discovered Wadlin viewing a film or show of any real quality. He gave the impression of deliberately eschewing features that displayed even minimal artistry in favor of bad B movies and worse TV, occasional aberrations like *The Westerner* excepted. On one occasion I'd even found him watching *Dusty's Trail*, which was *Gilligan's Island* for the mentally impaired. Admittedly, Wadlin hadn't been laughing, but that was like saying no one smiled at *Schindler's List*.

"Buker's not here," said Wadlin. "Hasn't been back since yesterday."

"Has anyone else been asking after him?"

"Only you. And I can't give you that key again. I'd be fired."

"Bobby, if you get fired, you can just rehire yourself. But in your position, I'd have fired myself a long time ago."

His eyes remained fixed on the screen, and on dead men made eternal.

"Insulting me won't change anything. I can't let you have that key."

"When's his rent due?"

"He owes from tomorrow."

I placed my card in the hatch.

"Call me when he gets back. Same if he doesn't."

"I'm not calling you."

I decided playtime was over for today.

"Bobby," I said.

Reluctantly he reached out a hand and drew in the card, like a trap-door spider settling for poor prey.

"Nobody likes you," he said, "not even me. And I like everybody."

I processed my hurt as I left. It proved easier than expected. By the time I hit fresh air, it was gone.

———

JO NILES, THE PAROLE officer who formerly had worked with Raum Buker, was at her desk when I dropped by the Department of Corrections office on Park Avenue. She was in her early thirties, and might have scraped five foot in heels. Her dark hair was cut very short, her ears ended in the slightest of points, and she wore glasses with wide blue frames. Her skin was a very deep black. The eyewear apart, she looked as though she could have stepped from a painting in Strange Brews, possibly the big canvas with the naked female elf and the dragon. I was considering buying that one for Angel and Louis, as long as I could deliver it in person and watch while they unwrapped it. It was absurdly expensive—it would have been absurdly expensive at ten bucks—but what price happiness?

"So you're Charlie Parker," she said, as I took a seat opposite her. "I thought you'd be taller."

"I get that a lot," I said, "along with 'I thought you'd be dead.' "

"We have to learn to live with wishful thinkers." She opened a note-pad on her desk. "Chris Attwood told me you were interested in Raum Buker. Have you been hired to investigate him?"

"Yes."

"By whom?"

"The current partner of one of his ex-girlfriends."

"Has Buker harmed her in some way?"

"Not that I know of."

"Has he harmed someone else?"

"If he hasn't, he will, but only on the basis of probability."

"But you have no evidence that he's committed a crime?"

"None, beyond the ones he's already served time for."

"Then what's the problem?"

"That," I said, "is what I'm trying to find out."

Niles pursed her lips and studied me through her lenses. If I ever found myself on probation or parole, I decided I didn't want her to be the one holding my chain. After only a few minutes in her presence, I was already examining my conscience and finding it wanting.

"Are you being deliberately evasive?" she said. "Because I've heard that said about you."

"It's a character flaw," I admitted. "It may even be a genetic one. On this occasion, though, I'm being straight. I'm as much in the dark as anyone as to why Raum has come back to Portland. All I can tell you is that I think he's scared of someone, or something. If I can establish the nature of the threat, I can determine how, or if, it impacts on my client's interests. But it's also my understanding that Raum has a plan in place to make some quick money, and it's unlikely to involve delivering bottles and cans to a redemption center."

"Do you know the nature of that plan?"

"My guess is criminal."

"That's funny. I was hoping you could be more specific."

"I'd like to be, but I can't. I'm going on previous experience."

Niles might still have suspected me of lying, either in whole or in part, but her questions were mostly for display. Attwood had asked her to help me, and in addition to being her superior, he was known to be a good guy. She'd have been foolish not to oblige, but she made a show of hemming and hawing, and creased her brow, just to let me know how much the effort was costing her.

"Raum Buker maxed out in New Jersey," she said, "so post-release supervision doesn't apply. It wasn't as if I could just call a PO and ask for this information." The crease deepened. "I had to get in touch with an ex-girlfriend, and I really didn't want to do that."

I produced a bottle of Moët from my bag and placed it on her desk. It had cost me fifty-five dollars at the liquor outlet in Portsmouth, New Hampshire, because I wasn't a chump: like half the state of Maine, I bought anything more expensive than box wine over the border. I'd been saving the champagne for one of those special occasions when only a striking inducement to bend the rules would suffice. To be fair to Niles, it did cause her brow to unfurrow some.

"Classy," she said. "I've also heard that said about you, if grudgingly."

"Just don't tell Attwood. I'd feel odd giving him champagne, like I'd have to produce a corsage as well."

"It can be our secret. I wouldn't want to cause you confusion with your sexuality." She put the bottle in a drawer and returned to her notes. "Buker shared a cell for the first three years plus change, with two different cellmates, but he was in protective isolation for the remainder of his sentence."

"The reason?"

"He intervened in a fight, and saved a guard from getting his skull fractured. According to my contact, Buker was trying to defend another inmate, and blocked a couple of hits to the guard along the way. Buker and the other inmate were segregated in the aftermath, just as a precaution."

"Any grudges?"

"Nothing personal," said Niles, "or not beyond the usual, because it's always open season on a guard."

"What about the second inmate involved?"

"Egon Towle, released three months before Buker. Sixty-three months under the Graves Act. He was convicted for the robbery of a coin dealership in Paterson, during which a firearm was produced but not discharged. Mandatory minimum of forty-two months, plus fifty percent for a prior, along with a parole disqualifier."

"So Towle maxed out as well?"

"That's right."

"Was he originally one of Raum Buker's cellmates?"

"Actually, it was Buker's cellmate who attacked Towle. His name was Perry Gudex, from Kentucky. Manslaughter, ten years. He was also a religious fanatic, borderline insane."

"Any idea what might have caused the beef between them?"

"Religion, of all things. Gudex was a Southern Baptist, and Towle was about as far from a Baptist as a man can get, Southern or otherwise. He was no fan of organized religion, and liked getting under Gudex's skin, until Gudex snapped."

"Where's Gudex now?"

"Still behind bars. He's not due for release for another five years."

"And Towle?"

"No idea. Like Buker, he isn't under post-release supervision. He can go where he pleases, but my contact says Towle's mother lives down in Ossipee, New Hampshire, and that was the address he gave when he was arrested in New Jersey."

"What about Buker's other cellmate?"

"Clu Angard. Three years for possession with intent to supply. Died of an overdose shortly after release."

I finished writing. I liked to keep notes. I rarely had to consult them, but putting things down on paper helped cement testimony in my memory.

"There is one more thing," said Niles. "I asked for a list of Raum Buker's permitted visitors, just in case it might be of help."

"And?"

"For the first three years, there was only one name on the list," said Niles. "A woman, Ambar Strange. For the final year, there were two."

"Who was the second visitor?"

"Another woman: Dolors Strange. I'm no detective, but instinct suggests they might be related."

"Sisters," I said.

"You know them?"

"I've only recently become familiar with them."

"Huh. The Strange sisters."

"You have no idea," I said, "just how."

XXXVIII

A t the Cracker Barrel by the Maine Mall, the server named Olivia had grown used to the odd man who had placed the identical breakfast order for the previous seven mornings in a row. It wasn't as though he was unusual in the consistency of his appetites. She had people in her section who'd been eating the same breakfast for years, sometimes even at the same table. A few of them wouldn't consent to eat at any other; if they came in and found their spot occupied, they'd insist on waiting until it freed up, or go for a walk and come back later. For her favored customers, the ones who always remembered to tip more than the minimum, she would even agree to call when the table was ready, and secure it for them with a little RESERVED sign.

The stranger wasn't quite so persnickety. He'd eat anywhere, just so long as his eggs were well poached and his apples weren't too hard. She didn't know his name, as he always paid cash, but she'd come to think of him as Mr. Beige, because he only ever wore faded shades of yellow, oatmeal, and brown, from the top of his trilby hat to the tips of his scuffed shoes. He rarely spoke, except to say please and thank you.

"The usual?" she would ask.

"Please," he would reply, and his voice seemed simultaneously to come from very near and also far away, as though it contained within itself its own echo. On the first morning she'd tried to make small talk with him, but he had only nodded and smiled before opening his newspaper. Now she just served him and collected her tip at the end, which was fine with her. He wasn't unpleasant to deal with, didn't try to come on to her, and added 20 percent without fail. There were worse customers to serve.

Initially, Olivia had liked the way he smelled. A couple of her regulars stank like they washed only at Christmas, but Mr. Beige wore a clean, old-fashioned scent. After the first two days, though, it had begun to bother her, because it stayed with her even after she finished her shift, clinging to her skin and clothing. She'd taken to showering again when she got home, and changing her underclothes—because the smell permeated even them—but it didn't do much good, and now she couldn't eat without some vestige of it affecting the taste of her food. She hoped the stranger would finish whatever business he had in town and go back to wherever he'd come from; that, or find another place to eat breakfast. She was considering salting his apples, or asking that he be assigned to another server, but he had to hit the road sometime, right?

Perhaps most peculiar of all, even allowing for his scent, his reticence, and his appearance—hands that were both swollen yet small; and his eyes, God, those *eyes*—were the newspapers he read. They were all out of date, and not by days, or even weeks, but years. A day earlier, he'd been reading about 9/11, and the day before that the headline had concerned Jimmy Carter and some hostages from 1979, before Olivia was born. The newspapers were yellowed yet crisp, as though they'd been carefully set aside unread back in the day, and only recently been unearthed. It was like meeting a character from *The Twilight Zone*, someone who'd woken from a long sleep and was trying to play catch-up on world affairs.

Olivia wished she could afford to take a few days off. With luck he'd be gone when she returned, and that scent with him. But times were tough, and the tips mattered.

"You okay, hon? You look tired."

It was Caitlin, one of the assistant managers. Caitlin had a daughter about Olivia's age, and this made her protective of Olivia, although Caitlin was nice to everyone at the Cracker Barrel. Caitlin's daughter lived with her father, for reasons to which Olivia was not privy. Caitlin struck Olivia as pretty chilled, so it was hard to imagine what domestic circumstances might have caused her daughter to choose to be with her father instead, unless he was even more chilled than her mom. Caitlin smiled with her mouth when her daughter came up in conversation, but her eyes stayed sad. Olivia hadn't been working at the Cracker Barrel for long enough to feel right about asking why.

"I'm okay," said Olivia. "But I haven't been sleeping so good lately."

Which was true. When she closed her eyes, she felt Mr. Beige begin to draw near.

"Bad dreams?"

"Yeah, something like that."

"You must have a guilty conscience."

For a moment, Olivia considered sharing her recurring dream with Caitlin. It had been coming to her for the last few nights, although it wasn't the same each time, but was instead a variation on a theme. She would sit up in bed, aware that someone was in her apartment, and see a shape occupying the chair by the window; or standing by her bookshelves, running a finger along the spines of the novels; or silhouetted in her bathroom door, staring at her from the dark. She could never see the intruder's face, because it was always in shadow, but she knew who it was, knew him by his trilby hat and his distinctive scent.

Except you didn't smell stuff in your dreams, but somehow it was always the odor of his cologne that finally woke her, and it would still be there when she opened her eyes, like a ghost in the room, before slowly dissolving away.

"I think I have to go home," said Olivia, suddenly. "I feel sick."

"Hon, we're kind of busy—"

"I know, I'm sorry," said Olivia, untying her apron. "I have to leave. I have to get out of here before I puke."

I have to be gone before he comes.

XXXIX

Kepler now had a name for the man who had been in Raum Buker's room: Parker, a private investigator. Kepler was curious to know who might have hired him, but the only way to establish that would be to confront Parker himself, and everything Kepler had learned about him suggested that this would not be advisable, not yet.

Kepler inspected himself in the mirror. He was applying ointment to the cuts that were now regularly blighting his face and hands, but they refused to heal, and these were not the only visible signs of his deterioration. Small, painful swellings had erupted in his armpits and at the base of his neck, so that he now had to keep the collar of his shirt unbuttoned. They resembled plague buboes, and he had a vision of his fingers and toes beginning to rot. The black joke shared with Reuben Hapgood—*it's not terminal*—no longer seemed quite so funny. It *was* terminal. Kepler was dying, and as he faded Raum Buker grew stronger.

He had hoped that Buker might have been foolish enough to keep in his accommodations at the Braycott some, or all, of what he and Egon Towle had stolen, but the room was entirely free of valuables, possibly because it contained no safe in which to store them. Meanwhile Buker didn't even bother locking his woebegone Chevy, and would surely have acquired a more secure form of transportation had he intended to use it as a mobile vault. Finally, Kepler had tried and failed to gain access to the house of Ambar Strange, the woman with whom Buker was said to be keeping company, but the fact that he was now living at the Braycott Arms suggested their relationship might have come to an end. If this was so, Buker was unlikely to have entrusted the hoard to her. Ambar also had an older sister, but Kepler had established that Dolors did not enjoy her sibling's level of intimacy with Buker. Where, then, was he keeping what he had taken?

How much easier it would have been had Kepler been able to confront Buker directly, but Kepler was weak and Buker was strong, while the very nature of the crime he had committed was offering him protection, even if he might not yet be aware of it. The result was that Kepler was being forced to circle, hoping that his reputation, and his presence in Portland, would be sufficient motivation for Buker to reach a settlement with him. But Buker had not responded to Kepler's overtures: *You can keep most of what you took. I want only this. It is important to me.* Emails sent to Buker's address went unanswered, and his most recent cell phone number was no longer in service. Soon, Kepler would have to make his move. Admittedly, the private investigator was an unwelcome complication, but all Kepler had to do was evade him.

Kepler felt the sands of his days slipping through his fingers. He stared at his reflection again and saw it change to the image of another man, also dying, this time by Kepler's hand. The man was laughing, laughing even as Kepler tore away strips of his skin.

He'll destroy it if you get too close to him, said the laughing man. *He'll destroy it, and put an end to you.*

XL

The morning dawned unseasonably warm for the third day in a row, presaging an early thaw. I called Will Quinn to ask if he'd had a chance to reach out to Dolors Strange. He told me that he'd driven over to see her immediately after our meeting at his home, and they'd spoken for two hours. The upshot was that Dolors admitted to feeling about Will the same way he felt about her, and they'd decided to resume their romance.

"What about Raum?" I said.

"He's definitely out of her life for good. She says that if her sister wants to keep seeing him, that's her decision, but she's advised Ambar against it. Buker and Ambar had an argument, and he hurt her arm. Ambar says it was an accident, but Dolors isn't so sure."

"I don't suppose I need to ask if Ambar reported the incident to the police," I said.

"I wouldn't waste my breath. I believe that was Ambar's view, too."

I thought that the next Thanksgiving with the Quinn-Strange households would be quite the occasion, and I'd need to have my excuses prepared well in advance in order to miss it.

"Did you tell Dolors that I would continue to work for you?"

"I did. Was that a mistake?"

"She'd have found out sooner or later. How did she take the news?"

"She told me I shouldn't have done it, and that I didn't need to go wasting any more of my money on a private investigator. She recommended I sever my ties with you immediately. I said I couldn't do that until I was sure she was safe. I suggested that if she was willing to answer any further questions you might have, it could help set my mind at ease."

I was pleased to see that Will had some backbone. It must have been all those years spent hauling lumber.

"I'm going to see her shortly," I said. "I first wanted to check that I wasn't about to squander an hour. I've had my fill of being cold-shouldered by the Sisters Strange."

"Would you like me to join you?"

I told him to stay right where he was. I might have been working for Will, but that didn't mean I wanted him by my side at all times, or made party to every exchange. In fact, depending on how forthcoming Dolors Strange was with me, it might be better for Will if I was sparing with what I shared, unless he was keen on listening to the intricacies of her past relationship with Raum Buker. Even I wasn't too sure I wanted to hear those, and I, unlike Will, wasn't planning on sleeping with her.

It was also the case that every time I thought I might be getting a handle on the Sisters Strange, it came apart in my hands. I'd watched Raum attempt to kiss Ambar Strange and be rebuffed, but there was to their manner more than a hint of enduring intimacy, and it was to Raum she had turned when she was worried about the damage to her door. While Dolors Strange now claimed to have excised him from her life in favor of Will Quinn, she had visited him at East Jersey State Prison, and spent time with him after his recent return to Portland. Dolors might already have explained to Will Quinn why that was, or she might have elected not to mention it for fear of casting a shadow over their reconciliation. Out of deference to their future prospects, it would be wiser to ask her without Will being present.

"I have a question for you," said Will, "since we're sharing."

"Shoot."

"How come you always refer to Buker by his first name? If I didn't know better, I'd almost have said you were intimates."

I hadn't even been aware of doing it, but Will was right.

"I've never liked him," I said, "but I've always felt sorry for him."

"Seriously? You must have better outlets for your sympathy."

"Easier ones, I'll admit."

"He's no good to anyone. He's bad through and through."

But that wasn't correct. I'd been confronted by profound human wickedness, and worse. Raum Buker undeniably possessed a streak of viciousness and spite, but not enough to damn him, not in my eyes, although it might be that I was growing more forgiving in middle age. I'd always believed that Raum was intelligent enough to recognize the failure of a human being he'd become, and could yet redeem himself. Perhaps, too, I saw some shade of myself in him: a man who had lost his parents too young, who had found himself adrift, who had succumbed to rage. If I were to condemn him entirely, might I not also have to condemn myself?

But I didn't like what I'd seen and heard at the Braycott Arms. That was a different Raum Buker. In fact, it might no longer have been him at all.

CHAPTER

XLI

One hour later, I returned to Strange Brews. The same New Age music was playing, and the same deranged fantasy art was making the walls look embarrassed, but Dolors Strange was absent, and an older woman I didn't recognize was tending the register. When I asked after the owner, she told me that Dolors had phoned in sick, and wasn't expected for the rest of the day. I ordered a coffee to be polite, and brought it back to my car. The coffee tasted flowery, although I shouldn't really have been surprised. I poured it on the ground and made a note to bill Will Quinn for it.

———

DOLORS STRANGE LIVED IN a single-story house off Broadway in South Portland. The city figured high on lists of the most desirable places to settle in Maine, but the compilers probably hadn't been thinking of her particular stretch of Broadway when they made their notes. It wasn't lousy, just dull and unkempt, but it covered more than 2,000 square feet, according to the property records, although this included the garage. At $230,000, the valuation was at the lower end of the scale, so Dolors owned a lot of house for her buck. It could have done with some TLC, because the woodwork was rotting in places. Will Quinn would certainly be able to oblige. Dolors might have been dating him for the discount.

In the days before the Gramm-Leach-Bliley Act, the Driver's Privacy Protection Act, and reforms to the Fair Credit Reporting Act, it was relatively easy for private investigators to obtain credit reports. Now it required signed waivers from the subject and tedious discussions of the definition of "permissible purposes." Backdoor lines of inquiry remained available, but they were expensive and carried with them the risk of the suspension of one's license and the threat of jail time. When it came to antagonizing the law, I'd already spent my nine lives, and a couple of others on credit. Wherever possible, I preferred to tread the path of righteousness. If I was going to be hanged, I wanted it to be for something memorable.

I called Will Quinn for a second time while I sat outside Dolors Strange's property.

"This is a delicate question," I said, "but how is Dolors doing financially?"

"I don't know all the details, but not great. She quietly remortgaged her home after that mess in '08 in order to keep Strange Brews in business. She's about breaking even, or so she says."

"You don't believe her?"

"In my experience, a business owner will tell you things are worse than they are, or better than they are, but never *how* they are. I think Dolors is putting a brave face on a bad situation, and with the remortgage she's carrying a lot of debt. I did offer to help her out."

"And?"

"My ear still hurts from the rebuff."

"What about Ambar?"

"Dolors owes her money, too. After they reconciled, Ambar also remortgaged her home, and put part of the cash into Strange Brews. She invested most of what was left."

"In what?"

"According to Dolors, in Raum Buker."

"And how did that work out?"

"You'd have to ask Ambar," said Will, "but I'd say they're worthless securities."

I thanked him, locked my car, and knocked on Dolors Strange's front door. I felt briefly guilty at the prospect of dragging her from her sick-bed, but I was here now, and had questions that needed to be answered. I let a minute or two go by before knocking a second time, with the same result.

I glanced around. Cars passed, but I saw no pedestrians, and nobody was paying me any attention. I left the front porch and walked around the exterior of the house. None of the drapes were closed, and I could see clearly into every room, the bathrooms excluded because of their frosted glass. Dolors might have been in there, but I didn't think so, because unoccupied houses have a particular feel to them. Finally, I took a look in the garage. It too was empty.

Which made me wonder just how sick Dolors Strange really was.

XLII

Ambar Strange's cottage was also quiet when I got there, with no car in the driveway. I assumed she was at work, which was the main reason I was at her home and not the dental practice. I parked in the driveway as though I was expected, in the event that any of the neighbors were paying attention, and went straight to the back of the house.

The damage to the glass and screen of her door had not yet been repaired. One of the lower panes was badly broken, the hole now covered with a piece of cardboard, and part of the screen was mangled, the way an animal might tear at a wire cage to escape confinement. I'd viewed the handiwork of some lousy burglars in my time, but this was rough by any standard.

I gently pried the cardboard from the glass before taking some pictures of the mess with my phone. By now I was feeling tired and hungry. Had Angel and Louis been around, I'd have arranged to meet them somewhere for dinner, but they had returned briefly to New York for one of Angel's regular medical reviews. I thought about catching a movie, but there was nothing I wanted to see. I missed Sam, and sometimes I missed Rachel, too. Generally I liked my solitude, but there were moments when it became hard to differentiate from loneliness.

I checked the images of the damage for clarity as I headed back to the car, magnifying the last of the pictures. It might have been the dying sunlight on the glass when viewed with the naked eye, or the angle from which I'd taken the photo, but I was noticing something I'd missed initially. I returned to the door, knelt, and examined the glass more closely. Among the scratches I thought I could pick out a semi-circle, and what looked like a "V" tilted on its side. Unless I was very mistaken, it resembled half the rune I'd found on Raum Buker's mirror. I pictured him scratching at his tattoo as he left Ambar Strange's property. Now I thought I knew why.

———

IN MY CAR, I accessed online the property records for Ossipee, New Hampshire. Emmeline Towle, mother of Egon Towle, who had been saved from a prison beating by Raum Buker, still lived in the area. It was about a ninety-minute drive from Portland to Ossipee, but it would have to wait until the following day. Nobody liked a private investigator showing up once darkness fell. Come to think of it, they didn't much welcome visits in daylight either.

I'd already looked into Egon Towle's criminal record. Prior to the spell in East Jersey State Prison that had brought him into Raum's purview, he'd been in trouble with the law on only one previous occasion, and that was down in Connecticut. Towle had been charged with larceny in the first degree for being in possession of a collection of rare coins. He could have faced up to twenty years in prison, and a hefty fine, but the judge, bless her tender heart, had deemed him suitable for accelerated pretrial rehabilitation on the grounds that Towle claimed to have been unaware of the true value of the haul, which came to almost $250,000. Towle had successfully completed the rehab program, vowed never to sin again, and the charge was dismissed. Five years later, he started his term at East Jersey, once more for a crime involving coins, which suggested efforts to rehabilitate him might not have succeeded unconditionally. He'd also graduated to robbery involving the use of a firearm.

I called Angel.

"How did the medical appointment go?" I said.

"I'm going to be with you all for the foreseeable future. Louis took the news like a trouper."

"Good, because I wouldn't be able to keep him amused on my own. What do you know about coin thieves?"

"They're boring," said Angel. "Seriously. They read boring magazines, have boring conversations, and keep company with the kind of men who make stamp collectors look like RuPaul. If you're talking about very rare coins, they're hard to sell, so they're usually stolen to order, or at least with buyers in mind. On the plus side, if you do have a buyer, then the goods are easily transportable, and will earn someone a lot of money very quickly for minimal risk. After that, the coins vanish into a private collection, although I've heard of some being used as collateral in drug deals, the same as stolen art. Why?"

"You ever hear of a guy named Egon Towle?"

"Nope."

"Could you ask around?"

"I can make some calls. How quickly do you want it?"

"By tomorrow. I'm planning to drive to New Hampshire to visit his mother. Towle may be living with her."

"Is this still the Raum Buker thing?"

"He and Towle were prison buddies."

"Well," said Angel, "there's no accounting for taste."

XLIII

I couldn't sleep that night. It was nothing to do with Raum, or the Sisters Strange. I knew this because of the familiarity of the restlessness, and what I understood it to signify: my dead daughter was near, or whatever part of her still inhabited this world.

It was cold outside, but not so much as to be uncomfortable, not with a warm coat and boots worn over my T-shirt and sweatpants: that strange weather again. I suppose I might have presented a sight had there been anyone other than Jennifer to witness it, but all was quietude, and no cars passed on the road below. I stood on my porch and surveyed the trees and the marshes, but could find no trace of her. It was like that with her. She was a manifestation more often sensed and felt than seen and heard, but I took comfort from it nonetheless.

"I'm okay," I said aloud to the darkness. "Better than okay."

Here is a truth, or as close to one as I can come: Those who have lost children will speak to them until death stills their own tongue. They will perceive their presence in a gust of air that passes briefly through a locked room, in the tinkling of a wind chime where there is no breeze, in the settling of boards that have long since found their alignment, and to these things they will give the name of a son or daughter. In grief we look for solace where we can, and in whatever we believe to be true. Who is to say that we are wrong, should this bring us peace and cause no harm to another? And if, as the years go by, we speak less often to the shadows, and these wordless visitations grow rarer, it is not that we are forgotten, or have forgotten in turn, but rather that the dead perhaps better understand the needs of the living than the living themselves, and are more cognizant of meaning and meaninglessness. For the dead, love has consequence, time has none, and absence lasts the blink of an eye.

From the tamarack tree, the black-crowned night heron soared into the sky and was lost to the stars.

CHAPTER

XLIV

The maid Floriana was late in attending to Mr. Kepler's room that morning. First there was a problem with her car, and then two of the other maids—cousins who shared an apartment, and consorted, in Floriana's view, with the wrong order of men—had come down with something, which meant that she spent the day running to catch up with herself and failing.

She knocked on Mr. Kepler's door and received no reply. Typically she'd have given a second knock, as the rules of the motel required, but she was weary and distracted, and the unease she felt whenever she approached his quarters had mutated into a deeper dread. She just wanted to give his *maldita habitación* a cursory cleaning and have done with it.

She opened the door. The first thing she noticed was a pair of ivory dice on the table beside the closet. It was the first time she had discovered anything of a personal nature in the room, beyond a toothbrush, toothpaste, a disposable razor, and a travel-size can of shaving foam. Next to the dice was a small clock with exposed workings and multiple dials on its face. Its numerals were from no alphabet that Floriana recognized, and the arrangement of the dials was so complicated as to make telling the time impossible for her.

Floriana touched a finger to the dice. They appeared to be very old.

She also noticed, after a moment, that their dots were oddly arranged. Instead of the opposite faces adding up to seven—1 and 6, 2 and 5, 3 and 4—the distribution was random. On the other side of 6 was 2, opposite 5 was 4, and 1 was paired with 3. The second die was different again: 4 and 6, 1 and 5, 2 and 3. She had never seen anything like them before.

As she drew back from them, she heard a sound from the bathroom. It was very slight, barely there at all, like the release of gas from a valve.

"Hello?" she said, but softly, so softly, even as a voice in her head told her it would be better if she left the room now, closing the door gently behind her, forgetting the dice, forgetting the noise. . . .

She peeked into the bathroom. Mr. Kepler was sitting naked before her, his eyes closed, seemingly asleep on the edge of the tub. His entire body, with the exception of his face, neck, and hands, was covered in tattoos, even down to his foreskin. They looked like symbols, or letters of an alphabet, but again, none that was familiar to her. At his neck, on his chest, and amid the sparse hairs of his groin, she saw swelling and blistering, and knew that here was a man enduring near-unimaginable pain.

Floriana backed away. She did not speak, and Mr. Kepler disappeared from view. She made it to the door, still lodged open with a wooden stop. She stepped into the hall and removed the stop, steadying the door with one hand and holding the handle down with the other so that it would make no sound when it closed. Only when the door had locked behind her did she release a breath.

And only then did Kepler open his eyes.

———

I SPENT THE MORNING at the Maine District Court, waiting to testify in an insurance case that was eventually settled on the courthouse steps. I had a book for company, they were billable hours, and there's something pleasant about being paid to read. When I was done, I grabbed coffee and a sandwich at the Crooked Mile on Milk Street, and tackled the parts of the *New York Times* that weren't depressing. I was just finishing up when Angel called.

"You were asking about Egon Towle," he said.

"Am I going to be sorry?"

"How about if I start by telling you that they call him 'Weird Egon'? "

"You know," I said, "I'm sorry already."

———

EGON TOWLE, ACCORDING TO Angel's information, didn't have faith in God, or not any incarnation of Him that involved itself in human cares, but he did believe in demons. He was fascinated by transcendentalism, theosophy, spiritualism, hermeticism, Kabbalah, neo-paganism, and witchcraft. He'd worked briefly in the library at East Jersey State Prison before it was discovered that he had somehow managed to have five occult volumes—including a modern edition of the eighteenth-century *Grimorium Verum, The Book of Ceremonial Magic* by Arthur Waite, and a treatise on occult warfare—smuggled in as part of a charitable donation from the collection of a defunct home for elderly spinsters. He also claimed to have infiltrated the Bilderberg Group and the outer margins of the British royal family, and to have personally forged President Barack Obama's birth certificate. Egon Towle wasn't just out where the buses don't run, he was out where no bus was ever likely to run, not unless he hijacked it first.

"So he's crazy?" I said.

"Oh, he's out of his mind," said Angel. "But he's also a very, very good thief."

XLV

Raum Buker had not yet returned to the Braycott Arms, and was overdue on his rent, yet Bobby Wadlin, who was not liable to demonstrations of kindness, did not immediately order his room to be emptied and cleaned. It was not that, as Wadlin's middle grew softer, so too did his heart: the organ in question was as hard as its surrounding arteries, and had atrophied to the size of a nut. No, it was more that the Raum Buker currently residing at the Braycott Arms was not the man familiar to Wadlin from memory and rumor, and he believed that caution needed to be exercised with him.

Wadlin had encountered plenty of disturbed individuals over the years, which was why he rarely emerged from behind his screen, not if it could be avoided. But plexiglass offered only so much protection, and even Wadlin was occasionally obliged to venture onto the city's streets. This was why it was important for him to maintain the fiction that he was merely an employee of the Braycott's absentee owners, not a principal shareholder in the operation, in order to avoid being accosted by unhappy tenants. Similarly, he avoided antagonizing the residents unnecessarily, and would call the cops only as a last resort. The second-last resort was a low-level bruiser named Tony Motti, who had once gone all of two rounds with Joey Gamache, the only Maine boxer ever to win a world boxing title. Joey had played around with Tony for a while before flooring him with a punch that Tony still felt when the weather turned cold. Now Tony worked security at the kind of bars that sane people avoided on the grounds that they required someone like Tony Motti to maintain a semblance of order, and helped landlords of Bobby Wadlin's stripe deal with recalcitrant tenants.

Raum Buker was not quite a problem tenant, and Wadlin sincerely hoped he wouldn't become one, because, in Wadlin's opinion, Buker was displaying signs of cracking up. One of the other tenants had complained that he was keeping him awake at night by shouting in his sleep. The tenant also mentioned to Wadlin that he thought Buker might be entertaining visitors after hours, because he was sure he'd heard someone else in there with him. When Wadlin had gone to check, he'd discovered Buker alone in the room. But that wasn't all. Standing in Buker's unit, Bobby Wadlin had smelled something burning.

"You lighting fires in here?" he asked. "Don't be smoking no cigarettes. You know the rules."

"I don't smell anything," said Buker, "and I don't smoke. I was asleep when you knocked."

He hadn't looked sleepy to Wadlin, and he didn't resemble someone bothered by an intrusion, only amused. But that smell—damn, it was like someone grilling bad bacon. If he hadn't known better, Wadlin might even have said it was coming from the man standing before him.

From that point on, Bobby Wadlin decided he wanted Raum Buker to clear out. Another deadbeat would be along to replace him soon enough, and it wasn't as though the income from one unit was the difference between eating and not eating; Wadlin and his relatives could take the hit. But he didn't want to give Buker cause for animosity, which was why he waited a few more hours before dispatching a maid to the room with instructions to gather up any personal possessions and put them in storage. If Buker came back and tried to pay in advance for another week, or even another day, Wadlin would tell him that the unit had already been rented to a new guest, and there was nothing else available. Wadlin was done with him. Buker was giving him the creeps, and not only Buker but also—

The phone beside him rang, temporarily derailing his train of thought and distracting him further from the action on his TV screen, namely Johnny Ringo's efforts to establish the truth about the outlaw Boone Hackett. He picked up the handset.

"Braycott. Manager speaking."

And an unwelcome voice said, "Why are you interfering with Raum Buker's room?"

CHAPTER

XLVI

The drive down to New Hampshire was uneventful, helped by the fact that I stayed at seventy-five and slowed anytime I saw a sports car that wasn't tearing up the road, the Maine State Police liking nothing better than to lurk in Mustangs and Chargers to trap the unwary.

I'd never been to Ossipee before. It was a conglomeration of villages sharing variations on the name, and located around Center Ossipee, "Home of the First Snowmobile," because somewhere had to be. Emmeline Towle lived on Moultonville Road, close to Lord's Funeral Home. Her house stood farther back than its neighbors, and was sheltered by evergreens. One car was parked outside the garage, a boxy blue Oldsmobile Cutlass from the 1980s, bearing a faded election sticker for a politician I'd never heard of—which, given the nature of so many of that species, was almost certainly the best kind.

I parked behind the Oldsmobile. As I got out, the front door of the house opened and a woman in her early fifties stepped onto the porch. Her hair was gray-blond and unwashed, and she wore a Howdy Doody apron that came down to her knees. Her right hand was buried in one of the apron's pockets. I was prepared to offer good odds that the hand was holding a gun. Get shot at often enough and you become adept at spotting the signs, if only as a belated survival strategy. I decided to stay by my car in the hope that the hand would likewise remain in her pocket.

"What do you want here?" she said.

"I was looking for Emmeline Towle."

"You're about two months too late."

"Why is that?"

"Because we buried her over at Chickville Cemetery."

I sometimes think life would be a lot simpler if we could press "reset" on any preceding ten seconds. In the absence of that facility, I'd have to keep working on my diplomatic skills, or start conversations by making sure the person I was inquiring after didn't happen to be dead.

"I'm sorry to hear that," I said.

"You can go drop off flowers if you like."

"I didn't know her that well. In fact, I didn't know her at all."

"Then you got nothing to be sorry for."

"Except your loss."

She untightened enough to nod an acknowledgment.

"You still haven't told me who you are," she said, "or what you wanted with my mother."

"I was hoping to talk with her about her son, Egon, or with Egon himself, if he happened to be around. My name is Charlie Parker. I'm a private investigator. It concerns a case I'm working."

At the mention of Egon, the shutters came down again, and her right hand altered its grip on whatever was in her apron pocket.

"Egon's not here—and before you ask, I don't know where he is, so you can be on your way."

"I'm not trying to create any awkwardness for you," I said. "Or him, not if I can help it."

"What other reason would a private investigator have for being on my property, other than to create awkwardness for someone?"

Which was a fair observation, even an astute one. The sun would soon be setting behind the trees, and I could already feel the evening chill creeping into the air after the temperate day. I'd driven for nearly two hours in roadwork traffic to the Home of the First Snowmobile, and I didn't even like snowmobiling. Neither did I especially like Raum Buker, or the Sisters Strange, and whatever Will Quinn was paying me wasn't enough to compensate for the toll the case was taking on my natural ebullience, so I decided to be honest.

"I think two women may be in danger because of their association with a man named Raum Buker," I said. "Your brother served time with him in East Jersey State Prison. They may even have grown close. Raum is congenitally dishonest, and your brother is a convicted thief. If they cooked up something between them for after their release, I'd like to know what it is. If they were in it together, it could be that they've drawn someone down on them by what they did, and those women are at risk of being caught in the crossfire."

Egon Towle's sister drew her right hand from her apron, and I instinctively backed up a step, as though that might have helped in the event of a bullet being fired. She saw the expression on my face, and lifted her hand to display a bulky vape pen. I breathed out while she breathed in.

"Did you think it was a gun?" she said.

"It's been known to happen. No offense meant."

"None taken. Anyway, it'd be hypocritical of me, seeing as how I left the gun on the console table inside the door. It's still within reach. You got some ID?"

I walked to the porch and showed her my license.

"It looks real," she said.

"I hope so. It took me hours to make."

She took another puff on the vape pen, and her reserve diminished.

"I suppose you'd better come in," she said. "Time will tell if I can help you after all."

3

Art is the final cunning of the human soul
which would rather do anything than face the gods.

—Iris Murdoch, *Acastos: Two Platonic Dialogues*

XLVII

E gon Towle's sister was named Eleanor, because, she said, her family had a preference for names beginning with the letter "E." There was no particular reason for this beyond eccentricity, which, as she noted, also began with an "E."

Eleanor Towle apologized for the condition of her home as she led me to the kitchen, although it struck me as perfectly neat and clean, if resolutely old-fashioned, right down to the Howdy Doody apron. She offered me coffee, and I made a point of never refusing coffee or tea in these situations, because it helped to establish some small bond of intimacy and informality. Declining often rendered an interview subject less likely to open up, although one had to be careful with alcohol. Then again, Eleanor Towle could have suggested a cup of arsenic and I'd have taken her up on it. Just because one accepted didn't mean one had to drink. There was a moral in there somewhere.

Only when the coffee was in front of me, served in a small, delicate cup, did I ask why she had a gun on her console table.

"Why does any woman keep a gun?" she said. "For protection."

"Did you have someone specific in mind?"

"I might." Her eyes roved over my upper body. "Do you carry a gun?"

"On occasion."

"Now?"

"No. If you think I'm likely to need one, I can go get it from the car."

"So I could have shot you, and there wouldn't have been a thing you could have done about it?"

She seemed to find the idea amusing, which was more than I did.

"By the time someone starts shooting at you," I said, "it's generally too late to do very much beyond ducking, bleeding, or dying. Then again, arriving on a stranger's doorstep with a gun in hand sends out the wrong message. It's a question of judgment."

"Well, you called it right on this occasion."

"I hope so. If you do decide to shoot me, I'll be very disappointed."

"If it comes to that, I'll shoot to kill from behind. I wouldn't want your last emotion to be disappointment."

She raised her cup to her mouth, but didn't sip from it, instead using the moment to embrace the opportunity to think before she spoke again. It gave me a chance to take her in. She radiated strength and sadness in more or less equal quantities. I thought she might be a hard woman to get to know, but an easy one to like once she'd decided to open up. I took in the kitchen, and the living room beyond. It didn't feel as though she belonged here, because everything in sight seemed part of an older dispensation. If she'd asked me, I'd have advised her to clear the contents and start again with an empty shell; that, or sell up and move someplace else. Were she to stay, the house would trap her in its web, cocooning her in memories while the past sucked her dry.

"Décor not to your taste?" she said, when my gaze returned to her.

"I'd speculate that it's not excessively to yours, either."

"My, you're honest." She tapped her cup. The porcelain chimed like a bell. "Everything you see belonged to my mother. Whatever there is of mine is elsewhere, out of sight. I haven't decided what to do with this house, but it won't be my call alone."

"Your brother?"

"The estate is to be divided equally between us. We just need to sit down with a lawyer and hammer it all out."

"Does that mean we can talk about Egon now?"

"I'm still weighing that up."

Her tone had altered gradually. She wasn't joking any longer, and her eyes were watchful for lies.

"We were speaking about guns," she said.

"We were."

"Have you ever been shot?"

"Yes."

"I thought you might have been. I could see it in your face when the subject came up."

"Because I flinched?"

"No, because you didn't. I think you're probably a brave man, Mr. Parker. I'd wager that you're also an honorable one." She put down her cup. "Yes, let's talk about Egon. How much do you know of my brother?"

"Not a great deal," I said, "beyond the fact that he served time for robbery, and narrowly avoided another term for possession of stolen goods. He also has some odd taste in reading material, and may, if you'll forgive me for saying so, be slightly unbalanced."

"You sure you haven't met him?" said Eleanor. "Because that's a strikingly accurate summation of his character."

"Guaranteed. Are you frightened of him?"

"Of Egon?" She laughed. "My brother wouldn't hurt a fly."

"Perhaps not, but he keeps company with men who would—and have."

She stopped laughing, which was a shame. She was a plain-looking woman, and the world weighed heavily on her shoulders, but she had a nice smile.

"Egon's a planner," she said, "but he's not strong, and he's certainly not intimidating. He's solitary by nature, and works better that way. He never was much good at choosing friends. That's probably why he ended up with none."

"I was told he had a reputation as an accomplished thief."

"Egon—" she began, and stopped. "Honorable or not, how do I know you're not just going to approach the police with all this?"

"You don't."

"But?"

"I'm not a law enforcement official," I said. "I'm under no legal obligation to report details of a crime, either planned or committed, unless directly asked about it in the course of a criminal investigation. A prosecutor or the police might contest that position, but any half-decent lawyer would shoot them down. That aside, I do have certain conditions: if it concerns an act of violence that can be stopped, or the abuse of a woman or child, historical or ongoing, I have a moral duty to act on that information—and a legal one, too, depending on the interpretation of the law, but the moral obligation supersedes all."

I waited. Sometimes—not often, but enough to make a statistical difference—you come across a person who wants to talk, and has been waiting to be asked the right questions. Frequently they're scared or angry, so dealing with them is a delicate business. I've found silence helps, but that requires patience. Uncomfortable with silence, the majority of individuals will seek to fill it, and unburdening has a lot in common with downhill skiing: once you start, it's very hard to stop.

"I don't know why I made coffee," she said. "I didn't want any."

"Neither did I."

That smile shyly revealed itself again.

"Aren't you wicked sharp?" she said. "If I drank liquor, I'd suggest we move on to that instead, but I never had a taste for it, and I got nothing stronger than soda in the house. You must think I'm real dull, living here in my spinster abode with a beater in the drive and not even a light beer in the refrigerator."

"I don't think that at all," I said, and I didn't. Eleanor Towle was smart and self-aware, but talking with her in these tidy but strangely gloomy surroundings, with my knowledge of her recently deceased mother and her crooked brother, it was possible to construct a narrative of her life that contained more than its share of disappointment and frustration. The choices she'd made—if she'd ever been given any real choices— had led her to this place, and it wasn't a happy one. Even had she been in a position to pursue better alternatives, her brother's actions would have leveled the scales, or tipped them against her. Life wasn't fair, but it was harder on some than others, and women, people of color, and the poor would always be among the most encumbered and restricted. Anyone who told you otherwise was a liar, and anyone who facilitated that injustice was a cheat. There endeth the lesson.

Eleanor Towle, the waters rising darkly around her, stretched out a hand for help.

"Egon made a mistake," she said.

"What kind of mistake?"

"He took something from the wrong man," she said, "and now that man wants it back."

XLVIII

Bobby Wadlin did something he very rarely did: he turned off his TV, leaving Johnny Ringo and Boone Hackett in limbo. He then made a call to Raum Buker's room and ordered the maid to leave everything as she'd found it, because they wouldn't be renting the space to someone new after all, not yet.

"But room all clean now, with fresh sheets on bed," said the maid, who was Chinese, or Vietnamese—some form of Asian, anyway. Wadlin liked to boast that he didn't see the color of a person's skin, which was only partly true: for him, there were just Whites, Blacks, Asians, and Everyone Else, and as long as they paid their bills and obeyed the rules, he had no quarrel with any of them.

"So?" said Wadlin. "That's what you're paid to do: clean, and make beds."

But he knew what the maid meant. The rooms were serviced twice weekly, unless they were being made ready for new guests, and unnecessary housekeeping impacted on her other duties. Also, she was a creature of routine, and disdained deviation. She and Wadlin had that much in common.

"Mr. Buker return?" she said.

"Damned if I know," he said. "Damned if he does, probably."

"What?"

"Nothing. Just put his stuff back where you found it."

Wadlin hung up. He wasn't exactly regretting accepting the money for permitting access to Buker's room to the sickly guy in brown, because making money was never to be regretted, but Wadlin wished the stranger had crawled off and died immediately after. It was troubling that he was aware of the attempt to clear out Buker's possessions, meager though they were. Wadlin supposed that someone must have told him, which meant he had eyes in the Braycott. Wadlin didn't like this one little bit. Trust, honesty, and discretion were required for the successful running of a rooming house for criminals, and any lapses depressed him. Wadlin went into his little apartment, lay down on his bed, and despaired of humanity.

XLIX

The story Eleanor Towle shared with me went like this:

Egon, her brother, was not a typical thief but a species of magpie, lured by shiny things, and coins in particular. Where this fascination had originated, she could not say. Their father, who had died when she and Egon were children, never had more than a couple of spare quarters to rub together, and the only items her mother collected were thrift-store knickknacks and the associated dust. Yet from an early age Egon had immersed himself in numismatics, driving Miss Dinah, the librarian at the public library in Center Ossipee, close to crazy with requests for books that would have been regarded as obscure at the New York Public Library, let alone her little athenaeum. Nevertheless, she had done her best for him, because she liked to encourage reading in the young.

It was probably for the best that Miss Dinah died before it became apparent that Egon's childhood hobby had developed into a full-blown adult criminal enterprise, but even in youth the first signs of it were apparent. Egon would check his mother's purse and change drawer for coins of interest, because he had memorized the Washington quarters that were worth more than their face value, and could identify a silver one by sight. If he discovered any such coins, he pocketed them, despite his mother's working two jobs to keep her children clothed and fed. Once that source had been exhausted, Egon convinced local businesses—diners, gas stations, candy stores—to permit him to sort through their quarters, informing them that he wished to assemble the best coin collection in the state. Because he was just a kid, they humored him, and in the beginning he would set aside the coins that interested him before diligently exchanging them for quarters of his own under the eye of the business owner. Gradually, he began to make a small profit from his efforts, then a larger one. One day, at Minty's Garage, he found two 1932-D Washington quarters in a jar of old loose change and Canadian coins that Minty kept on a shelf beside his containers of orphaned nuts and bolts. Egon used some of the money he made from selling the quarters to buy dinner for his mom and sister, but one way or another Minty got wind of what happened and came over to the house, where he raged on the doorstep about how the boy had cheated him, and demanded a cut of the proceeds. Mrs. Towle sent him on his way with a flea in his ear, noting that her son had exchanged like for like, just as he always did, and it wasn't Egon's fault if Minty didn't know the true value of whatever was sitting under his own nose.

But after that, word got around, and businesses in Ossipee weren't quite so willing to allow Egon access to their registers. Meanwhile a steady stream of locals began to make their way to the Towles' door, bringing with them bags of dusty coins in the hope that among them might be a Barber or Draped Bust quarter, something apparent only to the expert eye of young Egon Towle. Egon managed to bilk a few of these supplicants, although not for very much, while he traded more scrupulously with the brighter ones. Most, though, left disappointed, cursing grandparents and great-grandparents for bequeathing their descendants only small change.

But by now Egon wanted to leave greasy registers and filthy jars behind. He traded with a vengeance, exchanging a hundred low-value coins for one that might actually be worth retaining; and what he couldn't acquire honestly, he stole, often from small mom-and-pop dealers who still believed, despite any evidence to the contrary, in the fundamental honesty of people. Egon felt no compunction about plundering them. As far as he was concerned, "In God We Trust" contained an implicit warning about human duplicity. If one chose to ignore it, well, one couldn't say that one hadn't been told. By the time the majority of his marks even realized a coin was missing, Egon was long gone, and the coin in question would quickly change hands.

As a sideline, he also monitored obituary columns. Egon kept a record of collectors in the Northeast, and tried to be among the first at the door once the requisite time had passed following the final exhalation, ready to help widows dispose of coin hoards, as the bulk of collectors tended to be male. He would always arrive neatly turned out, under his arm an album containing photographs and cuttings of coins with doctored estimates, and an envelope filled with cash in the inside pocket of his jacket. Ready money helped, he had discovered. He was amazed by the number of men who died intestate, leaving wives and offspring to survive as best they could while lawyers tried to untangle estates. Show some of them a billfold and they'd be willing to sell whatever happened to catch a knowledgeable eye, even if they at first demurred because it had "sentimental value." From experience, Egon knew that sentiment, like so much else in life, could be valued in percentage increments.

And alongside the swindles, his thefts continued, growing in audacity. Only the most gullible of judicial observers would have read Egon Towle's criminal record and concluded that he had indulged only twice in acts of larceny. His was an ongoing, persistent endeavor, but one that frequently required long months of research and planning. He haunted coin shows, lurked on Internet forums and chat rooms as the business of collecting moved online, and learned the identities of the hobbyists who were careless about their security, as well as those less conscientious than the norm: the ones who would buy what he had to sell without question, so long as the price was right.

"Egon was good at spotting them," said his sister. "He had a nose for corruption."

But for all his efforts, he rarely ended up with very much money of his own. The stock of rare coins with real value was small, and even when he managed to secure a prize, he was frequently forced to sell it for much less than its actual worth because of the way in which it had been acquired. His biggest score was the $250,000 haul that brought him to the attention of the law in Connecticut, and he had been apprehended before he could move any of it. Also, Egon Towle was something of a collector himself, and would use any profits to obtain items for his own stash—but always legally, Egon being too clever to hold on to stolen goods for too long.

During that time, he continued to live with his mother and sister, except for his spell of incarceration in New Jersey. He dated neither women nor men, and spent his evenings at home reading coin books, occult esoterica, and the apocalyptic ramblings of assorted bunker dwellers, all while listening to avant-garde jazz.

"He was open with us about what he did for a living," said Eleanor. "I mean, it wasn't as though he could hide it after that business down in Connecticut. My mother was very disappointed in him, and decided the best course of action was to pretend it wasn't happening. If he gave her money, she thanked him and didn't mention it again. Egon's criminality was never a topic for discussion in our home. But he hasn't been the same since he was released from East Jersey," she added.

"In what way?" I said.

"He's sadder, but also harder. I suppose that's what prison does to some people, right? I thought it might have made him reconsider, but it hasn't. If anything, it's made him more committed to thievery. He knew that no one would give him a job because of his record, so what was the point of trying? I think he's decided he may as well keep going with what he knows. At least he got to spend some time with Mom before she died. He always did try to look out for her."

"And the occultism?"

"Yeah, we don't talk about that a whole lot, either," said Eleanor. "My mother was Episcopalian, so she didn't hold with the occult. Personally, I regard it as a weird joke. Egon always had funny ideas about the world, and he's never met a conspiracy theory he didn't like, but the occult thing has become more of a serious interest as the years have gone by. If I said he's curious about it on an intellectual level, that wouldn't be too far off the mark. Egon is really intelligent. He taught himself Japanese. He doesn't even know any Japanese people, doesn't like flying, and gets seasick in the tub, but still he decided to learn the language, and he only ever uses it when we go to a sushi bar."

I had my notebook open, but I wasn't taking notes. What Eleanor Towle had to say was interesting, but no more than that. I was letting her circle, allowing her to get comfortable before she settled. Now it was time for her to focus.

"Did he ever talk to you about a man named Raum Buker?" I said.

"Yeah, I know Raum some," said Eleanor. "I ought to. After all, I slept with him."

CHAPTER

L

Kepler, clad only in a towel, folded the copy of the *New York Times* and consigned it to the trash can in his motel room. The newspaper dated from May 2003, and its lead story reported the then president's contention that major combat operations in Iraq had come to an end. This, as subsequent events proved, was optimistic at best, and deluded at worst, especially when one took into account the history of the region, which no one in that benighted U.S. administration had done. But then, Kepler had a longer memory than was the norm, even if the gaps in it could be frustrating for him, requiring that they be filled in as, and when, he was able. Kepler's sanctuary in eastern Ontario was quiet and dark, and its occupant could sleep whole seasons away, like a spider in hibernation, waking only to feed as required. Long life was not an uncomplicated blessing or an unqualified curse, and even the oldest of trees required careful tending.

He looked at the clock by his bedside, with its runic symbols, its complications within complications, dials within dials. It was of his own design, and made sense only to him, but had it been monitored closely, even by one unfamiliar with it, the retardation of its workings would, in recent days, have become apparent. The movements were slowing, nearing cessation, and with it Kepler's time on earth would draw to a close, but he would not surrender without a fight. The application of gentle pressure on Raum Buker had produced no result, and Kepler had been on the verge of instituting more direct and painful measures when Buker had vanished. Now he would have to expend energy rooting him from his hiding place.

But Kepler was weak, so weak, and Buker's failure to return to the Braycott Arms was disturbing. If he had intended to relocate elsewhere, why had he not taken his possessions with him? One of the Strange women might know where he was, but to approach them directly would mean hurting them, and that would attract further attention. He had already left too many bodies behind, and would, in the end, add Buker to their number, not only because there might be no other way to force him to surrender what he had stolen but also to punish him for his effrontery. Yet Kepler remained concerned that, in a confrontation with Buker, he would come off the worst. By their actions, Buker and Towle had set in motion corruptive elements: Kepler could see and feel himself rotting. Buker was playing for time because he believed it was against Kepler, like a boxer keeping out of reach of a fading opponent's punches.

Kepler drew his laptop toward him and pulled up the screenshot of the private investigator, Parker. Kepler had lived too long, and put too many inquisitive men in the ground, to be worried by this latest incarnation of the breed. Here, though, was one adept at finding those who did not wish to be found. Kepler had been reading up on him, and Wadlin, the manager at the Braycott, had also been a useful source of information. If Parker was as good as he was said to be, there was a chance that he might already have found out that Buker and Towle were trying to sell stolen coins. He might even have established the identity of the coins' true owner, which had obvious perils for Kepler, but could equally be turned to his advantage. Parker and Buker, it emerged, had been involved in a confrontation at a bar called the Great Lost Bear, where the former was well known. Sometimes, Kepler knew, one had to cast bait upon the waters, and let the prey mistake itself for the predator.

Keeping his gaze averted from the mirror, so that he would not have to look upon his ravaged self, Kepler slowly, arduously, began to dress.

LI

E leanor Towle folded her arms and waited for my reaction to the news that Raum Buker had shared her bed. For a man with very few redeeming features that I could identify, Raum was quite a hit with women of a certain age. He ought to have published a book. There appeared to be no delicate way to broach the subject, so I decided to dive straight in.

"How familiar with him were you before you—?"

"Made the beast with him?" she finished. "I thought I'd save you the trouble of concluding the question, seeing as how you're looking so uncomfortable about it all. By the way, is that also disapproval I see on your face?"

"It's puzzlement. I struggle to see his appeal."

"I slept with him," said Eleanor. "I didn't say I was going to marry him. Anyway, he told me he had a woman up in Maine, so it wasn't as though I was planning our life together."

"Actually," I corrected, "he has two women up in Maine, or did."

"Tattletale. Are they the ones you're worried about?"

"That's right—assuming Raum wasn't sleeping with anyone else, which isn't beyond the bounds of possibility on current evidence. Did he happen to mention the name of the particular woman he was seeing?"

"Just the last: Strange. He thought I'd find it funny."

"And did you?"

"I might have found it funnier if he'd told me before I had sex with him."

"It must have slipped his mind."

"Must have. I reckon men's memories are flawed that way. How it happened was, he and Egon were celebrating, I joined in, and one thing led to another. There hasn't been a whole lot for me to celebrate lately, what with my mom dying and all, and I was grateful for the distraction. As for sleeping with Raum, I hadn't been with a man in three years. I'm not exactly inundated with suitors. Sometimes you take what you can get, and you're grateful for it."

"How did he end up here?"

"Egon invited him. It was the first time I'd met him, although I was already familiar with the name. Egon had told me about Raum during prison visits, and I'd seen him at a distance, although we'd never been formally introduced. He and Egon had become close—not in a freaky way, though. Well, everything to do with Egon is freaky, I guess, but you know what I mean."

"They weren't lovers."

"No. They didn't have much in common, not that I could see, beyond both being out of favor with the law, but somehow they got along, and Raum looked out for my brother. Later, after we'd done the deed, Raum told me that Egon had gotten him interested in all that occult stuff. In fact, I'd even have said that Raum was more committed to it than my brother, which is saying something. I mean, whatever his obsession, Egon never went and got himself a pentacle tattoo. He's too conservative for that."

"And what did you think of that tattoo?"

"What did I think of it? I thought it made him look like one of those goth kids who hang out by the movie theater at the Mountain Valley Mall. A man his age had no business getting a tattoo like that, and I told him so. I also figured it had been done with a dirty needle, it was weeping so bad. It was never going to heal either, not the way Raum was fussing at it."

"Did he tell you why he'd had it done?"

She puffed on the vape.

"I wish I still smoked," she said. "This damned thing just isn't the same."

Her eye came to rest on something to my left, and her face fell. I turned to look, and saw a photograph of a younger Eleanor between two older people, a man and a woman. I could see a little of each of them in her, possibly because they were one of those couples who, either through a quirk of fate or years of exposure, resembled each other deeply. Sunlight had faded the picture slightly. In time, if it wasn't moved, the faces might cease to be identifiable. I was reminded of the photograph in the room at the Braycott: Raum with his mom and dad, the color saturation degenerating, evanescing like memory. Funny how he and Eleanor Towle had found each other. Perhaps the two of them had more in common than I, or they, knew.

"Were they good parents?" I said.

She smiled.

"Yes, they were. My father, had he lived, wouldn't have let someone like Raum Buker set foot in his yard. But then I've never yet picked the right man for my bed, or the right man never picked me. It's this place—not the house, or not just that, but I've stayed too long in this town, this county. People get to know you. They put you in a little box, and you start to become whatever it is they've decided you are. Me, I'm Eleanor Towle, spinster. Good for a turn on a Saturday night, if there's nothing better on offer, and assuming I'd put out, but not someone you'd want to wake up beside for the rest of your life, or not even two mornings in a row." Her mouth curled with self-disgust. "Listen to me. You ought to be charging by the hour for this."

"I'm on someone else's dime, if that helps," I said. "Even if I wasn't, I don't have anywhere else to be right now, and I don't feel like driving back to Portland until the traffic has eased."

"You're kind," she said. "I haven't spoken properly to anyone since my mother's funeral, or not beyond Egon, and Raum that one night, and neither of them showed much interest in my sorrows. You were asking why Raum got the tattoo. He said it was for protection."

"Did he happen to mention from what?"

"Not what, but whom. And we're getting ahead of the story. We need to go back to why they were here to begin with."

"You said they were celebrating," I said.

"Yes, because whatever thievery they'd cooked up together had come off, I suppose."

She looked away, but I wasn't going to let her slip the hook so easily.

"You 'suppose'?"

"Okay, I *know*. Is that better?"

"I told you already: I'm not the police."

"But you look like police. I had a cousin who was a cop. It marks a person, if you can spot the signs. I see them in you."

"I was police, once."

"Where?"

"New York."

"You retire early?"

"Very."

"Don't want to talk about it, huh?"

"Not so much."

"Now you know how I feel."

"Touché. Let's get back to the celebration."

She rubbed the fingers of her right hand across her lips.

"Jesus, I wish I still smoked," she said again.

I waited.

"It was coins," she continued at last. "With Egon, what else would it be? Egon had heard about this guy. He was said to be a high-end collector, but real reclusive, and he made acquisitions largely from abroad, through agents or by remote auction, specializing in Greek, Roman, Persian, Chinese, and early British: coins mainly, but also religious artifacts, and the rarer the better. When he set his sights on a prize, he didn't like to be beaten to it. If he was, or if someone refused to respond positively to one of his approaches, he'd find another way to get what he wanted."

"By theft? Or violence?"

"According to the stories, he didn't steal, or not exactly. A coin worth, say, ten thousand dollars might vanish from a collection, but he'd leave something else as a replacement. It might correspond to only a fraction of the value of what was taken, but it would be an unusual item—an old cross, say, or an ancient Greek arrowhead. It wasn't a fair exchange, but it was an exchange nonetheless, and would only occur after any offers had been declined. We all find ways to ease our consciences. As for violence, that's a different matter. The antiquities market has its dark corners, and he wasn't above stealing from thieves and criminals, because they weren't true collectors, not in his eyes."

I had known a man like this once, a collector—no, *the* Collector. He, too, had operated by a code of his own, but he was gone now. I hoped.

"He was a legend in the trade," Eleanor continued, "or a bogeyman. A lot of collectors just laughed off the stories about him. Those rumors had been circulating for decades, and some dealers could recall their fathers, and even their grandfathers, talking about the same guy, or a version of him. I mean, that would make him really, really old, beyond anything possible, and he often used aliases, so no one could be sure it was the same person they were talking about. He was a campfire tale for people who don't like the outdoors. For a long time my brother, like so many of the rest, wasn't willing to accept that he even existed, until Egon did some homework and became convinced he was real."

"How?" I said.

"Because they shared some of the same interests, Egon and this guy—you know, the woo-woo stuff. Then someone else came forward, another collector. I don't remember his name, but he lived in northern Pennsylvania: Sayre, South Waverly, someplace like that. He filled in the blanks for Egon, or a lot of them."

"Why?"

"He wanted Egon to do his dirty work for him by stealing from the bogeyman, and Egon was willing to go along with it because the score promised to be big, and the mark wouldn't be able to report the theft to the police because of his own activities. If it wasn't the perfect crime, it was as close as Egon was likely to get."

"Aided by Raum, right?" I said.

"Egon doesn't like roughness. The gun that got him into all that trouble wasn't even loaded. So the Pennsylvania collector—Athens, that's where he's from, but his name didn't stick with me—provided the lure: an Indian coin, very old, which came with a provenance linking it directly to Alamelamma, the wife of an Indian ruler who threw herself from a cliff back in the seventeenth century, but not before cursing the Mysore kings."

I couldn't help but raise an eyebrow.

"Yeah, I know," said Eleanor. "After years of living with Egon, some of this shit had to rub off on me. They convinced a tame dealer up in Whitefield to list the Alamelamma coin, but selectively, and told him to keep it dangling until the right fish bit. He did, made the sale, and the delivery went to a PO box in Potsdam, New York, not far from the Canadian border. After that, they spent some cash to find out who was renting the box. It was a lot easier than Egon had anticipated, but perhaps this collector, who it turned out was based in Ontario, had become careless in his old age, although not so careless as to rent a box near his place of residence. By the time Raum got out, Egon had the plan in place. He and Raum hit the mark a week or so later, and that's what they were celebrating the night we slept together. They'd taken down the bogeyman and stolen his treasure, just like in a fairy tale."

"And does this bogeyman have a name?" I asked.

"Like I said, he uses aliases," said Eleanor, "but one in particular."

She was no longer smiling, and her gaze drifted past me to the gun on the console table.

"More often than not," she said, "he calls himself Kepler."

LII

E leanor Towle poured away the cold coffee and washed the cups. I caught her glancing at my reflection in the glass of the kitchen window, regarding, assessing. If her brother was anything like her, regardless of his eccentricities, he could be a force to be reckoned with. She was an intriguing woman. Of course, she was also a liar, if only by omission, but nobody was perfect.

I was listening carefully while she worked at the sink. I'd been listening ever since I entered her home. It's harder for a person to remain quiet and still than one might think, especially if they're trying to monitor a conversation going on elsewhere in a house, but I'd picked up no indications of another occupant. I believed Eleanor Towle to be alone. Wherever her brother was hiding, it wasn't here.

"What do you do for a living, Ms. Towle?"

"I'm a waitress at Phil's," she said. Phil's was a grill house up on Route 16. I'd passed its billboard on the way to the Towle house. The sign read PHIL UP AT PHIL'S!, a gag so worn even Goodwill wouldn't have accepted it.

"Do you enjoy it?"

"What do you think?"

"I've no idea. That's why I asked."

She set the cups upside down to drain, dried her hands on a dish towel, and turned to look at me.

"No, I don't enjoy it," she said, "but it's a job, the tips are okay, and they were real understanding when my mom was sick."

"Are you going to keep working there, now she's gone?"

"I haven't decided. Egon and I need to have that serious conversation about selling the house. I'd like to move away from here. Ossipee hasn't brought me much luck in life, Egon neither, but he's comfortable with the familiar. Given his druthers, he'd elect to be carried out of here feet-first."

If they sold the house and split the proceeds evenly, I guessed they might come out with $100,000 each, give or take. It wasn't a lot, not if she was hoping to make a new start somewhere else, but there were also the proceeds of the robbery to consider.

"What exactly did your brother and Raum Buker take from this man Kepler?" I asked.

"Coins. I told you."

But there it was, that little hint of evasion.

"Just coins?"

She tilted her head.

"You are good, aren't you?" she said.

"I've had practice."

"At picking up on what's unsaid?"

"That, and knowing when someone wants to finish a tale but is worried about how it might sound, or make them appear."

"I've got no concerns about the second part."

"What about the first?"

"Some," she conceded. "And it wasn't 'just' coins."

"I'm not following you. You mean they stole other items as well?"

"No." She practically grimaced with frustration. "Look, the majority were coins as you or I would understand the term—you know, gold or silver, Roman or Greek, the kind you'd find behind glass in a collection—but one wasn't."

"What was it, then?"

She shifted uneasily on her feet. We were closing in on the truth, or some rendering of it.

"It was Celtic," she said, "made of potin, from before the time of Christ. The coin was discovered in Essex, but may have come from elsewhere in the British Isles, or may not even have been minted there at all. It's hard to say, because it doesn't look like anything else from that time or place."

"What's potin?"

"It's a mixture of copper and tin, sometimes with lead thrown in."

"Valuable?"

"Sure, to a museum or the right collector. The guy down in Athens wanted it very badly, which was why he put up the Indian coin as a lure, and helped Egon and Raum target the bogeyman. You see, this particular potin coin was very special, even if it didn't look like it to me, not at first."

"You saw it?"

"Yes," she said, but she sounded tense.

"What was so unusual about it?"

She smoothed her apron while she debated what to share and what to exclude. There could only be two reasons for evasion: either she was scared, or she was trying to throw me off the scent. I thought the former was more likely, but that didn't entirely preclude the latter.

"Look," she said, "early British coins are fairly standardized. From what Egon has told me, they're based on gold and silver staters introduced to the British Isles by traders from Gaul, because you imitate what you see, right? That's why some of the first British coins had representations of Philip of Macedon on one side, for example, and a charioteer on the other. But then, as you go on, you find the coins becoming more distinctive, some with images of creatures, real and imaginary, like little works of art. It could be that the local shaman or chieftain might have been smoking something strong and had a vision, so that was what he wanted put on his coins. It makes them interesting, periodically unique."

"And what was on the coin Egon showed you?" I asked.

"A beast," she said. "Or more correctly, a demon."

I grabbed a pile of dust, and holding it up,
foolishly asked for as many birthdays as the grains of dust.
I forgot to ask that they be years of youth.

—Ovid, *Metamorphoses*

LIII

D ave Evans was preparing to head home from the Bear when Paulie Fulci approached him. Dave's late failure to remove Raum Buker from the premises had been forgiven by the Fulci brothers, if not entirely forgotten, helped by the fact that Raum hadn't returned to the bar since his altercation with them. The Fulcis were by now aware that he was holed up at the Braycott Arms, but sometimes a man is worth hitting, yet not worth the effort of traveling any distance to hit. Should Raum have been unfortunate or careless enough to stumble into their path, the Fulcis would have undone all the progress achieved by his periodontist, and also put some work the way of a good orthopedist.

"The man in the corner," said Paulie, "over by the specials board, I think there's something wrong with him."

"Wrong, how?" said Dave.

"Just wrong."

Any number of accusations could have been leveled at the Fulci brothers—and many had, not least in courts of law—but being poor judges of character was not among them. Their reactions might have been instinctive, and expressed in the simplest of terms, but they were very rarely mistaken. It was a consequence of their comparatively child-like perspective on the world and those who inhabited it. The Fulcis viewed behavior in terms of good or bad, kind or unkind, generous or mean, and distrusted any morality that was tolerant of compromise. And, Dave thought, who was to say they were wrong? Admittedly, their own past behavior was less than blameless, and even some of their more recent exploits gave cause for concern, but an undeniable sense of righteousness and honesty underpinned everything they did, which was more than could be said for a lot of folk Dave knew. The Fulcis' principal flaw was that they were easily led. Well, that and their hair-trigger tempers. And their willingness to use violence as a second resort, or even a first. Actually, now that Dave came to consider it, the Fulcis had a great many flaws.

So, although home was calling, Dave listened to Paulie, and used a check on the spelling of the evening's specials as an excuse to take a look at the patron in question. He was sitting directly under the board, and dressed in various shades of tan, cream, and brown from the top of his trilby hat to the soles of his two-tone leather brogues, like the subject of a sepia photograph come to life. He was wearing a brown tweed jacket over a tan vest, a yellow shirt with a yellow-and-beige tie, and cream moleskin trousers. A single red feather poked from his hatband, like a Native American scout imperfectly concealed amid arid slopes.

But glimpsed up close, the stains on his pants and shirt were plain to see, along with the fraying of his jacket cuffs, the missing middle button on his vest—his belly straining against the cotton shirt beneath, revealing coarse gray hairs—and the scuffing on his unpolished shoes. His chin was sunk on his chest, the brim of the hat concealing his face. He was breathing so regularly and deeply that Dave thought he might be asleep, and he gave off a hint of rosewater, along with something nastier that smelled like an outhouse in high summer. An empty yellow-and-black plastic ampule stood beside a glass of what resembled brandy, although when Dave asked around later, no one could remember having served him, and the glass was not from the Bear's stock.

Then he raised his head and opened his eyes, and Dave was

reminded of hinged shells unclasping to reveal the bivalves within, or single embryos at the heart of frog spawn. The globes were milky, one more than the other, and the irises were gray, the widening pupils dark and imperfect in their circularity, as if those same embryos had been coaxed into unfolding by the sudden influx of light. His hand shifted position on the table, revealing a pair of ivory dice that matched the color of his skin. When he spoke, his voice was so soft that Dave had to lean in close to hear it.

"Are you a gambling man?"

LIV

Evening was leaching into night, so Eleanor Towle lit a lamp on the kitchen table. The ancient heating system had rumbled into action, gurgling and hissing, and now the house sounded as though it were suffering from indigestion.

"So the design on this coin was distinctive," I said. "Is that what gave it a rarity value?"

Eleanor rested her chin on her hands. Her mood and tone had altered once more, and I could see she was becoming increasingly impatient, even angry. By inviting me into her home she had set in motion a chain of events that could end only with the revelation of more than she had originally intended to divulge. She wanted something in return, if just a brief respite from her loneliness. But the more time I spent in that house, the more oppressive its atmosphere became, especially now that darkness had arrived.

"You do ask a lot of questions," she said.

"It's why I'm here."

"Hardly seems fair. You ask, I answer. It's like an interrogation."

"Ms. Towle, I don't believe you're sharing anything you don't want to share."

"And why should that be?"

"Because you're worried."

"About what?"

"Your safety," I said, "and Egon's, too. You can't call the police because of what he's done, and I don't think it would ever have crossed your mind to hire a private investigator, because what is there to investigate but your brother's crime? You've taken a calculated gamble that my involvement is more likely to help than hinder, but each time I ask a question, I can see you reckoning for a couple of seconds before you reply."

"That's because I'm putting a lot of faith in you, and it's all one-way traffic."

"I think 'faith' may be open to debate. For every truth you share, you hold another back."

"Maybe you're not so kind after all. Are you married?"

"No."

"I'm surprised. I thought only married people were so cynical about the opposite sex. Were you ever married?"

"Yes."

"What happened?"

"She died."

"I'm sorry," she said, but it was a rote reply. "Do you have children?"

"One."

Two, but my dead daughter was none of her concern.

"A boy or a girl?"

"A girl. You were telling me about the coin."

She accepted that this was as much as she was going to get from me, or not without further concessions on her part.

"Yes, I was, wasn't I?" She lifted her head and rubbed the palm of her right hand with her thumb. "I held it, you know, but not for very long. I didn't want to."

"Why was that?"

She raised her right hand, displaying the palm. Even in the lamplight, I could see the tiny white blisters on her skin.

"I can't get rid of them," she said, "and they itch. I think I'll have to see a doctor, but what will I tell him? That I held an old coin for a couple of seconds before dropping it on the floor? That a presence manifested itself in those seconds, a presence that resembled the image on the coin, except viewed through mist, and afterward my skin began to blister? That I now have nightmares about contamination and disease, of the pustules bursting and small black worms emerging from the wounds?"

She closed her hand and placed it on her lap. Her eyes were very wide.

"What is the coin, Ms. Towle? Why is it so important?"

"It may not always have been a coin," she said. "Egon thinks it might have had another form at one point—a small effigy, or an amulet—before being turned into a coin. In the end, it doesn't matter. The shape may change, but its nature never does. It's both a disease and a remedy. It's a toxin and an antidote in one. It's not the coin that's important, so much as what it's supposed to buy."

"And what's that?"

"Time," she said. "An extension of your years. Because the coin wards off death."

"Eternal life?"

She laughed.

"No, not that—and who would want it anyway? You look skeptical, and it's an expression your face settles into without difficulty."

"Shouldn't I be?"

"Certainly. Nothing is eternal. Even God will vanish when no one is left to speak His name. Call it longer life, or a delayed death: years, decades. That would be enough for many. I know people who'd sell their souls for just an extra day." She paused. "My mother wouldn't have, but I'd have sold mine for one more day with her."

She kept her eyes fixed on the table, like a woman peering into a stagnant pool to gauge the depths of her own regret.

"I sense a 'but' coming," I said.

"Isn't there always? I thought I'd be married by now, but I'm not. I hoped to have children, but it didn't happen. I wanted my mother to keep on living, but she died. Life is written after the 'but.' The rest is just what might have been."

She wiped her eyes, even though they'd barely betrayed her.

"I'm a fool," she said. "Raum Buker rolls up here, and I take him to my bed. You arrive at my door, and I spill my guts to you. My brother is a thief, and brings his tribulations down on me. Damn all you men. I'm better off alone."

I wasn't about to disagree, and any straw poll of unhappy women would also have come down on her side. Men could be poor advertisements for their sex.

"The coin is its own price," said Eleanor, "or so Egon says, because that's the myth surrounding it. The coin infects, but it also staves off the consequences of the infection. It corrupts, but as long as you hold on to it, you'll slow the decay. But lose the coin and you're lost, too. The sands in your hourglass fall faster, your weakened system is exposed to the damage of the years, and the contamination begins to make itself felt. And all the while, whatever haunts that piece of metal starts looking for a new host as the old one begins to wither.

"If the coin isn't taken up again, the presence lies dormant, and waits to be rediscovered. So it's a fairy tale, although not one I'd want to tell a child, and most collectors had dismissed the story, even while they believed in the coin's existence—because it's changed hands in the past, although not since early in the last century, or not that anyone could swear to. The collector in Athens figured out that Kepler had the coin, and he wanted it. Egon and Raum were willing to get involved, because even if it turned out not to be the case, the rest of Kepler's collection would be worth the effort and risk involved.

"But they did find the coin, and if its history is all just so much baloney, there are still men who will pay a lot of money for it because it's old and uncommon. Egon is convinced it's the only one of that design ever to have been struck. To the right buyer, it's worth a low- to mid-six-figure sum, and that's before you add the value of whatever else Egon and Raum took from Kepler."

"But the Athens collector wanted the coin," I said, "or am I mis-understanding the arrangement? He had no intention of selling it, just adding it to his own collection."

"Which is why Egon and Raum double-crossed him," said Eleanor. "They calculated that by the time they disposed of their share, allowing for the vagaries of the market and what Egon always refers to as 'thief's depreciation,' they might be splitting two hundred thousand between them, if the stars aligned. They wanted more, and had a dealer lined up to take on the sale."

And there it was.

"Wouldn't there be consequences for reneging on the arrangement?" I said.

"I doubt it," she said. "The middleman dealer would keep quiet because he wanted the money—and some of the coins, too, because he was also a collector. The Athens collector is old, from what Egon told me, and he and Egon never met face-to-face. What's he going to do, call the FBI and tell them that the robbery he helped arrange didn't work out the way he'd planned? He'd have no choice but to suck it up."

Hundreds of thousands of dollars for one coin, aside from the rest, was a lot of sucking up to do. If I were Egon Towle and Raum Buker, I might be worried. An elderly man wouldn't have much to lose by point-ing the finger at them.

"Is the dealer aware of the source of the coins?" I said.

"What do you think?"

"Whatever happened to honor among thieves?"

"It died with Watergate, and it always did have a price. For most anyone, the proceeds from the sale of those coins would represent life-changing money."

I noticed the stress on the word "most," and the curl of her upper lip.

"But not for Raum and Egon," I said.

"No, not for them, because each of them is dumb in his own fashion. Egon will use his half to buy more coins. I might see a little of what he makes, but not much. Otherwise, his life won't change one bit, because he likes it just the way it is. As for Raum, if you gave him a skewer, it would turn to a corkscrew in his hand. That man was born crooked, and he'll die the same way. Money won't alter him for the better."

I was no longer listening. Her brother's character was of scant interest to me, and I was as familiar with Raum Buker's as I needed to be. What interested me now was this man Kepler, because if items so valuable had been stolen from him, he would undoubtedly be making efforts to retrieve them. He would be alert to any signs of his collection being offered for sale so that he could pounce on the seller. At the same time, he would be hunting the thieves, and my guess was that he was already aware of their identities, because every crime leaves a trail. If I was right, Kepler had made his presence known at the home of Ambar Strange, and in Raum's bathroom at the Braycott, yet he had not so far resorted to brute force.

"Has your brother found a buyer for the coin?" I asked.

"I don't think so. The problem is Kepler. No one is going to want to acquire that coin as long as he's looking for it. I mean, who wants to die for a myth?"

"So Raum and your brother will have to wait him out?"

"Assuming the story, unlikely as it sounds, is true," said Eleanor. "If it isn't, they'll be forced to rethink their strategy, if what they're doing even passes for a strategy."

She tapped a finger on the table, and the lamplight caught the gleam in her eye.

"But as soon as Kepler dies, the auction starts."

LV

At the Great Lost Bear, amid the sounds of music, conversation, and laughter, amid normality, Dave Evans stared at the pair of dice on the table. Like the housekeeper Floriana, he had immediately spotted the peculiarity of their manufacture, and could only guess at their antiquity. He thought they might have been made from bone—animal, he hoped, but possibly not. Whatever their origin, he recognized with absolute certainty that it would be unwise to touch them.

"I don't gamble," said Dave.

The stranger tapped his fingers on the table in time to a cadence only he could hear. He blinked heavily, his eyelids descending slowly and ascending more slowly still, as though the tarsal plates within were formed of lead. His eyes flicked wetly to Dave.

"I wasn't proposing a cash wager, just a game of chance," he said. "You win, you get to ask me a question. I win, I ask you. These are low stakes. The emperor Claudius once bet four hundred thousand sesterces on a roll of the dice."

Dave noticed that his voice was possessed of a peculiar reverberation, a form of distortion that gave the impression of two people vocalizing at once, each with a slightly different timbre.

"What do you have to lose," the stranger persisted, "except time?"

Dave had been in the hospitality business for most of his life. During those years he'd learned to spot badness early, because it saved a lot of aggravation. Some individuals, he knew, tried to disguise their iniquity, while others failed even to recognize the fact of its existence, so estranged were they from their own true nature. But then there were those who chose to advertise their wickedness, or could no more hide it than they could the color of their skin or the rise and fall of their breathing; were the very marrow of their bones to be examined, it would be adjudged polluted. With such men—for men they often were—it was best to avoid all discourse and dealings, but when faced with them, one could not display weakness. If they were hell-bent on confrontation, only courage would give them pause.

"With respect," said Dave, "I don't believe you have anything I need to know."

The stranger picked up the dice, shook them in his right hand, and dropped them on the table. They showed a double six.

"There was a gentleman in here a while back," he said. "I believe he was involved in a fracas. His name is Mr. Raum Buker. I'm eager to make his acquaintance. You think he might again be gracing your establishment with his presence anytime soon?"

"I don't believe you heard me right," said Dave.

"Oh, I heard you fine, but just because you're unfamiliar with the rules doesn't mean you're excused from the game. The game goes on. The game always goes on. The only issue to be decided is if you're a player or a pawn."

He shook the dice again. Once more they returned a double six.

"Has Mr. Raum Buker been a regular here since his return?" he said.

"Get out."

Shake. Throw. Double six.

"Or his women?"

Dave dearly wanted to eject this man personally, and with considerable prejudice, but so far he had done nothing more threatening than to ask questions. Close by, the Fulci brothers were hovering, because trouble recognizes trouble.

The dice were thrown once more. Double six: either this man was very lucky, or the dice were weighted.

"What about a man named Parker, a detective? Does he run with Mr. Raum Buker?"

"How about this?" said Dave. "I could remove you forcibly from that chair and deposit you in the parking lot, but it would be undignified for you and disruptive for our other customers."

"Or?" The dice were back in his hand.

"Or we could let the cops sort it out," said Dave. "As it happens, I think we might have a few in tonight, if you'd like to be introduced. But it's my conviction that you'd probably prefer to adopt an alternative strategy, which would be to walk away and never show your face in my bar again."

The stranger rolled the dice loosely in the palm of his hand.

"That's a sharp move," he said. "I hope you won't come to regret it."

Then, in a feat of legerdemain that Dave would remember until his dying day, he simultaneously moved the dice over and under the fingers of each hand, so that they appeared to float across the knuckles and adhere to the pads of the fingers in defiance of gravity. When he was done, he let them drop to the table before pressing the bottom of his glass against them in turn, until finally they split, each revealing a tiny piece of metal.

"They're all deteriorating." He spoke softly and sorrowfully, but not to Dave. "My Dutch and High Germans, my bristles and fulhams, my high and low men. What manner of rook am I now? None worth the name."

He finished his drink, dropped the empty glass into one of his misshapen pockets, and scooped up the fragments of dice, where they vanished in an instant, leaving only an empty palm.

"You were right not to play," he told Dave. "You have to be able to trust the dice, and the only dice you can trust are your own." He slipped a dollar bill under the beer mat. "If you see Mr. Raum Buker, or the hawkshaw named Mr. Charlie Parker, you can inform them that Kepler sends his regards. I'll be in touch with one or the other of them by and by."

With that he left, trailing the scent of roses and decay. The Fulcis monitored his progress gravely as one of the servers arrived to clean the table.

"What a creep," she said. She moved to dispose of the empty ampule, but Dave stopped her.

"I'll keep that," he said.

She shrugged and handed it to him, before picking up the dollar bill.

"Big tipper, too," she said, before examining the bill more closely. "Wait, is this even real?"

Dave took it from her. It was an old Blue Seal Silver Certificate bill in perfect condition, a type that had ceased to be produced in the 1960s. The series date was 1923.

"It's real," he said, "but old. Might even be worth a few bucks, if you ask around."

He returned the bill to the server.

"I misjudged him," she said.

"No," said Dave, as the door closed behind Kepler, "I think you were right on the money."

CHAPTER

LVI

ill Quinn knocked on the door of Dolors Strange's home but received no reply. He had already tried Strange Brews, but Dolors had not been seen at the coffee shop. According to Erin, the assistant manager, Dolors had phoned to say that she still wasn't feeling great and would be staying home. Now here was Will, flowers in hand, come to check on her, only to find the house empty. Neither was Dolors answering her cell phone.

Will sniffed glumly at the arrangement. It wasn't a cheap gas station purchase, but a proper bouquet bought at Harmon's Floral Company on Congress Street, with a ribbon and a card. He felt ridiculous standing on the stoop with no one to accept his offering, like an overgrown kid jilted on prom night. He considered leaving the flowers inside the screen door, but feared they might be crushed. Dolors, he knew, kept big planters beside the rear entrance to the house, the one that opened directly into her kitchen. The pots were empty at the moment, given the season, and he thought he might be able to leave the bouquet in one of them, where it could sit without being damaged or taken by the wind.

He opened his jacket to let in some air. He'd put on a sweater that morning, but the weather continued to play unseasonable tricks, and he now felt that he was wearing one layer too many. The ground was starting to thaw, even farther north. It had implications for his business, because he ran a small garden center alongside the lumberyard, and he wasn't yet fully stocked for spring.

Will poked at the bouquet. If there was no fool like an old fool, he thought, there was no old fool like an old fool in love. Had he enjoyed more experience and success with the opposite sex, he might never have found himself in this position: employing the services of a private investigator to look into the activities of a woman who had once shared her bed with a criminal, and in turn had shared that criminal with her sister; a woman, what's more, who had ended their nascent relationship upon that criminal's reappearance after a term in prison for manslaughter, this last detail being just one of a number of facts about Raum Buker that Dolors had elected to skate over or conceal completely. And yes, perhaps Will had been complicit in this, accepting that whatever prospect he had of maintaining a relationship with Dolors was dependent on permitting her to share or conceal as she saw fit, but it had placed him on the back foot from the start. All this because, one afternoon, he had spotted a customer by the mulch pile and decided to pass the time of day instead of leaving his staff to take care of her.

Will was in love with Dolors Strange, and believed she might have reciprocal feelings for him. At a stage in life when he had more or less given up hope of ever finding a companion, or even a regular dinner date, he had entered the orbit of an extraordinary, if eccentric, woman, and had no intention of letting her go. It was, though, a source of reassurance that he had the investigator on his side. He might no longer have been sure what it was he had hired Parker to achieve or find out, beyond establishing Raum Buker's reasons for being back in Portland, but he knew that a man could have worse allies in a time of disquiet.

Will arrived at the back of the house and stopped dead. The body of a squirrel was nailed to the door, its belly cut open and its innards coiled on the step. Its blood had been used to leave a figure like a stick man on the wood.

Will Quinn dropped the flowers and made a call.

LVII

I pressed Eleanor Towle for the name of the coin dealer who had conspired with Egon Towle and Raum Buker to steal Kepler's collection.
She knew it, even if she hadn't yet revealed it. She knew because she
was shrewd, and had become accomplished at seeing and hearing more
than she ever let on. Despite this, it took her a while to answer. Had
she been giving evidence on a witness stand, the obviousness of some
of her inner deliberations might have caused a jury to doubt the truth
of everything she said. I was disposed to be less censorious, because
by now I thought I had the measure of her: if she lied, she would lie by
omission, but she preferred to speak the truth.

"Nice to know that some details do slip by you," she said. "It's our
frailties that make us human. His name was Reuben Hapgood."

"Was?"

"He's dead. Killed in a fire."

"When?"

"A week or so ago, I think, at his store."

"What was the cause of the fire?"

"It's still under investigation, but the police have told the newspapers
that it may have been started deliberately."

This was the curse of living in a big country: a man in a contiguous
state could be burned to death by parties unknown, and one might

only find out about it by inadvertently making the right inquiry of a stranger.

"You didn't see fit to mention this until now?" I said.

"It may have nothing to do with what Egon and Raum did."

"Is that what Egon said, or what you've been trying to tell yourself?"

"Does it matter either way?" said Eleanor.

"I don't suppose it does. It doesn't even matter to Reuben Hapgood, not any longer."

"That's cold-blooded."

I resisted the urge to laugh in her face. It wouldn't have served any purpose, and might have brought proceedings to a premature end when questions remained to be answered. Eleanor Towle had degenerated in my estimation from intriguing to capricious, even downright shady.

I felt my phone vibrate in my pocket, but I didn't take the call. Whoever it was could wait until I was done here. I asked Eleanor if she had a picture of the coin, but she told me she didn't.

"Egon certainly has images of it," she said, "and Raum, too. They'll need them when the time comes to sell, just to convince buyers that they really do have it in their possession."

"But they won't start advertising it until after Kepler is dead."

"Like I told you, that's one chance they're not prepared to take. He's not a man to be underestimated."

"Why didn't Raum and your brother just dispose of Kepler and have done with it, instead of risk having him come after them?"

"Egon isn't the kind," said Eleanor. "Neither is Raum, for all his bluster."

I reminded her that Raum had done time for killing a man in New Jersey.

"He had no choice," she said. "It was self-defense."

"Witnesses differed on that."

"Then to hell with them. But—"

She hesitated.

"Go on," I said.

"What if Egon and Raum are convinced the myth is true," she said, "and the only way to get rid of Kepler is to keep that coin from him."

"Are you offering that as a hypothesis, or telling me it's what they believe?"

"Okay, I'm telling you. If they can avoid Kepler, they believe fate will take care of him, and fast. There, are you happy? You got your story, for what it's worth. You can accept or dismiss it, I don't care."

We were at the end. I wasn't going to get much more from her. I took out my cell phone and showed her the symbol I'd photographed in Raum's unit at the Braycott Arms.

"Have you ever seen anything like this before?" I asked.

She looked at the picture and visibly recoiled.

"Egon showed it to me, when he was drunk. That's a rune—Kepler's rune. It's a signature, or a calling card. Where did you find it?"

"In Raum Buker's motel room, and on the door of one of the women he was seeing up in Maine. Has Kepler been here, Ms. Towle?"

"No."

That made no sense. If Kepler was stalking Raum Buker, he also had to know about Egon Towle.

"When was the last time you heard from your brother?" I said.

"Six days ago."

"Before or after Reuben Hapgood went up in flames?"

"After," she conceded. "But not long after."

"So he went underground when Hapgood was killed."

"If you want to put it that way."

"Aren't you concerned for his safety?"

"Of course, but he was planning to lie low before Hapgood died. I'm not surprised that Egon hasn't been in touch. He told Raum to keep his head down as well, but I don't think Raum is the head-down type."

She was right about that much, given Raum's performance at the Great Lost Bear. If the Fulcis had managed to lay hands on him, he might not have had a head to keep down. But this part of Eleanor Towle's narrative was missing a link. If Kepler couldn't lay hands on Raum or Egon, and had already placed his mark on Ambar Strange's door, then why not put pressure on Egon's sister to find out what she knew? Unless—

"Do you have a number for your brother?"

"Yes."

"Have you used it lately?"

"No, because calls can be traced. Everybody knows that."

"Indulge me," I said. "Contact him."

"Not with you here. I'll call him later, when you're gone. I'll let you know how it goes. I give you my word."

"Will you tell him about my visit?"

"I don't see why not."

She was playing a dangerous game, and I wasn't convinced that she knew all the rules. With that in mind, the likelihood of her losing was high.

"Wasn't Egon worried about leaving you exposed to Kepler?"

"That's why I have the gun, but Egon was convinced that Kepler would weaken fast, assuming he could even figure out who was responsible for the robbery."

I tapped the image of the rune.

"I think, Ms. Towle, that your brother may have been gravely mistaken."

———

ABOUT FIFTY MILES TO the east, Ambar Strange moved through the confines of her Westbrook cottage, a distracted specter haunting its spaces. Her car was parked in the driveway, mud on its body and wheels. It looked as though it had been driven hard. From a thicket of trees, Kepler followed her form, and wondered where she had been until now.

LVIII

Eleanor Towle walked me to the door and stayed on the porch as I headed to my car. Logically, Kepler should have approached her, just as he had given Raum Buker intimations of his presence in the hope of frightening him into returning what had been taken, but Kepler had not. There could only be one reason: He was aware that Eleanor didn't have the coin, and the only way he could have known this was because Egon Towle had told him so. But Egon's testimony must have been very convincing to ensure that Kepler didn't go after his sister, which meant that if Egon wasn't already dead, he almost certainly wished he was. This, though, I did not share with Eleanor. If she was as bright as she appeared, or half as bright as she thought, she might have suspected as much already.

"May I ask one last question?" I said.

"I'm surprised you have any left, but go ahead."

"How many of those stolen coins did your brother entrust to you?"

The hall light shone behind her, casting her into silhouette and hiding her face from view. I heard her laugh, and the wind caught the sound and carried it away to the north.

"You're very perceptive, Mr. Parker, but you do rush ahead of yourself. If you ever get lonely, feel free to visit again. I wouldn't wait too long, though. I might be gone."

She stepped back into the hallway and closed the door.

———

I SAW THAT I'D missed a call from Will Quinn, as well as a text message from Dave Evans at the Bear asking me to call him as soon as I got the chance. Since I was working for Will, I got back to him first as I drove east, and listened as he described what he'd found at Dolors Strange's home.

"Have you managed to reach her?"

"Just now, after eight attempts."

"Did she say where she was?"

"Only that she needed some space to think, and had headed out of town for a couple of nights."

I could hear the doubt in his voice. He was asking himself if Dolors had been alone, or if she might not have brought along Raum Buker for one last turn on the merry-go-round.

"What about Ambar?" I said.

"What about her?"

"Did she leave town as well?"

"I didn't ask."

"Do you think you could find out?"

"I'll try."

"Do that. How did Dolors react when you told her about the dead squirrel on her door?"

"She asked me to get rid of it. When I suggested talking to the police, she told me she'd never see me again if I got them involved. I mean, what the hell is going on here?"

I told him I had some answers, if not enough of them, and I'd drop by later that night to go over what I'd learned. I also recommended that Dolors and Ambar find somewhere else to stay for a while, and even take time off work, if possible. I recommended the Inn at St. John, because I'd used it in the past when clients needed somewhere safe to hole up for a night or two. If Will mentioned my name, the staff would do what was required. He said he'd try to convince Dolors, and she could then talk to her sister, but he hung up a disturbed man.

If the police were drawn into this, I'd have to tell them about Eleanor Towle and her brother, and for some reason I felt a perverse sense of obligation to the Towle woman. She had been using me, feeding me enough information to set me on Kepler's trail in the hope that I might become another means of keeping him at bay, but she hadn't tried very hard to hide it and I thought the world would be a more diverting place with her in it. As for Egon, if by some miracle he answered his sister's call, and could be made to see sense, it might yet be possible to resolve the issue. Admittedly Raum remained a problem, but I hoped he could be persuaded to hand over some, or all, of what had been taken from Kepler—to save his own hide as much as anyone else's. Yet the situation was escalating, as indicated by the mutilated squirrel: a man who will hurt an animal is just as capable of hurting a human being, or even burning one to death, because there remained the fate of the coin dealer, Reuben Hapgood.

I pulled over to fill up at a gas station, and used the opportunity to look into the Hapgood case. Arson had yet to be confirmed, but Eleanor Towle's information placed me in an awkward position, because theoretically I was now in possession of knowledge that might aid a police investigation, even if it was only a name—Kepler—and a story about a stolen coin. If I went to the police with what I knew, any number of people could conceivably be dragged down as a consequence. It might have been that Raum Buker and Egon Towle—even, at a stretch, Eleanor—deserved no better, but the Sisters Strange would also find themselves under scrutiny because of their relationship with Raum. I had no way of knowing what the police might discover once they began digging into the lives of Dolors and Ambar, but the chance existed that they knew more than they had shared with Will Quinn or me. Even if they did not, as soon as the police began pulling loose threads from the tapestry of a person's history, it was difficult as all hell to put it back together again. Ambar's job might be lost, Dolors's business could go under, and the resulting resentments would endure. Call me a sentimentalist, but I didn't want Will Quinn to have employed me to ruin his life.

It might have been the wrong thing to do in the eyes of the law—actually, strike "might have been"—but I decided to give it twenty-four hours before talking to the police. If Raum and Egon Towle could be induced to hand over the potin coin at least, it would act as an enticement for Kepler, like placing meat at the heart of a snare. I think I wanted to catch sight of him. Maybe, like others who were privy to the stories about him, I wished to confirm he existed, and that all I had seen and heard so far—runic symbols on glass, tales of coins and extended lives—was not part of some elaborate hoax cooked up by Raum Buker and the Towles to shroud a straightforward crime of theft. Once persuaded of the fact of his existence, I could determine how to deal with him. If I failed to trap him, I would have no qualms about sharing with the police a redacted version of what I knew, once I'd had time to decide what to leave out. It was an imperfect solution, which made it a perfect one for an imperfect world.

———

THE TRAFFIC WAS LIGHT all the way to the Maine border, and even sparser from there. Eleanor Towle contacted me as I passed Newfield.

"My brother isn't answering his phone," she said. "My calls go straight to voice mail, but that's not odd for Egon."

"How long does it usually take him to respond?"

"That depends on his mood, but he always checks his phone before he goes to bed, and again first thing in the morning. He doesn't leave it on overnight. Egon likes his beauty sleep."

"Let me know when you hear from him," I said.

"And if he doesn't get in touch?"

There was no point in dissimulation.

"Then he's dead," I said. "I think you need to get out of that house, Ms. Towle, and you need to do it right now."

She hung up without saying another word.

LIX

I f, as seemed increasingly likely, Kepler had already tracked down Egon Towle, then it was Towle who had directed him toward Raum Buker. But Kepler was also aware of Raum's involvement with the Sisters Strange, which was why he'd placed his mark on Ambar Strange's door. He wanted Raum to know that Ambar was in play, and if Raum wasn't prepared to hand back what he'd taken for his own sake, he should consider doing so for hers. I pictured again the extent of the damage to her door. It had struck me as excessive and pointless at the time, but no longer: Kepler might have been responsible for the initial destruction, but it was Raum who had vandalized it still further in an effort to hide the presence of the rune.

Yet if Kepler had indeed located Egon Towle, he appeared more reluctant to tackle Raum directly. This wasn't surprising. From what I knew of Towle, he sounded as though he would have presented an easy target. Raum, by contrast, was many things, but easy wasn't one of them, and prison had only made him harder. So far, Kepler was avoiding a face-to-face confrontation, but that couldn't be put off for much longer. It made me more concerned than ever for the safety of the Sisters Strange.

It was only as I saw the exit sign for the Maine Mall and its motels that I realized what had been nagging me about the peephole in the door of Raum's unit at the Braycott Arms. Although it was getting late, I continued into the center of Portland and parked on the curb outside the hotel. The inner lobby door was closed, but Bobby Wadlin was at his post, bathed by the light from the TV screen. If he was pleased to see me, it didn't show, but then pleasure was probably an alien concept to him, unless it involved someone being shot from a horse.

"Has Raum Buker been back?" I said.

"No," said Wadlin, "but I'm holding the room for him, despite the demand—although you're shit out of luck, in case you're considering asking. I'm particular about my tenants."

I contemplated how low in life I might have to sink before I was forced to go knocking on the door of the Braycott Arms. Not quite so low, perhaps, as I might have to sink in order to be turned away.

"I need to take another look at his room," I said.

"It's late."

"Indulge me, Bobby."

"I don't approve of indulgence. Anyway, we got rules."

He tapped the sign forbidding entry to nonresidents after 5:00 p.m. The spelling of "visiters" had been crudely altered with a crayon. The sign now read NO VISETERS AFTER 5PM.

"I'm not visiting," I said, "because there's no one for me to visit."

"Come back tomorrow. Even better, don't."

One of the tenants appeared at the inner door. As he came out, I stepped in. Bobby Wadlin shouted after me as the door closed.

"I'm not giving you the damn key!"

"I won't need it," I said.

———

MOMENTS LATER I STOOD outside Raum Buker's unit and removed a small flat-head screwdriver from my pocket. I inserted the edge behind the lens of the peephole in the door and pushed. The outer part of the viewer popped onto the floor while the inner part remained in place.

Through the hole I could see a length of black wire. I used the screw-driver to ease it forward and felt the wire catch. I explored deeper, and the head caught on an edge of adhesive tape, and a cylindrical shape that must have been the power supply. I knew now why Raum's view was obscured.

Someone had installed a camera in his door.

LX

Kepler checked out of the motel by the mall. He'd already remained there too long, but staying had been easier than moving, physically at least. By night, though, his spirit, or some poisoned surrogate, chose to wander, leaving him with the memory of dreams that were not his own. The entity inside him was growing restive after too many years of his company, and it felt the pull of the coin. He thought it would be glad to see him die.

The peephole camera he had installed in Buker's room at the Braycott Arms was no longer functioning. From the final images, it was obvious that someone had discovered and removed it. Kepler was eager to establish who might have been responsible, but the fool manager, Wadlin, wasn't answering his phone. It couldn't have been Buker himself because Wadlin had been paid well to let Kepler know when, or if, he returned. Kepler doubted that Wadlin was clever enough to have spotted the device, but if by some faint chance he had, he'd also have been sufficiently streetwise to connect its presence to Kepler and forget he ever saw it. That left the private investigator, Parker, who very much was clever enough to uncover a hidden camera, which was another reason Kepler had seen fit to change accommodations. He had also ditched his old SIM card and replaced it with another. If Parker had been the one to find the camera, his next step would be to ask some awkward questions of the manager. Wadlin had a line of communication to Kepler, which could be used to track him, and Kepler did not care to become easy pickings for Parker.

The new motel wasn't any more luxurious than the old, but the rooms were marginally bigger, and the location was farther from people and commerce. In the bathroom, Kepler stripped naked and bathed himself gently. The action of the cloth was like sandpaper against his skin, so exposed and sensitive had his depletion made the nerve endings, but he liked to stay clean. When he was done, he put on some scent. The bottle was almost empty, but applying the eau de cologne was more a question of habit than necessity. He had been using it for so long that the odor had infused him, and he exuded the smell of rosewater and civet from his very pores.

Finally, Kepler stood before the full-length mirror on the door, the runic tattoos on his body like the errors of a life made manifest. He could no longer deny the progress of his decay by refusing to look upon it. On the bedside table, the exposed workings of the ornate clock whirred and clicked, but much, much slower than before. When the clock stopped entirely, so also would Kepler's heart.

And as he watched, something like a worm crawled beneath his skin.

LXI

B obby Wadlin was staring at the mechanism.

"What the hell is that?" he asked.

"It's a camera. Someone installed it so that it faced into Raum Buker's unit."

"Well, it wasn't me," said Wadlin. "Wait, did you damage the door?"

His concern for his property, allied to the expression on his face, made me inclined to accept Wadlin's denial of responsibility, but I wasn't about to let him off so easily.

"Who else has been asking questions about Raum?" I said.

Wadlin began to open his mouth, but I raised a finger to stop him.

"Bobby, if you lie to me, I'll know, and I'll tear that desk apart to get to you."

I saw him weigh an immediate threat to his well-being against a more distant one, and come to the correct decision.

"There was someone," he said. "He wanted me to tell him if Buker met with anyone, and keep track of his messages and movements. It was nothing parole officers haven't asked me to do in the past, and they don't pay."

"Who is he?"

"He didn't give a name, just an email address."

"Did he search the room?"

"I don't know. He might have. I didn't ask."

"Describe him to me."

Wadlin did. If this was Kepler, and Wadlin's description was accurate, Eleanor Towle had been right to refer to him as a bogeyman. He sounded as though he was only one step from the grave.

"I'll take that email address," I said.

Bobby extracted a square of notepaper from a drawer, scribbled the address, and pushed it through the slot in the screen. I looked at it, folded it, put it in my pocket, and prepared to wipe the dust of the Braycott from my feet.

"What address did you use to send your messages?"

"I made up a new one on Gmail," said Wadlin.

"I want that as well, and the password."

"You can't mean it. That's private stuff."

"Do I look like someone who doesn't mean what he says?"

Wadlin concluded that I didn't, and gave me the address and password.

"Look," said Wadlin, "you won't tell this guy I rolled over, will you?"

For a moment I thought he couldn't be for real, until I realized that he was.

"Of course not," I replied. I let Wadlin's shoulders sag with relief before adding, "He'll be able to figure it out for himself."

————

THE EMAIL ADDRESS USED by Kepler—random numbers, symbols, and letters—was temporary and anonymous, and generated by Guerrilla Mail. I knew because I'd come across the sharklasers.com domain name before. It would be untraceable, and set up so that the recipient was alerted any time a message came through. It was a reasonably efficient way to operate, and obviated the necessity for a phone number, which could more easily be traced and located.

I opened up Gmail, entered the details given to me by Wadlin, and sent a simple three-word message to the Guerrilla Mail account: *Buker has returned*. Then I sat back to wait. I spent close to three hours outside the Braycott Arms, my car positioned facing the side of the building so I could see anyone entering or leaving through the front or back doors, but none of those who came or went matched the description offered by Wadlin, and all appeared to be residents. Kepler wasn't coming. He had not taken the bait. I thought I knew why, but I was tired, and payback could wait.

,

I t was long after midnight when I got to Will Quinn's home, but he had waited up for me. He hadn't wanted to speak on the phone because he was a man who preferred to conduct serious business face-to-face. I shared with him most of what I'd learned that day, holding back my suspicion that Eleanor Towle might have been entrusted with some of the coins from the cache, although not the one Kepler was seeking most keenly. She was too streetwise for that, and may have given its myth enough credence not to want to hold on to it. Neither did I mention to Will the demise of Reuben Hapgood, because Will was distracted enough as things stood. In turn, he told me that Dolors hadn't been in the mood to talk about very much upon her return to Portland, and had barely glanced at the pictures Will had taken of the dead squirrel nailed to her door, or the bloodied mark on the wood.

"It was like it was nothing she hadn't seen before," said Will. "The mark, I mean. Maybe the squirrel, too, because who knows? But I thought the mark at least might have drawn her interest."

Not if she was already aware of what it meant, I thought, but this, too, I kept to myself. Just how much of his predicament had Raum shared with the Sisters Strange?

Will had failed to persuade Dolors to relocate to the Inn at St. John, which meant that Ambar was still at her own place as well. It couldn't be helped for now, but I thought I might make a final effort to change their minds the following day. Dolors had assured Will that she would keep her door locked and her cell phone with her at all times, and had instructed Ambar to do the same, but it didn't exactly equate to pulling up the drawbridge and calling out the guard.

"Does either of them keep a gun in the house?" I asked.

"Ambar does," said Will. "Dolors doesn't like firearms. She has pepper spray somewhere, she told me."

It was better than nothing, I supposed, assuming she could find it, and it retained some potency.

"Did you find out if Ambar had also been away?"

"Dolors said she went along to keep her company," said Will.

"Where?"

"North, somewhere."

"There's a lot of north. She wasn't more specific?"

"She displayed an aversion to further questioning, shall we say."

"I'm sure the police will take her sensitivities into account."

"Dolors has made her position clear on the subject of police involvement."

"You saw what Kepler did to that squirrel. Soon there will come a point where Dolors's feelings won't matter a damn, unless Raum does the right thing."

"All this over a coin?"

"People get stabbed to death for small change. That coin is worth much more."

"I have to confess," said Will, "that the whole story sounds bizarre to me. I mean, I accept that Buker might have developed some funny ideas while he was locked up, otherwise he wouldn't have got himself that damned tattoo, but it doesn't mean the rest of us are obliged to accept them as true."

"I believe that Raum and his partner, Egon Towle, stole valuable items from Kepler," I said. "The rest is irrelevant. Kepler is trying to avoid a face-off, which is why he put that fancy little camera in the peephole, in case Raum had stashed some of the takings in his room or decided to use it as a showroom for prospective buyers. If I was pressed, I'd put money on a miniature microphone or voice transmitter being hidden somewhere in the unit, because it's what I'd have done. That way Kepler would be able to listen in on at least one side of any conversation using his cell phone."

"But how did he gain access to the Braycott?" said Will.

"The surveillance camera on the back door is broken, so he could have bribed a tenant to admit him, but I suspect he just paid Bobby Wadlin to turn a blind eye. Wadlin denies that he let Kepler up there, but he'd deny his own name if there was a dollar in it. He's stubborn and ornery. I think it's all those westerns he watches."

"So what next?"

"I smoke out Raum, and try to persuade him to hand back what he took."

Will considered this.

"I hope you have a plan B," he said.

"That would be to trace Kepler, and convince him to keep his distance from Dolors and Ambar while I work on the Raum problem. The final and most sensible measure would be to go to the police right now, tell them everything I know, and let them figure the whole mess out, but Dolors will blame you for it. Also, if we go to the police, it's likely that Dolors and Ambar will get dragged through legal thorns, and they won't emerge unscathed, because no one ever does."

Will squinted at me. He might have been relatively inexperienced in matters of the heart, but that was about the limit of his ingenuousness.

"You think Dolors and Ambar know about the coins," he said.

"That's what the police will assume," I said, "because of their prior intimacy with Raum."

"And what do you assume?"

"That the police would be right."

Will rested his face in his hands. Not approaching the police went against every instinct he possessed. He was a good man, with faith in the institutions of law and justice, but he also had faith in me. I didn't want to tell him it might be misplaced, because honesty can be bad for business, so I sat back to see which way he might tilt.

"So where's this Kepler?" he said, finally.

In your face, due process.

"He must have a temporary base near here," I said, "even if it's only a motel room or an Airbnb. I'll start following up that angle in the morning—and I'll also be calling on Dolors again, so you can tell her to expect me. Feel free to divulge to her what I've told you. It might help focus her attention, and convince her to arrange a sit-down with Raum. Whatever she may say to the contrary, she has an idea of where he is, if only through Ambar."

"What about Egon Towle?" said Will. "Isn't he involved, too?"

"He was," I said, as I stood to leave. "Whether he remains so is open to question."

———

I WAS ALREADY HOME and half-undressed when I realized I had forgotten to get back to Dave Evans. I decided it could wait until morning, because Dave wouldn't thank me for calling him at such a late hour. Despite my tiredness I took a while to get to sleep. I knew I was handling this case improperly, and even the twenty-four hours I had permitted myself before involving the police constituted at least twenty-three too many. I could justify it on the grounds that the intelligence I had obtained was sketchy at best, and were I to run to the law with every tidbit I picked up, I'd become as much a fixture in station houses as the bars on the holding cells, not to mention a laughingstock. I hadn't even seen a picture of the rare coin mentioned by Eleanor Towle, and I was hesitant to believe the lore being peddled about

Kepler. I could accept that Raum Buker and Egon Towle might be coin thieves, and Kepler their victim, but that was the limit of my credulity.

More to the point, if I were to approach the police each time I entered a legal gray area, my career as a private investigator would come to a rapid close, clients expecting some degree of discretion in my dealings with them, if not absolute confidentiality. But the truth was that my curiosity had been piqued, and curiosity, as with cats, was the curse of my breed. So far, it hadn't killed me. Admittedly, it had come close on occasion, but close doesn't get you a cigar.

I stretched, and felt old pains sing out.

Wounds, maybe, but no cigar.

LXIII

Lucas Tyler was playing hooky. He didn't do this very often, only once every month or two, when the mood hit. His mother always covered for him because Lucas was bright: too bright for his class, too bright for his school, too bright for his town. He aced every test at Kingswood Regional, New Hampshire, and had his mind set on a degree in computer science and molecular biology at MIT. He planned to take the SAT in October, using the summer break to study, and was confident of nudging a score of 1600. It was a confidence shared by his teachers without reservation, because in addition to being bright, Lucas was a decent kid. His family income, which came from his mother, his dad being long dead, was well below the $90,000 cut-off point for the MIT scholarship. If he was accepted—and there seemed no reason he should not be—he would attend tuition-free.

Lucas drove a 1990 VW Golf he'd bought with savings from his weekend job at a home improvement store. He loved the car. Minor defects he could repair himself, and those beyond him were easily tackled by any moderately accomplished mechanic. It also had enough room to entertain his girlfriend, Annabeth, in relative comfort, neither she nor Lucas being above five seven in their stocking feet, and access to private space being an important detail to consider when you shared a house with your mom—especially a mom who volunteered at First

Congregational and still hankered for the days when married sitcom couples slept in separate beds.

The Golf was currently parked at the southern edge of the Heath Pond Bog Natural Area, concealed in a glade to shield it from the eyes of any passing cops who might be curious to check up on it, and then inquire as to why its owner wasn't furthering his formal education. Lucas liked walking in Heath Pond Bog because it was easy to avoid other people there. He had a favorite spot by the creek, where the branches of an old tree acted like the frame of a chair. He'd bring along some cushions, a flask of coffee, his satchel, and a sack lunch, and there he would read, listen to music, or watch the water flow by. It was good for the soul.

Lucas hadn't visited the creek for a couple of weeks. The weather had been lousy and cold, and anyway, he hadn't felt the urge. But a couple of boring days in class, followed by an argument with Annabeth that had resulted in what he hoped was only a temporary estrangement, had changed his mind. Now Heath Pond Bog was calling to him.

Lucas Tyler went to the bog for the last time that morning. He parked his Golf for the last time in the glade; removed, for the last time, his cushions and satchel from the trunk; and walked, for the last time, to his favorite tree. He caught the stench as he came within sight of the creek. Lucas had never smelled a dead body before, but some atavistic memory was triggered by the odor, and he knew, even before he found the remains, that this was no skunk or deer.

The man was naked, his hands cuffed over a low branch of Lucas's tree, and his legs tied together with wire that had cut deep into his ankles. The winter foliage hid him from anyone passing on the main trails, and the stink might have been missed if the wind was blowing in the right direction. He was small: although the branch was low, his bare toes still only scraped the ground. A bloodied gag drooped around his neck, leaving his mouth hanging open. After all, Lucas thought, even as his gorge rose, how can someone tell you what you want to know with their mouth all stopped up? On the other hand, you might have to muffle them while you convinced them to talk, just in case the screams attracted attention. Lucas didn't know how much convincing this man had required, but it had been enough to necessitate the removal of long strips of skin from his arms, his legs, his belly, and his chest. Lucas could see that, even with the bloating.

When he'd finished emptying his stomach into the creek, Lucas used his cell phone to dial 911. He knew he'd get into hot water with the school, even the police, but he couldn't walk away from this. When he had finished speaking to the dispatcher, he called his mom. Then he sat on a rock before the dead man and cried.

CHAPTER

LXIV

Will Quinn had provided me with Raum's latest number, via a reluctant Dolors, who had consented to disclose it only when he advised her that sharing it with the police would represent a worse outcome. But Raum wasn't taking calls, and the phone went to voice mail after four rings. I left a message asking him to get in touch, but more in hope than expectation. I then spent ten minutes chatting with my daughter on FaceTime over breakfast before managing to catch Dave Evans on his way to the Bear.

"A freak was in here yesterday asking after you and Raum Buker," said Dave. "Said he might be in touch again."

"Did he leave a name?"

"Kepler. If it's any use to you, we should have him on the security footage."

I told Dave I'd be right over. Before I could leave the house, a Google Alert informed me that the fire at Hapgood Coins & Collectibles was officially being treated as arson, and the death of its proprietor as murder. Witnesses were being sought, but so far none had come forward. Of course, it was possible that the killing of a coin dealer in New Hampshire had nothing to do with the recent theft of a valuable collection in Ontario, or the presence in Maine of both Raum Buker and the man named Kepler, but then it was also possible that the odds didn't favor the house, and the check really was in the mail.

I called Raum's number again from the car, and left a second message. I phrased it as delicately as I could, voice recordings being admissible as evidence in any legal proceedings, but I made it clear to him that I knew what he'd done; that the confirmation of the arson attack in Whitefield had altered the landscape, both literally and figuratively; and it was now about limiting the damage, because the time for an accommodation had passed. Kepler was very likely a killer, and if Raum came forward and shared what he knew about him with the police, Moxie Castin would do his best to ensure that any assistance offered would be taken into account when it came to sentencing. There was no way he was going to avoid jail time, although Moxie would negotiate for a minimum sentence, but if Raum cooperated, he might save the Sisters Strange from threat, because their involvement with him had put them in Kepler's sights. Finally, I made it plain that if he didn't contact me before close of business, I'd be obliged to go to the police and feed him to them, so it would be wise to speak to me first. In the meantime, I would continue to search for him, but not before visiting the Bear to take a look at the bogeyman Kepler.

CHAPTER

LXV

Vehicles from the Ossipee Police Department, the Carroll County Sheriff's Office, and the New Hampshire State Police surrounded Lucas Tyler's VW Golf, just as representatives from each of those agencies surrounded Lucas himself. The first words Lucas had said to them were "I didn't do it," because a person couldn't be too careful, not when it came to murder, but he hoped no one really suspected that he *had* done it. In the event that he required an alibi, Lucas was trying to remember everywhere he'd been for the last week, which turned out to be harder than anticipated. Nearby, two state police detectives were speaking to his mother, who'd left work to be with him. She knew that he sometimes played hooky, and was content to cover for him so long as he didn't do it too often—and more to the point, so long as he didn't get caught. Staring at the crests of three different law enforcement agencies, Lucas reflected that, short of the FBI and the NSA also becoming involved, he couldn't have been any more caught if he'd tried.

Lucas really wished he hadn't found the dead man. He was starting to worry about how it might affect his prospects for MIT should his name become linked to a murder investigation. But the police seemed interested only in whether he'd touched the body, and whether he'd noticed anyone behaving strangely in the area on his previous visits to Heath Pond Bog.

It struck Lucas that he still didn't know how the man had died. Having strips of skin excised from his body would have hurt—it would have hurt a whole hell of a lot—but it wouldn't have been enough to kill him, not unless he had a bad heart and the stress had pushed him over the edge.

As it happened, the cause of death—choking due to obstruction of the respiratory passage by a foreign body—would not be established conclusively until the autopsy, when the object lodged in the larynx was removed by the medical examiner. It was made from lengths of aluminum craft wire, tightly bound, and was shaped roughly like a stick figure of a man. Inserted into the hollow of the figure's head was an old bone die.

Kepler, signing his handiwork.

CHAPTER

LXVI

I sat with Dave Evans in his office at the Great Lost Bear, moving back and forth through the security footage from the night before. In none of the images could I get a clear impression of Kepler. It was as though he had been aware throughout of the location of the cameras, and had positioned himself to avoid their gaze as best he could. Nevertheless, I saw enough to be convinced of the singularity of his aspect, even without Dave's corroborating testimony.

"What about the medication you took from the table?" I said.

"I asked my physician about it," said Dave. "It's used to treat liver conditions. It makes sense, because he looked unwell, and I mean terminally unwell."

"And you say he wanted you to play dice with him?"

"Yeah, they were made from ivory, or bone," said Dave. "I thought I'd seen it all in this place, but obviously I was wrong. Do you know why he wanted to speak with you and Buker?"

"Raum stole a coin collection from him. Kepler wants it returned."

"Then Buker ought to hand it over, because this is not someone he wants to have taking an interest in him. How involved are you?"

"More than I'd prefer. You know Will Quinn, the lumber guy? He hired me to find out why Raum was back in town and hanging around the Sisters Strange, Dolors in particular. Will has feelings for her."

"He couldn't find an iceberg to latch on to instead?"

"The heart wants what it wants, but I'm beginning to wonder if the question should equally be why the Stranges have kept company with Raum. Either way, the answer is becoming clearer. It's love, money, or both."

"Damn," said Dave, "I'm not a detective and I could have told you that. What about the police?"

"Until recently, nobody had been hurt," I said, "except a squirrel, and that might already have been dead. I hoped I might be able to settle this without involving the authorities, but now I think Kepler may have killed a coin dealer in New Hampshire, and he could just be getting started. If I can't convince Raum to come in of his own volition, I'll have to talk to the cops today and let them decide the next move. In the meantime, you'd better hold on to that video footage. It could prove useful."

I left Dave and returned to my car, still without any sign of contact from Raum. I had believed that he cared to some degree for the Sisters Strange. I might have been foolish to do so, but a man gets tired of assuming the worst of people, no matter how intent they may be on proving him right. So either Raum didn't care, and never really had, or he was past caring, because there was a difference between not wanting to communicate and not being able to communicate. If Kepler had already found Raum, no one was going to be hearing from either man again. But until I was sure, I'd keep hunting for both.

———

I SPENT THE NEXT few hours making phone calls to Raum's former associates, including the two boneheads who had taken a swim in the Fore at the Fulcis' insistence all those years ago, and knocking on the doors of the ones who struck me as most likely to have remained in contact with him. Apart from pointing me in the direction of the Braycott Arms, none of them could tell me where Raum might be, and I didn't suspect them of lying. Again and again I was informed that Raum was an altered beast since his release from prison. It was in his eyes, his voice, his carriage. Whatever residual appeal his company might have possessed, even for the incurably felonious, was entirely gone. Raum's old acquaintances were minor grifters and thugs, just as he used to be. They might have been wary of him, but they had not feared him. Now, I learned, they did.

The most curious testimony came from a man named Tessell Forde, who was the kind of criminal more familiar with county jails than state prisons, and never felt comfortable behind a wheel until he'd first had a couple of drinks to steady his hands. Tessell lived in a crappy single room on Mellen Street in Parkside, an area of Portland that locals regarded as rough, but only because most everywhere else in the city wasn't. He'd run with Raum back in the day, but now he didn't run with anyone at all, and could walk only with the aid of a stick. Tessell might have passed for seventy, was understood to be sixty, but was, in fact, barely fifty. He subsisted on welfare and the proceeds of petty delinquency, and had never known even modest prosperity. Still, Tessell retained a curious sense of optimism despite the fact that life woke up every morning, yawned widely, and gave him a good kick in the ass before getting on with its day.

"Raum's sick," said Tessell, as he rolled a cigarette. An oxygen tank stood nearby, the connected mask dangling over the end of a bedpost. I didn't hear the hiss of gas, which was some small relief.

"What kind of sick?"

"He got him a defilement down in Jersey, body and mind both."

Tessell licked the paper and stuck one end of the roll-up in his mouth. It looked even slimmer than the match he used to light it, his pack of rolling tobacco containing little more than dust and memories.

"When did you last see him?" I said.

"Three or four days ago, first time over by the Braycott. I called to him, but he didn't recognize me." His hurt was obvious. "Me and Raum, we've known each other for many years, but he stared at me like I was a stranger. His eyes were all feverish, and even his voice weren't his own. If I didn't know better, I'd have said he was another man, and I'd been mistaken in my initial cognizance of him."

Tessell's father was a defrocked Catholic priest from somewhere up in Piscataquis County, and a quantity of the old man's loquacity and love of oratory had rubbed off on his son. A crucifix hung on the wall above Tessell's bed, the paint on Christ's feet rubbed away by the actions of beseeching fingers. I speculated on what Tessell might have been praying for. Whatever it was, it hadn't arrived, unless he had been petitioning solely for bad luck.

"But then he came knocking on my door that same night," Tessell continued, "and he was the old Raum again, or near as made no difference. He told me he was sorry about earlier, and gave me a pouch of tobacco and a bottle of Hobble Creek."

Hobble Creek tasted like grape soda that had been stored in a whiskey bottle. It was an indication of how tough times were for Tessell Forde that he sounded grateful for the gift, but conceivably it was the thought that counted.

"Raum told me he was going to be leaving town soon," said Tessell. "He had a mind to go west, he said, to take the Pacific air." Tessell frowned. "Then he asked me to examine his right eye."

"Why?" I said.

"He wanted to know if I could see anything wrong with it, said it was troubling him. Well, my own eyes aren't too good, so I had to get my magnifier, the one I use for reading. I put it real close, and peered at his workings." He took a deep drag on the roll-up, which shrank alarmingly in his fingers. "He had a worm in his eye, dug right in there."

Tessell spoke nonchalantly, as though it were a matter of course to him to discover organisms burrowed into the eyes of associates.

"A worm?"

"A little black worm, like a parasite, right in the corner. A tiny thing, couldn't have been more than the width of a thread and the length of the nail on my little finger. I told him what I was seeing, and he started to panic. I made him calm down while I found a pair of tweezers. I judged that I could get at it and remove it, because by then I'd already had a couple of shots of Hobble Creek. I got a hold on it, sure enough, but as soon as I pulled, Raum started to scream and near knocked me through the wall."

Tessell rubbed his chest, as though the impact still lingered.

"Naturally, I put away my implements at that point and advised him to consult a medical specialist."

The roll-up was now reduced to a fragment of paper. Tessell stared at it regretfully before stamping out the ember on the floor, adding another scorch mark to the collection. I didn't speak for a while, so absorbed was I by the image of an inebriated Tessell Forde attempting surgery on another man's eye. I tried to take consolation from the fact that whatever caught Tessell's attention might not have been real. Drink enough Hobble Creek and there was no knowing what one might hallucinate.

"Did Raum mention anything about coins while he was with you?" I asked once I'd recovered.

"Coins? No. He did gift me one more thing, though."

He reached beneath his shirt to reveal a gold cross on a chain, inset with five concentric circles.

"They represent the wounds of Christ," said Tessell. "I remember that from my father's sermons. Raum said the cross was ancient, and I'd take that for true. I never owned anything so primitive yet so pretty before."

He restored the cross to its place at his breast.

"I figure Raum came by it dishonestly," he said, although he remained remarkably sanguine about this. "No other way he could have acquired it, but it was nice of him to commit it to my care, even if it's unavoidable that I'll have to sell it. I already got enough crosses to rival Golgotha."

I found a twenty in my wallet and laid it on the table by the door.

"If I were you," I said, "I wouldn't tell anyone else about that cross, and I'd wait a while before I sold it."

"He didn't steal it from a Christian man, did he?" asked Tessell. "Because that would be wrong."

"No," I said. "Quite the opposite."

LXVII

D olors Strange was back at her coffee shop. This time, as promised, she didn't give me the bum's rush, and even offered me a cup on the house. We sat under a new painting of a naked woman playing chess with a wizard during a thunderstorm. Dolors caught me looking at it, or trying not to.

"Erin over there is the artist," she said, pointing at the girl behind the counter, the metal detectorist's dream. "All these pieces are her work."

"She has a very distinctive artistic vision."

"I didn't know you could be so diplomatic, Mr. Parker."

"Well," I said, "I want to get on in life."

I tried the coffee. It tasted just as flowery as last time. If I drank too much of it, I'd have to take an antihistamine.

"I presume Will has spoken to you about what Raum and his buddy Egon Towle may have stolen," I said.

"The coins? Yes, Will told me."

"Did you know about what they'd done before Will brought up the subject?"

Dolors shifted in her chair.

"Not until very recently," she said. "Raum said only that he would have money before too long, and he'd be able to pay back what he owed Ambar and me. But a few nights ago he checked out of the Braycott, came by the house, and said he'd have the cash soon. I'd heard that tune from him so often I could whistle it, and told him so, which was when he produced a gold twenty-dollar double eagle, dated 1905. He said it was worth five thousand dollars, and proved it by using his phone to show me a similar one for sale. After that, I believed him."

"And you hadn't asked him the source of these imminent funds before then?"

"I knew better than that. I'm not stupid enough to go inquiring of Raum about his activities, although I can't speak for Ambar."

The aside about her sister emerged with real bite. Relations between them were obviously deteriorating again.

"Did he tell you where he got the coin?"

"He told me it had originally been stolen, and he and Egon Towle had taken it from the thief along with a bunch of others. He said it was nothing more than justice being done, stealing from a crook. I can't say I agreed with him, but then Raum's appeal was never exactly based on his moral fiber."

"Did he mention this thief's name?"

"Raum said he went by lots of names."

"Try one."

"Kepler." But she said it reluctantly, and in a low voice, like one pressed into an unwanted invocation.

"And did Raum appear worried when last you saw him?" I said.

"His mood kept changing, like he was high on something. At times he'd come across as paranoid, then a minute later he'd be entirely calm—frighteningly so. The first Raum I recognized, but the other I didn't. He didn't even sound like himself. Were you aware that he hurt my sister?"

"Will told me about it. He suggested that it might have been unintentional."

"Unintentional or not, the old Raum would never have done that. He'd never even have put himself in a position where a woman might have gotten hurt."

I didn't offer the opinion that, had he shown the same restraint toward men, he would have avoided a lot of problems in life, including prison time.

"When you say he was anxious—"

"I assumed at first it was about the police. This is Raum we're talking about. If he wasn't dishonest, he'd be nothing at all. The police are a permanent hazard for someone of his vocation."

But she said it with a smile. Whatever Raum had, it should have been bottled and sold as scent to ill-starred men.

"Which is why you asked Will Quinn not to involve them."

"Yes."

"Do you still have feelings for Raum?"

"I have memories, a few of them good. For their sake, I won't see him thrown to the lions."

"And your sister?"

"Whatever happened between them, she feels the same way about keeping him out of the hands of the law. She did take him back to her bed, though, however briefly."

"You disapproved of her resuming their relationship?"

"I just didn't think he was good for either of us, and I didn't want him to come between us again."

"And has he?"

"Briefly, but we'll get over it. The money will help."

"You'll still accept funds from Raum, even knowing how he came by them?"

"I can't afford not to. I'm about to lose my business, and if I lose that I'll lose my home along with it. Ambar is also in debt, and can barely make her monthly payments. If a thief has to suffer so we can survive, I'll take that deal."

"That's very pragmatic of you."

"I'm a very pragmatic person."

I didn't doubt it.

"Where is Raum now?"

"He left town."

"Can you be more specific?"

"He's gone up to the County. He said he'd be safer there until all this had blown over, which was when I started to understand that it wasn't the police he was trying to avoid, because he assured me the theft hadn't been reported to them, and never would be. So I asked him straight: Who knew that he and Egon were responsible for the robbery? He assured me that no one did, not even Kepler."

"Raum was mistaken, because Kepler is here."

Dolors Strange briefly turned away from me so that her hair hid her face.

"Raum was mistaken about a lot of things," she said.

"Would you like to elaborate?"

"I'm sleeping with Will Quinn, not Raum. Is that clear enough for you?"

Go Will, I thought. *You're a braver man than I.* But I noticed that Dolors hadn't reacted with any great shock to the revelation of Kepler's presence in Maine.

"You knew Kepler had tracked Raum to Portland, didn't you?" I said. "Even before he nailed a dead squirrel to your door."

"I feared he might come, whatever Raum might have claimed to the contrary. Nobody gets away with a robbery like that, certainly not men like him."

"You do realize that Raum has put you and your sister in danger."

"But we don't have what Kepler wants."

"You should consider writing him a note to that effect. I'm sure he'll take your word for it."

"There's no need to be snide."

"Equally I might argue that there's no need to be naive. We're talking about a dangerous individual who may already have burned one man alive, and I'd speculate that hopes are also fading for Egon Towle."

"But Raum said that Kepler was dying," said Dolors.

"Everybody's dying, but like scripture says, without knowing the day or the hour. Those with a grudge can be surprisingly resilient. I wouldn't be relying on the prospect of Kepler's mortality as a guarantee of my safety, or anyone else's."

This gave her pause, and I was suddenly back in Eleanor Towle's kitchen, watching a sharp woman calculating odds.

"Have you a means of contacting Raum?" I asked.

"I gave Will his cell phone number. He was supposed to pass it on to you."

"He did, but Raum isn't picking up."

"He'll surface again once Kepler is dead."

Her certainty was striking, and I thought I understood why.

"Raum didn't just tell you Kepler was dying," I said. "He informed you of the existence of the coin, the one made from potin. You know why Kepler wants it back."

"What if Raum is right?" she said, and her eyes were bright. "What if that coin *is* special?"

I felt as though I'd wandered into the canteen of an asylum.

"Have you seen it?"

"Raum showed it to me. I held it."

"And?"

She splayed the fingers of her right hand before me, and I saw again a spread of white blisters.

"There's something to the story," she said. "I have faith in it now."

She spoke with the zeal of a new convert, the gold flecks in her irises shining like the flares of a black sun.

"What you may or may not have faith in is irrelevant to Kepler," I said. "I doubt he'll balk at hurting a woman to gain leverage. Raum needs to come back down here and return what he stole, or else it could go badly for everyone."

"That's Raum's decision, and he's already made his choice."

"You don't apprehend the seriousness of this. Raum is relying on a myth for protection, but that's all it is: a myth. Kepler may outlive us all, in which case he won't give up, and if he can't lay hands on Raum, you and your sister will be high on the list of alternates."

"I trust Raum to do what's right," said Dolors, with the faintest of shrugs, and I knew I was wasting my time.

"Did you and Ambar help him leave Portland?" I said.

She didn't bother with dissimulation.

"That was why he came to me," she said. "Ambar and I followed him as far as Houlton, and said goodbye to him at Monument Park. Ambar dumped his car at a mall in Lincoln, and I drove us both back to the city afterward."

Lincoln was in Penobscot County, south of Aroostook.

"Why did he want you to get rid of his car?"

"It was too conspicuous. He'll find another. Are we done, Mr. Parker? I have a business to save."

"I'd still advise Ambar and you to move out of your homes until I can find a way to bring this to a conclusion."

Dolors Strange reached out her right hand and placed it on mine. I moved it away, and not only because of those blisters. She didn't take offense. She was long past such sensitivities.

"But Mr. Parker," she said, "don't you see? None of this may be real. Egon Towle's sister told you a story and you believed it. A collection is supposed to be missing, but I've seen only two coins, one of which was gold—valuable, but not uncommon—while the other gave me a rash. The only coins that matter to me are in my register, and there aren't enough of them for my liking."

"Are you rehearsing a narrative for the police, Ms. Strange?" I asked, because this represented a change of tune from the new believer she had earlier professed to be.

"Let them come. I have nothing to hide."

"And Kepler?"

"Let him come, too."

There it was again: that certainty.

"What did Raum do with that double eagle he showed you?" I asked.

"Why, he took it with him, of course."

Her eyes challenged me to call her a liar.

"You and Egon Towle's sister may have something in common, Ms. Strange."

"Really?" she said. "What would that be?"

"You're both gambling on a game, the rules of which you don't understand."

"And do you understand them, Mr. Parker?"

I stood, and she stood with me.

"No," I said, "but then, I don't have anything at stake."

LXVIII

I f Raum Buker had gone to ground in Aroostook, finding him wouldn't be easy, which was undoubtedly the point. Even Mainers struggled to negotiate the County, and for Downeasters—those of us who lived along the coast—it resembled alien territory, a remote and socially conservative region set apart from the rest of the state. Huge tracts remained uninhabited, and in the St. John Valley it wasn't uncommon to hear French dialects spoken, given the area's cultural, historical, and geographical ties to Canada and the Acadian people.

If it would be hard for me to locate Raum, then Kepler, who was an outsider to both Aroostook and Maine, would have no hope at all. That was good news for Raum but bad news, I feared, for the Sisters Strange. I was now convinced that Kepler was quite capable of progressing beyond runes and disemboweled squirrels to more direct action, although it still wasn't clear to me why he might have killed the dealer Hapgood. The only reasons I could offer were vengeance—punishment for Hapgood's involvement in the theft and attempted sale of Kepler's stolen collection; caution—whatever Hapgood knew about Kepler, it was enough to justify silencing him; or the acquisition of information—in this case, the names of the thieves.

But Raum's pentacle tattoo symbolized that this wasn't only about money for him, but also reflected a deeper interest in the esoteric.

Eleanor Towle had indicated that Raum and Egon were proselytes, Raum more than Egon. There was, in addition, the testimony of Tessell Forde to consider. His story might have sounded peculiar in isolation, but I could view it through the prism of my own experiences with Raum, including our encounter outside the Braycott Arms. This was not the Raum Buker of old with whom we were dealing, but a transformed man: "sick" was the word Tessell had used to describe him, and I wasn't about to disagree. As for the parasite Tessell claimed to have glimpsed in Raum's eye, who could say?

While I wasn't yet prepared to accept Eleanor's tale of the coin as anything more than a legend, Raum Buker, Egon Towle, and possibly the enigmatic Kepler all believed it might be true. Of these, two were currently unreachable, but the third, Kepler, wasn't afraid to make himself visible, as evinced by his appearance at the Great Lost Bear. But if he'd shown himself, and asked after me, why had he not yet tried to make contact?

I called Moxie Castin and asked if his secretary could begin phoning hotels and lodgings in Portland and South Portland to see if they had any guests matching Kepler's name or description. I advised beginning with the chains and progressing to more upscale accommodations, because it was easier to be anonymous at conglomerate lodgings. Some might decline to provide such information, but it was worth a shot.

"I hope you're going to reimburse me for her time," said Moxie.

"You're such a kidder," I said, and hung up before he could ask for my credit card details.

In case Moxie's secretary didn't have any luck, I returned to the Braycott Arms. Bobby Wadlin was watching an episode of *The Life and Legend of Wyatt Earp*, which didn't look or sound as though it had improved with age.

"You owe me for what you did to that peephole," said Wadlin.

"You can add it to the rest of the damage," I said.

Wadlin tore his eyes from the screen.

"What damage?" he said, just as I kicked in his office door.

———

A LITTLE LATER, I sat in my car while Tony Motti glared at me from the entrance to the Braycott Arms. Wadlin had called him while I was still working on demolishing his door, but Tony was only good for ejecting drunks and collecting debts from people too frightened or ignorant to know their rights. Unless he could also do carpentry, he wouldn't be much use.

It had been stupid of me to take Wadlin's word on email as the sole means of contact with Kepler, and he might yet live to regret what he'd done if the police became interested. It turned out that Wadlin, perhaps wisely, was more scared of Kepler than he was of me. He had possessed a cell phone number for Kepler all along. The cell phone was the primary means of contact, Wadlin admitted, but only by text message, because the number was never answered. After I'd left the Braycott the night before, Wadlin had messaged Kepler to admit disclosing the email address to me. Now attempts to send text messages to Kepler's number were proving unsucccessful, and I got no result from feeding the number into a locator app, meaning the SIM had already been removed or destroyed so the user couldn't be traced.

I hadn't laid a finger on Bobby Wadlin, but only because it would have landed me in a cell, and he would likely have sued me into the bargain. But I knew what he'd done, and I planned to hold it over him, even if the law never got to hear about it. A pressure point might prove useful in the future, because I had no doubt that I hadn't seen the last of the Braycott Arms.

I was driving off when Moxie Castin's secretary got in touch to say that a guest named Kepler had been staying at one of the chain motels by the Maine Mall, but had checked out the day before. I asked her to keep looking, but I didn't hold out much hope. I had a feeling that when Kepler surfaced again, it would be for the last time.

I watched the sun mark the decline of the day. Within hours I would have to share with the police what little I had learned. It would represent an admission of failure on my part: failure to help Will Quinn, failure to protect the Sisters Strange, failure to save Raum Buker from himself, and failure to locate a man who couldn't have been more distinctive if he'd arrived in town with a brass band in tow. Some cases you chalk up to experience, but they take their toll.

In the aftermath, I would speculate on how long Kepler had been following me, but I thought it might have been since the night before. While I sat outside the Braycott Arms, Kepler had been nearby, my car in sight, the faintest outline of my form visible behind the windshield. By then he must have been in so much pain that sleep was beyond him, so he had distracted himself from his own extinction by observing a man who had mistaken himself for a hunter.

When he made himself known to me at last, it was almost a relief.

LXIX

I parked at my home and stood in the driveway as the winter sun was setting on the marshes. I had spoken with Will Quinn to advise him that, having achieved so little, I would no longer be charging him, and whatever else I might manage to do for him would be on my own time and at my own expense. I also told him I'd be speaking to the police before the night was out, and the Sisters Strange would be advised to have their stories straight by then, although it would be better if they came forward of their own volition. Eleanor Towle would just have to take her chances.

Will didn't make a final effort to talk me out of it. He thought, mistakenly or otherwise, that Dolors and Ambar would be fine, because he wanted to believe that they had done nothing wrong. I chose not to comment.

"I'll ask them both to meet me at Ambar's house," said Will. "I'm about to make a late delivery to Westbrook, so I'll be in the vicinity. If I can't talk them around, I'll go to the police with you. I'd go alone, but I get nervous around the law."

"That's because you're honest," I said. "I bet you also worry about being convicted of a crime you haven't committed."

"Don't even joke about it," said Will. "You know, I really wish Raum Buker had never been born."

"You're not the first," I said, "but the way things are going, you may be the last."

———

I HUNG UP AND checked my watch. Angel and Louis were probably already back in Portland by now. I felt the need of their company. Maybe the police could wait until morning, which would give Raum Buker and the Sisters Strange a final opportunity to see reason. I could even make the first approach to the Portland PD through Sharon Macy. We'd begun seeing each other again, if tentatively, so much so that both of us were reluctant even to acknowledge that we might be laying the foundations for something longer term. She'd been in Quantico, Virginia, for ten weeks, participating in an extended development course for law enforcement liaisons run by the FBI's National Academy, and had followed it with some downtime in Florida, but she was now back in town. I was careful about maintaining a professional distance between us to avoid complications for her, but in the matter of the Sisters Strange I'd done nothing wrong. I simply had information that might prove useful in the course of an investigation, one that involved police in another jurisdiction, and Macy was the primary point of contact between the Portland PD and outside agencies.

My phone beeped with an incoming text message. It came from a number I did not recognize, and contained only one word: *Kepler*. I called the number. Seconds later, a phone rang behind me.

I turned, and he was there.

LXX

K epler was dressed as in the video from the Great Lost Bear, all tans, creams, and browns, but his clothing hung more loosely than before, cut for a man with more meat on his bones. His cheeks were marred with lesions that did not bleed, and the skin around his eyes sagged as though his face was coming away from his skull. His eyes were so white that the world must have been little more than mist and shadows to him. But the gun in his right hand did not waver, and when he spoke, his voice was firm.

He killed the call and let the phone fall to the ground. I held mine in my hand, and kept my arms away from my body.

"Do you have a gun?" he said.

"Left side."

"Left thumb and forefinger only."

Awkwardly I removed the gun from its holster.

"Toss it into the bushes, and you can send your phone along after it."

I did as I was told.

"Now sit, legs folded beneath you."

I eased myself down, all under the watchful eye of his pistol. It was a Colt Single Action Army revolver, the gun that helped to tame the

West. Colt still made a modern version. This one looked old and worn, but well maintained.

"I've been reading about you," said Kepler. "You're a cursed man."

"If the rumors are true, so are you."

"You have been busy. Who's been telling you stories?"

He sounded genuinely curious, which was all the more reason not to answer.

"No one you've met," I said. "What do you want from me?"

"I want what's mine. I want what was taken."

"I don't have it."

"But you know who does."

"Raum Buker? You've sent him running, and I don't hold out much hope for your finding him. You should have gone to the police and told them what was done to you, instead of leaving your mark on doors and mirrors."

"I don't enjoy the attention of the law."

"Skeletons in your closet, or do you hide the bones elsewhere?"

"Sometimes," said Kepler, "I don't hide the bones at all. I leave them to burn, as you may be aware. Are you goading me, Mr. Parker? Because I wouldn't, if I were you. I am not a patient man."

"No, you're a dying one."

"But not dead, not yet. I have questions for you. Where is Buker?"

"I don't know."

On the road behind us, a truck roared by. Kepler used the noise to smother the sound of the gunshot, but it was still ferociously loud. The impact of the bullet blew grit into my eyes from two feet away. He had barely been required to move the gun more than an inch, and now its dark eye returned to me.

"I don't know where he is," I reiterated. "But I'm as keen to trace him as you are."

"I doubt that. Who are you working for? The Stranges?"

"I'm worried for their well-being." I saw no point in bringing Will Quinn into it.

"You ought not to have involved yourself with them. I suspect those women of perfidy. It is in the nature of their sex."

"I think you may be blinded by misogyny."

"And you by sentimentality. The great error of man has always been to underestimate the intelligence and cunning of women. In this, we are all sons of Adam."

"I can tell you that the Stranges don't have what you need," I said.

"And what is that?"

"A coin, an old and valuable one."

His head tilted to the right, like a bird debating whether to feed on strange carrion.

"Did Buker share its nature with you?"

"Like you said, I've been busy."

The head remained at an angle.

"No, not Buker, and not Egon Towle either," he said. "Did you speak to his sister? Yes, I'm sure you did. It would have been logical. But she doesn't have it either."

"Because Egon would have told you if he'd entrusted it to her," I said. "You made sure of that."

"Well done."

"Is he dead?"

"Very."

"Then let it stop here," I said. "I can find Raum. I just need time to convince him to return what he took, but to do that I have to be assured of the safety of Dolors and Ambar Strange."

"You may want time, Mr. Parker, but not for that alone. Are you seriously suggesting you won't go to the police with what you know about me?"

"No," I said, "I plan to tell them everything, but I'm also a realist. You know how to hide, and if the police fail to catch you, I don't want my clients looking over their shoulders for the rest of their days. The coins aren't important to me, but they're very important to you, and one more than the rest. If I find a way to retrieve it for you, I'll know my clients are safe. After that, the law can hunt you to its heart's content, and I'll be sure to book a good seat for the trial."

"How close are you to locating Buker, Mr. Parker?"

"He's gone north, to Aroostook County, which means you have no hope of tracking him. I do."

"You're lying. Buker is here, in Portland, near his women."

He cocked the pistol, and instinctively I raised my hands, as though my fingers might somehow ward off a bullet.

"I'm telling you the truth," I said. "Why would I lie? I have no reason to protect him."

Not for the first time, my life hung on the pressure of a finger. Slowly, Kepler eased the hammer down.

"Yes, why would you lie?" he said, more to himself than to me. "All right, Mr. Parker, we've spoken long enough."

Kepler reached into a pocket with his left hand and withdrew a plastic tie, already looped. He walked behind me, keeping his distance, the muzzle of the gun never deviating from my body.

"Hands extended behind your back," he said.

I stretched out my hands, but prepared to move in the hope that the action of pulling the tie tight might leave him vulnerable or off-balance for just a moment. The tie touched my wrists. I tensed.

A Colt Single Action Army revolver weighs about two and a half pounds. Wielded with enough force, it will fracture a skull. Kepler didn't hit me that hard, just hard enough to leave me seeing explosions in the sky. The plastic tie snapped taut as I fell. I lay in the dirt and listened to the sound of his footsteps growing distant, followed by a car driving west. I didn't lose consciousness, but the pain made me wish I had. After a while I got to my knees and threw up, before using the edge of my car key to cut the plastic. When I was free, I dug a couple of bandages out of the first-aid kit in the trunk, used them to stanch the bleeding from the cut on the back of my head, and swallowed two Tylenol dry. I retrieved my phone from the bushes and tried calling first Will Quinn, followed by Dolors Strange. Neither picked up.

I now had a choice between two numbers, and one of them was 911. I opted for the other, either because I wasn't thinking straight or because I was.

"Where are you?" I said, when the call was answered.

"Drinking cocktails in Terlingua," said Louis.

Terlingua was an upscale BBQ place on Washington Avenue, within walking distance of Angel and Louis's Portland apartment.

"How many have you had?" I asked.

"I've just ordered my second. Angel's still on his first."

"Cancel it, and pay the check. I need some help."

"Gun help?"

"Would I be calling you," I said, "if it was any other kind?"

―――――

FIFTEEN MINUTES LATER, I pulled up outside Ambar Strange's cottage. I'd managed not to throw up again while driving, but it was a close-run thing. The lights were on inside the house, but the drapes were drawn. Will Quinn's Jeep was parked in the driveway, as were Ambar's red Toyota and Dolors's old Buick. I rang the doorbell, but no one answered. Behind me, a black Audi pulled up at the curb. From it emerged Louis and Angel.

And inside the Strange house, the shooting began.

CHAPTER

LXXI

Kicking in a door is hard work, even without a mild concussion, so I let Louis take care of it. Angel was already running to the back of the house, gun in hand. The front door eventually surrendered, but we didn't go tearing inside. That was a very good way to get killed, and the shots had sounded as though they came from two different guns. I risked a cautious glance around the jamb into Ambar Strange's open-plan living area. Will Quinn was lying by the fireplace, haloed by its flames. I could see no sign of injury, and his eyes were open, but he appeared dazed and in pain. Dolors Strange was kneeling beside him, while Ambar was standing in the center of the room with a gun in her hands, the muzzle pointing in the direction of the kitchen and the open back door. The gun was shaking because Ambar was shaking, too.

"Ambar," I said, "don't shoot. It's Parker. I have two colleagues with me, one of them moving on the back of the house. Don't shoot them either."

She turned toward me, and the gun turned with her. I returned to the shelter of the doorframe.

"Put the gun down, Ambar," I said. "Please."

"Ambar, do as Mr. Parker says," said Dolors. "He's gone."

I chanced another look. Ambar, dazed, was lowering the gun. I walked over and gently took it from her hands, while behind me Louis advanced to the back door. The gun was a 9 mm Springfield XD, a good weapon for a woman, with minimal recoil and a long sight radius. With practice, she'd probably hit whomever she was aiming at in the confines of her home.

"Kepler?" I said.

Ambar didn't answer, but Dolors did.

"Ambar shot him," said Dolors. "There's blood all over the kitchen floor."

"Is he still armed?"

"He has a revolver. He fired it, but he was already hit by then. I don't know where his bullets went, but they didn't injure any of us."

"What about Will?"

"I think he's having a heart attack."

An acrid odor hung in the room that I couldn't place. I thought it might have been coming from the fireplace, but I didn't have time to consider it further.

"Call an ambulance," I said, and made for the kitchen door, skirting the wall because I didn't want to be a target for Kepler. Dolors was right: Ambar had wounded him. The blood was bright red, so there was serious trauma involved. Louis had paused by the sink and killed the kitchen light.

"Angel?" I said.

"Over to the right," said Louis. "He says someone just went into the trees."

Behind Ambar's house was a patch of undeveloped land where people walked their dogs under pines.

"Then we'll have to go after him," I said.

The containers for trash and recycling stood behind a low concrete wall to the left. It wasn't great cover, but cover nonetheless. I didn't waste time thinking, because if I thought about what I was doing I'd probably feel the pressing urge to stay where I was. Nothing discourages movement so much as the prospect of being framed in a doorway while an armed man contemplates taking a shot at you. I was out the door and hidden by the dark before I could draw another breath, Louis at my heels.

"He's hurt," I told Angel when we reached him. "But he's also armed."

"We could always wait until he bleeds to death," said Angel.

"Or until he gets away," I said.

"Pessimist. So we go?"

"We go," I said.

We moved in unison, running fast for the trees, spread out and staying low. The trail of bright blood was easy to follow in the moonlight, and harder to spot as we got into the trees, but at least the pines offered some cover. My eyes were growing used to the dark, and I thought I could pick out a pale shape slumped amid the shadows.

"I see him," said Louis.

"I have him too," I said.

I called Kepler's name, but he didn't respond.

"He's not moving," said Angel from somewhere to the left, and slightly ahead.

"Any sign of a gun?"

"On the ground, by his right hand."

We advanced, drawing closer and closer to the wounded man until at last we surrounded him. Kepler was lying with his back to one of the pines. The front of his body was drenched with blood, and his eyes were barely open. He did not react as Louis eased the Colt out of his reach. I could hear his ragged breathing. His mouth tried to form words, and I knelt to listen.

"Perfidious," he said. "I told you."

It might have been the scudding of clouds, or the shifting of the branches in the night breeze, but for an instant there was movement on Kepler's skin—no, not on, but under, so that the shape of his face was transfigured. Beneath his own features I descried those of another, the lines sharp and animalistic, the teeth jagged and keen, and I smelled, amid the man's floral scent, a hint of burning.

And then it was gone, and Kepler with it.

LXXII

We returned to Ambar Strange's house. Sirens were already approaching, so Louis and Angel ditched their weapons in the compartment beneath their vehicle's spare tire while we waited for the ambulance and police to arrive. I checked on Will. He was hurting, but still conscious. Close to the edge of the blaze in the fireplace I saw a small stain, and a melted residue. I thought it might have been liquefied metal. Over by the door, Ambar's tan Timberlands lay on their side, mud caking the soles and staining the leather.

The police came, and I told them all I knew, omitting only my suspicions about Eleanor Towle, because she already had enough sorrows of her own. I listened, in turn, as Dolors Strange described Kepler's sudden entry into the house from the backyard, and Ambar's reaction: two shots, one of which hit its target. The Sisters Strange denied all knowledge of the whereabouts of Raum Buker or whatever he might have stolen, admitting only that they had assisted him in getting to the County. A prosecutor with nothing better to do might have gone after them for aiding and abetting, but since Raum hadn't been wanted for any crime when the Stranges accompanied him north, that prosecutor would have been wasting time and energy. In the meantime, Ambar's shooting of Kepler would certainly fall under the Maine Criminal Code's definition of legitimate force and the right to self-defense. Kepler was dead, and that was the end of it.

But that night, as I prepared to sleep, I thought again of the residue in the fireplace. It was just what a small coin might have looked like after melting.

LXXIII

Kepler's death made all the papers and TV news shows, along with variations on the story of the robbery, yet Raum Buker did not emerge from his hiding place. Some said that he'd gone west after all, and started a new life with the proceeds from the sale of Kepler's collection. But if Raum was selling off treasures, he was doing so discreetly, and discretion was not a word that had ever previously been associated with him. This is what I now believe: Raum should never have come between the Sisters Strange, and would never leave the County.

I think he's still up there, buried as deep as the winter dirt would allow.

LXXIV

E ven in death, the man who called himself Kepler remained an enigma. His vehicle, a tan 1977 Cadillac Coupe DeVille d'Elegance, was found parked near Ambar Strange's cottage. It was empty apart from an old medical bag containing clothing, minimal toiletries, and a small, ornate clock with multiple dials, each now stopped at a different time. The numerals on the dials were subsequently identified as ogham, an ancient Irish system of letters. The clock appeared to be of Kepler's own devising, because no record of a comparable mechanism was ever discovered. The Cadillac was registered to a New Mexico limited liability company with a tax ID number from a ghost address that turned out to be another box number, this one in Mississippi. His South Dakota driver's license gave his name as Johannes Kepler, after the German astronomer and mathematician. The address on the license was a disused shack in Wall, owned by the same LLC. In the pocket of his coat were two pairs of loaded dice, made from bone that was later determined to have come from a young female. The dice were four centuries old.

Eventually, some weeks after Kepler's driver's license photo had first appeared in newspapers, a woman in Perth, Ontario, contacted the Portland PD to say that she thought she recognized the man in the picture. She knew him as Christopher Cattan, another borrowing from history: Cattan was a noted sixteenth-century geomancer, geomancy being the use of patterns in soil, stones, and sand to divine hidden knowledge. This Cattan, she said, was only an occasional visitor to Perth, and didn't socialize, but he kept a small house off Highway 7 on the road to Peterborough. Sharon Macy was dispatched to Canada to liaise with the Ontario Provincial Police, joined by Detective Peter Condell from the Pennsylvania State Police Bureau of Criminal Investigation, for whom the death of Kepler marked a likely conclusion to the Edwin Ellerkamp case. A warrant to search a named property, located by the Tay River, was obtained from the Ontario Court of Justice in Perth.

The house, Macy later told me over dinner at the Corner Room, was unprepossessing from the outside—a simple two-story building in wood and brick, the woodwork much the worse for wear, ivy embedded in the brickwork—but the windows and doors were strong, and it had an alarm system in place, although it did not activate when the police entered. Two armed OPP officers accompanied Macy, but it quickly became clear that the house was unoccupied. Inside they discovered a broken safe and shards of glass from display cases swept into a corner; portable storage racks for coins, all full; a library of books on numismatics and the artifacts of ancient civilizations; multiple bone dice of various ages, all weighted; and an entire room of shelves laden with Sunday newspapers going back thirty years or more, many apparently unread, and sealed in plastic in bunches of ten. The décor didn't look as though it had been refreshed since the fifties, and the walls were unadorned. There was no TV, no radio, and no phone, only books and old newspapers.

Upstairs, just one room was furnished as a bedroom, with a small double bed. A safe was concealed in the bedroom closet, although, unlike the main one downstairs, it had not been forced open. When a locksmith did gain access, it was found to contain $20,000 in assorted currencies, along with a range of official identification documents: passports and driver's licenses in a number of names, including Faber,

Galeotti, Bacon, and Dee, all four being historical astrologers or alchemists. The earliest of the paperwork dated back to 1924—a New York State driver's license in the name of William Backhouse—but the photos on each document showed some version of Kepler. The official explanation was that Kepler had belonged to a long line of dishonest men. Who was to say this was not close to the truth?

CHAPTER

LXXV

The Sisters Strange went back to their old lives, once all the fuss had died down. Ambar continues to work at the dental practice, and has had some improvements made to her cottage, but other than the occasional nice vacation, she doesn't lead an extravagant existence. Strange Brews is still in business, and has even expanded to new premises in Saco and Old Orchard Beach, although Dolors can normally be found in the original coffee shop in South Portland, surrounded by bad art, and maybe, at times, bad memories. She and Will Quinn don't see each other anymore. Will and I had a long talk about the Sisters Strange, and I voiced suspicions that he had perhaps only countenanced during sleepless nights, as Raum Buker's silence dragged on and on. Will is now dating Kestrel Carroll, sole detective at the Cape Elizabeth Police Department, and there are rumors of an engagement on the horizon. Will, it can safely be said, is over his fear of the law.

Eleanor Towle no longer lives in Ossipee. Last I heard, she'd moved to Florida, and I doubt I'll ever see her again because I don't like Florida. I spoke to her briefly in the days following the discovery of her brother's body, to express my condolences. She thanked me and hung up.

Sometimes Angel calls to say that an unusual coin has come on the market, either at auction or as part of an under-the-counter transaction. For the most exceptional items, the seller is often a woman, although not always the same woman in every case. The description of one frequent consignor matches that of Eleanor Towle, which would be understandable given her late brother's interests, but the other sounds a lot like Dolors Strange.

THE FURIES

1

The vast cities of America, the fertile plains of Hindostan,
the crowded abodes of the Chinese, are menaced with utter ruin.

—Mary Shelley, *The Last Man* (1826)

I

The Braycott Arms was a stain on the character of the city of Portland, a blight on its inhabitants, and a repository for criminality, both aggressively active and relatively passive, the latter frequently due only to the temporary requirements of a parole board. It had always been thus, even beyond recall. The Braycott was one of a number of railroad hotels that had sprung up in the vicinity of Union Station, now departed these sixty years, of which only the Inn at St. John and the Braycott survived. But while the former was comfortable, hospitable, and carefully maintained, the Braycott catered to those who were less than particular about their surroundings, and valued the company of rough men and rougher women over clean sheets and a peaceful night's sleep.

There was something almost admirable in the Braycott's commitment to anarchy and disrepute, a commitment that seemed to have been passed down from owner to owner along with the deeds and keys. The hotel first opened its doors on July 25, 1888, just one month after Union Station itself. By then Maine's embrace of Prohibition, which had commenced nearly seventy years before the passage of the Volstead Act, was tightening. The sale of alcohol was illegal in the state, which drove the business underground—literally, in the case of the Braycott Arms, whose principal developer, Normand Braycott, had the foresight to devise a bar in the basement, albeit one omitted from the official plans. Bribes rendered it largely immune from raids, except for cosmetic purposes, although a two-hundred-foot tunnel behind the keg storage bay was kept clear in case of real emergencies, with a point of egress in a Braycott-owned property on the other side of Park Avenue. Decades later, when the rest of the United States followed Maine's lead in attempting to dry out its population by force, the Braycott's tunnel and bar became a staging point for the rumrunners bringing liquor into Portland Harbor, where the bottles would be concealed in boxes of Moxie soda, later to become the state's official soft drink, possibly in part for services rendered to its populace during Prohibition.

The Braycott's decline commenced after the repeal of the Volstead Act. In common with many such downturns, it was gradual at first, but accelerated rapidly. So regular were the fights, the beatings, and the knifings in its bar, it was proposed, not entirely in jest, that the police should consider opening a substation there just to save money on gas. Eventually, after a commercial salesman was gutted in 1972 in an argument over a hat, and a woman was subsequently shot dead in a disagreement concerning the same commercial salesman—and, by extension, the same hat—the Braycott lost its bar license, and the basement den closed its doors to drinkers, never to reopen.

By then Bobby Wadlin was a year old, the youngest of three boys whose father, Eldon, was the most recent owner of the Braycott. Bobby, like his brothers, was born in the hotel, and knew every dusty corner of it, each crack in the walls and hole in the floor, each nightingale board and treacherous, squealing door hinge. When his brothers finally moved out, Bobby stayed on to assist his father and mother with running the place. He became the official face of the Braycott, a permanent presence behind the front desk, and consequently was with both of his parents when they died *in situ*: his father first, followed by Bobby's mother six months after, each of them passing away in the bedroom of their private apartment on the top floor of the hotel. The Braycott did not close its doors following the demise of either party, and Bobby Wadlin was absent from his desk only for the duration of the funeral services and burials.

But following the death of Wadlin *mère*, rumors spread that the hotel, much to the relief of the city fathers, was to be sold and demolished. The former was true while the latter was not. The Braycott was disposed of, but this was, in effect, a piece of legal chicanery that transferred its assets to a private company controlled, in all but name, by the Wadlin brothers and a sole sister-in-law. Bobby became an employee of said company, and the profits were split equally four ways, although thanks to a good accountant and a succession of crooked contractors, the Braycott appeared barely to operate in the black.

Yet Bobby had little interest in the finances of the Braycott beyond its day-to-day operation. Oh, he was no fool about money, and could have cited income and expenditure on demand, to the nearest dollar, but liquidity had value for him only as a means of keeping the Braycott secure. He would have worked at the Braycott for next to nothing, just so long as he was permitted to remain within its precincts and had sufficient funds both to feed himself and support his addiction to old westerns in every medium. He had turned the rooms behind the front desk into his private living quarters, the walls lined with shelves containing westerns on videocassette, DVD, Blu-ray, and even LaserDisc, although he no longer owned a functioning player. He possessed full collections of the works of Louis L'Amour, Luke Short, John H. Reese, and Nelson Nye, as well as partial sets of almost a hundred other writers, some of which he kept in room 13, which he used as a library and storage facility, many guests, no matter how hardened by life, being reluctant to check into a room with *13* on its door.

Bobby, though, had no truck with superstitions of that stripe, or any other. He'd lost count of the number of people who'd asked him if the Braycott Arms was haunted, given its long and ignominious history. Certainly no small number of occupants had died in the place, including his parents, the victims of the hat feud, and assorted drunks who had variously broken their necks on the stairs, choked on vomit, or, in one case, mistaken a window for a door and plummeted four stories to the ground. (Bobby had heard tales of drunks who'd fallen from great heights and survived thanks to alcohol-induced relaxation of the limbs, but relaxed limbs didn't count for much if one landed on one's head.) None of them, as far as Bobby was aware, had chosen to spend their afterlife in the environs of the Braycott, which was, he felt, their loss. When he died, Bobby hoped to be permitted to spend eternity in his beloved hotel or some celestial version of it, there to watch *The Virginian* and *The Rifleman* on endless loops.

After all, it was the little things that kept a man sane.

II

In the hallways of the Braycott, no clocks ticked. The orientation of the building, combined with the grime on the hall windows, meant that sunlight had only a modest effect on the state of illumination, and at night the weak bulbs made barely any difference. The hotel, therefore, existed in a permanently crepuscular state, like many of its inhabitants. Bobby rarely troubled the corridors after dark—to be honest, he rarely troubled them in daytime either—except when someone exceeded the permissible noise levels, refused to leave on the agreed date, took ill, or expired. Bobby's post was by the door, next to his television, where he sometimes spent the entire night. When he slept, he did so only for a few hours. He had never been a big sleeper, and the lack of proper rest did not appear to affect his mood or personality, both of which continued to leave much to be desired.

The housekeepers monitored the state of the rooms, and informed Bobby of breakages, stains that might be regarded as unacceptable even by the Braycott's lax standards, and furniture and appliances that had reached the end of their long usefulness. Such items were then replaced from the stock that Bobby kept in the basement, the inventory sourced from thrift stores, flea markets, yard sales, and the homes of the recently deceased during Bobby's sporadic forays into the outside world. During these singular periods of absence, front-desk duties were assumed by a woman named Abigail Stackpole, of whom the kindest thing to be said was that she might have been a handsome woman when she was alive. Abigail Stackpole was a desiccated body of uncertain years, and it was whispered that she and Bobby Wadlin were, or had once been, an item, despite a difference in age numbered in decades. It was to Abigail, and Abigail alone, that Bobby Wadlin was willing to entrust the Braycott in his absence, and she was one of only a handful of individuals with a full set of keys to the hotel.

If Bobby Wadlin was not a particularly warm human being, neither was he unduly cruel. He did not tolerate bums in his establishment, because a bum was a man who made a habit of not paying his bills—which Bobby viewed as both dishonorable and prejudicial to the efficient running of a business—but he was prepared to make allowances for those who had fallen, in passing, on hard times, even if such concessions seldom extended for longer than forty-eight hours. The Braycott had a handful of long-term residents, toward a couple of whom Bobby exhibited a degree of patience and protectiveness that might, in the hotel's dim light, have been mistaken for something approaching affection. But while he loved his hotel, he was under no illusions about the quality either of the institution or the preponderance of its guests. Taking up persistent residence at the Braycott was akin to permanent occupancy of a cemetery: it was a sign that your life had come to an end. The Braycott was one step above the street, and two steps from the grave.

Bobby also had his own peculiar code of chivalry, derived in part from his close study of westerns. He did not regard the Braycott as a suitable venue for unaccompanied ladies, and did his best to send any who arrived at its door in the direction of more appropriate lodgings. He did welcome female guests, because to do otherwise would have been against the law, but he favored those who looked like they could handle themselves, preferably women who boasted more tattoos than the Sixth Fleet, at least once he had ascertained that they were not prostitutes. This Bobby did by bluntly informing women suspected of commercial sexual tendencies that he didn't allow hookers in his hotel. If they were offended, then they shouldn't have been trying to check in at the Braycott to begin with. Otherwise, they could take it on the chin or, if they were hookers, find somewhere else for their hotbed needs. Children, meanwhile, were not permitted under any circumstances. The Braycott was no place for children, and Bobby didn't care for them anyway, blithely informing anyone who would listen that, while he didn't hate kids, he'd never been able to eat a whole one.

Which was why Bobby was surprised and annoyed to be woken from a doze shortly after 2 a.m. by the ringing of the internal phone, followed by the voice of Phil Hardiman in 22 complaining that a child was running up and down the hallway outside his door. Hardiman had recently been released from Maine State Prison after serving four years for a class A drug felony, and Bobby was quite certain that he would soon be returning to MSP for another four years at least, because Bobby knew a lifelong loser when he saw one. Now it appeared that Phil Hardiman was getting high on his own supply, or even someone else's; this, or he was enduring the kind of dreams that required some regulated form of pharmaceutical intervention to bring them to an end, in which case he needed to square matters with his parole officer, and fast.

"We don't have any kids staying in the hotel, Mr. Hardiman," said Bobby. "We don't permit them."

"And I'm telling you," said Hardiman, "that someone has snuck a kid into this shithole, whether you permit it or not. I can hear her, for Christ's sake! Up and down, up and down, and laughing all the while. She's driving me fucking crazy."

"What does she look like?" said Bobby. "I mean, is she real young, or—"

Hardiman didn't answer immediately.

"I don't know what she looks like," he said finally. "When I go into the hallway, she hides."

"She hides?"

"What are you, a fucking echo? Yes, she hides."

"Hides where?"

The Braycott's halls contained ten rooms on each level above the first floor, as well as one storage closet to which only the cleaners had the key, and which was kept locked under pain of immediate dismissal, because Bobby didn't want any of the guests selling his stock of towels, toilet rolls, bleach, and soap in order to buy bottles of Mr. Boston Wild Cherry Flavored Brandy. (Someone had once spilled a bottle of the same in 24, and the smell still pervaded it.) In other words, short of the stairwell or the elevator shaft, there wasn't really anywhere for a child to go.

"If I knew where she was hiding," said Hardiman, "I wouldn't be asking you to come find her, would I?"

"Did you check the stairs and the elevator shaft?"

"Yes, I did check the stairs and the elevator shaft, but it's cold and I only got my drawers on. Now, are you going to come and sort this kid out or aren't you?"

Bobby didn't believe there was any way a child could have been smuggled into the Braycott. While the hotel had a back door, it was kept locked. This was obviously a code violation, but Bobby's patrons couldn't be trusted not to sneak buddies, women, men, or farm animals up to their rooms. Furthermore, if a fire did start at the front of the hotel, Bobby would be available to open the door at the back, and if there was a fire at the back, Bobby would make sure everyone got out the front. There was access to the fire escape from every hallway window, and most of them opened. It wasn't rocket science.

"Are you listening to me, numbnuts? Hey!"

Hardiman's voice, which seemed to have gone up an octave, brought Bobby back to the issue at hand.

"I'll come up and take a look," he said, "but nobody else has complained."

Only one other room on Hardiman's floor was currently occupied. The two men in residence were not the kind to have a kid in their room.

If they did, even Bobby—no fan of the law—would have summoned the police immediately, because it would have boded no good for the child in question.

"If someone has sneaked a kid in somehow, I'll sort it out," he said. "But I still think you're mistaken."

"Just get it done," said Hardiman. "I need to sleep. I got business to conduct in the morning."

Sure you do, thought Bobby. *Maybe I should call ahead to Warren, tell them to have your usual cell ready.*

Hardiman hung up. Bobby found a flashlight, just in case he had to go poking in any unlit corners, of which the Braycott boasted an abundance, and left his sanctuary. This required him to unlock the security door and step out from behind his protective plexiglass shield. As was inevitable in a business, differences of opinion sometimes arose with customers. Since the nature of any number of the Braycott's guests tended toward the abrasive, it was best to maintain a line of separation from them.

Bobby peered into the elevator, but it was empty and hadn't moved from the first floor since the last guest had returned shortly before midnight. As a precaution, Bobby disabled it with his key and took the stairs to the fourth floor, giving the second and third a once-over along the way. He could hear snoring from at least one room, music playing from another, and one side of a telephone argument from a third, but the hallways themselves were empty. Even at night, a certain element of noise was part and parcel of the Braycott's ambience, but few guests ever made a fuss about it. Bobby knew this was because anyone who had spent time in stir grew used to sleeping with the accompaniment of clamor, and often struggled to rest soundly without it. If there really was a kid in the building, that might explain why Hardiman had been woken: it wasn't so much the disturbance as the fact that it was so incongruous, a sound unfamiliar from prison.

But Bobby remained convinced that Hardiman was imagining things.

He reached the fourth floor. Hardiman's room was at the far end, close to the north window. The other guests on that floor currently occupied room 29, over by the south window. They had registered as Lyle Pantuff and Gilman Veale, and paid in cash for three nights, of which this was the first. They'd requested a room with two beds, which probably meant they weren't queer, although one could never be sure. Bobby Wadlin didn't have any problem with gays so long as they kept their paws off him. He might not have been a conventionally handsome man, but he had something. He was pretty sure of it.

Pantuff and Veale, on the other hand, were grown-up versions of the shitheads who had made Bobby's school days a misery. Pantuff, the older of the two, had a reddish-blond bowl cut that ended just above the ears, with the rest shaved close. Combined with the dark sockets of his eyes, and thick pink lips fixed in a joyless grin, as though the nerves had been damaged during botched surgery, he resembled a clown, but not one at whom a sane person might have been inclined to laugh. Bobby Wadlin was used to dealing with men who had done time, and Pantuff had that vibe about him. But experience had also taught Bobby to categorize ex-cons according to their likely offenses—the thieves, the pushers, the grifters, the killers—and the years had only heightened his acumen. He figured Pantuff for, if not a sex criminal, then a criminal who liked to sweeten his jobs with sex. If you woke to Lyle Pantuff burgling your home, someone was likely to get raped.

Veale was younger and darker, like he might have some Black in him from back down the line, Bobby guessed. He looked more normal than his associate, although next to Pantuff a visiting alien would have blended into the scenery, but if you examined Veale's face more closely, the eyes were gray and insensate. Pantuff brimmed with malevolence, but at least it was energy, an animus. Veale's gaze, by contrast, was entirely without luster, so that his soul might have been excised by God at birth along with any interest in ordinary humanity. Persons like Veale, Bobby thought, had probably tended the ovens at Auschwitz.

Their lives were a constant exploration of depths of cruelty in order to evoke a feeble emotional response deep inside them, as a scientist might increase the voltage on a dead animal until a muscle spasmed.

Bobby padded softly to their room and listened at the door, but could hear no sound from within. If they were sleeping, they were sleeping quietly, like the dead. If there was a child with them, it, too, was now silent; but as Bobby had already decided, these were not men to harbor children in their hotel room, or not for long. He left Pantuff and Veale to their rest and began moving from door to door, investigating each empty unit for signs of a child, and finding, as anticipated, none. He proceeded to do the same with the remaining two floors—exploring unoccupied rooms, pressing his ear to the doors of those with guests— before concluding that Phil Hardiman had indeed been mistaken, which confirmed for Bobby that it would be best if Hardiman stopped taking drugs, began taking them, or altered the dosage of whatever he was on, because the status quo just wasn't cutting it for him.

Bobby returned to the front desk. He thought about calling Hardiman's room to inform him that the inspection had proved inconclusive at best, but decided to let sleeping users lie. With luck, Hardiman would have forgotten about the whole palaver by morning, but on the off chance that he wasn't aurally hallucinating, and one of the guests had managed to introduce a child into the Braycott Arms, Bobby would instruct housekeeping to keep an eye out for evidence of unauthorized occupancy.

By now Bobby was fully awake and feeling resentful about it. He might not have slept much as a matter of course, but he both needed and enjoyed the little rest he did get, and Phil Hardiman and his fancies looked set to deprive Bobby of it for one night. Still, he wasn't defeated. He heated a saucepan of milk, opened a box of Lorna Doones, cranked up his old VHS player, and inserted the expanded widescreen edition of Lawrence Kasdan's *Wyatt Earp*. Bobby figured if that didn't put him to sleep, nothing would.

CHAPTER

III

I t might have interested Bobby Wadlin to learn how close he'd come
to being killed that night, because his fruitless search for what was
most likely a nonexistent child had not gone unnoticed. When he'd
put his ear against the door of room 29, listening for noise and finding none, the barrel of a suppressed Beretta M9 had been leveled at
his head from the other side, because when it came to sleeping, lately
Gilman Veale made Bobby look like Rip Van Winkle.

As Bobby moved away from the door, Veale monitored his progress
through the peephole. Veale wondered what the hayseed from the front
desk was looking for. It didn't strike him that the reason for Bobby Wadlin's
presence in the hallway might be connected to his own inability to sleep.

Because Gilman Veale was being haunted by a child.

Once Veale was satisfied that he and Pantuff did not appear to be of
specific interest to the manager, he returned to the chair by the window
and placed the gun on the table by his right hand. Over on the far bed,
Pantuff was sleeping soundlessly. Pantuff could sleep anywhere, almost
instantly settling into deep slumber. Veale thought that, given his
druthers, Pantuff would opt to sleep his entire life away. When he was
awake, he was pure mean, but he was also sufficiently self-aware to recognize his own poisonousness. In idle moments, Pantuff even brooded
on it. It wasn't guilt, exactly, more a sense of his ongoing debilitation, like

a man given a terminal cancer diagnosis who becomes obsessed with the unseen progress of the disease. The only times Pantuff wasn't tormented were when he was inflicting suffering on another human being, and when he was unconscious. He never moved during the night, and would always wake in precisely the same position in which he'd begun.

Pantuff couldn't hear the child. He thought Veale was imagining it, which was odd because Veale had no imagination. To possess an imagination required a creative intelligence, which Veale lacked, along with anything resembling serious emotional engagement with the world. He had always been that way, even as a boy. His parents were ordinary working-class people, and would probably have loved him had he responded to them with any kind of feeling at all, even hatred, but they couldn't cope with his inability to engage. Veale had been examined by doctors, who, having speculated on some previously undiagnosed brain injury or hidden emotional trauma, were disappointed to discover neither, and instead settled for variations on autism and alexithymia, or "emotional blindness." Therapy was attempted, but if Veale had no interest in interacting with his mother and father, he had minus interest in speaking about himself with a stranger.

Gradually, though, he did commence a private exploration of his situation, based around provoking negative emotional and physical reactions in others and reflecting on the results. He started out with animals—cats, stray dogs, even rats if he could catch them, although it was hard to deduce a lot from the responses of a rat—before progressing to human beings. He also experimented with self-harm before deciding there wasn't a great deal to be learned from inflicting pain on himself, beyond the fact that it was uncomfortable and therefore better avoided. Hurting others, on the other hand, didn't give him pleasure either, but it didn't actively displease him, and he found exhibitions of fear, rage, and grief curious. He was interested in causing others to feel these emotions because it enabled him to bathe in their heat, so that what he lacked he was able to experience vicariously. This made Veale very employable in specialist circles, although it had also rendered him a marked man elsewhere: one could only inflict torment for so long, sometimes on the wrong people, before attracting a level of negative publicity, leading to a quiet consensus that the world might be better off without one's presence in it.

A similar conclusion had been reached about Lyle Pantuff, although in his case it was a result of his taste for sexual violence. These changes in their professional circumstances had forced the two men together, and they now functioned as a single, very effective unit. They worked for others only selectively, preferring to operate on their own initiative. They picked their targets carefully, specializing in larceny and extortion. Veale had moderated Pantuff's behavior to an appreciable degree, encouraging him to keep his sexual proclivities separate from his work whenever possible. Pantuff, in turn, had enabled Veale to explore the concept of companionship, because the former seemed actively to enjoy his society. Veale did not understand why this was—even Pantuff struggled to explain it—but he was prepared to concede that he might register Pantuff's absence if he wasn't around, which was as close as he'd ever come to caring about another human being.

Veale sniffed the air. The Braycott was more sanitary than he'd anticipated, but it reeked of desperation and neglect nonetheless. Still, that wasn't what Veale was trying to detect. The sound of the child— Veale didn't care to think of it as "him" or "her," since he wasn't yet prepared to admit that it actually existed—was accompanied by a particular redolence, a mix of healthy perspiration combined with what might have been talcum powder and chocolate. Veale had smelled it just a few minutes earlier, but now it was gone. It was an odor that was strangely familiar to him, perhaps from his own childhood. Objectively he considered the possibility that he might be haunting himself, and the child, which had so far revealed itself only as sound and scent, represented a sensory manifestation of some deeper psychological disturbance: a breakdown, for want of a better word.

Veale didn't like to think that he could be experiencing the initial stages of a larger collapse. He wasn't stupid. He knew he was unusual, although he was aware that those familiar with him and his work might have preferred to categorize him as aberrant, even insane. Whatever the diagnosis, Veale was prepared to accept that the internal mechanisms that permitted him to function effectively in the world were potentially fragile. Were they to weaken further, he was not sure he would ever fully recover. Sometimes he visualized his inner self, his animating principle, as a transparent box of black bugs crawling over one another in an endless cycle of birth, reproduction, fighting, and dying. Should the walls of that box be ruptured, Veale himself would be consumed.

He waited a few minutes longer to be certain that the hallucination, phantasm, derangement—call it what you will—had ceased for the time being before climbing back into bed. He closed his eyes. He had always dreamed, and never pleasantly, but since he had begun hearing and smelling the child his dreaming had ceased, or if it had not, he woke with no recollection of it. This added to his concern that he might be flirting with derangement, and that the barrier between his sleeping and waking lives had been irreparably breached. If that was the case, he could soon end up wishing to become more like Pantuff, and seek escape in oblivion. Should the disturbance persist, Veale decided, he would probably be forced to kill himself so that he could sleep forever. The prospect was vaguely consoling, and thus he drifted into insensibility.

———

VEALE WOKE TO THE sound of the TV news. Pantuff was awake, crouched like a gargoyle at the end of his bed. His skin was so pale that it almost glowed in the dark, and in a certain light approached translucence. Naked, he presented as less than human, evincing a greater genetic commonality with certain predatory creatures of the deep than with mankind.

Pantuff looked at Veale as he sat up.

"It feels like the end of the world," said Pantuff. "Fucking Chinese. I never even liked their food."

"Any change?"

"Sounds like the city of Portland could issue a stay-at-home order sometime soon."

"How strict?"

"People will still be able to move around some for essentials, but—"

"But there'll be fewer of them," Veale finished for him.

"That's right. And who knows? If this virus gets any worse, maybe they'll put more police on the streets, even call out the National Guard to restrict activity. We could get stuck here, or find ourselves being asked questions about our reasons for being in town, questions we'd prefer not to answer."

"And we don't want that."

"No, we definitely do not."

Both men had criminal records that would set alarm bells ringing if they were stopped as part of any routine check. Once they were on the local radar, it would be impossible for them to complete their work here.

Veale tested the air, but could smell only himself. He wanted to shower. By now Pantuff should have been up and dressed, but he'd become obsessed with the virus, which meant monitoring the news channels even when there wasn't any news, or none worth hearing. Veale wasn't as worried about the virus as Pantuff was. Whatever happened, he knew he'd be okay. Veale was kin to the cockroach, which was fine by him.

"We gave her until the end of the week to get the money together," he said.

"I'm aware of that. We'll have to tell her that circumstances have altered, and not in her favor."

"And if she doesn't have it all?"

"Then we'll take what she has," said Pantuff.

This wasn't a big score, but they weren't big-score guys. Big scores attracted greater attention. You got greedy, you got caught, and it wasn't as though they were running yachts, or had staff to pay. They drifted between forty-dollar motels and cheap trailer parks, ate at Denny's and buffets, and drank in bars where the special came in a plastic cup. They were survivors, and you survived by staying close to the mud at the bottom of the pond.

"What if it isn't enough?" said Veale.

"You're starting the day with a lot of questions."

"It's that kind of day."

Pantuff returned his attention to the TV.

"We could stage a burning," he said, "make a video, and send it to her. It would focus her attention if she kicks up, encourage her to try harder. Nothing like a countdown to set a body moving."

Veale had another question. It didn't bother him that Pantuff was showing signs of irritation. Pantuff, regardless of rest, wasn't a morning person. Anyway, Veale wanted an answer. He didn't like leaving issues unresolved, and was organized by nature. As Pantuff had said, circumstances had altered. The woman was about to be put under additional pressure, and when you pressured people, they grew unpredictable.

"What if she does something stupid?"

"She's a woman," said Pantuff. "All they do is stupid."

Pantuff hated women, which was why he liked tormenting them so much. Veale thought it likely that Pantuff wanted to torment this woman, too, because he'd missed his chance the first time around. It might even have suited him for her to renege on their deal. It would give him an excuse to go after her again.

"That doesn't answer my question," said Veale.

Pantuff got to his feet. He had his cell phone in his right hand.

"We destroy everything she cares about," he said. "We turn it to ash. Then maybe I'll rape her to death. Does that answer your question?"

Veale showed no surprise. He'd figured as much, but it was best to be clear.

"Yes," he said, "it does."

He stayed quiet while Pantuff made the call. He noticed that Pantuff's voice changed as he spoke to the woman. It became lower, almost a purr. Veale knew that Pantuff liked to talk to the women while he raped them, and he would have bet good money that this was the voice Pantuff used, because Veale could see him growing aroused. In Pantuff's mind, he was already inside her.

When the call was done, Pantuff entered the bathroom, closing the door behind him. Moments later Veale heard the shower running, although he knew Pantuff wasn't bathing, not yet. He was only using the noise of water to mask whatever sounds his body might be about to make while he was sitting on the john, and he'd left the TV on for the same reason. Pantuff was funny that way. He was embarrassed by the workings of his own body, yet he never insisted on separate rooms, even when they could afford them. Veale knew that Pantuff wasn't queer. He just didn't like being alone.

Veale continued half watching the news, and listening to talk of quarantine and sheltering in place. The idea of enforced seclusion appealed to him. It meant he wouldn't have to deal with people he didn't know. If there was an issue beyond his comprehension, Pantuff would be there to explain it to him. Otherwise, Veale could read— history, preferably, but only of the ancient world, when life was sim-pler—and take walks alone. Perhaps, by then, the child would be gone. He hoped so, because the idea of sequestration while the child was still with him did not appeal, not one bit.

The woman worried Veale in ways that Pantuff's misogyny preven-ted him from seeing. Veale didn't believe she was stupid. Her husband might have been—he wouldn't be dead otherwise—but she wasn't. So much had already been taken from her. In her position, Veale would be trying to find a way to guard against a double-cross. He might even have been considering a double-cross of his own. If they did decide to lean on her, she would have to be watched.

Unfortunately, there were risks involved in monitoring her, because she'd be alert to signs of surveillance. Pantuff would be in favor of them continuing to keep their distance, but Veale could talk him around. The issue was this: To whom might she turn? Not the police, because they'd be happy to see her squirm. She couldn't go to her husband's people either, since she was lucky they hadn't killed her along with him. It was possible that she could hire herself some muscle, but they'd be no match for Pantuff and Veale, not unless she went for the best—and the best cost money, which she claimed not to have. It was a quandary, and no mistake.

The toilet flushed, followed by the sound of Pantuff stepping into the shower. Veale killed the television, and with the absence of its background noise, his thinking cleared.

What if she does something stupid?

He realized he'd asked Pantuff the wrong question.

No, what if she does something smart?

IV

When Dave Evans called I was over by the Maine Mall, watching people pushing carts filled to overflowing with groceries, liquor, potato chips, and toilet paper. Elsewhere gun stores were having trouble keeping ammunition on their shelves, and even L.L. Bean had closed its doors, which was a sign of desperate times. The only thing missing was the voice of Orson Welles announcing that the Martians were closing in on New York.

"There's a woman here asking for you," said Dave. "She says she wants to hire you."

I had a backlog of calls to return, and most of my messages I hadn't even listened to yet. I guessed I'd be turning work down for a while, until it became clearer just how we were all supposed to function in this unnerving new world. I was going to struggle to tie up the cases I currently had on my slate, although three of them were corporates that could wait, and the fourth was legwork on a worker's comp case for Moxie Castin. I'd spoken to Moxie earlier that morning, and he took the view that delays would be inevitable. Civil suits would have to take a back seat to felony cases until a vaccine was developed or everybody died. Moxie confessed to me that the pandemic had made him philosophical, causing him to reassess his professional existence. To that end he had divided his client list into those he hoped would survive, those he hoped would die, and those he hoped would die slowly.

"Tell her to leave a number," I told Dave, "and I'll get back to her when I can."

My daughter Sam was in Burlington, Vermont, living with her mother and grandparents. I didn't want to be any more isolated from Sam than I already was. If I packed a bag, I could find a place to stay nearby. I might even be able to rent an apartment and—

"She says she did leave a number," said Dave, "and the call wasn't returned, which is why she's now in my bar."

Dave sounded fractious, which was out of character. I couldn't blame him. Everybody was fractious, so why should he be any different? Plus, he had a business to keep afloat, and staff to take care of. Right now he had more on his plate than a lot of other folk.

I heard a woman's voice in the background. Dave spoke again, repeating what had been said.

"She asked me to tell you that it's urgent," he said. "Also, she says her name is Sarah Abelli, but she used to be Sarah Sawyer. She's Nate Sawyer's widow."

"*The* Nate Sawyer?" I asked.

Dave relayed the question back to her.

"The very same, she says. Should I know who he was?"

"Better you don't," I said. "This can only mean trouble."

"With respect," said Dave, "it's not like anyone ever comes to you because they've struck gold. Now are you going to speak with her or not? Because I'm kind of busy trying to prepare for the apocalypse."

Outside Books-A-Million, a woman was loading the trunk of her car with boxes of discounted novels. Perhaps there was yet hope for humanity.

"Tell her I'm on my way," I said.

"I'll make sure she listens out for your trumpet."

"Wait," I said, "was that sarcasm?"

But Dave had already hung up.

V

The name Nathaniel Sawyer was not one usually associated with Italian mobsters, but this specific Nate Sawyer bucked that trend. He had operated as a bagman and enforcer for the Office, as the Patriarca crime family out of Providence, Rhode Island, styled itself. Sawyer's mother, Luciana Morati, had married Nate's father, Royce, more out of necessity than desire, the latter having run its course after a couple of unsatisfactory sessions in the back seats of cars, but not before she had conceived a son. Royce Sawyer was the runt of a once proud Connecticut litter, with looks but a dearth of charm, and expensive tastes but a lack of money. The marriage didn't last and Royce decamped to Australia, never to be heard from again. Luciana went back to her own people in Lenox Dale, with the shadow of a failed relationship hanging over her. Her son, Nate, screwed around for a while before eventually entering the orbit of the Office's Boston underboss Sam Ricci, otherwise known as Sam the Chef, since he operated out of the back of a restaurant on Route 1 in Saugus. The restaurant stood on the same lot as an impotency treatment clinic, so Sam Ricci was sometimes referred to as Sammy Dryfire, but only out of earshot of the man himself.

Nate Sawyer's mongrel heritage made him an outsider, but outsiders have their uses, especially in an organization like the Office. The Patriarcas had endured a succession of bad times: the jailing of the boss Peter Limone in 1968 for a gangland murder he didn't commit, resulting in thirty-three years in prison—ten of them on death row—before his release and a settlement of $26 million for wrongful imprisonment, which was small recompense for spending the best part of his life behind bars; the brief, disastrous reign of Raymond Patriarca Jr. in the eighties; and his successor, "Cadillac Frank" Salemme, turning government witness in the nineties upon discovering that some of his own associates had ratted him out to the FBI.

After this checkered history, and the media interest it attracted, the Office made a conscious decision to place a premium on discretion, and did its best not to draw attention to its activities. It never quite succeeded, but the intention was admirable, if nothing else about the Office was. Nate Sawyer played his part in all this, being regarded as a safe pair of hands, but he was also a louse: crude and cruel, a bully both inside and beyond the walls of his own home, a man who was only ever comfortable in the company of those more ignorant than himself. It probably shouldn't have come as any surprise when it emerged that Sawyer had been an FBI informant for the best part of a decade, ever since the Bureau had uncovered evidence of Sawyer's skimming from his employers that would have earned him a beating followed by a bullet behind the ear. Nate Sawyer had been more cunning than anyone suspected.

Regrettably for him, just as he was preparing to make the final jump to federal witness, followed by his absorption into the protection program, Sawyer killed an undercover policeman after what he claimed was the accidental discharge of his weapon during a robbery at a liquor warehouse in Gloucester, Mass. The fact that the cop had been hit three times didn't help Sawyer's case, and the subsequent revelation of his snitch past made him persona non grata with his own people, who now got in line with law enforcement and the FBI to make what remained of his life a misery, the Bureau in particular being profoundly embarrassed that one of its sources was a cop killer. Despite being held in protective custody at the state prison in Concord, Sawyer never made it to trial. Someone put thallium in his food, and he died on Christmas Eve, 2017.

Sarah, his wife—although by then in name only, their marriage having long become a celibate nightmare for her—probably didn't even register that he'd been murdered. Earlier that same week, her five-year-old daughter, Kara, had fallen down the stairs at their home in Revere, hit her head on a spindle, and died on her way to the hospital. In the space of seven days, Sarah Sawyer became a widow and the mother of a dead child. But by then she had been ostracized, tainted by association with her husband's activities. Her daughter's funeral was sparsely attended, and Sarah didn't even bother to go to Nate Sawyer's cremation. The story was that his ashes were claimed by the Office and fed to hogs.

Six months later, the bodies of two women were found buried under the part-dirt floor of the rented garage in which Nate Sawyer had formerly stored a 1978 Chevy Camaro. The first had been missing since 2014, the second since 2016. It wasn't clear if Sawyer had only recently developed an interest in killing women, or if these represented his latest victims. Sarah Sawyer, already a pariah in her community, now became an object of disdain, even hatred, beyond it. She must have known, it was whispered. If she didn't know, she must have suspected. And if she didn't suspect, she ought to have. With her husband dead, some of the blame for his crimes devolved to her. That left her with two choices: she could brave it out or disappear from sight. Wisely, she went with the second. I wasn't aware that she'd relocated to Maine, assuming she hadn't traveled all the way to Portland from somewhere else just to engage my services. If so, she was destined to be disappointed. I couldn't think of many reasons why I'd choose to involve myself in her difficulties. To be honest, I couldn't think of any.

By then I was turning onto Forest Avenue. I found a parking space outside the Great Lost Bear, but didn't immediately go inside. Instead I spent a few minutes boning up on the facts of the Sawyer case. His widow had been born Sarah Gaudiano. I wondered where Abelli had come from, unless the woman in the Bear was lying about her identity, in which case she was insane because no one in their right mind would claim a connection to Nate Sawyer if it wasn't true. But then, these were strange days.

VI

obby Wadlin was sitting behind his desk when Lyle Pantuff and Gilman Veale passed by on their way to find somewhere to eat breakfast. Unlike seemingly most of the population of the city, Wadlin wasn't panic buying or watching a news channel, but was immersed in an episode of *Alias Smith and Jones*, a series that Pantuff recalled vaguely but Veale, being fifteen years younger than his partner, did not.

Wadlin leaped to his feet as the two men came into view, or as close to leaping as someone as naturally indolent as Bobby Wadlin ever came.

"You gentlemen sleep okay last night?" he said.

"I slept fine," said Pantuff. "I always sleep fine. Must be my clear conscience."

That grin widened in a manner suggesting it would be surprising if he had any conscience at all, clear or otherwise.

"Why do you ask?" said Veale. His intervention surprised Pantuff, Veale not being one for unnecessary conversation. But Veale thought that Wadlin appeared agitated, and his original inquiry had an air of more than politeness about it.

Bobby Wadlin suddenly regretted opening his mouth. Pantuff might have resembled a sideshow freak, but it was possible to gauge the measure of him. By contrast, being regarded by Veale was like having a spider crawl across one's face.

"Another guest called to complain about a disturbance last night," said Wadlin.

"From our room?" said Pantuff.

"No, heaven forbid," said Wadlin. "From the hallway. Someone running around. He thought it might have been a kid but"—Wadlin tapped the notice on the plexiglass advising guests that minors were not welcome: it read NO KID'S ALLOWED—"we don't permit children at the Braycott, so he must have been mistaken."

Veale was staring at the sign.

"No kid's what?" said Veale.

"What?" said Wadlin. He had almost said "No kid's what what?" but stopped himself just in time for fear that Veale might feel he was being mocked.

"Your sign says 'No Kid's Allowed,' but it doesn't say what particularly of kids is not allowed. Toys? Games? Shoes?"

Bobby Wadlin did not have a fucking clue what the guy was talking about. The Braycott, he mused, really did need a stricter door policy. His utter bewilderment finally registered with Veale.

"You have a rogue apostrophe on your sign," said Veale. "You've made the word 'kids' into the possessive. You should correct it to avoid confusion."

Wadlin had a vague memory of someone else complaining about one of his signs. Maybe it wasn't just viruses that were contagious, but fucking pedantry, too. He considered informing Veale that he'd get around to the sign in his own good time, just as soon as the temperature in hell dropped enough, but common sense prevailed. When a man like Gilman Veale told you to fix something, you got it fixed, so Wadlin removed the sign and tossed it in the trash. He thought he might dispense with signs entirely in favor of making up the rules as he went along, which was what he preferred to do anyway.

Pantuff's eyes drifted to the TV screen, where Pete Duel and Ben Murphy were now running the details of a con with Walter Brennan.

"You know there's a pandemic, right?" said Pantuff.

Wadlin followed his gaze.

"Not in Wyoming Territory in the eighteen hundreds," he said.

"You must go out sometime."

"I try not to. I don't like it out there. Never did."

Given the current state of the world, Pantuff thought Wadlin might have a point. He asked Wadlin for some breakfast recommendations, and Wadlin suggested Marcy's up on Oak Street, although he advised that they only accepted cash, which made Pantuff like the place already. He only ever paid cash, and any cards he used were stolen.

Pantuff and Veale left Wadlin to his show, got in their car, and drove to Marcy's. Pantuff drove everywhere, preferring never to be more than a block from his vehicle. He'd gone to jail the first time because he'd tried to get away on foot after taking down a liquor store, and only a fool made the same mistake twice.

"You okay?" he said to Veale as they pulled up at a parking meter a few steps from the door of the diner. Anyone unfamiliar with Veale would have spotted no alteration in his demeanor since they'd left the Braycott, but Pantuff knew better.

"Wadlin was talking about a kid," said Veale.

"So?"

"So I heard the kid again last night, while you were sleeping."

Pantuff checked the street for police before exiting the car. He had one of those faces that couldn't have drawn more cops if it were shaped like a doughnut and covered with sprinkles. It was better not to provide the law with the opportunity to open a conversation. Only when he was satisfied that it was safe to do so did he open the door, get out, and put an hour's worth of quarters in the meter.

"And I say for the second time: So?"

"I've been hearing a kid ever since we targeted the woman," said Veale, falling into step with Pantuff. "You know that."

"You told me, and I believe you," said Pantuff. "For years after he died, I used to hear my father's voice. I heard it just like he was standing next to me. Strangest fucking thing, because he never used to speak more than two words a day while he was alive. But once he was dead, you couldn't shut him up. I must have missed him more than anticipated."

Veale didn't give a damn about Pantuff's dead father, and said as much.

"You don't have to be like that about it," said Pantuff.

They were at Marcy's by then, and Pantuff held the door open for a pair of young women to exit. In the space of a few seconds he had already followed them home, had a good time at their expense, and robbed their place of anything worth taking. He willed them to look back at him, because then he'd be able to see it all reflected on their faces, but they had more sense and kept on walking.

Pantuff and Veale took a table, and each ordered eggs, ham steaks, home fries, and coffee. They waited for the coffee to arrive before resuming their conversation.

"You're not trying to tell me," said Pantuff, "that a bum at the Braycott heard the same child you say you've been hearing. Look, someone sneaked a kid into that shithole, which is enough of a reason to have social services raid the place, but only after we're gone. The kid decided to stretch their legs for a while, because that's what kids do."

"In the dead of night?"

"Who am I, Doctor Spock? I don't know how a child's mind works. Jesus, I barely know how mine works." *And I certainly have no idea what goes on in yours*, although this Pantuff kept to himself. It wasn't as though Veale's feelings might be hurt—you had to have something approaching conventional emotions for that to occur—but Veale harbored an unfortunate tendency to take statements literally, and Pantuff didn't want to be woken in the night by his partner offering a considered assessment of his higher functions.

Their food came. It looked and smelled good, and Pantuff dove in. Veale pushed home fries around his plate. Pantuff tried to ignore him, although Veale had a way of not being ignored.

"What if it was us who brought the child?" said Veale.

Pantuff paused, a forkful of egg poised by his lips.

"What are you talking about?"

"I've only started hearing those sounds since we targeted the woman," said Veale. "What if it's her child?"

"Her daughter," said Pantuff, "is dead."

"I know that," said Veale.

His face showed no trace of embarrassment. It was another weakness to which he was seemingly immune.

"You think you and the bum at the Braycott heard the same child, and it's the ghost of the Sawyer kid?"

"Why not?" said Veale.

"Because it's crazy, that's why."

Reluctantly, Pantuff placed his fork back on his plate. He didn't like speaking with his mouth full. It was uncouth.

"Look," he said, "I'm not saying that ghosts do or do not exist. I can tell you that I've never seen one, but I've never seen Paris either, and I'm sure that exists, so I keep an open mind. I've also met people who claimed to have seen ghosts, and only some of them were nuts, although the ones that weren't nuts were drunks. I think you're jumping to some wild conclusions here."

Pantuff returned to his breakfast. He didn't want his eggs to get cold. In Pantuff's world, there were few things worse than cold eggs. Cancer, maybe, but if so, it ran cold eggs a close second. Eating also gave him time to consider how best to deal with Veale's problem, which was undoubtedly psychological and could therefore be added to the long list of Veale's other issues, even if this one needed to jump the line, since it related to the business at hand.

"I haven't seen a ghost," said Veale. "I've only heard one. I think perhaps I've smelled it, too, but I can't be sure."

Pantuff kept chewing. He wasn't going to be diverted from his breakfast. He was determined about that.

"You heard footsteps," he said, once he'd swallowed. "And you didn't hear footsteps where footsteps have no right to be. You didn't hear them walking up the walls, or on the ceiling. You heard them in a hallway, which is where folks walk, even little kids."

"But there were no kids. The manager said."

"The manager was mistaken. For Christ's sake, his clock stopped in 1889."

"He wasn't mistaken," said Veale. "I doubt there's a fissure in the walls that he doesn't know about."

"Then he could try filling some of them in," said Pantuff, "and get rid of the cobwebs while he's at it."

"Give me another explanation," said Veale.

"I can give you ten, a hundred. Tiredness, to begin with. Overwork. You could be running a fever. When I run a fever, I hear show tunes. I can't get them out of my head for a night, two nights, then they go away."

"I'm not tired," said Veale. "I don't have a job, and I haven't broken a sweat in days."

"Jesus!"

Pantuff threw his silverware on the table. What kind of world was it in which a man couldn't even enjoy his first meal of the day in relative peace? A few of the braver or more foolhardy diners glanced their way before wisely deciding to mind their own business.

Pantuff closed his eyes and took a deep breath. There was no percentage in getting annoyed with Veale. Veale didn't like shouting, expressly so when it was directed at him. After a certain point, his instinct was to put a stop to it. Raging at Veale was like throwing a ball against a wall: it just bounced back at you, but the more force you put behind it, the more likely it was to hit you in the face.

"Listen to me," said Pantuff, softer now. "I haven't heard anything, and the only times we've been apart lately is when one or the other of us has gone to the john. As for smells, all I get from that dump is old clothes and cheap sanitizer. Even if, by some quirk of the universe— and it's a big if, one that I'm only acknowledging out of politeness and respect—you were being haunted by the Sawyer kid, why should the guy down the hall have heard the child too?"

"Because it's real," said Veale, and he spoke so matter-of-factly that any reservations Pantuff might previously have entertained about his insanity vanished forever. "It's out in the world, so why wouldn't he hear it? You were asleep. And it comes at night."

The way he said those last five words made Pantuff's skin crawl, because for the first time since he'd known him, Veale sounded uneasy.

"Okay," said Pantuff, "you believe what you want. If it's true, all the more reason to get this thing taken care of quickly. And if it isn't, we need to get it sorted out anyway, just so we're not stuck up here with a virus and a million hicks."

He called for the check, and paid it with grubby fives and ones. The tip was just enough: not too high, not too low. He now regretted raising his voice earlier. In everything he did, Pantuff tried to pass unnoticed, even as his physiognomy and mien conspired against his best efforts.

"I think you're wrong about something else," said Veale.

"You keeping a list now?" said Pantuff. "We ought to get married, because this is like having an old lady."

Veale didn't want to marry Pantuff. He didn't want to marry anyone. If he married someone, he'd have to be with them always. Even if they didn't insist on talking to him, he'd know they were there. Veale considered there to be two general types of people in the world: mediocrities and everyone else. Both types were ultimately to be avoided.

"I don't need to keep lists," said Veale. "I have a good memory. And it's about the Sawyer woman. She's not stupid. I was the one shadowing her, and I could tell. She learned to hide it, I think because of her husband, but she's very smart."

Pantuff was already on his feet and moving toward the door. Veale followed.

"Then," said Pantuff over his shoulder, "she'll do as she's told."

"She has no reason to trust us," said Veale. "If I were her, I'd be working the angles. We should be following her."

"Then we risk being seen." Pantuff took a moment to check the street again before leaving the diner. He sighted a patrol car in the distance, but it was heading downtown, away from them. Portland, Maine, he had already concluded, possessed far too many police, with too much time on their hands. When he was happy the surroundings were clear, he led the way back to the car.

"If she's as smart as you say," said Pantuff, "she'll be keeping an eye out for surveillance. Wait a minute, what am I even saying? Fucking surveillance. We took a couple of baubles from her, some pictures. Sure, they have sentimental value, which we're looking to monetize, because otherwise we wouldn't be doing this, but 'angles,' 'surveillance'? No, it's a simple exchange. She knows we can't sell them, so why would we screw her over? She's the payday, no one else."

"But we're not going to return them, are we?" said Veale. "We are going to screw her over."

Pantuff started the car.

"If so," he said, "it's no more than the bitch deserves for keeping a rat in her bed. A killer rat, too."

Even Veale looked askance at him when he said this, given Pantuff's own treatment of women and his oft-expressed view that Nate Sawyer's victims had almost certainly asked for what had befallen them, if only for being dumb enough to let him get close. Veale thought Pantuff might have been envious of Sawyer. Pantuff had never killed a woman, but Veale knew he fantasized about it. He'd spoken about femicide often enough.

Pantuff was still hungry. It would play havoc with his mood for the rest of the day. Not even lunch and dinner would help, and now Veale was sowing doubts in his mind, which would further interfere with his appetite. But when Veale spoke, it was a good idea to listen. His unique psychological makeup gave him the clarity of an ascetic. He saw the world in black and white—well, principally black, but the point remained valid. Pantuff wasn't about to go so far as to accept that the Sawyer woman might be actively intelligent, but he was prepared to concede that she could be sneaky. In his world, "foxy" wasn't a compliment.

But they had increased the pressure on her once already, and might have to do so again. She could argue that she didn't yet have all the money together, and she probably wouldn't even be lying, painful though it was for Pantuff to admit. Yet by moving everything forward they would also restrict her opportunities for duplicity, and be able to slip into seclusion a day earlier.

"What are your thoughts?" said Veale.

"That we can proceed in one of two directions," said Pantuff. "We take whatever she can give us, even if it's less than we'd hoped for, and we vanish. That's the first."

"Or?"

"Or we pick up what we can now and come back for a second bite later, but that would mean returning some of the stuff. If we don't, we'll never get more money out of her. Give her a little when she pays the first time, and dump the remainder somewhere after we receive the second portion. I'd prefer to deprive her of all of it, but a man has to learn the art of compromise."

Veale shook his head.

"I don't want to come back here again," he said. "And I want all of what we took disposed of as soon as possible."

"So that you can stop hearing the footsteps of a child," said Pantuff. "Because that's what you hope will happen once we're rid of it, right?"

"Yes," said Veale, but it wasn't only that. He wanted the items gone before he stopped just hearing the child and began seeing it, too.

"Your superstitions are going to cost us money," said Pantuff.

"I'll make it up to you next time."

"I don't want that. I'm just saying, is all."

Pantuff pulled into the traffic heading toward the Old Port. He wasn't in the mood to return to the Braycott. Life was depressing enough without spending more of it in a dump like that, and being away from it would help Veale. Pantuff speculated on whether there might be a way for him to burn the Braycott to the ground at some time in the future. It wouldn't take much effort. The place was a firetrap as it was, and he'd be doing the city a favor.

"I'm wondering," he said.

"About?"

"Again, just supposing it is the Sawyer kid you're hearing, because I remain skeptical."

"Accepted. Go on."

"Do you think," said Pantuff, "that her mother hears her as well?"

The possibility had not crossed Veale's mind until now. He weighed it as they turned toward Commercial, the Fore River ahead of them. The bascule was open on the Casco Bay Bridge to allow a huge container vessel access to the sea. Veale had read that even the largest container ships sometimes had as few as twenty crew members on board. He had often pictured himself going to sea, losing himself in the immensity of oceans. If he could be entrusted with a task to be completed alone, a simple, repetitive action he could do well, his oddness might be accommodated. If he surrounded himself with those who did not speak English, it might not be noticed at all.

"Yes," said Veale, "I suspect she does. If I can hear the girl, why not her?"

The girl. He was starting to humanize the apparition. This displeased him.

"So the child must have a connection to what we took," said Pantuff, "a bond of some kind, or else why wouldn't it have stayed close to her? I mean, assuming it exists, which I don't."

"That's one explanation for what's happening."

"You have a better one?"

"Not right now."

"What I'm getting at," said Pantuff, "is we assumed the value of what we stole was purely sentimental, but what if it's more than that? Suppose a little of her daughter remains attached to those mementos—like, I don't know, a spirit?"

"What of it?" said Veale. "It doesn't mean she'll be able to get more money, even if we squeeze her."

"I don't want to squeeze her," said Pantuff. "I want to hurt her." He patted the fingers of his right hand on the steering wheel, tapping out a rhythm familiar only to himself. "We'll take whatever cash she's pulled together, then we'll destroy everything we took from her. We'll burn it, and what's left of her child along with it. We'll film it so she can watch it burn and know that the kid is no longer in the world. How about them apples, huh?"

"It sounds," said Veale, "like you're starting to believe."

But he didn't immediately agree with Pantuff's plan. He wanted time to examine it.

"Whether I believe or not doesn't matter," said Pantuff. "What matters is that she may believe. I'd really like to be sure, though."

He nibbled at a hangnail.

"Perhaps," he said, "we should find out."

VII

T he Bear was open as usual, although there was a palpable air of uncertainty and anxiety about the place. Even the Fulci brothers were not themselves, even if there were some who might have regarded any change as an improvement. The brothers had arrived early to help Dave repair some broken tables, but since they were responsible for breaking them to begin with—in a heated argument over a game of checkers—it was the least they could have done.

Dave stopped me at the host's station.

"I googled Nate Sawyer," he said. "I have to tell you, your client list gets more and more colorful as the years go by. I swear, if Jack the Ripper's widow came in here asking after you, I wouldn't be surprised."

"Where's the Sawyer woman?"

"In your usual office booth by the bar. You want coffee?"

"Sure, why not?"

"I'll send some over." He peered in the direction of the bar. "You have to wonder what kind of mess she's in to bring her here. Hard to think it's worse than what she's already seen."

"You'd be surprised."

"God, I hope not. I think the world already has an abundance of afflictions to be getting along with."

I left him to his burdens and headed over to the booth. Sarah Abelli, or Sawyer, was sitting with her back to the wall, facing out. She probably did that a lot these days, assuming she even ventured beyond her front door very often. Her head was bowed as she typed a message on her cell phone. She glanced up from the screen as I drew nearer, and I stopped in my tracks. I felt the breath catch in my throat, and was torn between the urge to walk away or to reach out and touch her face.

Sarah Abelli bore an uncanny resemblance to Susan, my dead wife. It was in her eyes, the curve of her cheekbones, and the shape of her mouth, but also in the way she held herself, even seated: a kind of relaxed elegance. The hair was different—longer, darker—and the face was slightly fuller, but had she and Susan been seated side by side, and the latter introduced as the younger sister of the former, no one would have demurred.

"Mr. Parker?" she said.

I found my voice. "That's right."

She rose and extended a hand. "I'm Sarah Abelli."

I hesitated only for a moment before shaking her hand. Her skin was very dry, with a rough, almost sandy texture. When I released my grip, I expected to see grains glitter in the palm.

"Thank you for taking the time to speak with me," she said, as she sat. "Are you okay? You look shaken."

"You remind me of someone I once knew," I said. "It took me by surprise."

"I hope it's someone you liked."

"Yes, it was."

Perhaps she saw something in my face, or heard it in my voice, but she didn't pursue the matter, and I was grateful for it.

"Well," she said, "I suppose that's better than the alternative."

A server arrived with two mugs, a pot of coffee, and some sweeteners and milk, because Dave knew that I preferred regular milk to creamer.

The server poured the coffee and left us alone again.

"I should tell you before we start," I said, "that I don't think I'm in a position to take on any more clients. Given the current situation, it's going to be difficult to fulfill the commitments I already have."

She ignored the sugar and milk—ignored what I'd just said, too, judging by the way she smiled—and tasted her coffee.

"I don't believe my problem will take up much of your time," she said. "In less than twenty-four hours it'll be over and done with."

"Even so," I said.

She held the mug in her hands and regarded me through the steam. Her expression changed, and I saw disappointment and anger swirl, not all of it directed at me. Sarah Abelli, I guessed, had spent many hours engaging in a process of self-examination, and had found herself wanting.

"Are you unwilling to work for me because of who I am, or more importantly, who my husband was?"

I didn't know enough about her to be able or willing to pass judgment on her, but I knew about the people Nate Sawyer used to run with, and the posthumous revelations about him didn't add to his appeal. Dave had been right when he said that we all had enough strife to contend with right now.

"Let's say that I'm aware of your late husband's associates," I said. "I'd prefer to keep them at a distance."

"I don't blame you," she said. "I've tried to adopt the same policy, circumstances permitting. I've even succeeded, for the most part. If it's a question of money, I can pay. If you're worried about people finding out you helped me, I can assure you that no one will ever know, just as long as your friend over there can keep a secret. And like I said, it's not as though this case is likely to drag on."

I added milk to my coffee. Some of the similarities to Susan were beginning to diminish, but the memory of that first impression persisted.

"Are you used to getting your own way?" I said. I meant it lightly, but she didn't respond in kind.

"No," she said, "I've never been used to getting my own way. My late husband broke three of my ribs, fractured two of my fingers, and once hit me so hard on the left side of my head that he induced a mild stroke in the occipital lobe, leaving me partially blind in one eye. I suppose I can consider myself lucky he didn't kill me, considering what he may have done to those other women. My guess is that he didn't want to have to go to the trouble of looking after our daughter alone."

She winced, and took a few seconds to collect herself. To give her time, I said, "Do you have doubts about his guilt?"

She welcomed the distraction, I thought, even if it didn't take her long to provide an answer. After all, she probably considered the subject every day.

"I'd like to believe that he wasn't responsible," she said, "if only for my own sake. I don't enjoy being a pariah for the sins of another. But I know what he was capable of, so it's likely he did kill those women, although it doesn't mean I wouldn't be happy to discover otherwise."

She set the mug down hard. Some of the coffee spilled on the table.

"Look what I've done now," she said.

I reached for a napkin, but she got there before me.

"I can take care of it!"

She was so loud that she drew the server's attention. I gave the slightest shake of my head, and the server turned away.

"I'm sorry," said Abelli. She finished cleaning up the coffee and set the stained napkins aside. "Are you aware of what happened to my daughter?"

"I read about it. I understand some small part of what you're going through."

"I hoped you might. That's why I came to you." She looked at me oddly. "You know," she said, "I think you're the first person who hasn't said they're sorry, or offered me their sympathies."

"That gets overused. It's well-intentioned, but I was never sure what it meant. Is this about your child, Sarah?"

And when I used her first name, her defenses fell away, and all that remained was suffering.

"Yes," she said, "or what remains of her."

VIII

S arah Abelli finally left for Freeport, Maine, three months after the deaths of her daughter and husband. Sarah's mother used to have a spinster aunt who lived on the outskirts of Freeport, and each summer she and Sarah, along with Sarah's two younger siblings, would take the bus from Massachusetts to spend a month with the old lady. Sarah's father would later drive up to join them for a week, entrusting the running of his beloved grocery store to his assistant manager, Theo, if by "entrusting" one meant badgering him constantly with telephone calls to ensure that he hadn't given away the entire stock to the undeserving poor, or allowed the whole place to go up in smoke. Upon her death, the aunt bequeathed the house to Sarah's mother, and she in turn left it to her children in her will. Sarah's brother and sister didn't have the same affection for the summer retreat as Sarah, and she bought them out in installments over ten years.

Nate Sawyer had rarely troubled the state of Maine with his presence, not unless a job required him to make the trip north. Neither was he bothered by his wife's increasing desire to spend time in Freeport as their marriage staggered on, since it gave him time to conduct his various casual liaisons and, as it later transpired, kill young women. In Maine, Sarah was known by Freeport residents simply as one of the "Abelli girls," since that was her aunt's last name. Following her husband's death, she submitted, through her lawyer, a petition form to a court in Massachusetts, seeking to use her aunt's name, and a hearing docket was fast-tracked. Within two weeks, following a closed-session hearing, she was officially Sarah Abelli. She now doubted if more than a couple of people in Freeport could have connected her to her late husband, and they cared enough about her to remain silent, especially after her daughter died.

"Why was the hearing docket fast-tracked?" I said. Changes of name could sometimes take up to six months to be certified by a judge or magistrate. But even as I asked, I could guess the reason.

"Because I told the police and the FBI as much as I could about my husband's activities without naming names, and in return they facilitated a degree of reinvention for me."

Bingo.

"That must have been a risky business," I said.

"It was. I spent a week planning what I was going to say, and rehearsing it with my lawyer. He, in turn, cleared it with, um, others in advance."

"The Office."

"Who else?"

I could understand why they might have been prepared to let her speak. Even the Office wouldn't want to be perceived as condoning sexual homicide by one of their number.

"How hard did the federal agents push?" The feds would have wanted more than the story of how the girls might have come to be buried under Nate Sawyer's garage.

"Pretty hard, but I only gave them what I was told to give."

"Did they ask you to testify?"

"It wouldn't have been worth the effort. Most of it was just hearsay."

"But?"

"Enough wasn't."

"Who did it damage?"

"Not the Office, but some people they wanted to see squirm on a federal hook. You know, annoyances."

That was a clever move, if it could be made to work.

"Does the Office know about your change of name?"

"We tried to keep it quiet, because that was part of the deal. But nothing is secret in Boston, or not that kind of secret. In the end, what does it matter? It's just me now. The rest is memories."

"Of your daughter?" I said gently.

"Yes. Of Kara."

CHAPTER

IX

"I replay it, you know," said Sarah Abelli, in the booth at the Great Lost Bear. "I try to locate the moments when I might have changed the outcome, so she'd still be alive. I stay with her upstairs, instead of going downstairs to call my sister. I insist that she come with me, instead of leaving her with her crayons and coloring book. I go to help her on the stairs when I hear her coming down, instead of staying at the kitchen table with a cigarette in one hand and the phone in the other. I react faster when I hear her fall. I explain what happened more coherently to the emergency operator. I use different words when I'm talking to Kara while we wait for the ambulance, words that lodge in her brain and keep her with me. I see all these forks in the path, these opportunities to alter the future, and they're tiny, seemingly inconsequential, yet because of those choices I made, the story ends with her dying in an ambulance."

I didn't interrupt, or offer consolation. I'd spent years tormenting myself in a similar way, except my choices appeared to lead inexorably to the killings of my wife and first daughter. It took me a long time to accept, if only partially, that the fault lay with the man who had taken their lives. Sarah Abelli didn't even have another with whom to share the blame, not unless it was God Himself. If she took that route, I wouldn't have begrudged her, and I don't believe God would have either.

By the time Kara died, Sarah Sawyer was the wife of a rat, soon also to be labeled a femicidal killer. As well as being ostracized by her community and her husband's former associates, she was also under pressure from the latter to explain where certain skimmed monies might have gone, because in addition to being a snitch and a murderer, Nate Sawyer had been thieving from his own people.

"A week after Kara's funeral," said Sarah, "two men I didn't know came to the house. They forced me into the back of a van, put a hood over my head, and drove me to a property by the sea, because I could hear waves crashing and smell salt, even through the hood. And that hood stank; it had been used before, maybe many times.

"I was led down to a basement. They cut off my clothes, left me in my underwear, and then one of them put his fingers inside me. He said they'd been assured they could do what they wanted with me, but if I told them where the money was, they might consider not raping me. Then they began hitting, punching. At one point, I blacked out. When I came to, there was another man in the basement, and I'm sure that I recognized his voice, because I'd met him a couple of times with my husband. Nate had introduced him to me as Luca, but I never found out his last name, because I never asked. He said that if I didn't tell them about the money, they'd dig up Kara's body and feed it to the same hogs who'd consumed my husband's ashes."

She took a moment, pursed her lips, looked inward.

"I married one of those men," she said, "the kind who would threaten to disinter a child and throw her to pigs. I slept with him, had a daughter by him—although Kara was always mine, never his. But how fucking stupid was I?"

There was no point in telling her that she couldn't have known, because she had known: the generalities, if not the specifics. She had simply elected not to acknowledge the fact. Sometimes, that's the only way we can survive.

"But if Nate did steal from them, like they said," she continued, "I didn't know about it. Sure, everything was cash with him, but that wasn't unusual, not in his circles. When I needed to buy something, the money was there. He wasn't cheap, and he didn't mind my putting a little aside for myself, but we're talking a low four-figure sum. I couldn't make them believe me, though. I thought for sure they'd do what they said they were going to do, and leave Kara's grave empty. Luca told the one who'd threatened to rape me that he could go ahead and do it if he wanted, and when he was finished, Luca would come back and talk to me again, to see if it had made me see reason."

Sarah kept her eyes fixed on me. She did not look away.

"The one who'd put his fingers inside me whispered in my ear about what he was going to do to me. He already had his hands on my breasts when there was a noise from nearby. I heard a door opening, and everything stopped for a while. When someone spoke again, it sounded like an older man. He said that he didn't want to see me hurt, that he had children of his own, but there was a limit to the protection he could offer. The money Nate stole had to be paid back. That was how it worked. It wasn't personal, just business."

In the end, she agreed to sign over her home to them—$200,000, with $50,000 plus change left on the mortgage—and they let her go. When she returned to the house, she found that it had been torn apart in an effort to discover some of her husband's hiding places. They'd succeeded, too, finding $5,000 in the wall behind the medicine cabinet and another $12,000 in the false bottom of the garage workbench.

"They gave me a week to move out," she said. "I arranged to have Kara's body exhumed and reburied under her initials, spoke to the feds like I was told to, and then came up here. I started to believe I might have been forgotten, but I was wrong."

She'd returned home from the gym a week earlier to another house that had been ravaged by intruders: upholstery and mattresses torn, clothing strewn across carpets, bookshelves stripped, and even the kitchen cabinets emptied of their contents, with opened boxes of rice and cereal upended on the floor. It was almost vindictive in its destruction, but thorough in its investigation. More of her husband's people, she thought, but if she informed the police, she would invite their scrutiny; anyway, the intruders couldn't have discovered anything of value because she had little worth stealing, and what she had was well hidden. It was only when she checked her bedroom for the second time that she realized what had been taken. Her reaction was to scream.

"I kept Kara's relics in a box," she said, "all those little things from her first years that I could save: her first booties, her first pacifier, the first tooth she lost, drawings that she'd made, photographs, even plaster casts of her hands and feet from the day we brought her home from the hospital. Everything I had of her, they took."

I could see she was determined not to cry in front of me. Her fists were clenched, and she was barely holding it together. Also, there was that rage again: had she been able to get to those responsible for the theft, she would happily have ripped out their hearts with her bare hands.

"I was about to call the police then," she continued. "I didn't care about my identity being revealed, or having my windows broken and being forced to move again. I just wanted Kara back. I had invested so much of myself, of *her*, in those things. They were my link to her. Without them, I'd lose her forever."

Watching, listening, I had the sense of words left unsaid and deeper emotions unexpressed. Perhaps it was only the natural grief of a mother who had lost her child, and an understandable shock and anger at the physical reminders of that child's former presence in the world being stolen. But no: I'd grown adept at identifying the hiding places, the silences, because that was where the truth so often lay. Sarah Abelli was concealing information. Whoever had burgled her house had taken more from her than mementos, however important they might have been to her.

"And did you turn to the police?" I said.

"I didn't get a chance. I received a phone call. I'm not sure how they got my number, because I'd changed it after leaving Massachusetts. I don't even keep my old bills in the house. Fewer than a dozen people have that number, and I trust them all."

"If you have a cell phone, the number can be found," I said, "no matter how sparsely it's shared. Tell me about the caller."

"He didn't give his name. He just told me that they had Kara's things, and I could have them back for fifty thousand dollars. I informed him that I didn't have fifty thousand. I barely have a thousand in my accounts, and my credit card is a hundred off its limit. I work at L.L. Bean and drive a ten-year-old car. I told him all that, but I think he already knew, and it didn't make any difference to him or his demand. He advised me to find a way to get the money together or they'd destroy everything they'd taken. He suggested I borrow against the house." She swallowed hard. "So that's what I did. The bank would only go to thirty thousand, so my brother and sister came through with another ten thousand each."

"I'm waiting for the 'but,'" I said.

"The caller got in touch again this morning. Now they want the money by this evening. The bank promised that the cash from the refinancing would be in my account by the end of the week. I've just been in touch with the assistant manager again, begging him to fast-track it for today. I said it was an urgent payment to cover medical expenses for my sister, and he told me that he'd see what he could do."

"Why are you telling me this?" I asked.

"I think they're going to double-cross me," she replied. "I'm convinced they have no intention of ever returning what they stole."

"Why do you say that?"

"Because they know who I am. They wouldn't have taken the Kara box otherwise. The caller said that he didn't think he needed to warn me against going to the police because they wouldn't have much sympathy for someone like me. And I could hear it in his voice: his spite for me, his amusement at my grief. Jesus, I pleaded with him, and he just laughed. He was getting off on my pain."

"And what is it you want me to do?"

"I want you to ensure that they give back what they stole from me, all of it."

I didn't reply for a long time. I had every reason not to become involved: the sense of panic on the streets; my urge to leave Portland for Vermont and my daughter; and the workload I already had, some of which I might be unable to complete for weeks, or even months, depending on the virus.

But most of all there was the Office. I'd long ago grown tired of trying to second-guess hoods, and my intervention in their dealings had never ended well. I also had bad memories of Providence, including crossing paths with what was once the Office's local competition, the Freudian nightmare known as Mother. Mother had seemingly scuttled back into the shadows, and her former territory was now the preserve of the Office, but the memory of that encounter persisted. Right now, sitting across from me and asking for my help was a woman whom the Office would have been happy to see suffer, and it was possible they'd already set about putting that wish into motion.

But she was also a mother mourning her lost child, and whoever was responsible for invading her home and removing her keepsakes of her daughter was guilty of a reprehensible act. I thought of Jennifer, my own dead child, and the tokens of her brief existence that I retained. Had someone taken them from me, I'd have hunted the culprits down and hurt them badly. If I didn't help Sarah Abelli, who would? If I turned my back on her, what moral authority would remain to me?

"You've sometimes been using the words 'they' and 'them' when talking about whoever stole the box," I said, "but if I understand you correctly, you've dealt only with one man."

"That's right, but he spoke in the plural all the time. I suppose he might have been lying to intimidate me further, but why bother? He had the Kara box, and that was enough. Also—"

I waited.

"I can't be sure of this," she went on, "because his voice was muffled over the phone—deliberately, I think—but this may be the same man who hurt me in the basement. His speech has an odd rhythm, as though he learned English as a second language, except he doesn't have an accent. If that's the case, it's possible that the other man who abducted me is also with him."

"Did you ever see their faces?"

"No, not really. They wore masks when they came to take me: see-through plastic, but with a distorting effect. It was like looking at images in a fun-house mirror. I barely got a glimpse, though, before I was hooded, and the hood remained in place until they brought me home. I don't think I'd be able to recognize them without those masks."

This wasn't good news. If it was the same men, there was a chance, even a likelihood, that they were working at the behest of the Office. The story was that Nate Sawyer had skimmed $500,000 over six or seven years, which was no small beans. Either that money remained hidden, its location taken to the grave—or rather, the digestive system of hogs—by Sawyer, or his widow was harder and more cunning than anyone had guessed, and had managed to keep some of the cash. Had she sold her home after her husband's death, she'd have made $150,000, give or take, although the deal with the Office had left her with nothing. But had she been able to hold on to the Office's money in turn for sacrificing the house, she might potentially have secured up to three times that amount, assuming her late husband hadn't spent it all. It was possible that someone in the Office had begun thinking the same way, and had tracked her to Maine. Holding her daughter's possessions for ransom would be a good way to test the waters. If she could access the $50,000 too easily, there would be more where that came from, and a second trip to a basement might be in order, this time one she wouldn't survive.

Helping her, though, would inevitably involve a conversation with the Office, which didn't appeal. These men had quick tempers, the world had no shortage of basements, and a hole in the ground would accommodate two just as easily as one.

"Were you given any way to contact them?" I asked.

"No, they always call from a blocked number, which means I have to answer every time the phone rings. I'm getting tired of people trying to sell me stuff."

"Have you been given instructions for the transfer of the money?"

"Not yet, but they told me to have it ready in cash."

That was useful. An electronic transfer would have been harder to trace. I knew someone who could do it, but by the time he'd found the end account, the funds would already have been dispersed. But hard cash meant the extortionists would be forced to come into physical contact with the ransom. It would leave them momentarily vulnerable.

"Won't the bank be suspicious when you ask for your money in bills?"

"Not if they've ever had to deal with the medical profession. Have you seen how much doctors charge? Some of them make the Office look like probity personified. Does this mean that you'll help me?"

"Being straight with you, I don't want to, but I'm not sure I could look myself in the mirror if I didn't. I do have one more question."

"Go ahead, ask."

"If these are the same men who tortured you, they may have been sent by the Office in an effort to establish once and for all whether you have the money your husband stole from them. My question is, do you?"

She held my gaze.

"No, I do not."

And I couldn't tell if she was lying.

X

Pantuff and Veale cruised past Sarah Abelli's Freeport home, but her car wasn't in the drive. A cat sat on one of the front windowsills, radiating resentment at being left out in the cold. Pantuff thought that Veale would probably have killed it were he alone, and it was lucky for the animal that it hadn't been in the house when they broke in. Veale had spoken in the past of his apprenticeship harming animals, and Pantuff had only recently been forced to warn him against setting spiders alight because he was convinced it made the room smell strange. Pantuff didn't like seeing animals in pain, only women. In his opinion, this qualified as a redeeming feature.

"I wonder where she is," said Veale.

"Getting our money, if she has any sense. We could call her and find out."

Pantuff wished there was somewhere nearby—a Starbucks, ideally, where a man might remain for hours without being rousted—in which one of them could have sat in order to keep an eye on the house, but the only Starbucks was on Main Street, surrounded by outlet stores. The Abelli residence was on Durham Road, way over on the far side of I-295, with no coffee shop in sight. Even stopping nearby for too long was likely to attract the attention of a neighbor or passing cop, which was why they had barely slowed as they gave the house the once-over. Out here in the boonies, people were too nosy for their own good. This was one of the reasons Pantuff hated small towns. The other reason was that he just hated small towns. He and Veale had also briefly scouted the woods behind the house, but couldn't find a spot that allowed them to get a good vantage point without attracting attention from people walking their dogs on the trails. Some days, you just couldn't catch a break.

"Let's call the bitch," said Pantuff. "I feel like lighting another fire under her."

———

SARAH ABELLI AND I went back over events in both Maine and Massachusetts. I asked her to tell me again about the men who had abducted and tortured her, this time concentrating on every aspect she could recall of their speech and appearance: height, weight, hair color behind the masks, whether they were left- or right-handed, and any distinguishing markings she might have registered, such as scars or tattoos. By the end, I had more to go on, but not much. I then made her recall what she could of the days preceding, and immediately following, the burglary, in case the men involved might have been keeping tabs on her and she'd spotted them, even if she wasn't aware of doing so. Again, we didn't come up with a lot, but Sarah thought she'd seen an old blue Chrysler LHS two days in a row, once at the Maine Mall and again at the Freeport Medical Center by the end of Durham Road. She remembered it because her father had driven the same model until his death, and she couldn't look at one without thinking of him. I made a note to check if the medical center had a surveillance camera, but even if it did, I doubted I'd be able to gain access to the footage: doctors didn't like private investigators examining the comings and goings of their patients.

"I don't suppose you were watching your rearview mirror on your way here?" I said.

She bristled slightly.

"My husband was a mobster," she said. "We spent our lives looking in the rearview mirror. I took precautions. I wasn't followed."

This I could accept.

"What now?" she said, as I closed my notebook.

"There's not much we can do until you hear from them again, and they tell you how the exchange is going to work. If they're professionals, they'll be very cautious. That could mean a moving drop—you open the car window as you drive by a certain location, dump the money, and keep going—with one of them watching you for the last couple of miles from another vehicle, just in case you've decided to play it clever, and the other waiting at the drop point to pick up the money. You won't be told the location until you're actually driving, and then only a few minutes before you reach it, so it can't be staked out in advance."

"But if I do that, how do I know I'll get Kara's things back?"

"You don't," I said, "and if your instincts are right, you never will, or not all of them. If you paid once, they may decide that you'll pay again."

"Well, fuck that."

But it was said more in desperation than defiance. She wanted her daughter's possessions returned safely, and her instincts told her this was now looking less and less probable, no matter how much money she paid.

"On the other hand," I said, "they're aware that you're unlikely to have contacted the police, and none of your husband's former associates will lift a finger to help you. If you were wealthy enough, you could go to some fancy private agency that specializes in dealing with problems of this kind for a premium, but they doubt you'd do that, even if you were sitting on your husband's money. Fifty thousand dollars isn't chump change, but neither is it a king's ransom: it's an achievable goal for all parties. As a rule of thumb, the trick is to figure out what the mark can afford, then add between ten and twenty percent to make them sweat. Ask too little, and you don't get taken seriously. Ask too much, and you risk attracting heat or coming away with nothing at all. It's all about finding the sweet spot."

"That's very interesting," she said. "It may even be true where I'm concerned, but where does it leave us?"

"It leaves us to establish whether the Office is involved, which is the main complicating factor. If the instruction to target you has come from Providence, there may be a way to open a dialogue, because fifty thousand isn't the endgame."

"I was telling you the truth," she said. "I don't have Nate's money."

"The Office's money," I corrected. "It's an easy mistake to make, but you lost a house because of it."

"And if this isn't coming from the Office?"

"Then we may still have some leverage, but let's set that aside until we can find out for sure."

I asked for her address, her cell phone number, and the keys to her house, front and back. I then excused myself for a moment and pulled up a map of Durham Road, followed by a Google Earth image of the locale. Merrill Brook ran more or less parallel to Durham Road for a time through woodland before skewing northwest after Richards Lane. It looked like it might be possible to come at the Abelli house from the rear via the brook and woods without being noticed. The trees might even have made a reasonable spot from which to watch the house.

I found Tony and Paulie Fulci and told them I had a job for them if they wanted it—which they did, because the word "no" didn't feature in their vocabulary where I was concerned. I asked Tony to get a copy of the keys made before taking a ride out to Sarah Abelli's house in Freeport. He should park a short distance away, watching out for a late nineties Chrysler LHS in blue, then work his way east through the woods from Merrill Brook toward the house, but only once he was sure that nobody was keeping watch on it. At that point, he was to enter through the back door and station himself somewhere that gave him a clear view of the road.

I instructed Paulie to be ready to follow Sarah Abelli once she left the Bear. Tony could drop him at their family home on the way to Freeport, allowing Paulie to pick up one of the less obtrusive family vehicles— that is, not the monster truck—and get back in time to stay with her. I advised them both to arm themselves, the Fulcis having avoided the loss of their gun rights by never being convicted of a crime carrying a sentence of longer than a year in prison, although they preferred to travel unarmed. When one looked like the Fulcis, guns were an unnecessary encumbrance. Paulie said he'd borrow his mom's car, which was currently a cream Kia Soul, although he admitted that part of him would die inside. I then returned to the booth and my new client.

"I'm not sure how much you know about me," I said, "but I don't always work alone, and I have people I can call on if required. As it happens, they're all in town at the moment, which is good. I can't guarantee a positive outcome for this, because the other side has most of the cards, but the odds in our favor will be increased by involving these men."

"I'm happy to pay whatever is needed," she said.

"Good, because two of them are already in motion, one of whom will be waiting in your home when you get there. His name is Tony. He looks more frightening than he is, but admittedly that's touch-and-go in the wrong light."

"Why does he have to be in my house?"

"An extra pair of eyes on the surroundings, and security in case these men decide to come collect their ransom in person. Do you keep a gun at home?"

"No, I don't like them."

"Well, Tony will be armed, so I'd appreciate your tolerance. Next, I need your phone and your code."

She handed over her Android phone, and I installed both Flexi-SPY and Call Recorder. The latter was mostly a backup for the former, because FlexiSPY would allow me not only to listen in on any calls made or received but also to record them. The app would additionally function as a microphone, which would be useful if we came to the point where Sarah was required to be in her car alone, enabling us to remain in contact. It also contained a location tracker, so as long as the phone was in her possession, I'd know where she was.

"I'll now be notified whenever you receive a call," I said. "Don't answer immediately because I may require time to join. I've set the app to monitor all calls, but if they're not relevant to what's happening, I'll stop listening. This also gives me access to your email and SMS, so if you have a problem with that, let me know now."

"You can look and listen all you want," said Sarah. "I don't have a personal life, not unless a book club counts."

"Nevertheless, it's important that we're clear on the access I have. I want you to stay here for a few minutes until Tony returns your keys, and I tell you that it's safe to go. When you leave, you'll be followed by a cream Kia. That'll be Paulie. If you have any doubts, just look for a big guy exuding shame. He couldn't really be inconspicuous if he tried."

Over the past few months, Tony—always the more thoughtful of the brothers—had begun to display signs of serious character development, including the ability, if not to blend into his surroundings, then at least to find surroundings in which he didn't look as though he might require a zoning permit. Paulie, by contrast, remained Paulie. Asking him to maintain a low profile would be like putting a hat on a bear and calling it a disguise.

"What will they be watching for?" asked Abelli.

"The Chrysler, or any other vehicle that seems to be taking an interest in you or your place of residence. If you're right about that car, the simplest solution to all this would be for us to locate it, talk to whoever owns it, and convince them to return your daughter's things before heading on their way."

"Just like that?"

"We can be very convincing."

"So your reputation would suggest."

"Don't believe everything you read."

"I didn't have to believe all of it," she said. "Ten percent was enough."
I let that go.

"But if we're not lucky," I continued, "and these guys manage to keep their heads down, we'll have to go along with whatever they tell you to do, and make sure we get our hands on at least one of them before they melt away. Then we propose a different exchange: they hand back the money and the items they stole from you, and in return we don't involve the police or resort to more violence than necessary. But first, as I told you, we have to establish the extent of the Office's involvement."

There was nothing more to discuss for now. We agreed to a fee for the job, which Sarah Abelli offered to pay in advance. She opened her purse to display an envelope of bills. I told her I'd take half now, half when we were done. I knew that the Fulcis were hurting for money, and paying them cash for their efforts would be best. She counted out the bills, all twenties, some fresh and others looking like they'd been retrieved from under sofa cushions, which still didn't mean that some of them hadn't been skimmed from the Office. I gave her the Fulcis' numbers and made sure she entered them correctly in her phone, because I didn't want communication problems if anything went wrong. I waited with her until Tony returned the keys and departed, and Paulie confirmed that he was waiting outside the Bear. We gave Tony time to get to Freeport, and then she left. Even the way she walked reminded me of Susan, and I had to force myself to keep a grip on the present. The weight of my past was heavy enough already without adding to it further.

Dave drifted over as the door closed behind her.

"Should I ask?" he said.

"Someone stole her dead daughter's possessions," I said. "Pictures, mementos from her infancy. They're holding them for ransom."

It took Dave a few seconds to find his voice again. When he did, a fraction of his faith in the world had been excised forever.

"What type of person would do that?" he said. "I mean, who would even think that way?"

Maybe, I was tempted to say, the type of person who would also threaten to dig up the same child's remains and feed them to hogs, but Dave didn't need to hear that.

At that moment, my phone rang. I glanced at the display, and saw an incoming call to Sarah Abelli from a concealed number. FlexiSPY was justifying its subscription.

"It seems like we're going to find out," I said.

XI

P hil Hardiman wasn't an early riser, and in any case had never struck Bobby Wadlin as a morning guy—or an afternoon guy, an evening guy, or much of a night guy, professional dealings apart. He negotiated life as though the good stuff were surrounded by an electric fence, and it was his destiny to fling himself futilely against it until death eventually arrived to relieve him of the burden of even trying. Narcotics dulled the pain, but he'd fallen into the cycle of selling so he could keep using, only to find that his personal appetites meant he was barely breaking even. By the nature of junkies, this meant he would soon find himself in the red, requiring him to indulge in various iterations of larceny in order to make the cut. His stay at the Braycott Arms was serving only to postpone the inevitable return to even less welcoming state-funded accommodation.

Now here he was, bleary-eyed, bad-tempered, and hovering before Bobby's desk, complaining again about the kid who had disturbed his night's rest, and looking for a refund or discount on some or all of his remaining stay at the Braycott.

"I'm telling you for the last time," said Bobby, "there is no kid here."

To be fair, Bobby wasn't absolutely certain of this because housekeeping hadn't finished checking all the rooms, but he was close to certain, and Hardiman was no one's idea of a reliable witness. If it were

Christmas, he would probably have claimed to have heard Santa Claus. Bobby wasn't sure what the man's drug of choice might be, but regardless of the specific weakness, he knew enough about hopheads to attest that their mental faculties tended to take a hammering as the years went by.

"And I'm telling you I heard one," said Hardiman, except Bobby could see that he was wearing Hardiman down, causing him to doubt himself, whatever his bluster might suggest. Spotting this, Bobby made a move to seal the deal.

"Look, here's what I'll do," he said. "If housekeeping finds evidence that someone has sneaked a kid into the hotel, I'll refund you half a night's rent to make up for the sleep you lost. But only—*only*—if housekeeping comes up with the goods. The owners will raise hell with me for it, but I'll take the heat because fair is fair. Is that enough for you?"

It obviously wasn't, but Hardiman accepted that it was the best he was going to get. He knew, too, that the stuff about the owners was just so much bullshit, and a portion of his rent was going straight into Bobby Wadlin's pocket. In fact, Hardiman didn't trust Wadlin to tell him about the kid even if housekeeping did find them. He wouldn't have put it past Wadlin to smuggle the kid out with the dirty laundry just to save himself having to open his wallet.

"I got things to do," said Hardiman. "I'm already late because of this."

"Don't let me keep you," said Bobby, leaving unspoken the admonition that the junk wasn't going to buy and sell itself. He was all set to put Hardiman out of his mind and return to *40 Guns to Apache Pass* when Esther Vogt popped up. Esther was one of the Braycott's oldest residents, and also the longest-standing. She'd rented a room at the hotel back in the late 1990s, following a fire in the old duplex in which she'd been living for thirty years with her husband, a German-born builder named Adolf. ("Jewish lightning," she always alleged. "They blamed him for the Holocaust.") Adolf died soon afterward of emphysema, Esther banked the insurance money, and a temporary stay at the Braycott gradually became a permanent one, Esther discovering she didn't need as much space as before now that her husband was no longer around to clutter the place with his junk—or, indeed, to incite further retribution from the Chosen People. Also, following many sheltered years spent in the company of a man who had spoken only to agree with her, she enjoyed the experience of sharing accommodation with more expansive characters, and now functioned as a den mother to the Braycott's inhabitants. She was eternally cheerful and helpful, and the years did not appear to be dimming her light one iota. Bobby Wadlin couldn't stand more than three minutes of her company, and what she said next permanently deducted at least two from that limit, not least because it brought Phil Hardiman scurrying back to the desk.

"Mr. Wadlin," she said, "I believe someone may have brought a child into your establishment."

XII

As instructed, Sarah Abelli gave me enough time to find somewhere quiet to listen in on the call. The voice on the other end of the line was male, and didn't sound young. The accent wasn't out of Massachusetts, and contained a trace of the South, but with a strangeness to it, as though he might have been the child of immigrants.

"Mrs. Sawyer," said the man, "I hope you're keeping well."

"I told you already, I don't go by that name anymore."

"Just like I told you that I don't care. You know, you really ought to modify your attitude, or else I'll wipe my ass with those pictures of your little girl."

"You're a poor excuse for a man," said Sarah.

I realized that I should have stayed close to her for the call. I'd heard and seen this happen before. Sometimes, when a person in trouble managed to convince the police to become involved, or engaged a private investigator, their courage took a boost. Antagonizing the men with whom she was being forced to deal would not serve Sarah Abelli well, but she appeared to recognize this herself, because when she spoke again the fire in her had been dampened.

"Then you won't get your money," she said, "and we'll all have come out of this with nothing."

"Except that there's always more money somewhere," he said, "but what we have of yours is strictly one-of-a-kind, and I don't see you squeezing out another child anytime soon. What are you, forty, forty-one? Hard to find a man who'd waste the jizz on you."

I knew then that Sarah was right: even if she handed over the money, she'd never see her daughter's possessions again. Here was someone who enjoyed humiliating women. The thought of Sarah Abelli mourning the loss of all physical traces of her dead child would help keep him warm until summer came.

To her credit, she kept her temper.

"Are you done insulting me?" she said. "Do you want to get around to why you're calling again?"

"Just checking where you are. Figure you must be out getting our money."

So they'd been by the house and noted that her car wasn't there. That was good. We had a potential idea of the color and make of their vehicle, which meant that one of Sarah's neighbors could have noticed it. If nothing else, we might be able to confirm how many people we were dealing with.

"I have it for you," she said, "or I will, in a few hours."

"Good. We wouldn't want any misunderstandings, not for your daughter's sake. You know, sometimes it's almost like she's here with us. You ever get that sense, Mrs. Sawyer?"

I counted the silence that followed: it lasted a full five seconds.

"My daughter is always with me," she said, but her voice was too even.

"Not lately, I'll bet. We look forward to doing business with you. We'll be in touch again about the arrangements. Goodbye, Mrs. Sawyer. If I see your little girl, I'll give her a pat on the tush from you."

He hung up. Barely a minute later, Sarah Abelli returned to the Great Lost Bear. That was smart of her, I thought. Her immediate reaction might have been to call me, but she hadn't.

"Did you hear all that?" she said.

"Every word, and I have a recording of the call in case this ever gets to a court of law."

"We never discussed what I was supposed to say—you know, whether I should draw them out, or try to get information from them."

"Because I didn't want you to do either of those things. If you did, you'd have given us both away."

"That doesn't sound like you think very much of me."

"Not true," I said. "I wanted you to act naturally, or as naturally as possible, under that kind of pressure, because then the caller would do the same. He did, and we now know a little more about him. He's from the South, but probably first-generation American; he's mature; and he's a misogynist. He was also out at your place not so long ago. I'll need the names and phone numbers of your neighbors on the road, on the off chance that one of them might have noticed the car and its occupants."

"I can make those calls. You have enough to be getting along with."

"Okay. Finally, you were also clever enough not to use your phone when you were done, but instead to come back in here and speak to me in person. I don't have any doubts about your intelligence, Ms. Abelli."

Suddenly, her phone rang once, as did mine: FlexiSPY again, the call coming from a concealed number. It didn't ring a second time.

"It's what I would have done," she said. "If the number was engaged when I called back, I'd figure that the contents of the conversation were being relayed to a third party, and I was being set up."

"Did that come from being married to a mobster?"

"No," she said, "it came from being married to a man who was compulsively unfaithful."

I played back the conversation in my mind, circling those five seconds of silence.

"When he asked you about your daughter, and whether you felt her near—" I began.

"Don't you feel your daughter near," she said, "the one who died?"

I didn't reply. This wasn't a conversation I wanted to have with a stranger, or with anyone. Sarah's face was a mask as she watched me, but I saw that pain had clustered in her eyes, her grief as sharp as shards of glass. I could not have said how, beyond the experience offered by my own loss, but I believed I was looking at a woman who spoke to her dead child in the night, and heard something in the darkness answer back.

"Go home, Ms. Abelli," I said. "I'll do my best for you and your daughter."

She nodded once, and I wondered if she understood me at least as well as I did her. I considered warning her against antagonizing the men with whom we were dealing, but decided she'd already learned that lesson, and it would make no difference anyway. At least one of them already hated her, if not for who she was, then for her sex. I didn't tell her that I was now convinced they would cheat her. That suspicion had already begun hardening inside her before she ever came to see me.

If the opportunity presented itself, I thought, it might be pleasurable to hurt them.

XIII

Pantuff and Veale sat in their car outside the Goodwill store at the Falmouth Shopping Center, watching a bum push a cart filled with his possessions. The bum moved with a sense of mission, his back straight, his head erect, and a surgical mask dangling from one ear. Pantuff felt a peculiar sense of resentment toward him.

Pantuff had not spoken since ending the call with the Sawyer woman. Veale could tell that he was thinking hard, and had elected not to disturb him.

At last Pantuff said, "I think she's been talking to someone about us."

———

PAULIE FULCI STAYED WITH Sarah Abelli's car as she headed up to Freeport. He kept an eye out for a late nineties blue Chrysler LHS, which meant that he reacted to any blue vehicles he saw along the way. It made the ride tense, and not a little challenging, but he enjoyed having a purpose, even if he prayed that none of his acquaintances spotted him behind the wheel of the Kia. It was also a tight fit for him, and he was starting to feel claustrophobic. He didn't know anything about the woman he was following, or why he was following her. He knew only that she'd turned to the private detective for help, and that help had been given, which was enough for him.

Paulie didn't follow her all the way to her home, but stopped by the Freeport Medical Center and let her proceed up Durham Road alone. His brother had called to say that he had her car in sight so Paulie could be sure she was safe. He killed the engine and tried to make himself comfortable. Tony called him a second time to say that the woman was now inside and all was okay. Paulie's mother had left an audiobook of a Bill Loehfelm novel in the car, so he put that on to pass the time. Paulie had never been to Staten Island, where the novel was set. Pretty soon into the audiobook he was thinking that, if he ever did visit, he'd bring a gun.

XIV

I spoke briefly to Tony Fulci when he called to confirm that Sarah Abelli was back under her own roof. Earlier he had made a brief recce on the woods by Merrill Brook, as instructed, but had seen no one acting strangely, and found no location that would have permitted an unrestricted view of the Abelli house without drawing attention to the watcher. He had also approached some of the people using the nearby trails who, once they'd recovered from the shock, informed him they hadn't noticed anything out of the ordinary, although I suspected they had the good sense not to add that at least they hadn't until Tony showed up. Meanwhile, Sarah had been calling her neighbors to ask if they'd spotted a blue car on the road that morning, or anyone acting suspiciously near her property, but so far no one had seen anything worth mentioning.

As I hung up on Tony, Dave Evans appeared once again on the horizon, looking like a servant who was regularly being forced to impart bad news to the king and was growing weary of the whole exercise.

"You really need to get an office," he said. "Or a hotel room, given the number of women currently asking after you. There's another one at the host's station. She says her name is Marjorie Thombs, and she, like all the rest, has been leaving messages you haven't answered."

I was tempted to ask Dave to lie on my behalf, enabling me to slip out the back door. I'd already informed Marjorie Thombs once that I didn't think I could be of much assistance to her. She'd been disappointed, but had taken the news reasonably well. She and I had been at Scarborough High together, although we hadn't moved in the same circles. She had never been unkind, just distant. She was good-looking, popular, and graduated in the top 10 percent of the class, meaning she got her name in the *Press Herald* and made her parents proud. Upon those less fortunate than herself she had bestowed occasional smiles like gold coins from the hands of royalty.

Since I'd never gone to a high school reunion, any knowledge I obtained about SH alumni came from chance encounters or obituary columns. I'd lost track of Marjorie Thombs until she reached out to me in the summer of the previous year. Marjorie had married too young, raised a kid, got divorced, ditched her office job at MaineHealth, and trained to be a psychotherapist, specializing in families and troubled couples. Unfortunately, Melissa, her only child, was intent on being a bad advertisement for her mother's business. She'd taken up with a guy named Donnie Packard, who for years had been a fixture in the local police logs for the kind of apprentice work that promised more serious offending at a later date: OUIs, operating while license suspended or revoked; unlawful possession of a scheduled drug; and criminal mischief. His record, therefore, consisted of transgressions likely to earn him a fine or ten days in the county jail, and a label as an irritant to society in general, and the police in particular. Lately, though, and as anticipated, I'd noticed Donnie upping the ante with unlawful sexual contact and domestic violence, the latter almost certainly involving his girlfriend, Melissa. Marjorie Thombs would obviously have preferred her daughter to find someone better, which wouldn't have been too difficult, but Melissa appeared either unable or unwilling to extract herself from the train wreck that was her relationship with Donnie Packard.

I'd tried talking with the daughter as a favor to the mother, but the conversation had lasted about as long as it took Melissa to tell me to mind my own business, which wasn't long at all since she'd only had to use two words. I returned to Marjorie to notify her that I'd already exhausted all my options, since engaging with Packard would be as pointless as discussing morals with a shark. It wasn't a tangle in which I cared to involve myself any further. People had to be free to make bad choices, and it was possible that Melissa Thombs actually loved Donnie Packard, in which case beating the shit out of him in an effort to encourage him to seek pastures new—as Marjorie Thombs had suggested, in a roundabout way—would only compound an already unfortunate situation. I gave Marjorie the names of a couple of people who might be of more help to her daughter, if she could be made to see some sense, including Molly Bow at the Tender House women's shelter up in Bangor, then walked away from the whole affair. I experienced a twinge of guilt, but I'd learned long ago that walking away was often the next-to-worst option, the worst being not walking away.

"What the hell, I'll talk to her," I told Dave. "But after this, I'm gone, and I don't care if Jesus himself comes asking after me."

My priority now was Sarah Abelli. Anything else was a distraction I didn't want and wouldn't countenance.

From a distance, Marjorie Thombs looked as fresh and elegant as I remembered, because she'd always been destined to age gracefully. Up close, though, it was obvious she hadn't been sleeping as well as she should, and there were lines on her face that I couldn't recall from last year—dry now, like old riverbeds, but cut by anguish.

I hadn't even managed to speak before she opened her mouth.

"He's going to kill her," she said, and she started to cry.

CHAPTER

XV

Bobby Wadlin was beginning to suspect that everyone in the Braycott was going crazy, and was intent on dragging him down with them. The Vietnamese women whom he paid in cash to work as housekeepers had reported that they'd found no trace of a child in the rooms they'd cleaned, although they hadn't gone into any room on which a DO NOT DISTURB sign was hung. There were three of these, they said. One was room 11, currently home to a drunk named Max Sapon, and Bobby didn't think that old Max was a candidate for having a kid anywhere near him, not unless the kid was 50 percent alcohol. The room would have to be checked regardless, for fear that Max had accidentally mistaken a kid for a bottle of Admiral Nelson's Spiced Rum and brought it back to kick-start his day. Max Sapon rarely surfaced to awareness before noon, so Bobby instructed one of the housekeepers to ignore the DO NOT DISTURB sign, hold her nose to ensure the fumes didn't get to her, and take a quick look around while Max was still too far gone to know any better.

The second room with a sign on the door was 38, in which a couple named the Sussmans was staying. They'd checked in for a few days to attend a funeral, and were so old that it would hardly be worth their while leaving the cemetery afterward. Bobby guessed they were afraid to move from their accommodation unless it was absolutely necessary, and might have pushed the furniture up against the door as well, because better safe than sorry. They were up there now, pissing their britches at the sound of approaching footsteps, but Bobby thought that if he called the room and told them he needed to fix something, they'd let him in. Mind you, if they were willing to let him in, they didn't have anything to hide, including a child.

Which left the final room, 29, the one occupied by Lyle Pantuff and Gilman Veale. Bobby knew that the Pantuffs and Veales of this world didn't put a DO NOT DISTURB sign on their door and not mean it, and would be sure to take it amiss were someone to ignore it. Then again, what they didn't know couldn't hurt them, and while what passed for Bobby Wadlin's conscience was barely a flicker in the void of his soul, it did allow for some small protective instinct when it came to children, one that now also extended to himself. If it turned out that Pantuff and Veale did in fact have a child in their room, and that child was there under duress—which was more than plausible, Pantuff and Veale not striking Bobby as the paternal or avuncular types—then the ramifications might be severe for the Braycott. Should Bobby be discovered to have ignored claims that a child was on the premises, and the child came to some harm, he'd be tied up with lawyers until doomsday.

Esther Vogt had returned to her quarters, and Phil Hardiman had gone off on urgent narcotic business, although not before reminding Bobby that the Vogt woman's contribution to the debate might have clinched the deal on his requested discount. Very reluctantly, Bobby once again opened the door separating his desk and apartment from the rest of his kingdom, removed his key chain from his belt, and locked the front entrance. He then placed a handwritten sign against the glass, indicating that the desk would be unattended for a short time and advising anyone waiting to enter, or claim their room key, to have some "patiens."

One of the housekeepers, Thi, returned to say that Max Sapon was still lost to the world, and his room contained no children, empty bottles not counting as offspring. Bobby then called the Sussmans and asked if it would be okay for one of his staff to enter their room in order to check for a possible leak. They didn't sound enthused by the prospect, so Bobby threw in an offer of some complimentary cookies and a bag of potato chips, and they acquiesced. Bobby and Thi went upstairs, and Bobby waited by the Sussmans' room while Thi performed a search on the pretext of examining the pipes. He was really hoping that the Sussmans had smuggled a grandchild in with them because then he could have avoided entering room 29. Much to Bobby's disgust, God didn't elect to smile on him, or was otherwise occupied, because the Sussmans hadn't even unpacked their suitcase, and the bed was barely used. Thi told Bobby that she thought they might have slept on the comforter. If they had, Bobby hoped they'd done so fully clothed, because the comforters got laundered only every couple of months. He shuddered to think what might have shown up on one of them under UV light.

With nothing else for it, he ordered Thi to get back to cleaning, and to make sure that she stayed away from the lobby. The last thing he wanted was for Pantuff and Veale to return to the Braycott, demand entry, and return to their room while Bobby was still inside. That would not end well for him.

Then, like a condemned man ascending the scaffold, he made his way to room 29.

CHAPTER

XVI

I didn't ask Dave to bring coffee for Marjorie Thombs, or even a glass of water, but sat her down and took the time to listen to what she had to say. According to her testimony, Donnie Packard's disposition had deteriorated considerably in recent weeks, as had his behavior toward his girlfriend. If he'd left bruises in the past, he'd made sure they were in places where they wouldn't be seen, but now Melissa Thombs was sporting marks on her face and arms—or had been when last her mother saw her, because Packard was also discouraging Melissa from meeting her mother, or anyone else. Only considerable perseverance had enabled Marjorie to gain access to her daughter, and then just briefly. Packard had even taken to confiscating Melissa's phone to ensure she couldn't make or receive calls on the sly, and when her mother did manage to speak with her, Packard listened in on their conversations. Melissa had succeeded in calling her mother a couple of times from pay phones, but their exchanges were inevitably hurried, and it was hard for Marjorie to get her to open up. All Marjorie could say for sure was that Packard's current drug of choice was Spice, or synthetic marijuana; he was doing as much of it as he could afford, and at the highest potency. And while Melissa, she thought, was finally coming around to the idea that Donnie Packard might not be a keeper, he had now made her a virtual prisoner in their home, so her opinion was incidental.

Despite its name, synthetic marijuana is unrelated to marijuana itself, and its effects are completely different. Even relatively low-strength Spice heightens anxiety, and stronger doses induce paranoia and psychosis. If Donnie Packard was doing as much of it as Marjorie Thombs claimed, he stood a good chance of killing himself. More unhappily, he might end up taking his girlfriend with him.

"She wants to leave," Marjorie said. "She told me so when we last spoke, but she's frightened of what he'll do to her if she tries and fails. And even if she does get away, she's convinced he'll come after her. Now we're being advised to remain at home because of this virus, but she can't stay locked up with him for however long it lasts. She just can't."

"Have you spoken to the police?" I said.

"I tried, but there was nothing they could do. They went to the house, but Melissa assured them she was okay. A woman officer went into a room alone with her while the other cop stayed outside with Donnie, just so Melissa could speak without fear of him overhearing, but she stuck to her story. Sometimes I think that, while she wants to get away from him, she still cares enough not to want to see him get into any more trouble with the law."

It wasn't the first time I'd heard a variation on that tale, and I was certain it wouldn't be the last. Whatever her reasons for remaining, they wouldn't stop Melissa Thombs from being dragged down into the depths by her boyfriend, there to drown alongside him. Donnie Packard's reputation revolved around various synonyms of the word "mean." I'd passed him in courthouses and bars, and once watched him being arrested on Fore Street after he'd tangled with a doorman and come off worse. Nothing about him had ever impressed me, but dealing with him would still require a degree of caution. He'd always been undisciplined and unpredictable; addiction would only have made him more so.

I realized I was already approaching this as though I'd taken on the case. It seemed that I couldn't even trust myself.

"Do you know if Donnie has a gun?" I asked.

Packard's conviction for domestic violence, dating back to the previous August, meant he was prohibited from owning firearms or ammunition under the Lautenberg Amendment.

"I asked Melissa, but she wouldn't say."

"Which means he does," I said, "and is ignoring the ban." Criminals: at least when they broke a law, it wasn't out of character.

Marjorie Thombs stared down at the handkerchief in her hands. It was white, made of cloth decorated with red roses, and looked like it had been stolen from the heroine of a Harlequin romance.

"I don't know what to do, Mr. Parker," she said. "I just don't."

It felt odd to have her address me so formally, but then she was approaching me out of desperation. She was a supplicant, and all supplicants bend the knee, yet I wished she'd never come here to lay the burden of her familial misery on the table between us. Intervening in a domestic dispute always involved a very particular order of hazard, but this one sounded as though some form of violence would be unavoidable. To begin with I was on thin ice, legally speaking, and had no right to enter a dwelling uninvited, even if it was to help a woman suspected of enduring psychological and physical abuse. Of course, I might arrive at the house to find Melissa Thombs alone, her bags packed and a one-way ticket to Anywhere But Here already bought and paid for, in which case I'd stop off to buy us both a scratch card before dropping her at the bus station. More plausibly, Donnie Packard would be with her when I arrived, and would naturally object to someone coming onto his property in an effort to deprive him of his chattel. Finally, as I recalled from my time in uniform, even a woman filled with fear and hatred for her partner was capable of baring her claws to protect him if she saw force being required to subdue him.

And yet I couldn't turn away from this, no more than I could have turned my back on Sarah Abelli's pain. I dearly wanted to, but I couldn't.

"I'll see what I can do," I said, and the tension went out of Marjorie Thombs so quickly that her forehead was in danger of hitting the table.

"Thank you," she said, and started to cry again, but we didn't have time for that.

"I need you to contact Melissa," I said. "If we can do this with her cooperation, it'll be easier for everyone involved. But I have to warn you, I have another case that's going to take up most of my immediate time and attention. I can't promise that I'll get your daughter out today. I'll try, though."

"That's enough for me. What do you want from Melissa?"

"First of all, are they living in an apartment or a house?"

"A house: what used to be Donnie's mom's place up in Yarmouth. She left it to him in her will. It's a hovel, which is the only reason he hasn't sold it. Well, that and Melissa as the voice of sanity, because she knows that if he sells the house, they'll be out on the street, what with Donnie's habit and all."

"Does it have a yard?"

"Yes."

"Where do they keep the garbage cans?"

She looked thrown.

"Out front, I think, under an old tree."

"Okay," I said, "it would be best if I had a direct line of communication with Melissa, because it may be that we'll have to do this fast, and without a whole lot of notice. I'm going to arrange to have a phone dropped behind those garbage cans"—I glanced at my watch—"by six, or seven at the latest. I'd ask you to do it, but I'm worried Donnie might see you. You'll just have to find a way to let Melissa know the phone will be there. She needs to pick it up, mute it, and find somewhere to hide it. Once night falls, I want her to keep it on her person. It'll be as small a model as we can find, and there'll be a text message on it with instructions for how we're going to handle her escape. When she feels it vibrate, that'll be the sign we're ready for her. She can tell Donnie that she has to throw out trash, or get some air, whatever it takes. Then all she has to do is run to the car and we'll drive her away. She'll have to leave all her possessions behind, but we can retrieve them later."

"You make it sound so simple."

"I'm trying to be optimistic, because if she can't leave we'll have to go get her, and that will be messier. If she hasn't appeared within ten minutes of that first contact, the phone will vibrate again. We'll have someone at the back door and someone at the front. She has to get to one of those doors and open it. That'll cover us legally because it can be argued that we were invited to enter, even if Packard decides to kick up later, although my guess is he won't, not if he's holding Spice and an illegal weapon. So that's the second-best course of action."

"Which leaves?" said Marjorie Thombs.

"The third of four, on a very sharp sliding scale. Melissa knows we're waiting, but she can't reach the door, and we have to force our way inside. Now the likelihood of someone getting hurt has increased considerably, and I'd prefer to avoid that for all our sakes."

"And the final recourse?"

That was one I really didn't want to contemplate, but it would have to be anticipated.

"You fail to get in touch with Melissa, she has no idea what's being planned, and we have to decide whether or not to go in cold. I'd be very reluctant to do that, because now someone is certain to get hurt."

"Possibly including my daughter."

"Yes."

Marjorie considered this.

"Well, then," she said, "I'd better be sure to contact Melissa."

"That would be a big help," I said, with admirable understatement.

Of course, I hadn't really shared the worst outcome with her, because that would only have added to her worries. What if we managed to enter the house only to discover that Melissa Thombs had changed her mind about leaving, and suddenly we were faced not with one hostile actor but two? At least I wouldn't be alone. Misery loves company, and I knew just the companions.

XVII

B obby Wadlin knocked on the door of room 29 before entering. Even though the registered occupants were, he was certain, elsewhere, one couldn't be too careful. Bobby had learned that lesson way back, when he'd walked into what he assumed was an empty room at the Braycott, the guests having already checked out, only to discover three naked elderly people, on whom he'd never before set eyes, engaged in an act of sexual congress so bizarre that it continued to haunt his dreams a decade later.

Nobody answered Bobby's knock at 29, though, and he could hear no sounds from inside. He made sure the hallway was empty before inserting his key in the lock and opening the door.

"Hello?" he said, but there was no reply. Bobby slipped inside and closed the door behind him. The room smelled musty, but then all the rooms in the Braycott smelled musty, except for the ones that smelled of something worse than mustiness, thanks to their occupants. The drapes were partly drawn, permitting Bobby to see without having to turn on the main light. The twin beds were made, and two overnight bags lay open on the floor. Both were packed, the clothes inside neatly folded.

He took a look in the bathroom and saw that it was empty. All the towels had been used, but that was hardly surprising, the Braycott's towels being rough, thin, and pretty much unfit for purpose, unless that purpose was sanding a wall. Those staying at the inn for any length of time, or with previous experience of its hospitality, typically ended up supplying their own. Bobby then checked under the beds and in the closet, but found only dust. It was obvious to him that room 29 did not contain a child, or anything that might be associated with one: no toys, no diapers, no mess. Whatever else Pantuff and Veale might be hiding—and Bobby was in no doubt that they were hiding something, because everybody at the Braycott had something to hide—it wasn't a kid. Yet Phil Hardiman and Esther Vogt claimed to have heard a child, and unless they were more committed than most to the conspiracy to drive Bobby Wadlin mad, or were both independently crazy in the same way, there was a child somewhere on the premises. It was baffling.

Poking his nose around the Braycott's occupied accommodations, even those with DO NOT DISTURB signs on the doors, didn't bother Bobby Wadlin: this was his hotel, and if anything, the guests were the intruders, not he. During his years in charge he'd seen everything in these rooms—drugs, weapons, sex dolls, dead bodies—and had kept his mouth shut about most of it, the bodies excepted. It paid to be discreet, especially when a significant proportion of one's guests had criminal records, and demonstrated an admirable commitment to adding to them. But Bobby really didn't want to dawdle in 29, because he felt as though he were leaving traces of himself—scents, skin cells, stray hairs—that Pantuff and Veale might detect and follow back to their source.

His hand was reaching for the door handle when he noticed the spare blankets at the bottom of the closet. Every room had the same pair, and they occupied the same space, but these appeared fuller than the norm. Bobby squatted, poked a finger at them, and struck a hard object. He unfolded the blankets to reveal a vintage Sunshine Toy Cookie tin in red, gold, and greenish blue ("Joy Cookies for Kiddies Cut in Toy Shapes"). This one, Bobby thought, must have dated from the fifties, and might have passed for an antique among people who didn't know any better. He picked it up, shook it gently, and heard a sound that didn't come from cookies.

Bobby eased off the lid and peered inside, moving the contents around so that he could see them more clearly. The box held a child's wrist rattle, a pacifier, a tiny pair of scuffed pink shoes, a white rabbit about the size of his clenched fist, plaster casts of small hands and feet, a silver box containing a single baby tooth, and an envelope. Bobby opened the envelope and flicked through the photos it contained: perhaps two dozen in all, a record of the development of a little girl. In some of the photographs she was with a woman, probably her mother, but there was no sign of a father. Bobby didn't set any particular store by this. Often the simplest explanation was the right one, and someone had to hold the camera. If not the father, then who else? He checked the backs of the pictures, but there were no names or dates, nothing to offer a clue as to who the woman and child might be.

Bobby restored the items to the cookie tin, and replaced it exactly as he'd found it, the blankets along with it. He used the peephole to make sure the hallway was clear before leaving the room, closing the door securely behind him. He then returned to the front desk, where two long-term guests, the Huffs, were peering unhappily into the lobby from outside. Bobby let them in, offered what might have passed for an apology as long as nobody examined it too closely, and retreated to his lair. There he made himself a cup of coffee with a shot of brandy to calm his nerves, and thought about what he'd found in room 29.

He was now even more perplexed than before. The objects in the cookie tin were not the possessions of a child, but those of a parent. While Bobby might not have wished either Pantuff or Veale as a father on even the worst kid in the world, it was not beyond the bounds of possibility that one of them had sired a daughter and retained enough affection for her to keep with him some remembrances of her childhood. But if Phil Hardiman and Esther Vogt were correct, a female child had been heard running around the Braycott the night before. The only evidence suggesting the existence of such a child lay in room 29, but did not extend to food, clothing, or the girl herself. It really was most peculiar, and so preoccupied was Bobby by this mystery that even the prospect of a western did not distract him from it for almost an hour.

XVIII

E sther Vogt was seventy-six years old, but remained physically and mentally acute, and believed she might even have grown more so since her husband's death, Adolf Vogt having been a quiet, somewhat indolent man with the intellectual curiosity of a piece of whitebait. Esther had loved him in her way—not deeply, and with a certain practicality that only occasionally extended to obvious affection—but his death had not impacted greatly on the level of social and intellectual discourse in her life. Like many widowed women of her acquaintance, bereavement had caused her to reexamine her priorities, and her attitude to the years remaining to her. She became a Friend of the Portland Public Library, joined a dining club, became an accomplished candlepin bowler, and even took to entertaining—and being entertained by— the occasional handsome older gentleman, because no one ever died believing they should have enjoyed less sex. Some of her new friends had pressed her to seek alternative accommodation in one of their retirement communities, but Esther liked the Braycott. It had an edge to it, and a lot of personality, and she had spent far too many years in a marriage with no edge or personality whatsoever.

Of course, the Braycott had its downsides, not least its manager, Bobby Wadlin. Esther considered him a fool, but a sly fool, and one whom it was better not to antagonize. She knew he didn't like her, but she regarded him as being predisposed against liking anyone at all, Abigail Stackpole excepted, and then only because Abigail had slept with him once or twice without throwing up immediately after. Esther knew Abigail a little from their shared aqua aerobics sessions, and it seemed as though she had some kind of genuine affection for Bobby Wadlin, baffling though that might appear to anyone else. Then again, as Esther's best pal, Rosemary, liked to point out, Abigail Stackpole was hardly beating off suitors with a stick and therefore had to take her pleasures as they came.

So Esther Vogt stayed on the right side of Bobby Wadlin even as, behind his back, she grew more and more familiar with the ways of the Braycott. Thanks to Abigail Stackpole's carelessness, Esther had contrived to have made for herself copies of the keys to the front and back doors, as well as the storage closets and the basement. The former didn't contain a great deal worth taking, although the liquid soap was of a surprisingly high quality—Wadlin, she figured, must be getting it from the back of a truck, because he certainly wasn't paying market price—but the basement was a treasure trove, one with which even Bobby Wadlin was not intimately familiar as it was so full. Esther had grown accomplished at sneaking items from it up to her two-room apartment: rugs, pictures, lamps, even one very comfortable armchair, although she'd barely managed to get it into the elevator unaided, and had spent the trip between floors fretting in case Wadlin should choose that moment to make one of his rare forays into the environs beyond his desk. If the housekeepers noticed the enhancements to the standard décor, they either elected not to comment or just assumed that crazy old Esther was ransacking thrift stores in order to individualize her quarters, their silence guaranteed by the regular weekly tip Esther left in an envelope on her pillow. She'd even been tempted to sell one or two of the basement items, including an art deco mirror she was convinced might be worth a couple hundred dollars, but that would have been stealing, and Esther Vogt was a borrower, not a thief.

Now she had returned to the lower regions of the Braycott because she'd managed to spill ink on one of the rugs—Esther still wrote with a fountain pen, like a civilized human being—and didn't trust the housekeepers not to bring the stain to their employer's attention, tip or no tip. It wasn't a very handsome rug anyway, and had looked a lot better in the basement than in her room, even with the lights turned low. She was sure the maroon imitation Persian that she'd spotted during her last visit would work much better.

Entering the basement, Esther noticed that someone else had been down there recently. She could see marks in the dust where some of the furniture had been moved, and a small bathroom mirror with a painted frame lay broken on the floor, fragments of the glass catching the light from the hall bulb. It was unlike Wadlin to leave glass on the floor, she thought, and the housekeepers knew better than to make a mess and not clear it up, especially as Wadlin might dock their pay just to teach them the necessity of respecting another person's property. She decided to come back later with a brush and pan to take care of it. She didn't want Wadlin to take it into his head to change the lock.

Esther reached by instinct for the light switch, but nothing happened. She tried flicking it a couple of times—because that was what you did when a light didn't work, and you didn't have to be an electrician to know it—but the room remained dark. Here, then, was a problem. It wasn't as though she had a replacement bulb at hand, and even if she had, she'd still need a ladder to change the busted one. Neither could she exactly go to Bobby Wadlin and inform him that the basement required a new light bulb so she could appropriate one of his rugs to replace another soiled by her.

At least she had her cell phone in her pocket. The flashlight wasn't great, but it would suffice. Once she'd switched the rugs, she'd have to live with her current furnishings, at least until Wadlin got around to changing the bulb himself. She sidestepped the broken glass and went looking for the maroon rug. When last she'd seen it, it had been standing rolled by the far wall. She shone the flashlight in that direction and it caught the rug just where she remembered it, between a squat mahogany dresser with a decorative floral pattern and a four-drawer chest that she wouldn't have permitted to be placed in her room even had someone paid her to accept it, so ugly was it.

Esther began making her way carefully through the furniture and bric-a-brac, managing to avoid barking her shin more than once, although since this was against a cast-iron umbrella stand, it hurt. A lot. She reached the rug and tested the weight. It was heavier than it looked, but she decided she could just about manage it using both arms, with the cell phone held in her right hand to light her route back to the door while bearing in mind where that umbrella stand lay in wait. The rug smelled mildewy, but baking soda would sort that right out. Nearby she spotted a floor lamp she thought might serve nicely as a reading light, but it would have to wait. To be honest, her rooms were becoming cluttered. If she persisted in adding to them, a time would come when her unit began to resemble the basement itself.

As she started to make her way out, she reflected that it was a pity this space had been reduced to a storage facility. It maintained traces of decoration from its former incarnation as a bar: orange fleurs-de-lis patterns here, patches of red flock wallpaper there, and a couple of old taps lying on top of a dusty beer barrel. A section of brass foot-rail ran along one of the walls; why Wadlin hadn't sold it, she didn't know. A 1940s Four Roses Bourbon clock, its hands stopped at 5:30 and its numbers now faded from gold to black, hung above the shadow of shelves that had probably once held bottles. Esther could imagine music playing and people dancing, even during Prohibition, safe in the knowledge that the thick walls, combined with whatever bribes had been paid, would ensure the party could continue without fear of interruption by the police.

And if they did come, there was always the tunnel. Its entrance was still visible, a cave-like opening that had once been hidden behind paneling. It had long since been blocked up, but only four or five feet into the tunnel itself, creating an alcove that could be used for more storage. It remained dark, though, even when the basement light was on. The position and angle rendered it unfavorable to illumination, so whatever was stored in there was set to remain undisturbed since it couldn't properly be identified. While the basement was cool, the area around the old tunnel mouth was cooler still, and in winter one could feel chill air coming from it. Esther guessed that, in common with every other job in the Braycott, its closure had been completed cheaply and imperfectly, and the materials used had begun to crack and decay. The rats had probably found a way through, because there were rodents down here. She'd seen and heard them, but their presence didn't bother her as long as they didn't go running across her feet. Esther, a lifelong vegetarian, believed they had as much right to be there as she did—more, even, as she wasn't supposed to be in the basement at all, while rats were accepted, however reluctantly, to be part of the lifeblood of old places. God alone knew what they fed on, she thought. She supposed a rat would eat just about anything. Bugs, mice, other rats . . .

One of them was scuffling around in the tunnel right now. She could hear the ticking of its claws against the stone. It was big, too, by the sounds of it.

And then the rat laughed.

XIX

I arrived at Angel and Louis's apartment shortly before 1 p.m. Louis answered the door and told me that Angel was lying down.

"Is he ill?" I said. Angel's health remained a matter of constant concern for both Louis and me, despite the most recent all-clear. Angel also remained prone to tiredness, as well as periods of deep depression. But in common with a certain type of invalid, he hated being asked about his health or having it remarked upon, and so we watched him while pretending not to watch, and worried for him in silence.

"He's hungover," said Louis. "He drank a few bottles of some ale called Dinner last night, and woke up this morning looking like he'd been hit by a train, or possibly two, both heavily loaded with alcohol."

I was impressed, albeit in the way one might be by a rank amateur who had decided to go a couple of rounds with the champ. Dinner came from the Maine Beer Company in Freeport, and was an Imperial IPA, which was basically an IPA that had been put on a course of steroids. I seemed to recall that it was more than 8 percent ABV, and felled grown men the way lumberjacks felled trees.

"Where is he?"

"On the couch, dying."

I entered the living room to find the patient as described.

"Put me out of my misery," Angel whispered.

"Any last words?" I said.

"None that I'd want to be remembered by."

He managed to open one eye.

"My world is coming to an end," he said. "I consider it a mercy killing."

"I need your help," I said.

He closed the eye again.

"I had a terrible feeling," he said, "that you were going to say something along those lines . . ."

————

ANGEL MANAGED TO DRAG himself to the kitchen table. Louis cooked up some bacon and eggs, which Angel kept down, along with a couple of glasses of water, a handful of ibuprofen, and a concoction that combined two types of ginseng, ginger, brown sugar, and borage oil. I was conscious that time was limited, but I cared too much about Angel to force him to face the day without a fighting chance. At the end of it all, he admitted to feeling better, if only because the chances of feeling worse were relatively slim. By then I had brought them up to speed on Melissa Thombs and Sarah Abelli.

"So," said Louis, "Nate Sawyer's widow. Do you pick your clients solely on the basis of how many people would like to see them dead, or do you also take into account their ability to pay?"

"I don't think the Office wants Sarah Abelli dead," I said.

"Only because she can't pay up if she's a corpse," said Angel.

"She says she doesn't have the money her husband stole."

"And you believe her?"

"For now. She wants those relics of her child returned to her. I think that if she had the money, she'd pay the asking price for them. But she's right to be skeptical about the likelihood of getting those possessions back, whether she ponies up or not. The Office may not be set on making a corpse of her, but they'd be happy to see her suffer for her husband's failings."

"Assuming the Office is involved," said Louis.

"Which is what I need to find out before this turns any nastier."

"I hate Providence," said Louis. "Always have, even before the business with Mother."

"Any news on that front?" I asked.

"From what I hear, she never leaves that big old house of hers, and her people have deserted her. Someday someone will come by and find her dried husk curled up in a corner. They can just set fire to it, save the cost of a funeral."

"One might say that we did the Office a favor by involving ourselves in her life," I said.

"That's one way of looking at it. I'm not sure the Office balances its books that way."

"Looks like this is a chance to find out."

Louis finished his coffee and swirled the grounds in the dregs.

"Boston is still in transition after what happened with Sawyer," he said. "Last I heard, the Office had appointed a guy named Dante Vero as its interim boss in the Northeast, but he won't last. He didn't want the job to begin with, but he wasn't given a lot of choice in the matter. Dante is one of life's backroom boys. He's a family man, solid but cautious. He doesn't make the papers, doesn't take unnecessary risks, and doesn't have a reputation for violence. Dante's the guy they send in before they send in the other guy."

"Like Luca, the one who threatened Sarah Abelli with digging up her daughter's corpse?"

"Exhumation isn't Dante's style. It's interesting that she says someone stepped in just as soon as her kidnappers were about to progress to rape. To me, that sounds like something Dante would do. He's no pushover, and the Office still took her house, but watching a woman being sexually tortured wouldn't sit easily with him."

"Will he talk to me?" I said.

"He's a hard man to get to directly. He doesn't use phones: not cell phones, not landlines, nothing. He's a throwback to another age, and what happened with Sawyer has only made him more set in his ways, but that's one of the reasons why he's never done serious time. I know some people down there, as do you, but nobody from Dante's circle, if you'll forgive the pun. If there's a clock ticking, and you need a straight answer, it would be better to find a more direct route to him."

I thought about this.

"Moxie has been giving work to a man named Mattia Reggio," I said. "Driving, document pickups, that kind of thing. Reggio used to run with Cadillac Frank, although that was a long time ago. Moxie likes the idea of having a former hood on the books, and Reggio's reputation isn't far off Dante Vero's: the guy they sent before they sent in the other guy."

"Yet I detect hesitation on your part," said Angel slowly, and very, very carefully.

"Well, look who woke up," said Louis.

"I've been listening," said Angel. "I was just staying quiet until the swelling in my brain went down." He returned his attention to me. "Am I right about Reggio?"

"I don't deny that he's been respectable for years," I said, "and he's never let Moxie down, but I don't like him. No particular reason, just a feeling—well, except that he's always chewing gum, which he's been known to leave on dashboards and the underside of tables, including Moxie's. It's the weirdest thing, like a nervous tic, or a dog marking its territory."

"And, gum offenses aside, you don't want to be in his debt," said Louis.

"I'd prefer to keep him at one remove, that's all."

"You could go through Moxie," said Angel.

"No," I said, "if Reggio has to be asked, I'll do it."

"What about the other thing," said Louis, "the Thombs girl?"

"Once I know that Melissa has the cell phone, we can work on getting her out, even if it's late tonight. It would be better not to delay."

I took out my phone. I had Mattia Reggio's number stored in it at Moxie's request, although I'd never used it. Now, with time pressing, I called him.

CHAPTER

XX

For a moment Esther Vogt was convinced she'd misheard, and the sound from the tunnel was not, in fact, laughter but the tinkle of crystal disturbed by old Mr. Rat. Then it came again, clearer now, and she recalled the footsteps that had disturbed her rest the night before, just as they had woken Mr. Hardiman. She could tell that Bobby Wadlin hadn't believed them, even with their independent accounts, and she had to admit that it had seemed unlikely, even to her. After all, no responsible parent would bring a child into an establishment like the Braycott Arms, and even an irresponsible one might have thought twice about it. But it was possible that a kid could have sneaked in: a run-away seeking shelter, although the footsteps she'd heard were small and light, and runaways tended to be older kids. And what kind of runaway, having succeeded in gaining access to the Braycott, would then risk being apprehended by skipping along its corridors in the dead of night?

"Hello?" said Esther. "Is someone there?"

Which was a foolish question, because obviously someone *was* there, but it was the best Esther could come up with under the circumstances. She realized she was still holding the rug, and considered setting it aside in favor of something that might serve as a weapon, should one be required—although given that she was an arthritic woman in her late seventies, any such armament would be of limited usefulness.

She stood before the entrance to the tunnel and was surprised by how black it was. She couldn't recall it ever appearing so dark. It was as though whoever was hiding in its recesses had somehow wreathed themselves in gloom.

"I don't mean you any harm," said Esther. "I think I heard you in the hallway last night, and Mr. Wadlin, the manager, may be looking for you. He'll get to searching down here sooner or later, so you ought to be gone by then. He's not a very understanding man."

Even in the dimness, and with her poor eyesight, she thought she detected movement, shadow shifting over shadow like the swirling of dense smoke or the writhing of dusky snakes. It struck her, with a strange objectivity, that these were entirely negative comparisons, and ones not usually associated with a child, runaway or otherwise. She saw herself as she might have appeared to the presence in the tunnel: a vulnerable old woman, wearing slippers with her overcoat, leaning on a rolled-up rug for support.

"It's not good for you to be down here alone," she continued. "It's cold and damp in this basement, and there are rats and bugs. You don't want to get bitten."

The shape in the tunnel was now becoming more apparent to her. It was small, and she thought it might have been crouching on all fours, like a cat ready to pounce. The image caused Esther to take a step back, and it seemed that the shape moved forward in turn, so that what little light there was briefly caught what might have been a face before the presence receded again. It was a child, a little girl, probably not more than five or six years old.

Any thought of securing a weapon receded. She would have no need of it, not for a child so young. My God, Esther thought, how did she even get down here? Unless she'd somehow entered when the door had been left open, perhaps by Bobby Wadlin, and then found herself locked in when it was closed again. These old walls were thick, and it was possible that her cries for help might have gone unnoticed.

"Oh, honey," said Esther, "why don't you come upstairs with me? I'm sure I can get you safely to my room without us being seen. I have candy and cookies, and milk in the refrigerator. You can have something to eat and tell me all about whatever happened, and we'll set about finding your mom and dad. Because you do have a mom or a dad, right?"

The child made a sound, but whether of agreement or disputation Esther could not tell.

"And if you're really all alone," said Esther, "we'll look for someone who can help you. It'll be all right, I promise. What I do know is that you can't stay here."

Esther drew herself up to her full height of five two.

"I won't let you," she said firmly. "It's not right."

The child jumped, and the shock was so sudden that Esther barely had time to register its pale features, its lank hair, and the odd angle at which its head hung, before her heart exploded in her chest. She toppled to the floor, her consciousness consumed by a pain so overwhelming that it had weight and mass, and a gravity that was crushing the life from her.

"Boo!" said the child, as Esther Vogt died.

XXI

Mattia Reggio sounded surprised to hear from me, and then not overjoyed upon being told why I needed his help.

"A lot of the guys I knew are gone now," he said, and gum clacked loudly. "The ones that aren't dead are behind bars, and the ones that aren't dead or behind bars are trying to stay that way. It's all new faces, new names."

"Not all," I said.

He didn't answer. I let the silence hang.

"I worked out of Boston," he said at last. "Back then Providence took the lead, and we deferred to them. Now I think it's more Boston, but the Sawyer thing burned a lot of fingers, so maybe the chain has become fucked up."

"Did you know Dante Vero?"

"Yeah, I knew Dante, although I was closer to his uncle, Marco."

"Is Marco still around?"

"No, Marco died in Devens about ten years ago. Liver failure. Last time I saw Dante was at the funeral."

Devens, or FMC Devens, was a federal prison in Massachusetts that operated as a medical center for inmates with health problems, whether physical or psychological.

"Are you and Dante still on speaking terms?"

"I guess, within reason."

"I hear he has an aversion to phones," I said.

"Dante has an aversion to risk," said Reggio. "He doesn't open his mouth unless he has to."

"Even to you?"

"Even to me."

"How would you go about making an approach?"

"Marco's only sister, Elisa, is still alive, or was last time I asked. She never married, and wouldn't have left the old neighborhood. Dante is the kind of man who'd keep an eye on her, make sure she was doing okay. If anyone can get a message to Dante quickly, it's Elisa."

"If you could reach out to her, I'd appreciate it."

I heard Reggio exhale long and hard. I knew he didn't want to do it, and not only because no particular warmth existed between us. If the Office had targeted Nate Sawyer's widow, then Reggio's involvement with a man acting on her behalf, even if only as an intermediary, would earn him a black mark in someone's ledger.

"I'll make the call," he said, finally.

"Thank you."

"In return, I'd like to ask you something."

"Go ahead," I said.

"Maybe I'm speaking out of turn, but I get the feeling you don't like me. I never did anything to alienate you, yet you treat me like I got shit on my pants. I was wondering why that might be?"

I didn't try to deny it. It would have humiliated both of us.

"I don't know," I said, "but I'll think on it."

"You got some balls," said Reggio, and hung up the phone.

"Well?" said Louis.

"He'll do it."

"Is he happy about it?"

"Not so much."

"Are you?"

I stood to leave.

"Not so much, either," I said.

CHAPTER

XXII

antuff and Veale had been in the game for long enough to know that the hardest part of any job was the waiting period that preceded it. Keeping busy helped: going to a movie, playing pool, anything to remain distracted. Sleeping worked, too, if one could manage it. Younger, inexperienced guys struggled with that last one because they were so wired, but Pantuff, as previously noted, could sleep anywhere, and Veale had learned the value of at least closing his eyes and trying to relax. The plan, therefore, had been to return to the Braycott and kick back, but that was before Pantuff became worried that Nate Sawyer's widow might be laboring under the misapprehension of being a smart bitch.

This was a problem that needed to be addressed.

———

PANTUFF WAS GRINDING HIS teeth as he drove, which was what he did when under stress. He was grinding so hard that Veale expected him to begin spitting pieces of enamel before too long.

"The question," said Pantuff, "is to whom she's been talking."

That was how Pantuff spoke. He used formulations like "to whom" and "of whom," and even occasionally quoted lines from poetry and plays, although Veale had noticed that they were always the same lines, which led him to believe Pantuff probably didn't know more than a handful. Pantuff had spent a year at some midwestern liberal arts college before he was shown the door for unspecified transgressions. From what Veale knew of him, Pantuff's misconduct probably involved girls. Had he committed such acts now, he might have been arrested and charged, but back in the last century educational institutions had taken a more pragmatic approach to rapists and molesters. Reputation was everything. Well, institutional reputation was everything. A woman's reputation counted for considerably less. Actually, Veale thought, maybe things hadn't changed very much after all, not that it bothered him either way.

"Could be her sister or brother," said Veale, "or a friend. Someone close."

Not that Veale had any personal experience of this, being without siblings and virtually without friends, Pantuff excepted. But even if he was in trouble, he didn't think he'd ask Pantuff for help, not unless it was really bad trouble. He'd just sort it out himself by dealing with whoever was causing him difficulties—or was it "whomever"? Jesus, he was spending too much time in Pantuff's company—until they either stopped causing them or died, whichever came first.

"Or the cops," Veale added, "but you didn't think that was an option for her."

"It's always an option," said Pantuff, "but one she'd be reluctant to choose. As for friends, or the kind of friends that might concern us, she lost them when it was discovered that her husband had turned snitch."

"She might have made some new ones since then."

Pantuff ground his teeth again.

"No, not her, not with her past. She's reinvented herself. She may even have learned about human behavior from her time with her husband, even if only not to make the same mistake twice."

A shard of enamel came off a tooth at last, as Veale had anticipated. Pantuff plucked it from his tongue and held it up for his partner to see.

"Look at what she made me do," he said.

It was a big piece. Veale thought Pantuff might feel some pain the next time he drank something hot or cold. Pantuff flicked the fragment of tooth to the floor, and Veale could see him testing for a cavity with his tongue.

"There was always the chance she'd look for help," said Veale. "It's nothing we can't handle."

"True," said Pantuff, "but unknowns bother me, and I don't like that she doesn't trust us."

Veale considered this a little rich, given that they'd broken into her home, taken all she had left of her dead child, and were now planning to double-cross her. He kept this opinion to himself, along with the fact that the Sawyer woman's not trusting them made him respect her more.

Pantuff signaled left.

"Let's run the route one more time," he said.

So they did.

XXIII

I called Sharon Macy on my way to pick up a burner phone to be dropped at the house that Melissa Thombs shared with Donnie Packard. Macy and I continued to grow tentatively closer, ending what Louis had once described as the longest dry spell since that of the Chicago Cubs. Yet while we were drawing closer, we had, by unspoken mutual agreement, stopped short of calling it an actual relationship, or making it public. Some of this was natural wariness on both our parts, complicated on Macy's side by the inadvisability of letting it be known that a Portland PD detective with responsibility for liaising with other law enforcement agencies and the governor was sleeping with a private investigator who many of those same agencies—and parties in the governor's office—believed should be behind bars.

Oh, and complicated on my side by the fact that my deceased daughter apparently spoke to the living one, and she and some vestige of my dead wife continued to move through this world. This, though, Macy and I had not discussed. There were some conversations better left to another time, or preferably left altogether.

Macy answered on the second ring.

"The world is going mad," she said.

"The world was always mad. It just wasn't quite this frightening for most of us."

"If you're calling to propose to me before the end times, I can't guarantee you're going to be pleased with the answer."

"That's so ambiguous," I said, "that I think I'll leave the question unasked for now. How about we discuss Donnie Packard?"

"Jesus, I don't want to marry Donnie Packard. If that's the choice, I guess you'll have to do."

"I'll get started on my wedding speech," I said, "once I've stopped choking up. In the meantime, Donnie is living with a woman named Melissa Thombs, except she doesn't want to live with him anymore, or so her mother claims. But Donnie is the possessive type, and is reluctant to let her leave—again, according to her mother."

"Let me guess: Melissa Thombs doesn't want to turn to the police."

"There have been police interventions in the past, and Donnie has a domestic violence conviction because of one of them, yet she's stayed. I don't profess to understand why. The situation now appears to have worsened, but not so much that she wants the police involved again."

"Are you going to try to get her out?"

"That's the idea, but preferably quietly, and without Donnie realizing until she's already good and gone."

"Where are they living?"

"Donnie's mom's old place in Yarmouth."

"The mother's deceased, right?"

"Died of shame. It happens."

"If his name is on the deed to the house, you'll have problems with criminal trespass. And if you go in there armed, a prosecutor could hang you out to dry."

"Like I said, we're hoping to avoid entering the property. If forced, we aim to have an invitation from Melissa Thombs."

"And you're telling me this because . . . ?"

"If it does go south, we may need a sympathetic ear. I'm not asking you to intervene, but I'm looking for advice."

I hated even asking Macy for that much. Unspoken between us was that we would not risk compromising each other professionally. And that was another odd thing: I still thought of her as Macy, just as she still called me Parker. That might change as, or if, the relationship continued, but who could tell?

"My *advice* would be to walk away," she said. "Removing a woman from a domestic nightmare is always messy, and rarely goes smoothly. Even cops draw straws for those assignments. There are some who are really good at dealing with them, but it's a combination of nature and training, and someone—usually the male abuser—will still end up bleeding or in cuffs. It's not a job for a private investigator, not even one as skilled as you."

"Melissa Thombs's mother thinks Donnie may be close to killing her, and any shelter-in-place order could be enough to tip the balance."

"Then the daughter really needs to go to the police."

"We're talking in circles here. If the police show up at the door, there's no guarantee Melissa will leave with them, and Donnie will be alerted. He may even take it out on her once that door is closed again."

I was by now outside the little strip mall store that sold cheap burner phones, both used and new. I had often been tempted to have a button made for these visits. It would read I AM NOT A DRUG DEALER.

"You do pick them, don't you?"

At least I detected some affection amid her frustration.

"You're not the first person to have said something along those lines to me today," I said. "And for what it's worth, her mother picked me. I knew her in high school."

"An ex?"

"I might have wished, for about two seconds, and I doubt it took her even that long to dismiss me from her list of prospective suitors. Also, since we're engaging in full disclosure, I did try to speak to Melissa Thombs once before, but didn't get very far. You have no idea how reluctantly I'm reinvolving myself in this."

"I'm beginning to have an idea," she said. "When are you going to make your approach?"

"Tonight, with luck. I have a plan."

"I'd expect nothing less. If you're committed, and I can't talk you out of it, I'd suggest notifying Yarmouth PD formally when you're outside and ready to go. I'll find out who's on duty tonight, see if there's anyone who's particularly adept at dealing with domestics, and have a quiet word with them. But you do not—I repeat, do *not*—enter that property without the consent of either Melissa Thombs or, unlikely as it may be, Donnie Packard. If you do, and one of them gets hurt, you'll lose your license, and possibly your liberty, too, and I won't come visit you in Warren. You'll also be putting my career at risk, because I won't necessarily be able to ask whomever I spoke with to remain silent about my intervention, nor should they have to."

That was more than I'd expected, or had asked. Anyway, I had no intention of entering the Packard property without permission. Even on the ride over to the cell phone store, I'd decided that if Melissa Thombs didn't walk out of the house under her own steam, I'd postpone the effort to remove her, and find another way to help her as soon as I could.

"Agreed," I said. "And thank you."

"You owe me dinner."

"I've been saving my Denny's coupons for a special occasion."

"And I bet you wonder why women aren't lined up around the block to date you."

"It's still cold out there. Come summer, you'll see."

"Call me before you go to the Packard place. Is that your main focus for the day?"

"There's one other thing."

"Do I want to hear the details?"

I looked at the cell phone store. Standing outside was a man in his early twenties who, if he'd been wearing my button, could have crossed out the "not." I thought about Sarah Abelli and her dead child.

"No," I said, "you really don't."

The life of the dead is placed in the memory of the living.

—Marcus Tullius Cicero, Ninth Oration

XXIV

P antuff and Veale had blackmailed people in the past, and twice participated in kidnappings. The first of the abductions had gone well, in that the ransom was delivered successfully and the hostage released relatively unharmed, but the second had ended badly: no money, two of their associates apprehended, and a dead hostage. In neither case had Pantuff and Veale actually instigated the actions— they had been contractors only, working as part of a larger team—but the second incident had taught them that involvement in kidnapping wasn't worth the stress or the risks involved.

But they had also picked up valuable lessons about the mechanics of physical ransom payments, the most important of which was to keep moving. This meant no fixed drop-off points for the money: no holes in trees, no cases left on park benches, and no phone booths—assuming one could even find a suitable phone booth in this day and age. Neither Pantuff nor Veale was a bitcoin guy, and they didn't have the contacts to guarantee trustworthy or untraceable electronic transfers. Mostly, though, they liked the kind of money a man could hold in his hand and spend in a convenience store. In their world, cash was king, and always would be.

For the purposes of the drop-off they had selected a location in Androscoggin County, close to the border with Cumberland County, because there was nothing like even minor jurisdictional issues to screw around with law enforcement. There Lisbon Road branched into Shiloh Road as it crossed the county line, which then passed over a small stretch of water, Pinkham Brook, not far from the big Shiloh Chapel. That was where the drop-off would occur, and where Pantuff would be waiting. A short distance farther on from the brook was a quiet dead end, which was where Pantuff would leave the car. He had already made a dry run from the brook to the dead end—metaphorically, if not literally, the brook being harder than anticipated to negotiate without getting his feet wet—and had encountered no obstacles. With the money safely in hand, he would cross back into Cumberland County, picking up Veale along the way. As long as they could avoid the state police, they'd probably be okay.

While Pantuff was shivering in the damp and dark, Veale would be otherwise occupied. Nate Sawyer's widow would be instructed to drive a roundabout route from her home in Freeport: first south to Portland, then west toward North Windham, before gradually being brought back north to the drop-off point. Veale—in a '98 Honda Civic for which $750 cash had already been paid, and which was currently parked at a chain motel out by the Maine Mall—would first fall in behind her when she was thirty miles from the drop-off, and only to note the vehicles running behind and ahead of her. He would then cut away and pick her up again ten miles closer to Shiloh Road, where he would once more check the vehicles near the Sawyer woman's car. Finally, he would be sitting tight on a side road when she came within five miles of the drop-off. By that point it would be clear to him if she was being followed, and a determination would be made of what further action to take.

Pantuff and Veale had no intention of getting into a gunfight with cops or private operators. Veale thought the simplest solution, should the widow have sought outside help, would be to use the Civic to block Shiloh Road where it crossed the brook. The small-time crook from whom they'd acquired the car, who had himself picked it up from a wrecking yard for small change, suffered instant amnesia as soon as the money was in his wallet, so there were no anxieties on that front, especially if nobody got hurt during the ransom pickup. If by some miracle of sleuthing the Honda was traced back to the seller, the goon knew better than to give an accurate description of the man who'd purchased it. He might have been troubled by amnesia when required, but Pantuff and Veale were not.

As for the relics of Sawyer's dead daughter, she would be told that they'd be waiting for her in a box by the side of the road shortly after the drop was made, once it was confirmed the money was in the bag. And there *would* be a box, because Pantuff would place it where it was supposed to be before making for the brook. Of course, the box would be empty when she finally opened it, unless Pantuff decided to leave a little souvenir of his own. He'd discovered a dead rat in the Braycott's parking lot, and had bagged it before hanging it deep inside a thornbush, because he thought a dead rat might be appropriate for Nate Sawyer's widow. Pantuff had considered taking a dump in the box, but if anything went badly wrong, he'd be leaving a wealth of DNA for the police to find. If he went down the gift route, the rat would have to do.

The plan wasn't perfect, because no plan ever was. They would be at their most exposed after the money was thrown from the car, when Pantuff was still on foot. If any outside intervention was going to occur, it would happen then, but Veale would be ready and waiting to assist. Nevertheless, this was a weakness that needed to be addressed.

"What do you think?" said Pantuff, as they sat in the car on the Lisbon Falls side of Pinkham Brook.

"I think it would be simpler if I picked you up once you have the money," said Veale. "We should forget about the other car. If we do, it'll cut minutes from our exposure."

"But if she does have people with her, we'll have no way to stop them from following us."

"I've been working on that. There's a place out by the mall that sells those driveway spike strips—you know, the ones to stop drivers entering a property, or to puncture the tires if someone tries to steal your car. Wouldn't take but a few seconds for me to lay them behind us, assuming she does have someone following her."

"Huh," said Pantuff. "Yeah, that might work. Simpler is always better."

But it remained far from ideal. What if she was staying in touch with a tail by cell phone, or there was more than one car assisting her? He shared his concerns with Veale.

"Do you want to call it off?" said Veale, and was surprised to hear himself say the words, almost as surprised as he was to accept that a part of him wanted to. *It's the footsteps I've been hearing*, thought Veale. *They're the reason I want to walk away.*

And having admitted this to himself, he was prepared to concede yet more. He had tried and failed to dismiss the sound of a child moving in the night as an echo, and a smell of talcum powder and more as something coming through the vents or blown in from the street. He was now resigned to the bleak reality that he was being haunted, and this burden had fallen on him alone, because Pantuff was not similarly troubled. Veale could read the older man easily, and didn't believe he could, or would, hide such a source of disturbance from him.

Veale was not superstitious, and did not have faith in any god. At the same time, he had always believed the world to be stranger than it first appeared, because otherwise it could not have accommodated a man like himself. And he held a memory from childhood, one that had never faded, the truth of which he had never doubted, a recollection of waking from sleep the night after his mother's burial to feel a weight on his bed, the scent of her perfume strong in the room, and the lightness of her touch as her lips brushed his forehead as though to say good-bye to him for the last time. In that moment, he had often reflected, the abnormality existing within him, the otherness, had transitioned from dormant to active, for in the days that followed he had begun experimenting in earnest with the infliction of pain.

Now, it seemed, another revenant had entered his life. But if the child had been lured, what was the cause? It could only be the box of relics, as he had suggested to Pantuff. Some aspect of the child, some essence, had attached itself to them. He and Pantuff had stolen more than pictures, a tooth, a toy. In taking all that remained of the girl beyond her moldering bones, they had brought with them her—Veale struggled to find the right word: "spirit"? "soul"? No, he felt instinctively that this was not correct. "Shade" or "specter" would be closer to the mark, but remained inexact. He shifted in his seat, the fingers of his right hand clutching and unclutching, as though to wrest the letters, the syllables, from the air. Then it came to him: "sprite." The dancing, the laughter: light, but darkness too, because every child harbored a shadow self. Veale knew this better than most.

But did the mother really know it too? Was that why she wanted those possessions back so badly? Because they weren't just tokens of her child: they *were* her child. Did the same phantasm that was now haunting Veale also cavort through the rooms of the Freeport house at night, and regard her sleeping mother from the darkness?

If so, what was to be done? Pantuff would never agree to hand back the items, not even if the money was paid as agreed. In Pantuff's mind, the relics were forfeit. It was a wonder that he had not already destroyed them: only the necessity of being able to confirm to the mother, if required, that they remained safe had prevented him from taking that step.

Veale released a sigh that was like a dying breath. Total destruction was the solution. Pantuff was right about that, though for the wrong reason: he wanted to destroy the woman's life, but Veale wanted more. By burning the items they would consign whatever was left of the child to the flames, and Veale would be free of her. He tried to picture himself emptying the contents of the box into a bonfire, followed by the box itself. He could almost see himself doing it.

Almost.

"Hey!" said Pantuff. "Are you listening to me?"

Veale had been so absorbed that he'd failed to hear Pantuff's reply, and was forced to ask him to repeat it.

"I said we don't walk away, not until we have our money."

Veale nodded. "And I'm okay with burning what we took," he said. "We don't give it back to her."

"Were you ever not okay with it?" Pantuff asked.

Veale shrugged. "I had to give it some thought."

"So what brought about the decision?"

"The child. I want her gone."

Pantuff stared at him. A smile cracked his face, and then he was laughing, laughing fit to burst.

"Man," he said, once he'd regained control of himself, "you want to see her burn. You're hard, my friend." He whistled in admiration. "You're as fucking hard-core as they come."

I bought the cell phone that was to be passed on to Melissa Thombs, and input one number—my own—into its memory, because everything would run a lot smoother if I could find a way to communicate with her directly before we tried to get her out of the house. Now it was a matter of Melissa's mother letting her know that the phone would soon be in place. According to Marjorie, Donnie Packard had never relished her company, and in the past would have left her and Melissa to their own devices, but as his paranoia increased he had taken to remaining in the room with them, even if his attention was focused primarily on his phone or whatever happened to be on TV at the time. When Marjorie had something important she needed to tell her daughter, or be told in turn, conveyance was by way of a note folded small and pushed behind a chair cushion.

Marjorie Thombs called as I was filling a to-go cup with coffee at Panera Bread.

"I got the note to Melissa," she said.

"Any chance that Donnie might have noticed?"

"None. He was half-asleep when I slid it under the cushion. I was nearly tempted to make a break for it then and there with Melissa, but Donnie opened his eyes and looked at me, and I swear he was daring me to try it. He's like a rattlesnake. You think he's reposing, and then he up and bites you."

"And the trash cans haven't been moved?"

"They're still halfway between the house and the sidewalk. Donnie was taking them in from the street when I arrived, dressed in a wife-beater with his pants hanging halfway down his ass like he's some kind of hood. I hate that man, I truly do."

I thanked her for her efforts and hung up. I could tell she wanted to talk more, but I couldn't oblige her. I needed to get the phone to Donnie Packard's house. Once that was done, I could put Melissa Thombs out of my mind until later and focus on Sarah Abelli's problem. On reflection, I had decided not to ask Paulie Fulci to deliver the phone. Apart from my wanting him and his brother to remain close to Sarah's home in case the blue Chrysler took another pass at it—or worse, its occupants decided to pay a personal call—Paulie, as had already been established, was not an inconspicuous person. If I sent him to the Packard place, it would be as though someone had just abandoned a refrigerator on the street. I drove to the Great Lost Bear and paid one of Dave's servers fifty dollars to drop off the phone. I'd packed it in bubble wrap so she could just throw it if she had to. The priority was to ensure that it landed out of sight behind the trash cans in the yard. In fact, lobbing it might be preferable to entering the property, since the latter put her at risk not only of being seen by Packard but also by one of his neighbors. If he had a good relationship with any of them—unlikely, but anything was possible—they might mention that they'd noticed a stranger near his trash, which wouldn't be good.

I took a moment at the Bear to catch my breath. Around me, the usual business of the bar was being conducted, but there was an edge to it. I remember my grandfather describing to me how he and his father and mother had listened to the news of the Japanese attack on Pearl Harbor on a radio at a gas station as they were coming home from a church service. The hours between the attack and the declaration of war the following day had, he said, felt like being in limbo. The world had changed, and soon it would change again. They knew what was coming, and so the period between the assault on December 7 and Roosevelt's signing of the U.S. declaration of war at 4:10 p.m. on the eighth had an air of unreality about it, a hiatus between the past and a future with which it could have nothing in common. Being in the Bear that day, with the pandemic at our doors, I thought I understood for the first time what my grandfather had meant.

My phone rang, and I saw Mattia Reggio's name on the screen.

Time to go.

XXVI

Mattia Reggio had killed only one man in his life. He had never spoken of it to anyone, not even to his wife, Amara, and he both loved her and trusted her implicitly. He did not believe she would have thought less of him, had she known. She was the only woman he had ever slept with, and he was her only man. If she liked to remark to old friends that she had married young, but unfortunately her husband had lived, she did so within earshot, and would tip him a wink as she spoke. He might sometimes have frustrated her, but she never questioned his judgment. She understood that for much of his life he had engaged in criminality and consorted with men of violence. She knew, too, that he had inflicted harm on others when necessary, although only as a last resort. Mattia Reggio had a reputation as a calm man, and the voice of reason when others counseled rash acts. At home, it was Amara who had been forced to take on the role of disciplinarian when their children overstepped the mark. She could not recall Mattia ever raising a hand to them. To be fair, he was never required to. When he spoke, the kids had always paid attention, and acted accordingly. Only in his absence did they test the boundaries.

But if the relationship between husband and wife was one that seemed almost perfectly complementary, it was not without its secrets. Amara had learned that if Mattia wished to share something with her, he would tell her in his own time, and without prompting. He was a man who was comfortable with silence, and thought before he opened his mouth—a rare quality in his gender, she reckoned. She recognized when he was troubled, and had learned how to subtly alter the contours of their existence to permit him the space, both physical and emotional, to process whatever he was feeling. And if, in her more melancholy moments, she reflected that she had spent far more of their marriage trying to figure out her husband than he had in contemplating her nature, it was a small price to pay for a happy life, and she could at least console herself with the fact that virtually every married woman she knew could claim the same experience.

So it was that, had Mattia chosen to share with her the details of the killing, she would have been able to tell him, unaided, the date on which it had occurred, and what he had been wearing when he returned home that night. She could have detailed how he smelled, and spoken of the red stain behind his left ear, a smear of blood that had vanished by the time he came to bed, by then not only showered but also wearing some of the English Leather aftershave she had bought him for Christmas, even though he had not shaved since morning. She spent the following three days watching him brood, his face changing only when he left the house, just as if he were slipping on a mask in order to be able to consort with his peers, to be hung on the rack with his cap and coat when he came back in the evening.

On the fourth day, the clouds broke, and some version of normality was restored, but it was the beginning of the end of their life in Boston. It happened gradually—almost to avoid drawing attention to any particular time or incident, one might have said—but within a year Mattia Reggio had severed his ties with the Office, and he and his wife had moved to Portland, Maine. By then their children had already left home, and Mattia had suffered one mild heart attack, so the big men in Boston and Providence understood—or appeared to understand, because with such beings one could never be sure—why he might have wanted to find a new and less onerous path in life.

But had they known of the man he had murdered, it might have been a different tale. His wife would have become a widow, and Mattia would not have lived to see the birth of his grandchildren, because his own people would have killed him to prevent a war. It would have been quick, and he wouldn't have known a whole lot about it, if he was lucky. He might not even have seen the gun or heard the shot, and his demise would have occasioned some regret. Because of who he was, and the respect in which he was held, the necessity of a closed casket might have been avoided. It was the exit wound that would have made the mess. A .22, then, close up, fired at the temple or the back of the skull, where the bone was thinner; one shot, two at most. Actually, he probably *would* have felt it: the first one, at least, while it rattled around inside his skull. The second would have brought any pain to an end.

Mattia hadn't gone looking for trouble. In fact, he'd been trying to prevent the deterioration of an already perilous state of affairs. Mattia thought of the individual responsible almost as a kid, even though he was twenty-five, but that was because of the way he was behaving. Alessandro Angioni was hooked up with the Genoveses, running rackets for them in Springfield, Mass. But Angioni was ambitious, a hothead, and elected to regard territorial boundaries as purely optional. Alessandro Angina, the Office began calling him, because he was such a pain, but both Boston and Providence preferred to avoid a confrontation with the Genoveses, though some grayhairs speculated that Angioni wasn't acting solely on his own initiative, and was being given a long leash by his bosses to test for weaknesses in the Northeast.

Matters proceeded uneasily in this way for a time, until a girl named Donna Sirola caught Angioni's eye. Donna's family were ordinary Springfield folk, and the closest they'd ever come to breaking the law was crossing at a red light. They bought their pastries from La Fiorentina and their groceries at Frigo's, and knew the staff of the Italian consulate by name from social gatherings. The father was a security guard at Smith & Wesson, the mother a nurse at Mercy Medical. Donna was their only child, majoring in elementary education at Western New England University. She didn't have a boyfriend, didn't want one until she'd settled in at college, and even when she did get around to going out with someone, he wouldn't look or act like Alessandro Angioni.

But Angioni wanted her, and his attentions quickly began to make life miserable for her. He knew her class schedule, where her friends lived, where she liked to go for coffee. He knew her car, the used VW Beetle her parents had bought her when she was accepted into WNE, and no matter where she parked it, he would find it, and often be waiting for her nearby when it came time for her to go home. She gave up driving to class, and either took the bus or grabbed a ride with classmates, but this didn't stop Angioni from shadowing her. Her parents were afraid to go to the police because of who he was, and when her father tried to speak with him at the Mule, the dive bar off Main that was his preferred haunt, Angioni laughed in his face. That evening, an envelope addressed to Donna's father was left in the mailbox. It contained a business card for a funeral home, with his name written on the other side.

The Sirolas were distantly related to Mattia Reggio's wife: cousins of cousins, but it was enough. Mattia was asked to intervene, but they'd all been ordered by the Office to maintain a distance from Angioni. Wheels were grinding. People were talking to people. In a few weeks, once it could be done without anyone losing face, Angioni might be reined in, or preferably sent someplace else: Jersey, South Florida, fucking Cuba, who cared? As long as it wasn't anywhere the Office would have to deal with him.

But Mattia didn't think the Sirolas had that kind of time, because the word was that Angioni was tiring of the chase, and was now of a mind to teach Donna Sirola a lesson. After all, the Sirolas were nobodies. If, as he put it within earshot of a waitress at the Mule, he "reamed the bitch," the most he could expect was a slap on the wrist and an order to pay compensation to the family. Angioni was making money for the

Genoveses. Say what you liked about him, but he had the golden touch, and talent invited tolerance.

The next day, Leo Sirola called Mattia Reggio and asked to meet with him in Boston. Over take-out coffees by Revere Beach, Leo said that he was considering shooting Alessandro Angioni.

"I didn't hear that," said Mattia.

"I got no choice. He's talking about raping my little girl."

Leo's voice caught. His hands were trembling so much that he was spilling his coffee. Mattia wouldn't have put it past him to go through with what he was threatening, but he'd probably end up winging Angioni, even at close range, assuming he could hit him in the first place. It wasn't like on TV, shooting a man. Mattia knew of experienced button guys who'd missed a shot from a few feet away, because who knew what might happen in the seconds between producing a gun and pulling the trigger? And human beings were startlingly resilient, particularly the ones, like Alessandro Angioni, you really wished weren't so dogged. Unless they went down straight off, there was a good chance they'd either run, in which case you'd be forced to run after them, and few things were more likely to attract attention than a man with a gun chasing another man who was bleeding all over the sidewalk while screaming his guts out for all he was worth; or almost as bad, they could come at you, leaving you wrestling a wounded man for a gun, getting his blood all over you, and possibly one of your own bullets in the foot or belly for good measure. These outcomes were not only undignified but also a surefire way of ending up before a judge, either terrestrial or divine. Mattia reckoned Leo Sirola's chances of punching Angioni's ticket at somewhere between zero and less than zero, which meant that Leo's concerns for his daughter would be unlikely to trouble him for much longer, because the only thing worse than killing Angioni would be failing to kill him.

"I'll see what I can do," said Mattia.

He didn't tell Leo that he'd already tried to exert his influence on the Sirolas' behalf. He'd let it be known that they were family, and he didn't like family being harassed, but the message wasn't getting through. What was going on between the Office and the Genoveses was capo to capo stuff, so whatever he said was merely passed up the chain, and nothing ever came out the way it should when you played Broken Telephone.

But Mattia couldn't have Leo Sirola hanging around outside the Mule, waiting for Alessandro Angioni with a gun assembled from parts smuggled out of the Smith & Wesson factory, like some lethal version of that old Johnny Cash song "One Piece at a Time." And should Angioni make good on his threat against Donna, Mattia would have difficulty sleeping at night, assuming Amara didn't smother him for failing to prevent the rape from happening in the first place.

If Mattia couldn't approach Angioni through the usual channels, he was still hopeful of being able to reach some accommodation with him unofficially. Rape would count against Angioni, didn't matter how much he was bringing in for his bosses. He had a successful career ahead of him, if he could control his impulses. Failure to do so would see him imprisoned or dead, because that was what happened to men with poor impulse control in their line of work. Mattia had met Angioni a couple of times, but always in group situations, where the young cub felt obliged to act up. One on one, without an audience, Mattia believed it might be possible to steer him away from a course of action that could only harm him in the long run.

So he'd asked Leo Sirola to give him a couple of days, telling him that he was convinced he could find a way to ensure Donna's safety without recourse to putting a hole in Angioni.

"And if you're wrong?" asked Leo.

"I'll help you bury him myself," said Mattia, words that would come back to haunt him.

XXVII

L ater Mattia would try to convince himself that he had not traveled to Springfield that night with the intention of killing Alessandro Angioni, and everything he had said to Sirola, and Mattia's version of what followed, represented the truth. He had been set only on conversation and conciliation, because that was how he preferred to work; and if Angioni could not be made to see reason, Mattia would call in favors from his bosses, favors that would cost him professionally, but might be worth the price. He would even try to frame the trip solely as a reconnaissance mission, with the actual confrontation to come a day or two later, even though he was almost as familiar with Springfield as he was with the North End.

But as the years went by, lending a clearer perspective to Angioni's death, he became reconciled to a self that was both more and less than he had believed it to be. He grew to accept that from the moment news had reached him of the stalking of Donna Sirola, maybe even from the time Angioni had arrived in Springfield and begun flexing his muscles, he had known how this story would end. Angioni would never be open to compromise, which meant that violence would be required; and since Angioni would, if given the opportunity, meet violence with violence—with the approval of the Genoveses, who would choose, possibly for pragmatic reasons, to regard an assault on one as an assault on all—the response required to deal with him would have to be terminal, and secret.

It was to the misfortune of both men, but more particularly Angioni's, that Mattia Reggio should have marked his quarry shortly after getting to Springfield, although even this had been to a degree preordained. Angioni, already grown complacent in his fiefdom, had developed routines, one of which was to walk from his apartment on Magazine Street to his beloved Mule, usually via Lincoln and Federal, sometimes by way of State, on those evenings when he was in town. Thus Mattia passed Angioni as the latter neared Magazine Park, giving Mattia time to turn left onto Lincoln and park in the shadows. By the time Mattia walked back to the corner, Angioni was only a few feet away. He glanced once at Mattia, but initially failed to recognize him. Only as he was about to continue on his way did his features change.

"Hey," said Angioni, "what are you doing here?"

"I was hoping we could talk for a minute," said Mattia.

"I don't do business on the street."

"This isn't business. It's more of a personal matter."

"Then we can talk about it over a drink. Nobody will bother us."

"I don't drink."

"Don't drink alcohol, you mean," said Angioni. "You drink, like, fucking water, and soda, right? You're not made of fucking sand."

There they were, barely seconds into what was set to be the most important negotiation of Angioni's life, if only because it would be the final one, and the man couldn't even keep a civil tongue in his head. Any remaining hope Mattia might have entertained about dealing with the Angioni problem without bloodshed vanished in that instant. He looked around, but the streets were quiet, despite the presence nearby of churches, a high school, and Springfield Technical Community College. Even God, Mattia thought, didn't want Alessandro Angioni to live for very much longer.

"Actually," said Mattia, with a flick of his right wrist, "I got a lot of sand."

He stepped forward, put his left hand on Angioni's shoulder, and stabbed him hard in the chest. The knife was double-edged, very sharp, and Mattia knew exactly where to put it so it wouldn't stick. He lodged it deep, twisted once, and pulled it free before hitting Angioni twice more, virtually in the same spot. He had to move his head fast to avoid being hit in the face by a gush of blood from Angioni's mouth, and could feel his right hand and the sleeve of his coat growing wet and warm. By the time he withdrew the blade for the third blow, Angioni was dying, although he was still on his feet. Mattia slipped his left arm around Angioni's waist and half-carried him to the car. He saw people approaching down Lincoln, but still some distance away, so he took a chance on opening the trunk and dumping Angioni inside, resting him on the double lining of plastic garbage bags taped to the sides. Angioni shuddered as he died, and Mattia noticed the tears on the young man's cheeks. In all his time with the Office, Mattia had never seen anyone die violently before. It had never struck him that a dying man might have time to cry.

Mattia dropped the knife on the plastic before removing his coat and throwing it on top of the body, then closed the trunk. He'd kept the coat buttoned in the hope it would catch most of the blood, and it had. He spotted a little on his pants, but they were black cotton and he wouldn't have noticed the droplets if he hadn't been looking for them. More blood glistened on the right sleeve of his dark shirt, which was wet halfway to the elbow, and his right hand was entirely red. He could have worn gloves, but he was worried about maintaining his grip on the knife, and felt more secure doing the job bare-handed.

Mattia got in the car. The group of pedestrians was drawing closer now. They were young, and two of them were carrying guitars in cases. Mattia checked the rearview mirror. He could see the blood on the sidewalk. He'd taken Angioni in a patch of gloom between streetlights, but blood was blood, even in the dark, and it had a way of being detected by smell when it was fresh. He wrapped his red right hand in the rag he used to clean the windshield and pulled away from the curb as soon as another car turned onto Lincoln, Mattia falling in place behind it. None of the kids paid him any attention, so caught up were they with one another. One or more of them might step in the blood when they reached the corner, but by then Mattia would be out of sight. He kept an eye on them until he made the next right, then forgot about them forever.

Only as he was leaving Springfield did he begin to tremble. Despite his reputation as a moderating influence, he had, when left with no alternative, delivered beatings, leaving men with cuts, bruises, even broken bones, but he had never pummeled someone into unconsciousness, and had always made it clear to the Office that he wasn't in the business of killing. No one judged him for it. Mattia Reggio was acknowledged to be a hard man, in his way, and was not alone in distancing himself from wet work. There were others who found murder less distasteful, some who were untroubled by the act, and a handful who actively relished it, although all sane men kept a distance from such individuals. Now, as he drove, a fever sweat breaking on his face and the urge both to vomit and void his bowels verging on the overwhelming, Mattia wondered at how easily and quickly he had moved from being a man who refused to kill to becoming a killer.

The rag on his hand was now soaked through with blood, so he dropped it in one of the poop bags kept in the car for dog walks. He used a bunch of wet wipes to get rid of as much of the rest of the gore as he could before placing these, too, in the bag. He spotted a Starbucks up ahead, pulled into the lot, and headed for the men's room, a plain black canvas shopping bag in his right hand. He barely made it inside in time to get his pants down, thankful only that the sink was close enough to the toilet that he could also expel whatever was left in his stomach without leaving a mess some poor wage slave would have to clean up. When he was done, he washed his face, took off his shirt with the bloodstained sleeve, and replaced it with a similar clean one from the bag. He then made sure his hair was tidy, sprayed some air freshener, and went to the counter, where he asked for an iced tea that he didn't want because someone who came into a coffee shop, used the bathroom, and ordered from the menu was more likely to be forgotten than a man who entered, used the john, and left without ordering anything. But the iced tea would also help clear the taint from his mouth, although Mattia thought the tea would have tasted pretty vile to him anyway, even if he hadn't just puked in a sink. He didn't get Starbucks, and never would.

Mattia made sure that his lights were working and the tires were still okay before driving away, even though he'd performed the same check before departing for Springfield. It was better to be certain. If he was pulled over by the cops for a busted bulb, and they ran his plate, his name would light up like Christmas. Next thing he knew, some statie in a big hat would be asking him to open the trunk, and Mattia Reggio would be looking at life without the possibility of parole, although with Angioni's blood on his hands he'd be lucky to survive long enough to make it to trial.

Mattia continued east, avoiding tolls, as on the outward journey, so as to avoid leaving a record of his route. He knew where he was headed, which was back to Revere. He'd passed the building site on his way to the rendezvous with Leo Sirola: a new office block with a couple of retail outlets on the first floor. The Argent, they were calling it. The Office was taking its cut from the construction, the way it did: high-bid contracts, materials redirected and sold on, and a handful of guys on the payroll, none of whom would ever be seen in person. Easy money, some of it even clean. It all added up, with nobody getting hurt and the contractors able to sleep soundly at night knowing there would be no walkouts, no sugar in gas tanks, no cement mixers suddenly going missing, and no fires either during or after the build. Mattia was more aware than most just how much it all added up because he was the one who took care of many of the collections. The foundations at this one were due to be laid the next day, which was conceivably one of the reasons Mattia had decided to go talk to Angioni that evening instead of waiting a while longer, because it was funny the little nuggets the mind stored away.

There was no security guard. The site wasn't big enough to justify the expense, and the money being paid to those phantom employees also bought a very particular form of insurance, the kind that discouraged trespass. Mattia parked at the rear of the construction project, away from the road, and opened the trunk. He used another poop bag to pick up the knife, removed the duct tape that was keeping the garbage bags attached to the sides of the trunk, and carefully folded the ends over the body after first dousing it in bleach as an extra precaution. He then took the roll of tape and sealed the plastic at the ankles, thighs, chest, and neck, before placing two additional bags over the remains, one from the head down, the second from the feet up, and sealing the join with more tape. Finally, he hoisted the body from the trunk and carried it in a fireman's lift to the pit at the center of the excavation. The hole was big, with a pool of muddy water at the bottom. The water was just deep enough. Mattia laid Angioni down, produced the knife, and stabbed at the plastic to make some holes in it—and, for good measure, Angioni—to help the body sink faster and stay down once it did. When he was done, he kicked it into the pit. Angioni hit the side once before landing with a splash. The water closed over him, and he was gone. Mattia sent the knife after him.

After that, he didn't hang around. He returned to his car and drove home, stopping only to consign the shopping bag containing the bloodied shirt, rag, and wet wipes to a packed dumpster that smelled as though it already had at least one dead body of its own inside. When he reached the house, he killed the engine and sat quietly for a while. The shakes were still hitting him, but in receding waves. A part of him, the aspect that remained childlike and always would, wanted to confess to his wife what he'd done. It wanted to be held, consoled, and reassured. But Mattia knew that he could never tell Amara what had happened. Not only did he not wish to encumber her, but also to share would be to involve, and she needed to be kept at one remove. He had no doubt she would have forgiven him; she might well have decided there was nothing to forgive, given Angioni's nature and what he had intended for Donna Sirola. Regardless, the knowledge would have altered Amara, forcing her to pretend ignorance, to act naturally rather than be natural, and therein lay the risk. Someone like Alessandro Angioni didn't just vanish without questions being asked, and those sent to inquire would be attuned to dissimulation.

Mattia knew that he would be high on the list of suspects. He had erred in asking that Angioni be warned to back off. Mattia had displayed an interest in Angioni's fate, and one never displayed that kind of interest. It would have been noted, and would be recalled. The Office would not be sorry that Angioni was gone, thorn in the side that he was. What remained to be seen was how much cooperation the Office was willing to extend to the Genoveses in order to avoid conflict, and how hard the Genoveses might be prepared to push if they felt the Office could be protecting one or more of its own people.

What Mattia had going for him was that, the construction gods being willing, Alessandro Angioni's body would never be found, and therefore his ultimate fate would remain forever a mystery. Oh, the Genoveses could be reasonably sure that he was dead, men like Angioni not being disposed to go dark voluntarily, either fleetingly or permanently, or not without good cause. But an element of uncertainty would remain, and as long as it did, their options would be limited. Even the Genoveses would struggle to justify avenging a murder they couldn't prove had occurred, not unless they managed to force a confession out of the culprit.

Mattia's whole body trembled again. He could take a beating, if it came down to it. As long as Angioni's body was not discovered, and no witnesses materialized from Springfield, the Genoveses would be left fumbling like blind men.

He unfolded himself from the car, locked it, and went into the house. Amara appeared at the kitchen door and could tell instantly that something was wrong, but she knew better than to try to draw it from him. When he showered that night, the water was at first tinged with pink, but soon ran clear.

CHAPTER

XXVIII

It took forty-eight hours for the Genoveses to start worrying about Angioni. Like all those who live in fear of betrayal, their main concern was that he might have been induced to turn federal witness, but all such inquiries came up negative. Whoever had him, it wasn't the FBI's Strike Force unit, the section of the Boston office responsible for investigating organized crime in the region, and it certainly wasn't any of the state authorities in the Northeast. By then the foundations were already being laid at the Revere Beach site, and Angioni's body was encased in cement.

Within a week, the Genoveses began looking at outside enemies, particularly those whom Angioni might have crossed. It was a long list, discretion and diplomacy not being part of his limited skill set. Two men picked up Leo Sirola as he was leaving the Smith & Wesson factory and broke a couple of his ribs, but even when they threatened his daughter with the same fate that Angioni had once planned for her, he didn't buckle, and so they ruled him out. Finally, in the second week, they commenced circling Mattia Reggio.

"They want to talk to you," said Dante Vero, as he and Mattia walked along Parmenter Street drinking coffee from Polcari's, Vero with a package of meat from Sulmona's under his left arm, carefully sealed so the blood wouldn't leak.

"Because I asked about the Sirola thing," said Mattia. There was no point in pretending he didn't know why.

"You ought to have let it run its course."

"I had a problem with that. You would have as well, in my position."

"Yeah, but how much of a problem did you have with it?"

"Are you asking if I killed Angioni?"

"I'm not asking anything," said Vero. They turned left onto Hanover. Mattia noticed that Vero was keeping his eyes fixed straight ahead. "But the Genoveses are going to want to know if you killed him, so you'd better have an answer prepared."

"I didn't kill him," said Mattia.

"Which would be the right one."

"If that's what happened to him."

"You think he changed his name and entered a monastery? The Catholic Church has enough on its plate. No, he's dead, and whoever took care of him was smart enough not to leave the body where it could be found."

"Not yet."

"Not ever."

"You seem very certain of that," said Mattia. "You sure you didn't kill him?"

"That's not even fucking funny. But it was a pro job, whoever did it. To make Angioni vanish quietly like that, you have to be smart *and* lucky."

"Two men," said Mattia. "Even three."

"That was the Genoveses' thinking."

" 'Was'?"

"It didn't make sense to them. Angioni pissed off a lot of people, but not enough to want to put him in the ground. That means it was personal, which was why they beat up on the father. You heard about that?"

"I heard."

Vero stopped at the Prince Street intersection and removed the lid from his cup so he could drain the last of the coffee.

"We're vulnerable right now," he said. "We need the Genoveses off our backs."

"I understand," said Mattia, as a gray panel van pulled up to the curb.

"You keep in mind that answer you gave me," said Vero.

Mattia didn't even try to resist as a sack was placed over his head and he was bundled into the van.

CHAPTER

XXIX

They worked Mattia over hard, but not as hard as they might have. The Office had consented to pressure being applied, but no bones were to be broken, and any injuries were required to heal quickly. But there was also the fact that he was Mattia Reggio, the man the Office sent when hopes of a nonviolent solution to a problem still remained. He was a talker, a negotiator. He wasn't a killer. Everyone knew that.

On the other hand, he had cause to want Angioni out of the way. He'd asked for something to be done, but the Genoveses weren't about to rein in their golden boy in western Massachusetts, not while he was earning for them. In that situation, a man might be tempted to take matters into his own hands. Was that what happened? they asked Mattia. Did you try to talk to Alessandro? Except maybe he didn't listen. They could understand that. Alessandro didn't listen to most people, and barely paid attention to the bosses if he thought he knew better. He had a way of raising a man's temperature, of turning a conversation into a confrontation. You couldn't throw a stone in parts of the Northeast without hitting someone who was taking blood pressure medication because of Alessandro. They'd made efforts to warn him about it, encouraging him to modify his behavior. His provocations were low-level, not enough to invite punishment, but if Alessandro didn't get a handle on them, they threatened to escalate. So his bosses could appreciate how someone like Mattia, a mature individual with a reputation for restraint, might have felt forced to deal with him, because even the fucking Dalai Lama would eventually have resorted to kicking the shit out of Alessandro, and Buddha himself might have been tempted to take a crowbar to him. Did it play out that way? they asked. Did you start by talking, and next thing Alessandro was pushing you, getting in your face? You hit him and he went down, banged his head on the sidewalk and started bleeding from the ears. Or did you think, you know, fuck it, and shoot him? God knows, you wouldn't have been the first to consider it. If you tell us the truth, we can work something out: reparation, whatever. You must have money put aside. You can take the hit. How about it? Come clean, and we can all go home.

But Mattia didn't come clean. He stuck to his story. He didn't know anything about what might have happened to Angioni. He hadn't seen him in weeks, didn't want to see him. The guy was an asshole. They'd said it themselves.

They told him his car had been spotted in Springfield. He told them it couldn't have been because he hadn't been anywhere near Springfield. Didn't he want to know who saw it? they asked. No, said Mattia, because if he wasn't in Springfield, they were mistaken. Whatever, or whomever, they thought they'd seen, it wasn't his car, and it wasn't him.

So where had he been? they asked. Where had he been when? he replied. If they wanted to know everywhere he'd gone, and everyone he'd spoken to, since Angioni dropped off the map, they might as well shoot him now because he didn't keep a diary. If the feds were going to lock him up, he'd make them work for it. He wasn't about to leave a confession on his desk.

Everyone laughed at that, then someone hit him again.

It went on for a day and most of a night. It was still dark when they eventually returned him to his home, but there was light in the east. They helped him from the van, and two of them made sure he could stay upright unaided before they rang the doorbell. Amara answered within seconds, because someone would have made a call: Dante, probably, telling her not to worry, it was just a conversation, though she'd have known better. Amara wasn't dressed for bed, and he guessed that she'd slept on the couch in the living room, if she'd slept at all. She wanted to be ready in case she got another call, in case he never came home. But now he had been returned to her, and she held him close, burying her face in his neck, his chest, smelling blood, sweat, and worse. She didn't care. He was hers, and he was back in her arms. She helped him up to the bathroom, took off his clothes, dressed his wounds, and dosed him with ibuprofen, whiskey, and a sleeping pill, to hell with the potential risks of mixing them. Her face was the last thing he saw before his eyes closed, and it was all that he could do not to weep.

The next day, for reasons he could never explain, he bought his first pack of gum since childhood, and he hadn't stopped chewing gum since.

––––––

AMARA HAD GUESSED. OF course she had. From the moment questions started being asked about Alessandro Angioni, she'd made the connection. The way she looked at Mattia changed. She saw what he'd done, because no one fathomed him as she did, but nothing needed to be said, and nothing ever would. Even in the years since, the dead man's name had never once come up between them. Angioni's fate remained unknown, and Mattia thought that even Dante Vero had only fleetingly, and halfheartedly, suspected him of involvement. Mattia had been offered up to the Genoveses more as a gesture of appeasement than anything else, and he had come through, which was why no one objected when he announced his intention to walk away and make a new life in Maine. Mattia Reggio had been a stand-up guy. He'd done the right thing.

But he knew the truth, and his wife knew it. And here was the other thing, the worm that twisted in Mattia's belly: the investigator named Parker knew something of it, too.

Mattia kept a relic of Padre Pio in his car. It was a fragment of cloth from one of the saint's robes, sealed in a small brass locket attached to a chain with a crucifix. It had been a gift from Leo Sirola, Donna's father, and was one of the few physical objects treasured by Mattia, who was utilitarian about possessions. Padre Pio, it was said, could see into the hearts and souls of men, particularly during the examination of conscience required by the sacrament of confession. No sin could be concealed from him, and therefore no forgiveness was possible through him without complete honesty.

Parker, Mattia believed, possessed some version of the power of divination, because when he looked at Mattia, Parker perceived his sin; not every detail of it, nor the identity of the victim, possibly not even the exact nature of the crime, but he was aware that Mattia was engaged in an act of deception, one that involved violence and death. It was as though his gaze contained UV light, so that blood, or the faded stain of it, appeared to him as a kind of adumbration. It was the private investigator's gift, rendered sharper by the blood Parker himself had spilled, and the secrets he kept.

The result was that, for the first time since the night he had killed Alessandro Angioni, Mattia felt the urge to confess. He wanted to tell Parker what he had done—not for absolution, but for understanding. This was why Parker's rejection pained Mattia so much. Parker didn't trust him, but if he knew what Mattia had done, and why, he might change his mind. Parker, Mattia believed, saw only the shadow, not the reality of the man who cast it, not the truth of him.

But Mattia could not tell Parker about Angioni's death. If he had not shared the facts of it with his wife, he would not do so with a stranger. Rather, he was determined by his actions to prove Parker mistaken, to show him that he was worthy of his confidence, his respect, even his friendship. This was why, at Parker's instigation, he had reached out to his old comrades, men whom he had studiously avoided since retreating to Maine. He would do the right thing, and in doing so would earn Parker's respect.

Mattia Reggio believed himself to be a good man, but one who had committed a single terrible act—even if, when his time came, he would stand before God and tell Him that not to have acted, not to have intervened, would have been much worse. Mattia would call God on this. Because how often had He disdained to intervene, failing to stop innocents from suffering? God, Mattia thought, had spent too long without someone to criticize His behavior. It was Mattia Reggio's opinion that a lot of the tribulations in the world would have been solved if God had a wife.

Parker might have understood, had Mattia been able to open up to him. Parker did not stand by. Parker intervened. Perhaps when they grew closer, and Parker learned to trust him, Mattia would speak with him of what he had done. He would tell Parker of Donna Sirola's children, how she was married now, but still teaching. Mattia had seen pictures of the kids, twin girls. Leo Sirola had emailed some images to him shortly after they were born. Afterward Mattia had called Leo from a pay phone and warned him never to make contact again. He didn't care what Leo knew, or thought he knew, or even if he didn't think or know anything at all. The Genoveses were always alert, always listening.

This, too, Parker might have understood.

XXX

I answered Reggio's call.

"I got word to Dante," he said, "and he got word back to me."

"What did he say?"

"He wants to meet, in person."

"Mattia, there's a clock ticking on this."

"It's how Dante does business. He's not going to talk about Nate Sawyer over the phone, not even on a burner."

"Then where and when?"

"He's prepared to split the distance: Portsmouth. There's a bar called the Hitch Knot. It's run by a friend. He can be there in two hours. So can I."

The prospect of a rendezvous in a bar run by a friend of the Office didn't exactly fill me with happiness, not if Dante Vero's people were involved in the shakedown of Sarah Abelli.

"I think you should stay away from this, Mattia. You've done enough."

I meant it, and still I detected hurt in his silence.

"But tell Dante I won't be coming alone," I said.

"I doubt," said Reggio, "that he'd expect anything less."

XXXI

The server from the Bear, Lucie Barnes, was certain that she'd managed to stash the cell phone behind the trash cans at Donnie Packard's place without being spotted by anyone in the house. But as she was leaving the yard, she almost ran into an old woman pushing a small brown dog in a carriage. The dog was missing its right front leg, although the wound was long-healed. It seemed to be perfectly happy where and as it was, as though losing a leg was a small price to pay for being pushed around in a carriage for the rest of its life.

"What were you doing in there?" said the old woman.

"I thought I saw a kitten," said Lucie, "but it was really a rat."

"Must have been visiting Donnie Packard, then. Probably a relative. You ought to stay out of there. He's mean."

"I won't be going back."

"Yeah," said the old woman, as she recommenced pushing her dog, "that's what they all say."

———

I CALLED ANGEL AND Louis and told them of the imminent meeting with Dante Vero down in Portsmouth.

"I doubt he's going to kill you," said Louis. "That would be an over-reaction on his part."

"It does leave a lot of possibilities between alive and dead," I said.

"True. If the Office is involved in what's happening up here, Vero will start by warning you off. If you don't listen, he may take the step of rendering you unable to intervene. The Office has no shortage of places it can stash someone for a few hours. Best-case scenario, they'll order in pizza, let you watch some TV, then release you once the money is handed over."

"Which is why you're going to come with me."

"So I can watch TV and eat pizza, too?"

"If that's what we end up doing, I'll regard our mission as a failure. But I don't believe they'll try that with us."

"Good," said Louis, "because we can never agree on toppings."

The only reason for the Office to target Sarah Abelli would be to establish if she had access to the money stolen by her late husband. But even if she paid the ransom, it wouldn't definitively answer that question, because the sum being demanded wasn't sufficiently large and she had access to other funds, thanks to her siblings and the bank. There was a chance that, having forced her to pay once, they might come back for a second attempt, and so prove she had deeper reserves of cash on which to draw, but it struck me as a flawed strategy. Sarah wasn't stupid. After being ripped off the first time, she'd know there was little hope of retrieving all of her belongings, not unless she was prepared to dangle on a string for the rest of her days, so she wouldn't pay.

And I was also a factor. I didn't like what was being done to her, which was why I'd elected to involve myself. I would be reluctant to abandon her. If Dante Vero had any sense—and all indications were that he did—he wouldn't want me dogging his heels. He'd have to do something about it, but the price he'd pay for any violence would be high, because he knew force would be met with force. That, at least, was my hope.

I told Louis I'd drop by in the next few minutes. Before I hung up, Louis asked if Mattia Reggio had offered to accompany me to the meeting with Vero.

"He did," I said. "I turned him down."

"Why? He came through for you."

But I could tell that Louis had an end in mind here.

"You know the answer," I said. "He's not someone I want at my back, especially not if it involves some of his former associates."

"I asked around about Reggio," said Louis. "Judiciously."

"And?"

"You ever hear of a Genovese hood named Alessandro Angioni? He operated out of Springfield, Mass."

"No."

"Well, no one else has either, not for a long time. He disappeared over a decade ago, evaporated. There are some who believe Reggio might know what happened to him."

"Reggio didn't have that reputation," I said.

"Which may be why he got away with it. The consensus is that Angioni was no great loss. Someone would have taken care of him eventually. Could be Reggio got there first."

"Why are you telling me this?"

"It's just interesting, is all. Mattia Reggio may be more than he appears to be."

"That's what worries me," I said. "I'll see you in ten."

XXXII

Pantuff and Veale were nearly at the Braycott Arms when they saw the flashing lights of the vehicles in the lot. Their immediate reaction was to turn tail, until Pantuff spotted the ambulance and surmised that whatever else they might have done, they hadn't hurt or injured anyone, not so far.

"What do you think?" he asked Veale, as they pulled up to watch the show from a safe distance.

It took a while for Veale to respond. Pantuff thought he had been reserved on the ride back, even for him, but Veale got like that sometimes. Moods descended on him, and often wouldn't lift for days. Pantuff had long ago decided that Veale's problem was thinking too much, which often equated simply to brooding.

"Could be somebody fell down the stairs," said Veale.

"Or got shot. Fucking place is full of ex-cons. I've been in jails with fewer criminals."

Two police cars were parked beside the ambulance, along with an unmarked Crown Vic that screamed "Detectives!" Pantuff needed to use the john, but he'd hold it in until his bladder burst before identifying himself as a guest at the Braycott to a bunch of uniforms and plainclothes. He'd be better off climbing straight into the back of one of those prowl cars and requesting a cell with a view.

"We ought to have stayed someplace else," said Veale.

"Nobody asks questions at the Braycott," said Pantuff.

"They're asking them now."

"Not of us."

A gurney was wheeled from the front entrance, its occupant covered from head to foot. The two paramedics ran it straight to the open rear doors of the ambulance, where the wheels folded up and the gurney slid gently inside. Pantuff detected no great sense of urgency from the cops, which led him to believe that they were looking at the aftermath of an accident, not a crime. That was good. It meant no one would be knocking on doors to make inquiries of, or about, any guests. He said as much to Veale, but his companion's attention was elsewhere, distracted by a line of elementary school kids being led along like ducklings by a pair of young female teachers. Each child held on tightly with one hand to a loop of ribbon attached to a rope.

"You considering adopting?" said Pantuff.

But Veale didn't answer, so Pantuff left him to it.

———

VEALE WATCHED THE CHILDREN cross the road and disappear from view. None of them resembled Kara Sawyer, and yet somehow they all did.

Veale didn't want to return to the Braycott Arms. Given the opportunity, he'd have blown it sky high, along with everyone and everything in it, and it wouldn't have cost him a moment's sleep. As they'd drawn closer to Portland, he'd felt a pressure growing in his skull, which had become real pain by the time the hotel came in sight, and what had at first sounded like the distant crashing of waves, or the hissing of gas, now resembled a whispering, except Veale couldn't make out the words, not yet. But he would be able to, he knew, as soon as he set foot in the Braycott, because he was sure that what he was hearing was the voice of a dead child, the one who was waiting for them inside—no, for him. Pantuff couldn't hear it, only he. Kara Sawyer was trying to talk to

Veale, but he didn't want to listen. Whatever she had to say would be of no consolation to him.

"I might go for a walk," he said suddenly.

"Where?" said Pantuff.

"Anywhere. I got a headache. Walking might help get rid of it."

"You're not running out on me, are you?" It was said as a joke, but underpinning it was the recognition that, at some point in the future, it might have to be said in earnest. They trusted each other as much as any men of their stripe could, which meant that they did not really trust each other at all.

"When I plan to leave, you'll know about it," said Veale.

But he was as close to abandoning his partner as he'd ever come. The only thing preventing it was the money. Veale wanted his half of the fifty thousand. Without it, he wouldn't be able to survive for long, not unless he planned on busing tables or cleaning restrooms—or the criminal equivalent of the same, which was knocking off convenience stores and mugging old ladies. Veale wasn't above either, and in the past he'd done both, but it was subsistence living, like feeding off dead matter. The $25,000 would elevate him, and his needs were few.

"So walk," said Pantuff. "But don't go trying to reach any horizons."

Pantuff hated sounding like Veale's mother, but he had his routines and didn't like them to be disturbed. He knew that he wouldn't be fully at peace without Veale nearby, not until the job was done and she was safely in their possession. As long as Veale was tramping the streets instead of sitting on a bed or chair in their shared room, Pantuff would be on edge. It wouldn't come between him and a nap, but his sleep might not be as restful as he desired.

"I won't," said Veale, as he got out of the car.

"You sure it's just a headache?"

"What else would it be?" said Veale.

"I don't know."

"Well then."

Veale closed the car door and walked away. Pantuff returned to scrutinizing the Braycott. The ambulance was pulling out of the parking lot, followed by one of the prowl cars and the unmarked Crown Vic. Pantuff decided to stay where he was until the last of the cops were gone. He now barely noticed the discomfort in his bladder. He was contemplating Veale. He wondered if the time hadn't come for them to go their separate ways. If it had, Pantuff's obligations to his partner would cease. Pantuff was no mathematician, but he saw that $50,000 would last him nearly twice as long as $25,000, allowing for the natural exuberance and temptation to spend that came with finding oneself with more funds than anticipated.

And it wasn't as though he'd miss the sparkling conversation.

CHAPTER

XXXIII

Melissa Thombs had retrieved the cell phone from behind the garbage cans while disposing of some take-out food containers that had begun to smell particularly rotten. It was now hidden, for the time being, in a box of tampons. Donnie wouldn't look for it there—not because he was averse to searching through even her most intimate belongings, but because he had already gone through her things the night before during one of his rages, and he wouldn't have the energy for another rampage, not for a day or so. If the private detective did not arrive to help her that night, as her mother had suggested he would, Melissa knew she would have to get rid of the phone. Donnie would find it otherwise. He had a dog's nose for contraband.

And if he discovered the device, he would hurt her.

She'd tried stashing a spare phone once before. She thought she was being clever by concealing it inside the body of one of the speakers for the little bedroom stereo system that only she used. She first made sure the phone was switched off, of course. It was there, she assured herself, only in the event of an emergency. The screwdriver she used to tighten the frames on her glasses just about fit the heads of the screws on the speaker, but she'd left them slightly loose once the phone was in place, to make it easier to get to if, or when, it was required. Perhaps that was how Donnie figured it out, by spotting the loose screws. He never bothered to share that detail with her. He was too busy putting his booted foot on the back of her head and slowly pressing her face into the carpet until she thought she'd suffocate or her skull would crack, whichever came first. Only when it seemed as though one outcome or the other was imminent did Donnie take his foot away, because he always knew how hard to push, to twist, to press, to hit. Or he used to: lately, his judgment had grown impaired. The last time he'd choked her, she'd lost consciousness. This had never happened before, and it was then she realized that, ultimately, he was going to kill her. When she came around, and her head had stopped hurting, he made her lie flat on the floor for four hours, with her arms outstretched and her face still in the carpet, during which time he watched two movies on the portable TV in the bedroom. Each time she moved, he would stand on her head again. That was about as bad as it had ever got, but even the incidents that weren't as bad were bad enough.

A brief lull in the abuse had occurred following the intervention of the police. Donnie promised her he'd change, that what had happened was a wake-up call. And he did try, for about a week, if one was prepared to accept that psychological and emotional bullying unallied to physical force represented progress in a relationship. It sort of did, Melissa supposed, even if it didn't last.

Why didn't she leave? It was a question she used to ask herself a lot. She had tried to give Donnie up, but that was in the beginning, and she'd always returned to him because she loved him, and sometimes problems got worse before they got better, right? Except there seemed to be no limits to how miserable life with Donnie could get, and the upswings were only the blips of a fading heartbeat. Later, he would dare her to leave. "Go," he would say. "There's the door. Collect all your shit and go back to your momma. I won't stop you."

She took the bait—once. She managed to get as far as opening the front door before he dragged her back. It was February, and in retaliation he locked her in the bathroom with the radiator off, taking the valve with him so she couldn't turn it on again, and leaving her with only a thin blanket for warmth. She spent the night in the bathtub, and on cold nights the memory of it returned to haunt her bones. After that, when he invited her to leave, she elected to remain seated, and silent.

But that still didn't explain why she'd remained. She tried not to dwell on it, because any answers she came up with didn't serve to make her feel better about herself or her situation. Yes, she was frightened of Donnie, and even if she left him, she knew he'd come find her. Getting out of the house would be only the beginning, and her terror of him would likely increase thereafter; at least when she was living with him, she knew where he was. The idea of a life spent looking over her shoulder did not appeal.

But Donnie could also be kind, when he chose. That was what was so confusing: somewhere inside him was a better man. They'd gone to a movie together the previous week, and for drinks and a hamburger after, and he'd been the way he was when they'd first started dating: funny, tender, caring. She also remembered that she used to feel safe around him, because nothing scared Donnie. He wasn't big, but he carried himself as though he was, and he communicated a physical threat, a potential ferocity. For someone like Melissa, who was small and shy—natural prey for a certain type of predator—having Donnie to watch over her was akin to being under the protection of a bodyguard. By the time she discovered that Donnie, too, was a predator, and his violence could, and would, be turned against her, it was too late.

And who else would take her now? She was damaged goods. She even had his name tattooed on her wrist, dumbass that she was. He had branded her as his own. Except that wasn't true, because she had consented to it. She might even have suggested it, so in love with him had she been. It didn't matter that he hadn't done the same. He didn't object to tattoos on women, he told her, or not the right tattoos, but he wasn't about to get any of his own. His skin was too white, he said, and he thought pale white guys with tattoos looked like trash. Upon consideration, Melissa had decided he was right. Her skin, by contrast, was sallow, and her ink looked classy against it—well, apart from consisting of Donnie's name, which spoiled the effect. If she got away from him, she could have it removed, but it would leave a scar. That wouldn't be a disaster, though. It would serve as a reminder, not that she'd need one. Call it a penitential mark.

Donnie was currently lazing in his armchair, his left leg hanging over one side, the fingers of his right hand tapping and jerking. He was always fidgeting now, always moving; even in his sleep, he was a mass of twitches. He smelled sour, too. It was another fault to add to the growing list. It helped her to hate him.

The private detective, the one hired by her mother, would come for her. He would spirit her away. She would start a new life, somewhere Donnie would never be able to find her. She would never see Donnie again.

Or . . .

The private detective, the one hired by her mother, would come for her. He would spirit her away. She would start a new life, but Donnie would come after her. He would commence with her mother, forcing her to tell him where she had gone. He would hurt her mother, and then he would hurt her.

Seated behind Donnie, Melissa worked on her hate.

CHAPTER

XXXIV

I spoke to my daughter Sam on the phone while I waited outside Angel and Louis's apartment. She was bright and chatty, and I was reminded of how much I missed her. I thought again about finding somewhere to stay near Burlington, just in case things got as bad as some people were suggesting they might, but while Sam was in Vermont, my life was here: my home, my job, what friends I had, and what might be a new relationship with Sharon Macy. I also knew that if I moved to Vermont, even temporarily, I would be doing it more for myself than for Sam. She had her own life, her own routines, and a mother and grandparents to watch over her. My presence, however novel and welcome it might seem initially, would soon become an imposition, and potentially a problem for those around her. I decided to stay where I was. If difficulties arose, I would be able to get to Vermont in four hours, and I knew how to work my way around roadblocks.

From where I sat, I could see some of the islands of Casco Bay, and the ferry pulling away from the dock at Peaks. I wondered if the inhabitants of the islands felt safer away from the mainland, and the farther, the better. Most distant of all was Sanctuary, but I wouldn't have moved out there even if we'd been facing bubonic plague instead of COVID-19. I knew enough about what had happened on that island to make me want to keep well away from it. It was said that Sanctuary's ghosts were quiet now. Some claimed they were at rest, while others tried to pretend they had never existed. Whatever the truth, Sanctuary was its own place, and anyway, there were enough ghosts on this side of the water for those with a mind to look for them—and sometimes, for those without.

Angel and Louis emerged from their building. Behind them the sea roiled, and the sky was gray, yet I couldn't help but smile. I found solace in the company of these men.

"All set to make the day worse for some bad guys?" said Louis, as he got in the front seat and Angel climbed in the back.

"Always," I said.

"Then let's go."

XXXV

The traffic was heavy in both directions as we drove to Portsmouth. Angel's hangover had been downgraded from life-threatening to miserable, and now he just wanted the day to end so he could return to bed, sleep off what was left of the pain, and wake up the next morning intent upon never sinning again. We kept the music low, in deference to his suffering.

The Hitch Knot stood at the end of Junkins Avenue, and looked like what it probably was: a bar for locals, with a menu to which the word "experimental" could be applied only if the option of sweet potato fries was one's idea of cutting edge. Oddly, I couldn't recall ever having noticed it before, despite being a fairly regular visitor to Portsmouth. The bar blended into its block, so that unless it was a destination, the eye would skate over it. Even the name was barely visible, and the only concession to theories of design was a brass version of the knot that gave the place its name, which hung from a rail above the door. But if Mattia Reggio was right, the Hitch Knot was also somewhere Portsmouth cops didn't frequent when off duty, although one could be sure they kept an eye on it. If Dante Vero felt safe conducting his business there, then its connections to the Office ran deep.

We parked outside, put our cell phones in the glove compartment, and had a brief discussion about weapons. We didn't want to come across as actively hostile, but nobody likes being a pushover, and Louis's warning about the Office's penchant for basement hospitality had stuck. In the end we decided that sometimes even the NRA was right, and it was better to have a gun and not need it than vice versa. A sign on the front door read CLOSED FOR PRIVATE FUNCTION. Either we were about to gate-crash a wake, or Dante Vero didn't want any witnesses or eavesdroppers. I could feel myself tensing up. Walking into these situations was never pleasant, and the more often I did it, the greater was the likelihood that one day I wouldn't walk out again.

I'd been expecting the interior of the Hitch Knot to be functional, but I was wrong. Money and care had been put into its furnishings: brass fittings, dark wood, red upholstery, and illumination bright enough to allow a newspaper to be read without inducing a headache, but subdued enough for intimacy. Five men waited for us inside, not counting the bartender, who had long white hair, a long white beard, and a face to match. He seemed unimpressed by our arrival, which put him on a par with the rest of the welcoming committee. One of them, the largest, was sitting at the bar, while the remaining four were congregated around a table halfway down the room. Dante Vero, recognizable from some brief Internet research, was second from the right, a medium-sized man dressed like a construction worker: jeans, checked shirt, and a padded jacket, topped off with a weathered Red Sox cap. He looked as though he wished he were somewhere else, which, if what was said about him was true, counted as his default mode of being. Some men are born to lead, and some have leadership thrust upon them. The hunch in Vero's shoulders, and his expression of weariness, suggested the weight of responsibility rested heavily on him, and he'd surrender it with gratitude the first chance he got.

The guy at the bar dropped from his stool, and we all waited a moment for the floor to stop shaking. He came toward us with a bug detector in hand, and swept it over each of us before turning to Vero and shaking his head.

"I suppose you're carrying," said Vero.

"We are," I said.

"Hardly worth asking you to hand them over, is it?"

"We wouldn't have bothered bringing them if it was."

Vero glanced at his companions and made a gesture of resignation with his hands.

"Then I guess you can hold on to them," he said, "if they mean that much to you."

Behind us, the man-mountain locked up, monitored by Angel. He'd dozed on the ride down, and was sharper now.

"You don't mind if my friend here takes a seat by the door?" I said, indicating Angel.

"He can sit anywhere he likes," said Vero. "But if you're worried about being stopped from leaving, that's not why we're here."

"We're not worried," said Louis, speaking for the first time. The ambiguity of the statement brought a smile even from Vero.

"Then take a seat. If you want something to drink, Saverio over there will provide."

"Coffee might be welcome," I said, as Louis and I joined the quartet at their table. The bartender stroked his beard, but didn't make any move to oblige until Vero gave him the nod, after which he sprang—or shuffled—into action. At the rate he was moving, we'd have been better off asking for the coffee iced. Angel stayed at the table closest to the door, keeping everyone in sight. The man-mountain stared at him for a while, as though trying to figure out why God would have bothered making anything so inconsequential, before returning to his perch.

Of the four men, I recognized only one apart from Vero: Luca Zamboni, or Luca Z, as he was known. Luca Z was about fifteen years younger than Vero, and had been in line for the position that the latter now occupied before the bosses in Providence opted for a more cautious, conservative hand to steady the ship in the Northeast until a more permanent solution could be found. Luca Z had taken the decision reasonably well, because he knew his time would come, perhaps even as soon as Vero was permitted to stand down. Until then he had been instructed to shadow the older man, thus providing some steel to underpin Vero's softer approach. Luca Z was also the one who had been prepared to allow his associates to rape Sarah Abelli. If the opportunity ever arose to do him an injury without bringing the wrath of the Office down upon me, I'd take it.

The others at the table—one older than Vero, one younger than Luca Z—struck me as a consigliere on the one hand, and a driver-cum-errand-boy on the other. The more senior of the pair was regarding Louis closely, the way one might some rare species of animal about which one had heard much, and which might give cause for concern if roused. He had sad, rheumy eyes, and hair that had thinned to wisps. He was also the most formally attired of anyone in the bar, which meant that he was wearing a tie.

"Is it Lew-is or Lou-ee?" he said, before introductions had been made.

"It's Lou-ee," said Louis. "My people came from Evangeline Parish, Louisiana, way back."

"Really? Because I heard both, Lew-is and Lou-ee."

"Then some of the time, you heard wrong."

"I like to get names straight. It's polite, you know?"

"I know," said Louis. "But you have the advantage over me when it comes to names."

"This is Adio Pirato," said Vero. "To my left is Luca Zamboni, and the young man here is Anthony. Mark, over by the bar, you already met."

Anthony and Mark clearly didn't merit last names. The only people who mattered were Vero, Luca Z, and Pirato, with their staunchly Italian nomenclature. I vaguely recalled the latter, maybe from gossip or court reports. If I had retained some memory of him, it was almost certainly with good cause.

"I've been interested to meet you gentlemen for some time," said

Pirato. "That's quite the reputation you've established for yourselves. Frankly, there are a lot of people who would pay good money to see you end up as landfill."

"Are you tempted?" I said.

"Not me. I figure only my next of kin would get to spend the bounty."

Which settled the matter. I can't say I wasn't relieved, although I couldn't speak for Louis. He was probably feeling sorry that they hadn't tried. Luca Z might have been inclined, if only to prove a point. Up close, I could practically hear his fuse sizzling.

The coffee arrived. A TV was playing over the bar, the sound muted. More pandemic news.

"You believe this shit?" said Vero.

"It doesn't look as though I have much choice," I said.

"The president says it's nothing to worry about," said Anthony. His voice was cracked and high, the tone of arrested adolescence.

"The fuck would you know about it?" said Luca Z. "You don't even vote."

"If I did vote," said Anthony, "I'd have voted for him."

"Yeah, and if you played Powerball, you'd be a millionaire by now. Mook."

I glanced at Louis. This was what happened when half your operation was ratted out, and even some of the smarter ones ended up in jail.

"My grandmother," said Vero, ignoring both of them, "she could remember the Spanish flu of 1918. They were dropping like flies, she said, and the sick were left to rot in their beds. Over in New Calvary, the gravediggers were tipping the bodies straight into the graves from the open coffins so they could be reused. Never thought it would happen in my lifetime."

There was silence, then Anthony said, "Is she still around?"

"Is who still around?" said Vero.

"Your grandmother."

Vero peered at him, reluctant to believe that a human being in his employ could be so dumb. "No, she isn't around," he said. "Do I look like Methusaleh to you?"

Anthony sighed, folded his arms, and gave every indication of removing himself from the colloquy, which was no great loss to the history of discourse. From memory, Anthony meant "praiseworthy" in Italian. If this Anthony wasn't a grave disappointment to his parents, I didn't want to meet them.

Pirato poured coffee for Louis and me. His hand was very steady.

"You know," he said, "after you leave, the cops, and no doubt the feds, too, may come asking why you were here."

"Bible study," I said.

"What about your friends? Are you going to claim that they're students of God's word also?"

"I'll say they came along in case of doctrinal disagreements."

Pirato glanced past me to where Angel was seated, still looking sorry for himself.

"Even that one? He strikes me as unwell."

"He always looks that way."

"Hey—" said Angel.

But everyone ignored him.

"Well, I hope you know your scripture," said Vero.

It was time to get down to business.

"I remember something about bearing false witness," I said, "but I'm not sure it would apply in the case of Nate Sawyer's testimony, since all the evidence suggested it was true."

"Sawyer is dead," said Pirato. "He's yesterday's news."

"Yet here we are, all at the mention of his name."

"He caused us a great deal of inconvenience, and hurt a lot of good people."

"I think your definition of 'good' may be open to dispute."

Luca Z opened his mouth to take issue, but Pirato waved a hand at him, so he closed it again. I recognized that Pirato was operating as more than an advisor here. Both Vero and Luca Z were deferring to him, which meant that, as far as this meeting was concerned, Pirato was the eyes, ears, and mouth of the Office.

"We're not here to discuss semantics," he said. "Why did you need to speak with us so urgently about Sawyer?"

"Because he may be dead, but his widow remains alive."

"Fucking bitch," said Luca Z.

Pirato and Vero scowled at the intervention, but didn't bother to contradict him.

"What about her?" asked Pirato.

"Certain items have been stolen from her. They're being held for ransom."

"What items?"

"Mementos of her dead child, possessions that are of no value to anyone but her."

"And she's employed you to retrieve them?"

"That's right."

Vero's scowl deepened.

"So what's that to us?"

"Nate Sawyer stole money from the Office, and it's never been located. There are people in your organization who believe that his widow may know where it is. Pressure has been applied before, along with a degree of pain. We want to make sure that it isn't being applied again."

"Pain? I heard only that she was questioned about the money before being released unharmed."

Dante Vero's eyes flicked toward Luca Z, who shook his head fractionally. Pirato, who missed nothing, registered both tells.

"She was sexually assaulted and threatened with rape," I said. "The men responsible also promised to dig up her daughter's remains and feed them to hogs if she didn't tell them where the money was."

I didn't bother adding that they'd then forced her to sign over her home. Pirato must have been aware of that much, but the expression on his face indicated that the rest was news to him. He wasn't so much of a sentimentalist as to be shocked by allegations of sexual violence, but he was old-school enough to disapprove of disinterring a grieving woman's child and throwing the corpse to animals.

"She told you this?" he said.

"That's right."

Pirato turned to Vero. "Did you know about it?"

Vero, to his credit, didn't even flirt with evasion.

"I was there. It got out of hand. I put a stop to it before it could go any further."

"And these were some of our people?" said Pirato.

"No." It was Luca Z who answered this time. "We brought in outside contractors."

Vero twitched, and Luca Z corrected himself.

"*I* brought them in," he said. "I'd been told that one of them specialized in dealing with women. It may be that I didn't fully grasp the implications."

"Or you didn't want to," said Pirato.

"I didn't have a whole lot of choice. We had guys behind bars, others in hiding, and most of the rest under surveillance—and the ones who weren't being watched were afraid they might be. We needed to come up with cash for lawyers, for wives and children. We thought Sawyer's widow might know what he'd done with the money he stole from us."

Vero spoke up.

"And nobody we knew wanted to do what had to be done," he said. "Her husband might have been a thief and a rat, but she was mourning her dead kid. Luca is right: we were in a jam, and we didn't have time for niceties. Scaring her some was the right way to go. It just went south fast. The men involved were vermin, and should never have been allowed near her, but it's not all Luca's fault. I should have paid more attention to the details."

I kept quiet. Great guy that he was, Dante Vero had waited until long after one of the men had put his fingers inside Sarah Abelli before deciding that enough was enough. He could tolerate molestation, up to a point, but he didn't want to have to witness a rape.

Pirato took some time to mull over what he'd heard before turning to me.

"So where are we with this?" he asked.

"My belief is that the same two men may be responsible for targeting Sawyer's widow," I said. "I also doubt they have any intention of returning what they took. They don't strike me as individuals of high moral character. I sense malice to them."

I looked first at Dante Vero, then Luca Z. I let my eyes rest slightly longer on the latter, and made sure Pirato saw it.

"This is going to end badly for them," I continued, "because that's the way they're calling it. If someone from your organization is involved, now is the time to say so. We don't want blowback, not if it can be avoided, but if it's a choice between that and letting these men deprive a mother of all she has left of her dead child, we'll accept the consequences."

Pirato stared at Dante Vero and Luca Z.

"Well?"

Vero shook his head.

"No," he said. "On my mother's life."

But Luca Z hesitated.

"I didn't set them on her," he said at last, "and I'm not in communication with them."

"Go on," said Pirato.

"After that thing in the basement, one of them asked what kind of finder's fee there might be—you know, if they discovered where that fucking Sawyer had hidden our money."

"A finder's fee?" said Pirato. "What were you planning to do, put a notice in the window of a grocery store?"

"What did you take that to mean?" I asked Luca Z.

He addressed his reply to Pirato, not me.

"That they might make another run at her, if the chance arose," he said. "If they did, and she confessed, they knew we'd find out sooner or later. They couldn't just walk away with the cash. They'd have to come to us with it, and accept whatever cut we gave."

And perhaps that had been their plan, at least for a while, until they decided that it might be easier to target Nate Sawyer's widow and see how much money they could get out of her without involving the Office. I wondered when they'd come up with the idea of taking her daughter's things. It had the mark of a crime of opportunity, unless they'd somehow found out about the items from someone familiar with her. When they'd entered her home, it was probably in the hope that she might be holding some of the cash there. When that turned out not to be the case, they were sufficiently resourceful, or callous, to figure out another way to make her pay by using her grief against her.

"Who are they?" I said.

"I'm no rat," said Luca Z.

"Listen to me," I said. "Your organization doesn't need any more attention from the police or the FBI, but that's what's going to happen if this thing runs its course. We aim to take these men alive, although I can't guarantee it, and then what they did, and who they targeted, will be revealed. You're telling us that nobody in this room was aware of what was happening. That might be true, but it won't stop people from speculating otherwise, and it could be enough to instigate a whole new cyc of investigations, because the law likes nothing better than an excuse to go nosing around in the enterprises of crooked men. And even if that doesn't happen, you'll be associated with a crime that will do your reputations no good, not even among your own kind. Stealing the remembrances of a dead girl from her mother? Murderers will cross the street to avoid you."

Pirato didn't appear noticeably bothered by this, since murderers probably already crossed the street to avoid him, but Dante Vero had the decency to look mildly ashamed.

"You got kids?" said Louis to Pirato.

"Yeah, I got kids."

"Grandchildren?"

"Those, too."

"You care about them?"

"Sure I do."

"Then why are we still talking about this?"

Pirato brushed some grains of sugar from the table into an open palm, and set them in his saucer.

"Tell him," he said to Luca Z.

Luca Z knew when he was beaten. There might have been some small hope for him after all.

"Their names are Lyle Pantuff and Gilman Veale," he said. "Pantuff is older, and he's the one who likes hurting women. He's the talker. Veale is younger and quieter. I don't think he's particular about who he hurts."

"How did you find them?" I said.

"I asked around. They came recommended."

I didn't care to consider how one might go about finding someone who specialized in torturing women, or a go-between who might be in a position to offer suggestions, and how they might know this in the first place. Life was already bleak enough.

"How did you get in touch with them?"

"They contacted me, after I put the word out. I got a call, and we met at a bar in Somerville. I went through what had to be done, told them where to take the woman, and they pulled her from her home the next day."

"So you have a number?"

"Not anymore. They don't like leaving a trail. They only occasionally work for hire. They're self-starters, pulling down small scores."

"Scavengers," said Pirato.

Luca Z shrugged.

"How long have they been working together?" I said.

"A couple of years, I think."

"Are they shooters?"

"Not if they can avoid it, but they're not above killing, Veale especially. The guy I worked through, he knew of a couple of bodies, and was willing to bet on more."

"Who is he," I said, "this mysterious figure who knows about bodies?"

"No," said Luca Z. He shook his head, and sought support from his elders. "It's one thing giving up Pantuff and Veale, but another to make trouble for one of our friends."

"You haven't given me anything but two names," I said, "and they're no good to me unless I can lay hands on the men who use them."

"But Luca is right," said Pirato. "There are limits here."

"We could get word to them," offered Dante Vero, "order them to hand over the stuff they took and walk away."

"Perhaps you could ask them to make a donation to charity as well," said Louis.

"Or they could write a note to say they're sorry," said Angel, from by the door, "and throw in a gift card from Macy's to make up for the trouble they've caused."

Vero raised an eyebrow and smothered a smile.

"Those men don't work for you," I said to him. "They have no obligations to you or your organization. According to the mastermind here, he can't even get them on the phone without bringing in an adult to help dial the number."

"Don't fucking talk about me that way," said Luca Z, but he spoke too loudly. There was no substance to it, only bluster. Everyone knew it, even Luca Z himself.

"What I'm saying," I continued, "is that I don't trust these thieves to do the right thing, or even the smart one, if they're contacted by you or an intermediary. Neither do I trust any of your people to enforce a penalty on them if they renege on a deal, and by then it will be too late because they'll have dumped or destroyed this woman's possessions."

"And we'd be of a mind to take that amiss," said Louis.

"Yes," I said, "we really would."

"Then what would satisfy you?" asked Pirato.

"We deal with them, and in our own way. Your part will be to help us locate them. If you can't do that, even with your best efforts, then we'll settle for whatever number they're currently using. If we have the number, we can snare them."

"And that's all? That will be the end of it?"

"As long as my client isn't bothered again."

Dante Vero made a sucking noise through his teeth.

"Some among us still think she has our money," he said.

"Then swallow the loss, because even if she does have it, you're not getting it back, not after this."

Pirato wagged a finger at me.

"You know," he said, "I now grasp why so many people would be happy to see you dead."

"You're getting off easy," I said, "and I think you realize it."

"I don't agree with this," said Luca Z. "I say we tell them to go fuck themselves and take our chances."

Pirato eyed him wearily.

"You swear too much," he said. "You should consider modifying your language in company. As for whether you agree or not, it's immaterial. You got us into this mess, you and Dante both. You made two strangers privy to our difficulties, then set them loose to exploit that knowledge however they chose. Now that mess has to be cleaned up, and you're going to do your share of the sweeping."

"Our contact," said Vero, "will know we broke faith if Pantuff and Veale are taken down."

"Then you'll have to ensure that he appreciates the reason for it," said Pirato. "It might be easier than you think. They're bottom-feeders, and were born to be eaten by bigger fish. After they're gone, others will come along to take their place. We're never going to run short of their breed."

"What if they take our decision personally?" said Luca Z.

"Then their end will come sooner. But if they're wise, they'll swallow their medicine like men and chalk it up to experience. It's business, that's all. Make the call, Luca. Say that we need them for a job, something urgent, with good money to be paid fast. I leave the wording up to you. When you're not swearing, you can approach eloquence."

Luca Z took out his cell phone and rose to conduct the conversation in private.

"No," said Pirato, "do it here, where everyone can listen." Then he threw Luca Z a bone, just to pretend that it wasn't because he didn't trust him. "It will assure our guests of our good faith."

The rest of us waited in silence while Luca Z found the number in his contacts. Beside him, Dante Vero couldn't hide his displeasure, although it wasn't clear if he was bothered by Pirato's order or troubled by his own proximity to someone careless enough to keep a torturers' intermediary among his cell phone contacts.

We listened while the call was answered, and Luca Z did his wise-guy shtick, with still more swearing, before getting down to business. He stayed on-message throughout, from what I could tell, but I was relieved that Pirato had insisted on an audience for the exchange. I wouldn't have trusted Luca Z to park my car without stealing my spare change. Obviously Pirato was of a similar opinion, and might well have held it long before he arrived at the Hitch Knot.

"Do you know where they are?" Luca Z was asking the intermediary. "Why? Because they're no use to me if they're in Seattle, or fucking Alaska, that's why." Luca Z took in the reply. "How close? Uh-huh, uh-huh. You got somewhere I can call them at? There's money in this if they can get it done quickly, and I'll make sure you're taken care of as well. You know I'm good for it."

He snapped his fingers in the air and made a writing gesture. Dante Vero produced a ballpoint pen, and pushed that day's copy of the *Boston Herald* toward him. I watched as Luca Z scribbled a cell phone number above the masthead. I was already entering it on my own phone before he'd finished setting down the final digit.

Luca Z ended the call. He looked to be on the verge of flinging his cell phone against a wall, but restrained himself.

"That was bullshit," he said. "He's never going to talk to me again, and if he spreads the word, no one else will either."

"Then we make sure he keeps his mouth shut," said Vero. "We can do that. We're not the Rotary Club."

But I was barely paying attention to them as I entered the number on my tracker app. The SIM in the cell phone held by Pantuff and Veale was constantly transmitting data, even when it wasn't in use. That made it vulnerable to geolocation. The app wasn't perfect, but it could narrow a cell phone's position down to a block, or even a building. This time, though, I'd have known where these men were holed up even if the app had been able to offer only the most general indication of their whereabouts, because there was only one hotel in that locale.

They were staying at the Braycott Arms. Of course they were.

———

PIRATO WALKED LOUIS AND me to the door of the Hitch Knot, where we joined Angel. We were out of earshot of the others.

"I can't say it was a pleasure doing business with you," said Pirato, "but it was less painful than it might have been—for all of us."

"Except Luca," I said.

"He'll get over it."

"I wouldn't be so sure."

"You worried for yourself?"

"It was just a general observation."

"Structures up here," said Pirato, "they're in transition. These have been hard years. Stability is required while we rebuild. I've been tasked with making it happen."

"I'd wish you luck," I said, "but it would go against the grain."

"I can see how it might." He took in the three of us. "You appreciate that this is a favor you were owed, and we're even now."

"A favor?" I said, although I thought I knew for what.

"We had an agreement with Mother down in Providence," said Pirato. "She didn't encroach on us, and we paid her the same courtesy. It wasn't ideal—for us more than her—but the alternative wouldn't have been worth the aggravation. We were waiting for her to die, except her idiot son started to get ideas above his station, and she indulged him. Then you three came along and solved the problem for us."

"We didn't touch her son," I said.

"You didn't have to. You simply made what happened to him inevitable."

"You ever hear from her?" said Louis.

"Mother doesn't make social calls, and doesn't receive them either. If what I hear is true, she has dementia, or it may be that what you forced her to do drove her insane. Me, I'd suggest a woman with those capacities was deranged to begin with."

He patted me on the shoulder.

"Time for you to go now. When you see Mattia Reggio, mention to him that I said hello. Tell him I was over at Revere Beach not so long ago."

He unlocked the door of the bar to let in some light.

"I looked at the Argent," he said, "and thought of him."

CHAPTER

XXXVI

Veale spent a couple of hours walking the streets of Portland, and when he wasn't walking he found places to sit, observe, and brood. He didn't know the city, had never been there before, and suspected he would never return once he and Pantuff had completed their business. Veale didn't like cities at the best of times, even ones as small as this, but he'd also had his fill of people, so the pandemic might have been arranged with him in mind. He planned to stock up on food and supplies and find a place to wait it out. He supposed that, if he and Pantuff could afford a unit big enough, they might not even have to see each other very often; or they could go to a trailer park and rent adjacent units. But as he walked, Veale began more and more to conceive of a life without Pantuff by his side.

In the meantime Veale's headache hadn't gone away, and neither had the damn hissing. *No, call it what it is. Call it speech. And you could understand the words, if you chose, regardless of proximity to that damned hotel, but you don't want to listen, not yet. You will, though, you will.* He'd bought some painkillers at a gas station and swallowed them dry, but they hadn't helped. Finally, when his feet began to ache, he resigned himself to returning to the Braycott Arms.

———

THE MANAGER, WADLIN, WAS sitting at his desk, another western playing on his television. He barely bothered to acknowledge Veale, who
remained standing at the plexiglass, unspeaking.

"Your buddy already went up," said Wadlin. "He's got the key. If you
want a second, you'll have to pay another security deposit."

On the screen, natives were being picked off by soldiers hiding
behind adobe walls. The film was in black and white, so Veale knew
how it was going to end. The cavalry only ever lost in color, except in
that Errol Flynn movie about Custer. Veale produced a twenty-dollar
bill and slid it over.

"I'll take that second key," he said, "in case my friend is sleeping."

Wadlin made a big show of being inconvenienced, though he only
had to move his chair about six inches in order to open a cabinet and
withdraw the spare. The twenty disappeared into his pocket, the key
was dropped in the drawer, and Wadlin returned to his western.

"I knew a guy once," said Veale.

Wadlin's eyes didn't leave the action, but to Veale the manager's mind
was elsewhere, and he was looking less at the screen than through it,
following images only he could see.

"You don't say."

"He was Black," Veale continued. "He told me that, when he was
a kid, his old man used to take him to the Apollo Theater in Harlem
to watch westerns as part of the show, and when the Indians shot a
cowboy, the audience would cheer."

Wadlin found the clicker and paused the movie.

"Why would they do that?" he said. He sounded genuinely puzzled.

"Because they were Black," said Veale, "and the cowboys were white."

"But there were Negroes in the cavalry, too," said Wadlin, who
remained unreconstructed, and was only woke first thing in the morning. "Buffalo soldiers, they called them, I think on account of the
buffalo-skin coats they used to wear in winter, or maybe their hair.
When it came to the Indians, everyone was on the same side."

"Not in Harlem," said Veale.

"No, I guess not. But then, they didn't have many Indians in Harlem." Wadlin hit the clicker again, and the killing resumed. "You're covered for one more night," he said. "If you're planning on staying longer, payment in advance would be appreciated."

"We're about done here," said Veale. "We won't need the room beyond morning. Could be we may even be gone come nightfall."

"Well, don't forget to return both keys, that's if you want your deposits back."

Veale considered throwing the keys in a river, and fuck the deposits, if only to cause Wadlin a little inconvenience. The man reminded him of a pale toad.

"What was all the fuss earlier?" said Veale. "The police, and the ambulance."

Wadlin inhaled so hard that his shoulders touched his earlobes.

"One of the long-term guests had a heart attack down in the basement," he said. "An old woman. She was dead before the medics got to her. Very sad."

Veale didn't think it was so sad, if she was old. Old people died. To Veale, they had no other function. Only the circumstances interested him.

"What was she doing in the basement?" he said.

"Stealing."

"Stealing what?"

"Furniture for her room. It was full of stuff that shouldn't have been there, all taken from our basement. Pictures, lamps, rugs. Seems housekeeping was turning a blind eye. I'd fire a couple of them as an example, if I didn't need them so bad."

"Doesn't sound like stealing to me," said Veale. "More like redecorating, which the rooms could do with."

He could see Wadlin thinking about objecting to the slur before deciding it had the ring of truth to it.

"Doesn't mean she could go helping herself," said Wadlin. "And look where she ended up because of it: in a body bag." He tapped the clicker meaningfully with a long fingernail. "Anything else on your mind?"

"That kid you mentioned earlier," said Veale, "the one that was running around during the night. You hear anything else about it?"

"There was no kid," he said, but Veale caught something in his face. It wasn't a lie, exactly, but there was confusion, anxiety.

"The old woman," said Veale, "they have any idea what caused the heart attack?"

"I'm no doctor," said Wadlin, "but my diagnosis would be that it was probably her heart."

Veale was immune to sarcasm. It passed him by. This was one of his strengths, although since it didn't register, he didn't recognize it as such. Right now, he just thought Wadlin was even dumber than previously suspected.

"I mean," he said, "could something have scared her?"

"Like what?" said Wadlin.

There it was again, Veale thought: edginess. Veale had been witness to it often enough to be able to spot it, even when it was concealed.

"I don't know," he said. "Like a child, maybe?"

Wadlin flinched, and Veale knew for sure.

"I got things to do," said Wadlin.

He got up, killed the TV, and retreated to his private quarters. Veale stayed where he was, staring at the scarred security screen and thinking that Wadlin was a prisoner of the Braycott, but didn't know it or didn't care. The exchange with the manager was the longest he'd had with a stranger in years. He'd been killing time, postponing his return to the room.

He also realized two other things. His headache had gone, which was good. But he could now hear clearly the voice in his head.

Which was bad.

Very, very bad.

XXXVII

B obby Wadlin waited behind the door of his apartment, one ear pressed to the wood, until he was sure Veale had gone. Even then Bobby did not immediately resume his post. If someone wanted their key or their mail, they could goddamn well wait. He went to his bedroom, opened his bedside table, and took out a spray bottle of Bach's Rescue Remedy. Abigail Stackpole had recommended it to him a while back, when some of his guests were proving unusually recalcitrant. He'd been skeptical about the Rescue Remedy at first. As far as he could tell, it was made up of flowers, but it worked, although Bobby suspected this might be a result of the placido effect, like the singer. Whatever the reason, since he wasn't a drinker, and didn't hold with heavy narcotics, Bach had become Bobby's go-to guy in times of stress. He spritzed his mouth five times. Bobby just wanted this day to be done. He'd already dealt with one fatality, endured more unwanted conversations than a man could bear, and wasted valuable time searching for an elusive child.

At this, Bobby knocked back another five shots of spray.

Old Esther had been right, Phil Hardiman too: there *was* a child in the hotel, but it wasn't one that Bobby was in any hurry to meet again. The Braycott might have been old, but until today, and unlike so many institutions of similar vintage, Bobby had been convinced that it had no ghost stories to share. Perhaps because the surroundings were so deficient, even spirits didn't care to mope around inside its walls for too long for fear of becoming depressed. As a result, Bobby had never been frightened of the Braycott at night, or certainly not because of the dead, although some of the living might have given him pause for thought.

But he didn't think he'd be going back to the basement, not for a while.

———

IT HAD BEEN A hell of an afternoon for Bobby, what with the fuss over Esther Vogt and all—not that he'd be grieving excessively for her, although nobody liked to lose a tenant who paid on time, even one as occasionally vexatious as she. One of the housekeepers had discovered the still-warm body and raised such a hollering and lamentation you'd have figured her for Mary Magdalene stumbling from Christ's empty tomb, except in this case the vault was most certainly occupied, even if the spirit had definitely departed. The police and paramedics had found no signs of foul play, with the medics being of the view that old Esther had probably suffered a sudden cardiac arrest, a conclusion supported by a search of her room, which revealed enough medications to start a pharmacy, including antiarrhythmics and ACE inhibitors.

After the professionals had finished their business, Bobby took a brush and pan down to the locus of all the activity with the intention of clearing up the mess they'd left, including some broken glass and a busted chair. He'd planned to take pictures of the damage for the insurance company, because he knew an antiques dealer who might be prepared to produce inflated valuations in return for a few bucks. Bobby thought he could also find a couple of other pieces that were already broken long before the first responders started moving stuff around. His insurance policy had a bitch of a deductible, but if he assembled enough exaggerated estimates, he was certain to come out ahead while getting rid of some junk.

Unfortunately, the replacement bulb, inserted to aid the removal of the body, had blown, which meant Bobby had to go dig out yet another and retrieve the ladder, because he'd need decent illumination for the insurance photos. Once he'd located both, and a flashlight, he returned to the basement, picked his way to the heart of the room, and cleared enough space to erect the ladder. He climbed up carefully—he didn't want to end up going ass-over-tit and have to summon 911 for a return visit—and positioned the flashlight so it was pointing at the ceiling. Bobby hoped he wouldn't have to replace the light fitting, because every nickel counted these days.

He had just begun removing the spent bulb when the ladder shook.

———

IN HIS COZY APARTMENT, with its shelves upon shelves of movies, novels, and reference volumes, and its biographies and autobiographies of western stars, Bobby Wadlin—for the first time that he could recall—no longer felt comfortable or safe. Something had been stolen from him in that basement, never to be recovered, but the Braycott itself had also been tilted on its axis, its dimensions altered, if not beyond recognition, then in such a manner as to guarantee that its precincts could no longer be negotiated as before. It was as though Bobby's beloved hotel had been replaced with a simulacrum that was almost, but not quite, identical: a foot narrower here, an inch lower there; a doorway where once there was a wall, a step where none had previously existed. His sanctuary was gone, wrenched from him in a matter of moments, pulled away from beneath him like—

Like a ladder.

He set aside the Rescue Remedy. He felt a bit calmer already, but he thought it was more that he wanted, *needed*, to be pacified than the combination of ingredients he had ingested. It was already dark outside, although its impact on the interior of the Braycott was set to be marginal, given its natural tendency toward sepulchral gloom. But

Bobby was now looking at the darkness in a different way: not as a product of the sun going down, or the effect of the accumulated dirt on the windows, but as an atmospheric state generated from within, a dreadful caliginosity with its source to be found in the basement, its principal animus a new and uninvited guest.

———

THE LADDER: BACK TO the ladder.

At first, he took the shaking to be his own fault. He must have misplaced one of the supports so that it rested on the edge of an old rug, or stood in one of the slight depressions that pitted the floor. In removing the bulb, he had caused his weight to shift, and the ladder to teeter. Yes, that was it. He'd have to proceed slowly, but it wasn't worth climbing back down again, because the light fixture was just within reach—

The ladder rattled hard again, but this time he felt the impact from below. Someone had thrown their weight against it, causing it to sway more sharply. Bobby managed to hold on to the grips, but the old bulb slid off and exploded on the floor, and before he could stop it, his flashlight went the same way. It did not break, but instead came to rest pointing toward the door, lighting his way back to safety.

"Who's there?" said Bobby. "Goddammit, you better quit fooling around. I got a gun, and I'll use it."

He didn't have a gun, of course. He liked guns in Westerns, preferably when they were in the hands of Audie Murphy or Gary Cooper, men you could trust, but he didn't hold with them as a general principle. He'd spent long enough at the Braycott to realize that most guns were in the possession of people who couldn't be trusted with a water pistol.

Bobby listened. Whoever was fooling with him was delicate on their feet. All that junk—sorry, antique furnishings—in the basement, and he still hadn't heard the approach. They might as well have materialized beneath him, so stealthy had they been. Whatever their method, he needed to get back on firm ground, and fast. Once he had the flashlight in his hands, he could get a good look at them. Just to his left, but out of reach for now, was a brass lamp that would serve as a weapon. He risked moving his right foot, searching for the rung below so he could begin his descent.

Which was when the light in the hallway went out.

———

FROM HIS APARTMENT, BOBBY heard someone come down the stairs and pass by the front desk. There was the sound of a key being deposited in the slot, and the main door opening and closing. He didn't bother going to his window to see who it was. They'd left the key, which was the important thing. After that, they could do whatever the hell they liked.

Bobby sat on the edge of his bed. His hands were shaking and he was trying very hard not to throw up. He'd left part of himself in that basement, and he wasn't sure that he was ever going to get it back.

———

SO THERE HE WAS, as good as marooned in the dark, with only the beam of the flashlight for comfort, while someone intent on causing him harm lurked amid dead folks' furniture. Bobby could call for help, but it wouldn't bring anyone running, not unless they were on the first floor and listening hard. For the present, he was on his own.

His right foot found the rung it was looking for, and the left shifted position to join it. A scuffling noise came from nearby. Bobby twisted, squinting into the shadows, and in the beam of the flashlight he caught movement, small and pale; a rat or mouse, perhaps, except it was the wrong shape, and pink, not gray. Bobby stayed where he was and peered more closely.

It was a foot, the toes poking from holes in what looked like white stockings, although the limb was too slight to belong to an adult. This was a child's foot, but the nails were long, almost like claws, and the surrounding skin was filthy and wrinkled. Bobby saw that it had receded from the beds, which was making the nails appear elongated, because no child naturally had toes that ended in talons. The one from the big toe was missing, and the exposed bed was rotten and black.

That was when Bobby understood, and he wondered how one went about reasoning with the dead.

"Don't hurt me," he said. "I don't mean you no harm."

The foot was withdrawn from the light as its owner realized that it had been spotted.

"I just came down here to fix the light," Bobby continued, "but if you prefer the dark, that's okay, too. I can leave it be."

The foot appeared again. Bobby reacted, and once more it was pulled back into the dark.

Jesus, he thought, *it's playing a game.*

He had little experience of children, and hadn't joshed with one since he was a child himself. Neither was he a sensitive man, because he had no interest in people beyond their ability to pay for rooms in his hotel, and the relative levels of convenience or inconvenience he might incur as a result. But here, in a basement that was just a couple of batteries away from total blackness, he instinctively felt that this presence, although it might not mean him harm, could still cause it. It was fooling with him for its amusement, but its grin had sharp teeth. That joke with the ladder could have broken his neck if he'd landed badly, and he thought old Esther Vogt might have made the acquaintance of this same visitor shortly before her heart exploded. Bobby didn't want to die with the specter of a child hovering over him. He didn't want to die, period, but he very much did not want it to happen under the current conditions.

The ladder was trembling, but the child had nothing to do with it. It was trembling because Bobby Wadlin was trembling also. Somehow, he made the effort to smile.

"Peek-a-boo," he said. "I see you."

The foot briefly stabbed the light, and he heard laughter. He moved a rung farther down the ladder, and the laughter stopped. Bobby closed his eyes and prayed.

"I have to go," he said. "I got things to do, a hotel to take care of. But you can stay down here, if you like. Most nobody comes into the basement, except me."

And Esther Vogt, of course, but Esther wasn't likely to be rummaging for buried treasure again, not unless she was so attached to the Braycott that she decided to try a postmortem spell of holing up in it. Bobby had an image of a storage room filled with ghosts, a subterranean vault of phantasms who couldn't afford to haunt anywhere more refined. He was forced to stifle a giggle.

I have embraced madness.

In the dark, the child ceased its playacting. They'd come to it now, Bobby knew: blackness or light, and the former, if the cards fell that way, would be perpetual for him, just as it was for Esther. He negotiated the final rungs, and his legs were unsteady as he set both feet on the floor. He kept his eye on the beam, trying to memorize the obstacles illuminated by it, because if it went out, he was going to run. If the child wanted him, he'd make the little shit fight for the pleasure.

In the hallway the bulb came back on, its glare reaching out like a hand to swallow up the finger of brightness from the flashlight. The shapes of the movables in the basement came into focus, but where the child had been Bobby could now see only a reading chair with the stuffing bleeding from one arm. He thought the child might even have been sitting in that chair, because it was low enough for its feet to reach the floor.

He picked up the flashlight, but resisted the temptation to shine it around, just in case it should land on something he did not wish to see.

"Thank you," he said, as loudly as he could. "I'll be on my way."

He packed up the ladder and carried it with him to the hallway. The basement bulb still hadn't been replaced, but he wasn't going to worry about that. It would be a while before he chose to venture back down here again, at least unaccompanied. He'd been considering hiring a handyman on a part-time basis anyway, because he wasn't as young as he used to be, and he had to admit that the Braycott was starting to look frayed around the edges. He knew a couple of do-it-yourselfers who'd be glad of the work, cash on the barrelhead, and one of them could start in a day or two. Bobby would add installing a new bulb in the basement to the list of tasks, but a clearing out of some of this old stuff wouldn't hurt either. The Lord alone knew what might be hiding among it, he would tell the guy: rodents, cockroaches, anything.

Anything at all.

CHAPTER

XXXVIII

Donnie Packard was leaning against the jamb of the bedroom door, his stare sometimes following Melissa, monitoring her movements, before turning inward to traverse another landscape. He'd been smoking Spice earlier in the afternoon, and the fishy smell drifted to her from where he stood, but he was coming down from it, his heart rate almost back to normal, the blinding headache that had left him screaming reduced to a dull throb. She'd locked herself in the bathroom to get away from him. Had the pain in his head not been so bad he might have tried to bust the door from its hinges, but he'd resorted only to kicking it halfheartedly a couple of times before sinking to the floor and mumbling to himself for an hour. He terrified her when he was like that, but she felt a different fear of him now. Somehow, Donnie was scarier when he was in control of himself.

"What are you doing?" he said. It was the first time he'd spoken since appearing.

"What does it look like I'm doing?" she replied, as she dropped a pair of his dirty boxers into a laundry bag. "I'm cleaning up after you, like I always do."

She instantly regretted the barb. There was no cause to goad him. He was perfectly capable of moving from calm to fury without her help.

"No, I mean, what are you doing behind my back?"

It took all of her self-control not to react.

"I don't know what you're talking about. You're looking at me. I'm in front of you."

"Don't get slick. I saw you and your mother earlier. I was watching you, listening to you. You weren't acting natural, neither of you. What were you two sly bitches cooking up?"

Melissa continued gathering clothing, progressing from jocks to socks. He hadn't always been so slovenly, just as he hadn't always been so paranoid and violent—or an addict, which might have explained a lot. But the deterioration had been gradual, not sudden. It had sneaked up on her, trapping her like briars that surrounded her in a forest because she'd remained in one spot for too long. And the question returned to her, the same one that would be asked if, or when, he finally got around to killing her: Why didn't she leave him? Well, to hell with that. How about asking why *he* was the way he was? Why put all the responsibility for her fate on her?

But she had a satisfactory answer to the big question at last. It had come to her earlier, as she sat on the bathroom floor, waiting out the effects of the Spice. She hadn't left him because she hadn't been sure that she wouldn't return to him if she did. Now she was ready. She was done with him. Was it because her mother, by hiring the private detective, had given her an out? She conceded it had acted as a catalyst. A hand had been extended to her at the right time, just as she was finally starting to lose her grip, with a void waiting below. There are times when we need someone to say, "I'm here. The first step is down to you, but once you take that step, you won't be alone. So how about it?" It was an exercise in trust, like the teamwork exercises for field hockey back at Scarborough High, when you folded your arms across your chest, closed your eyes, and allowed yourself to fall backward. In that moment, a voice in your head screamed that you'd made a terrible mistake, until you fell into the embrace of another.

But she had yet to permit herself to fall, and now Donnie was staring at her, all vacancy gone from him. He understood her. He understood her so well. How could she ever have hoped to escape from this man?

"We were just talking," she said. "You were there. And don't call her a bitch, or me either."

He rolled spit on his tongue. Had her mother been present, he might have expectorated in her face.

"I know she wants you to leave me," he said.

She detected no trace of self-pity. He wasn't whining. It was presented solely as a statement of fact. If she retreated, if she tried to disavow it, he'd be on her in an instant. He'd tear her apart.

Melissa dropped the laundry bag.

"Can you blame her?" she said. "Do you even see what this place has become, how it looks, how it stinks? Why wouldn't she be worried? Why wouldn't she want me to leave? This isn't what she wanted for me. Hell, this isn't what you wanted for yourself. Jesus, Donnie, how did we ever let it get so bad?"

This wasn't what he had been expecting. She wasn't sure that he'd even noticed how nimbly she'd sidestepped his suspicions. She picked up the laundry bag and flung it at him—but not hard, not with real anger. He caught it instinctively, and she found it within herself to smile.

"Look, why don't you help me tidy up some?" she said. "We can open the windows and let some air in before it starts getting too cold."

She waited. She could see his better self trying to gain the upper hand. When it did, she felt a brief surge of warmth toward him. Without saying anything more, he began clearing the floor of his discarded clothing, adding a couple of empty beer cans along the way.

See? she thought. *This is why we stay. This is how they manipulate us. And this is how we die.*

XXXIX

We were already on our way back to Portland. The traffic hadn't eased any, and progress was slow.

"Is that crosspatch still managing the Braycott?" said Louis.

"Bobby Wadlin?" I said. "Sure, and he will be until he dies. After that they'll scatter his ashes on the carpets."

"Someone ought to knock that place down, with him inside, dead or otherwise."

"Then we'd have to go poking around in dark corners for half the ex-cons in the state anytime we needed to talk to them—us, the police, parole officers, social workers, bail bondsmen, lawyers. Think of all the time that would waste. At least with the Braycott in business, we know where to find them."

"Probably should have been the first place we went looking for whoever stole the child's things," said Angel from the back seat.

"Yeah," said Louis, "like hiding corpses in a cemetery."

"Are you sure those names didn't mean anything to either of you?" I said.

They both shook their heads.

"Scavengers," said Louis. "Pirato had that much right. We start keeping track of their kind, we'll have no room left in our heads for anything e. So what are you thinking?"

"We take them at the Braycott," I said. "No point in letting them run around loose if we can trap them instead."

"You figure them for reasonable men?"

"I figure them for pragmatists: unpleasant, but practical. The fifty thousand isn't in their hands yet. If it was, it would be enough to make them fight. With luck, we can convince them to walk away while they still can."

"We've never had much luck like that before," said Angel, which was true, if unhelpful.

"There's always a first time," I said, "even for us."

"Do you trust Luca Z not to try to warn them?" asked Louis.

"No, but I trust Pirato not to let Luca out of his sight until we resolve this."

"I doubt Pirato is going to be returning to Providence anytime soon," said Louis. "He probably already knew Dante Vero was weak, but now he also knows that Luca Z's judgment can't be relied on. I'd say that the Office's succession issues in the Northeast remain unresolved."

"Thankfully, they're not our problem."

"They might be, if Luca Z finds a way to wriggle out from under Pirato's heel and assert himself. The way you run, you'll cross his path again, and he's one to hold grudges."

I didn't reply. It was a worry for another day.

"What do you think Pirato meant by that comment about the Argent building?" I said.

"No idea. Reggio may be able to enlighten you."

"Could be I'm not concerned enough to ask."

"That might be for the best," said Louis. "There was definitely a cold undertow to Pirato's message. But then, that old man is pure ice."

XL

I n Portsmouth, Adio Pirato walked in step with Dante Vero, the others behind and ahead of them. Luca Z was to the fore, walking with Anthony, while Mark took up the rear.

"If you have something to say," said Pirato, "now is the time."

"It was mishandled," said Vero.

"With Parker?"

"No, before, with the Sawyer woman. By us. By me. I apologize."

"You're too hard on yourself. We put you in a difficult position, one you didn't ask for and didn't want. The greater error was ours, compounded by the poor watchdog we placed with you."

They saw Luca Z peer back at them over his shoulder. Pirato had asked him to give them some privacy, and now he was desperate to know what they might be talking about, because he was convinced—rightly, as it turned out—that it involved him. Luca Z had also been ordered by Pirato to hand over his cell phone. The pause before he consented had been one of the longest of Dante Vero's life.

"He may learn," said Vero, although his tone held no particular conviction.

"Some do, some don't." Pirato sounded untroubled either way. "And you, Dante, you've been a good captain. This difficulty up in :tland apart, you've kept the ship steady, but it's time for you to take a step back—with a token of recognition for your efforts, of course."

"That's not necessary," said Vero. It was what was supposed to be said, like politely demurring at a compliment, but in his case it was sincerely meant. To be able at last to jettison the encumbrance of leadership would be sufficient reward.

"Nevertheless," said Pirato.

"And who will take my place?"

"For the time being, that duty will fall to me. I don't mind leaving Providence behind." Pirato briefly reverted to Italian to speak of his dead wife. "*Mia moglie, che riposi in pace, non c'è più ora.* But as you know, I have a daughter living up here. I like her husband, and I love my grandchildren. I can find somewhere near them, but not too near. One does not wish to impose."

Vero knew that all this had probably been under discussion for weeks. What Pirato had seen and heard at the Hitch Knot only confirmed for him the wisdom of the final decision. Few would object, and then—if they were wise—solely in the privacy of their own hearts. Even Luca Z would know better than to kick at the installation of Pirato.

"Do you ever think about dying, Dante?" asked Pirato.

Vero was thrown by the sudden change of subject. When a man like Adio Pirato asked one about dying, it was usually wise to listen, just in case the question might have an imminent, personal relevance.

"Some days," said Vero.

"I think about it every day, more and more. I imagine I will continue to think about it until, at last, I have no thoughts at all."

"Do you fear it?"

"I fear the manner of it. Dying, I expect, will be hard—although, *se Dio vuole*, not for long."

"And what brought this on, Adio?"

"I think it was meeting Parker," said Pirato. "It's rare that a man lives up to his billing, but I feel he did. You don't agree?"

"It may be that I was not watching him as closely as you were."

Pirato tapped the index finger of his right hand against his cheek-bone.

"It was in the eyes," he said. "You know, it was once posited that the eyes of the dead retained an image of their final sight, so that a murderer might be identified by an examination of the victim's retina. I have a different theory: that the eyes of the living, if forced to look too much on death, become altered by it."

"Like undertakers?"

Pirato laughed.

"Or certain men of our acquaintance," he said. "But that's different. That's staring at the faces of strangers, or the unloved. This Parker, he was forced to look on his dead wife and child. What he saw is imprinted on him still. It has made him what he is."

"And what is that?"

"I'm not sure," said Pirato. "I know only that it is nothing I would wish to be, and I would not care to share his dreams."

XLI

V eale stood at the basement door. The hallway was scattered with the detritus of an emergency: discarded wrappings, a near-empty roll of adhesive bandage, the plastic protective cover from a syringe. He had no idea why such materials should have been required if the old woman was already dead. Possibly, he thought, the medics had tried to resuscitate her. If so, they should have saved their energy.

The door was locked, but locks had never been a deterrent to him, and a couple of hard kicks dealt with the obstacle. The basement smelled musty, but beneath it hung a harsh medicinal odor. Glass crunched under his feet as he entered, and he saw that a broken mirror and a cracked framed print of a lighthouse lay against the wall to his left. He supposed the damage was caused by the medics as they tried to get to the woman. The light from the hallway didn't extend much farther than a couple of feet. When he tried the switch by the door, nothing happened. He took out his phone and used its flashlight instead. He'd read how users could be tracked through their cell phones, but the only person who had his number was Pantuff. Veale had seen no reason to share it with anyone else. Anyway, even had he wanted to disseminate it more widely, he would have been reduced to writing it on a bathroom wall, because he spoke to no one but Pantuff, if it could be helped. He also left the business side of the operation to his partner, who was more sociable, or less particular, depending on one's perspective.

Veale shone the flashlight across the basement. It was filled with used furniture, most of it dull, devoid of vivid color. An area had been cleared close to an alcove at the rear, presumably where the old woman had been found. Veale had forgotten to ask Wadlin her name, but it was of no consequence, since it wasn't as though he was going to be invited to deliver her eulogy. He walked to where she had died, picking his way over a lamp, an umbrella stand, and a busted chair along the way. Before him lay the alcove, like the entrance to a cave. He pointed the beam at it, but the light failed to penetrate its depths. The murk swallowed it up, so that all he could see were shadows fading to black.

But amid those shadows, something moved. He heard it, and felt in turn its interest in him. It was regarding him, but not with pleasure, because he had sinned against it, against its mother. Its hostility caused his skin to prickle, and the whispering that had been troubling him for days suddenly ceased entirely, for he was now in the company of the one who had been calling to him, the dead child. In that instant, in the quiet and dark, Veale understood that destroying the relics would not put an end to it, because it was not for him to dismiss it from this world. If he tried, it would find a way to punish him. It was both beyond and within him. It had wormed its way into his consciousness. He could not force it to leave. It would have to depart of its own volition, and it did not wish to, not yet.

It, not *she*. This, too, he comprehended: he would no longer vacillate between the two. The presence in the alcove had sloughed gender and name, and what was left was a sexless amalgam of love, grief, and fury, at once both an autonomous being and the construct of another. All Veale's conceptions of existence, the structures and connections both received and self-created, fell away; he shed them like scales, leaving his essence exposed and acutely vulnerable. He foresaw how it might feel to die here, in this cold place, at the hands of something that was once a child. For the first time since his youth, Veale was frightened, both of the pain that was imminent and what might come after.

Now it was approaching, cleaving the gloom. He could perceive the shape of it, its paleness against the black. The child had been buried entirely in white, even down to its stockings, but its feet had worn through them, and bare toes poked from the tatters. Its hands were black with dirt and dust, but still he could not make out its face. It remained blurred, chimerical, leaving only the impression of eyes and a mouth, like holes cut in gray fabric. Onward it came, until it stood before him in a space created by mortality. Slowly Veale directed the light from the phone toward the floor, for he had seen enough. The child was obscured once again, only its silhouette persisting, as of an image briefly glimpsed against the sun.

And then Veale felt it brush by him, its fingers barely touching his. They were dry and cool, but not unpleasantly so. When he turned, it was already gone from the room, but he saw that it was waiting for him to follow, the hallway light flickering in its presence. He knew what it wanted. He thought that he had always known, ever since he had woken to the sound of its footsteps dancing outside his room, ever since it had chosen to reach out to him and not to Pantuff. He had tried to ignore it, but like all children, it would not be ignored.

Veale raised the phone and used the glare to help him navigate his way back to the door. He did not want to injure himself, not now. If he were to trip and fall, the child would have no patience with him. It would return, he knew, the door closing behind it, and he would spend his final moments alone with it.

But he made it to the hallway without incident, and heard the child already ascending.

Veale followed the sound.

CHAPTER

XLII

Donnie Packard was staying close to Melissa Thombs, following her around like a dog that had nipped its owner and now sought to make amends for its behavior. He arrived with a bucket and cloth as she was mopping the bathroom floor, and set about cleaning the toilet, a task that she could never recall his having undertaken before. After a couple of hours they had the place resembling something like a home again. Donnie opened beers for both of them, and ordered her to take a seat at the kitchen counter while he prepared his once-in-a-blue-moon specialty, spaghetti with meatballs, which even Melissa had to admit he did well. He found a Grover Washington playlist on Spotify, and soon he was humming to himself while he chopped onions and carrots, crushed tomatoes heating in a saucepan beside him. The knife was very sharp, and he was making fast work of the vegetables. The onions weren't bringing him to tears, but then Melissa had never witnessed him cry, not once, and she'd been with him when he'd buried friends.

It was only as he was boiling the spaghetti that she realized why he was acting this way. It wasn't atonement, but ongoing observation. He was trying to read her, to guess her intentions. He wanted to keep her near because that little alarm bell in his paranoid mind had been set off, and it wasn't about to stop anytime soon. In his way, he was a marvel, possessing an undeniable emotional acuity, except tuned only to the negative, and entirely devoid of empathy. Its sole purpose was self-preservation.

And sex would follow; this, too, she knew. He would take her, and keep her there beside him afterward. She could try to refuse him, which rarely worked, depending on how intent he was. Claiming it was her time of the month wouldn't stop him, because he kept track of her cycle. If she went to bed with him, she'd have no hope of keeping the cell phone to hand. Even if she found a way, she'd never be able to get away from him once the signal to move came through. Donnie slept lightly, and would wake to the beating of a moth's wings.

The smell of cooking, the heat of the kitchen, the taste of the beer in her mouth, all instantly became oppressive to her. There was dampness on her brow, her back, and under her arms. She burped, and the regurgitated alcohol flooded her mouth, tainted by an astringency that caused her to retch.

"I'm sorry," she said.

Donnie glanced at her.

"For what?" he said.

But already she was throwing up on the kitchen floor.

CHAPTER
XLIII

We were passing Kennebunk Service Plaza when the tracker app on my phone indicated that Sarah Abelli was receiving another call from an unknown number. It came through via Bluetooth on the car radio: the same voice as before, with that poisoned song of the South to it.

"Do you have our money?"

Pantuff, I thought: the torturer of women, the one whom Luca Z had described as the talker.

"Yes," said Abelli, "I have it. Do you have what you stole from me?"

"I'm going to send you some images. They'll be time- and date-stamped, to put your mind at rest."

"It may take more than that, but it's a start."

Pantuff laughed.

"You have spirit," he said, "I'll give you that. It's a shame we were stopped from getting more intimate with each other back in Boston. Who knows, you might even have enjoyed it."

"I doubt that."

"Well, I'd have enjoyed it, and fifty percent is better than nothing. You're responsible for your own pleasure. I think I read that in one of those magazines they leave in dentists' waiting rooms. If it's true, it gets me off the hook—and if it isn't, I wasn't so worried to begin with. But hear this, missy: If you try to fuck us over, not only will you never see your trinkets again, but down the line, months or even years from now, I'll come find you, and I'll rape you before I start cutting you. Do you hear me?"

"I hear you."

"In two hours I want you to be sitting in your car with the motor running. You put the money in a garbage bag, tie a knot in it, then find a duffel bag big enough to take it, one that zips up tight. You have something like that at home?"

"I do."

"Good. Leave it on the passenger seat beside you, and keep the door unlocked. Before you know it, our business will be concluded."

He hung up. Seconds later, three photographs were sent to her phone, mirrored on the app. Louis flicked through them. One was a picture of a vintage cookie tin, while the second displayed its contents. The third showed an erect penis, held in a hand that was also clutching a photograph of Sarah Abelli's dead child.

———

I SPOKE TO HER as we reached the Portland city limits.

"I was wondering when you'd call," she said. "I assume you heard that last conversation?"

"And I saw the pictures."

"They're animals."

"Barely. Is Tony still with you?"

"Yes. I've been teaching him to play chess."

Beside me, Louis's brow actually furrowed in shock, like a primatologist who has just discovered the text of *Hamlet* on a monkey's typewriter.

"I hope you're letting him win occasionally," I said. "He can be a sore loser."

"Are you trying to lighten the mood, Mr. Parker?"

"It would be difficult to make it any darker."

"Well, the effort is appreciated, but you can stop now. I want to kill these men. I loathe them for what they've done, and for what they want to do."

"Which is?"

"To leave me with nothing."

"We're not going to let that happen."

"I want to believe you, but it may be too late. By the time I get in my car, only memories will be left of my daughter."

She was a strong woman, but the days had taken their toll. At some point a person required more than general reassurance.

"It may not come to that," I said. "We know who they are, and we have an idea of where they're staying. We're on our way there now."

"Okay," she said, and I heard her voice catch.

I killed the call. Louis was looking again at the photos sent to her phone, in particular the last of them.

"We may have to inflict damage," he said.

I took the exit for Congress.

"Even if we don't have to," I said, "we will anyway."

XLIV

B obby Wadlin, fortified with so much Rescue Remedy that he believed he might already be half blossom, had made himself a cup of coffee and returned to the lobby. The TV was off because he couldn't focus on a western for the present, an indication of how disturbed he remained. He'd dug out a CD of thirties and forties torch songs, which suited the ambience and his mood, and set it playing softly in the background. He'd positioned his chair so that it faced not the door, but the hallway to his left, and the stairwell leading down to the basement. He didn't want to keep his back to it. It struck him as unwise. Bobby hoped the child wasn't planning on taking up permanent residence down there. He didn't think his nerves or his sanity could take it.

The Braycott's front door opened and three men entered. Two of them hung back while the third approached the desk. It had, without fear of contradiction, been a lousy day for Bobby. Had he been asked, he could have come up with few misfortunes, short of serious illness or his own demise, guaranteed to make it much worse, but among them would have been a visit from the man who was standing before him. Bobby closed his eyes.

"Lord," he said, "kill me now."

CHAPTER

XLV

I waited until Bobby Wadlin reopened his eyes before I began speaking. He looked disappointed to discover that I was still there.

"Don't think I'm not tempted," I said, "but I wouldn't want to leave a mess."

"Why? It's never stopped you before."

Wadlin stood and pointed past me to where Angel and Louis were watching him with nothing approaching interest.

"And I've heard all about those two as well," he said. "I don't want their kind in my place."

"That's prejudice," said Angel.

"So sue me."

"That would be the less appealing option."

Angel unbuttoned his jacket, revealing the butt of a pistol. Louis advanced and tapped the plexiglass with a knuckle.

"Nope," he said to Angel, "not bulletproof."

Wadlin sat down again. They might have been joking, but they might not. Even I didn't know for certain.

"What do you want?" he said.

"We're looking for two men. We think they might be staying here."

"You know I can't give out that kind of—"

Louis knocked again, this time with the muzzle of his gun.

"What are their names?" said Wadlin.

"Lyle Pantuff and Gilman Veale."

Wadlin gave every impression of wanting to crawl under his desk.

"It would have to be them," he said.

"Where are they?"

"You just missed one of them: the younger one, Veale. He left about ten minutes ago. I saw him drive off."

"What kind of car?"

"A blue Chrysler."

"And Pantuff is still up there?"

"Far as I know. What did they do?"

"They stole."

"That hardly makes them unique," said Wadlin. "Half the people staying here are thieves, and I don't even want to know what the rest are guilty of."

"Disregard for hygiene, at the very least," I said. "What room?"

"Twenty-nine. Fourth floor. To the left, end of the hall."

"Get the key."

Wadlin located the key recently surrendered by Gilman Veale and handed it over.

"You're coming with us," I said.

"I'm not helping you bust in there."

"You're certainly not staying down here."

"I won't warn him that you're coming."

"You say, but I'm not about to bet a bullet on it."

Already Angel was locking the main door. He added the sign indicating that the front desk was going to be unattended for a while.

"You know you spelled 'patience' wrong?" he said.

Wadlin glared at him.

"All the signs here are spelled wrong," I told Angel. "It's part of the singular character of the institution."

"Maybe you're dyslexic," said Angel to Wadlin.

"I'm not dyslexic," said Wadlin, as he emerged from behind the desk. "I just don't give a shit."

XLVI

Melissa Thombs was in the bedroom she shared with Donnie Packard, lying on her side with the comforter tucked under her chin and her stomach still churning. Donnie, unfortunately, was with her. She'd had just enough time to hide the new cell phone under the mattress before he arrived. In the interim, he'd thrown away all the half-prepared food in a fit of pique, and was now sitting on a beanbag, supplementing his diet with a bag of Munchos and a can of Old Style. For a moment Melissa had believed he might be concerned about her, but that passed as soon as she saw the manner in which he continued to scrutinize her, as though daring her to proceed with whatever plan she and her mother had cooked up between them.

She turned her back on him, but could see his reflection in the window. He hadn't tried to force himself on her, which was something. Melissa had deliberately neglected to wash her mouth out after puking, and neither had she changed her T-shirt. It would be enough to keep Donnie at bay. He might have tolerated, even contributed disproportionately to, a state of squalor in the house, but he liked her to be fresh for him.

Melissa let her right hand hang over the edge of the bed, one finger tucked beneath the mattress to touch the phone. It was muted, but she'd feel it vibrate if a message came through. What then, though? Because it hadn't escaped her attention that Donnie had positioned the beanbag near the bedroom door.

"I love you," he said.

She didn't turn around, didn't even reply.

"Did you hear me?" he said.

He wasn't going to let it go unacknowledged.

"Yeah, I heard you."

"You're supposed to say you love me too."

"I just threw up, Donnie. Right now, all I feel like doing is dying."

She regretted the last word as soon as it was out of her mouth.

"I don't want you to do anything but say it," Donnie persisted. "Say you love me."

She detected a new note to his voice, distant and discordant, like the trumpet blast of an approaching horde that would crush her as it passed.

"I love you, Donnie," she said.

She listened to his breathing. It sounded labored, the inhalations and exhalations of a man struggling to restrain himself from committing an act both shameful yet devoutly desired, and Melissa knew she was as close to being killed by him as she had ever been.

But Donnie did not move, and soon she heard the crunch of a potato chip in his mouth.

"I'll always be here," he said. "I won't leave your side, not ever."

She stroked the cell phone with a fingertip.

"Not even," he added, "in death."

XLVII

I took the stairs to the third floor, Bobby Wadlin behind me, Angel and Louis at his back, just in case Wadlin's nerve failed and he tried to make a break for safety. The Braycott had an old cage elevator that ran up and down the center of the main stairwell, which wound around it. If anyone decided to summon the elevator, we'd know, but it remained unused. The hallway was empty when we reached it, but we could hear some Neil Diamond coming from one of the rooms.

"Must be Pantuff," whispered Wadlin. "There's no one else staying down that end."

He was trying not to look at the guns in our hands.

"Listen to me," I said. "You're going to knock on the door and identify yourself. When Pantuff answers, you say that you don't want to alarm him, but a police officer just came by to ask about a blue Chrysler that was seen in the parking lot earlier, and this is something that ought not to be talked about in the open."

It wasn't the greatest of pretexts, but the key wouldn't be much use to us if Pantuff had set the security bolt, and it was better than trying to kick in one of the Braycott's heavy doors while he prepared to take a shot at us.

"What if he won't open up?" said Wadlin.

"Let's hope it doesn't come to that," I said, with feeling. "And try to keep your voice from shaking."

We followed Wadlin down the hall, the old runner muffling our footsteps. A wrinkled DO NOT DISTURB sign had been placed on the handle outside room 29. Neil Diamond stopped playing, followed by a jingle for Pure Oldies 105.5 and the first bars of Sam Cooke's "You Send Me." Louis and Angel took up position to the left of the door, far enough away to stay out of the limited range of the peephole. I went to the right, where the recessed entrance to a storage closet provided some concealment. When we were ready, I nodded to Wadlin. He steeled himself, and knocked.

"Mr. Pantuff?" he said. "It's Mr. Wadlin, the hotel manager."

We waited, but nobody answered. I signaled to Wadlin to try again. He knocked harder this time.

"Mr. Pantuff? I'm sorry to bother you, but it's important."

Still nothing. I moved forward, took the key from Wadlin, and motioned him to stand back. As Angel and Louis advanced, I used the wall for cover while inserting the key into the lock as quietly as I could with my left hand, then turned the handle. The door opened easily. No bolt or chain was in place. I nodded at Wadlin.

"Mr. Pantuff," he said, "are you okay?"

But I already knew that he wasn't. A certain smell comes with violent death: blood, and worse. I was aware of it now. I entered the room but didn't let my guard down. Just because there's a dead body doesn't mean that the person responsible isn't keeping the corpse company. I checked and cleared the bathroom before risking a glance into the bedroom itself. The remains of a man lay on the nearer of the two beds. He was wearing a T-shirt, underwear, and socks with a hole in one heel. His throat had been cut, probably while he was facing the wall, judging by the spatter. On the floor between the beds sat a Sunshine Toy Cookie tin with its lid removed. From what I could see, the contents were still in place: a collection of remembrances of the short life of a child.

Louis appeared beside me.

"Pantuff?"

"That would be my guess."

"Looks like the partnership has been dissolved," said Louis.

"Tell Wadlin to call the police," I said, "but keep him out of here. Have Angel escort him downstairs. Just get a description of Pantuff from him first, just to be sure."

Louis left me. I could hear Wadlin objecting to being hustled away, but I didn't want him to see what was in the room: not so much the body, but the cookie tin and what it contained. I pulled a pair of plastic gloves from my pocket. I'd promised Pirato I'd do my utmost to keep the Office's name out of this, and it would be in my best interests to hold to my word, but I was also worried about Sarah Abelli. If the tin was taken as evidence, she'd have to come forward to claim it. Questions would be asked, and someone in the Portland PD would connect her to her late husband. Her name would find its way to the media, and her life in Maine would be over. I was about to interfere with a crime scene, but it wasn't going to make much difference to the outcome.

Louis returned.

"It's Pantuff all right," he said.

If Veale had killed his partner, I wondered why he hadn't taken the cookie tin with him. Conceivably he felt he couldn't proceed with the plan alone, but it wouldn't have been beyond him to recruit some help if required, even at short notice. Then again, he had just slit a man's throat, so it might have been wise to put some distance between himself and the body, but that still didn't explain why he had to leave the tin as well. The mother was willing to pay to have her daughter's relics returned, and that situation wasn't likely to change, so why not see how events played out?

I put the lid on the tin and handed it to Louis.

"What if they catch Veale, and he mentions it?" he said.

"Mentions what?"

"You know, I think I've already started to forget."

"Make it disappear, please."

And he did.

XLVIII

I called Sarah Abelli from the hallway while I waited for the police to arrive.

"I have your possessions," I said.

It took her a few seconds to reply.

"Thank you. And the men who took them?"

"One of them, Lyle Pantuff, is dead. His partner, Gilman Veale, is in the wind. There was a falling-out between thieves. I'm going to have to insist that Tony and his brother stay close by you for the time being, until Veale is located."

"Will I have to talk to the police?"

"Not unless you want to."

"But—"

"For a number of reasons, I'd prefer that they didn't know about you or the nature of what was stolen. For now there is no cookie tin, and I was looking for these men in connection with an ongoing larceny investigation. The police might push me on it, but I doubt they'll push too hard. Should they decide to, we may have to muddy the waters. I'll try to claim client privilege on behalf of my lawyer, and he'll backdate a contract and have you sign it, but that would be a last resort. If, or when, they catch up with Veale, I'd be surprised if he opens his mouth.

But if you have a problem with this, I can return that tin to the room before the police get here. There's still time."

"No," she said, "I'd like to be kept out of it, and I have no difficulty in signing anything that might help avoid police trouble for you—or me."

I told her I'd do my best to get the tin back to her before the night was out, but I had one more client to take care of, so it might have to wait until morning.

"If you can, I'd like to have it returned as soon as possible," she said. "It doesn't matter how late you call, I'll wait up."

But I didn't think that would be necessary. I said goodbye and called Paulie Fulci as the first emergency lights bathed the parking lot below. I gave him the short version of what had occurred, and asked him to get in touch with Louis about retrieving the tin and getting it back to Sarah. I knew she wouldn't have any peace until it was safely in her hands.

Two uniformed officers emerged from the stairwell. I had just enough time to make one last call, this time to Moxie, before the questions commenced.

XLIX

As it happened, the interviews that followed proved reasonably straightforward. Bobby Wadlin had seen Gilman Veale leave before we arrived, and was with us when the body of Lyle Pantuff was discovered. Both men had records, neither ever having been in line for a good citizenship award, and Wadlin was able to provide the license plate number of the blue Chrysler in which Veale had driven away. It was found dumped by the Maine Mall a few hours later, but there were no reports of any other vehicles being stolen in the vicinity at about that time, which meant that Veale might have had another car waiting, or had arranged to be picked up. Whatever his means of escape, he was probably gone from the state by the time the Chrysler was discovered. Angel, Louis, and I all gave statements to the police—mine more detailed than theirs, since they claimed to have been asked to come along only as backup, which was largely the truth—and we were then free to go. I was pressed to name my client, but only half-heartedly. I referred the inquiry to Moxie.

Sharon Macy called as we drove toward Yarmouth, and the house occupied by Donnie Packard and Melissa Thombs. By then, it was closing on midnight, and I felt as though I hadn't slept in days.

"So was what happened tonight at the Braycott the other thing I didn't want to know about?" said Macy.

"It was."

"Thank God I wasn't on duty. This thing of ours, it's going to cause complications as it continues, assuming it does."

Louis glanced at me from the passenger seat. He was definitely smirking, but from the back seat I heard actual laughter.

"Hey, are you alone?" said Macy.

"Not quite."

"Damn it. Call me back when you are. Jesus."

She hung up.

"Ha," said Angel. "You got in trouble with your girlfriend."

———

THE DRAPES WERE DRAWN on the windows of the single-story Packard house as we drove by, but I could see lights burning. We parked just out of sight, and I texted Melissa Thombs to let her know that we were waiting for her. Angel took the wheel while Louis and I moved to the sidewalk, so we could be ready should Melissa emerge with Donnie Packard close on her heels. I was hoping she'd just walk out the front door while he dozed on unawares; if she did, I'd make a donation to charity in the name of St. Jude. We gave her five minutes, but she didn't appear, which meant we were going to have to get her out the hard way.

"Well?" said Louis.

I didn't want to knock on the door and confront Donnie, not at this late hour, because he wouldn't answer it without a weapon close at hand. Our best bet would be to distract him in order to give Melissa time to get to the door. We had already watched a red fox trot by the side of the house, a dead rodent in its mouth. The animal hadn't triggered any motion-activated lights.

"You think you can go around the back and throw a stone through one of the windows?" I said.

"You mean without getting shot?"

"Preferably, although it's your call."

"Yeah, I can break a window."

Louis moved into the yard, and I followed. We were about halfway to the house when the front door opened. Melissa Thombs stood framed against the light. She was wearing a long-sleeved T-shirt and gray sweatpants. Even from a distance, I could see she was covered in blood.

L

L ouis and I stood before Melissa, both of us already armed.

"Are you hurt?" I said.

She shook her head, and stood aside to let us enter. The door opened straight into the living room. Behind it was a small kitchen, accessed through an alcove, with a serving hatch on one side that doubled as a dining counter. Donnie Packard was sprawled on his back in the opening, dressed only in his underwear. Like Melissa, he had a lot of blood on him, but it was all his own, and most of it had come from the wound in his chest. The carving knife responsible lay close by.

"He found the phone," said Melissa. "He wasn't going to let me leave. Not tonight, not ever."

I looked at her. She put her right thumb in her mouth and began sucking on it like a child. She seemed to have forgotten her hand was bloody; that, or she no longer cared.

Louis closed the front door, but I barely registered the sound. I was thinking of what lay ahead for Melissa. If you believe the law treats men and women equally, you're deluded, willfully or otherwise, because the same gender injustices apply there as elsewhere. Most courts fail to take a history of abuse into account when sentencing women for violent crimes against their abuser. Even when the defense produces an expert witness, the prosecution can seek to invalidate the testimony by arguing that the woman failed to leave the relationship when she had the chance, and that's assuming the judge permits the evidence of historic abuse to be presented to a jury to begin with. On average, women lose self-defense cases 25 percent more frequently than men, and justifiable homicide cases 10 percent more often. The system is inherently misogynistic, tainted by a male fear of the rage of women that dates back to Clytemnestra, Judith, and Medea. Now Melissa Thombs was going to jail, perhaps for decades, all because we had been a few minutes too late to help her.

"Where does Donnie keep his gun?" I asked.

"What?" said Melissa. Her eyes were dull with shock.

"His gun. Where is it?"

"In his bedside table, the one on the left. It has a false back. Tap it hard enough and it comes away."

I pulled back on the plastic gloves I'd used earlier to search the room at the Braycott. I went to the table, pulled it from the wall, and struck the back. As Melissa had said, it detached. In the revealed space sat a battered Hi-Point with a taped grip. I checked the magazine. It was full, but the chamber was empty. I racked the slide, chambered a round, and brought the gun to the living room.

"Was Donnie right- or left-handed?" I said.

Melissa took her thumb from her mouth. "Right-handed."

"Have you ever handled this gun?"

She shook her head.

"You're sure?"

"Yes."

I touched the gun firmly to the dead man's fingers, making sure I got an index print full on the trigger, then placed the weapon on the floor by his right hand, but away from the bloodstain.

"I don't understand," she said, but I thought she might be starting to.

"You killed an unarmed man, Melissa. It doesn't matter what he'd done to you in the past, or what you claim he was going to do to you in the future. By the time you get out of prison, you'll be a middle-aged woman if you're lucky, and an old one if you're not. But that's one version of the story."

I stared down at my second corpse of the evening.

"So why," I said, "don't you tell me another?"

———

I CALLED MOXIE CASTIN for the second time that evening and informed him that we had arrived at the Packard house to find Melissa Thombs had stabbed her partner in self-defense. A gun—an illegally held weapon, given Donnie Packard's domestic violence conviction—was lying by the body. Moxie said he'd be right over, and warned us to hold off on calling the police until he got there. But I didn't need to be told because I wasn't a fool, or not that kind of fool anyway.

Louis went outside to wait with Angel. I stayed with Melissa. She sat with her back to the body, but I sat facing it. Call it some version of penance. What should you do when every choice you're offered is the wrong one, when every compromise you have to make will cost another piece of your soul? Donnie didn't deserve to die, but neither did Melissa deserve to go to prison for decades because of what she'd done—not if she was telling the truth about what had happened, although that should have been for a court to decide. Yet if the courts can't be trusted, what then? If the system is fractured and prejudiced, how can justice have any meaning?

The doorbell rang. I answered it. Moxie stood on the doorstep.

"Okay," he said, "you can make the call now."

LI

Melissa Thombs was taken to Yarmouth PD headquarters and was set to spend most of the night there, but she would have Moxie by her side. The gun was the clincher, he said, as I walked him to his car so he could follow Melissa to Middle Street. No prosecutor would want to stake their reputation on this case, not with an unlicensed weapon in the possession of a domestic abuser. It meant that Donnie Packard's history of violence would have to be acknowledged, and juries were less likely to convict if presented with that kind of evidence.

"Death caused 'while under the influence of extreme anger or extreme fear brought about by adequate provocation,'" he said, quoting the Maine Criminal Code, "is an affirmative defense to a prosecution."

"Meaning?"

"She won't do time," said Moxie, "not as long as her story stands up. And it will, won't it?"

He attended me closely.

"Yes," I said, "it will."

———

IT WAS CLOSE TO 3 a.m. by the time I got home. I'd missed four calls from Sharon Macy, the last only moments before I'd left the Packard house. I called her back as I was taking off my shoes.

"That's a hell of a night you've had," she said. "Two bodies across two cases is a lot, even for you."

"If you're going to give me a chewing out," I said, "can it wait until morning?"

She relented.

"I suppose so," she said. "Are you okay?"

"No," I said, because I really wasn't.

"Do you want some company?"

"I think I just need to sleep. Tomorrow, though, if the offer still holds."

"It should be good for twenty-four hours—the promise of a lecture, too. Good night."

I turned off the lights and went to my room, but I didn't sleep, not for hours. I tried to catch up with the news on my laptop, but all the talk was of viruses and death, and after a time I could take no more of it. Instead I sat at my window and stared out at the marshes. Doing wrong, even in the name of a greater good, had stolen my peace. I'd done it too often. It was becoming habitual. I feared that it would cost me in the end.

At last I hid my face from the dark, and waited for the dawn.

3

The starlings wandered
Till three hawks took them
And now my agents
Have caught the cripple.

—Les Murray, "Property"

LII

S arah Abelli sat on the floor by her bedroom window, the vintage cookie tin by her side, its contents spread around her. She was weeping, because she was about to say goodbye.

Behind her, the child danced, but it made barely a sound and cast no shadow. Her grief had willed it into being, summoning it from another place, but what had come to her was no longer entirely her daughter. It was a vestige, and an adumbral one. Sarah would not have called it malevolent, because that was not a word she was capable of applying to her child, but it had lost its grace. What remained was a creature of unbridled will.

But now she was about to send it back, and afterward she would mourn her loss in a different fashion.

"I have to let you go," she said to the child.

The child ceased its capering. She felt it draw close. She looked to the window and it was there, its reflected face all bedimmed.

"When those men had you," Sarah continued, "I thought I would die. I can't go through that again. If the other one were to return, if he were to succeed again, I don't know what I would do. I kept you here out of selfishness, because I couldn't bear to be without you, but I will have to find a way, for both our sakes. I love you very much, and I will see you again very, very soon."

Her body contorted with the pain of parting. She wondered how she could even begin to live with such emptiness.

"But before you go," she said, "there's something you must do."

And she spoke the final words.

In the glass, the child laid its hand upon her, and Sarah felt a coldness at her shoulder.

And then it was gone.

CHAPTER

LIII

Gilman Veale had driven north, pausing only to refill the tank of the Civic when the warning light came on. His picture, he knew, was already being circulated. Come daylight he would have to be off the road and in a place of safety. He and Pantuff had split non-perishable food and other supplies—medicines, a pair of little camping stoves, sleeping bags, spare clothing from Goodwill—between the trunks of the Civic and the Chrysler, with the option of consolidating again later if they were forced to abandon one car or the other. Veale knew the Maine woods some, because he'd sought refuge there in the past—not from the law, just from other folk: Stockholm, New Sweden, Long Lake, Cross Lake, those were the locales with which he was familiar. If he went deep enough, he could find an abandoned trailer or an old camp and bury himself until some of the fuss died down. The Civic would have to be disposed of; he didn't trust the seller to remain quiet once it emerged that the car had been sold to a murderer. Worse came to worst, he'd make a run for the Canadian border; it was porous, and he could cross on foot. He still had some contacts in Montréal and Québec, but Canada had no shortage of places in which a man could curl up and pupate before emerging again in a different guise.

Veale continued along Route 1, through Littleton, Monticello, Bridgewater, and Presque Isle. Just before Caribou, he headed west, taking roads barely mapped until the sun began to touch the trees. Near Carson, he found what he was looking for: a cottage with boarded-up windows and a hole in its roof, on land with a FOR LEASE sign so old it might as well have been written in Sanskrit. He parked the car out of sight of the road, and broke into the house through a back window. It smelled of decay, but a couple of the rooms were dry and habitable. He unrolled the sleeping bag, made a pillow from some old sweaters, and slept until night came around again.

———

VEALE WOKE TO THE sound of movement. It was too big for a rodent, and too rhythmic: more like skipping, or dancing. The child had come.

"I did what you asked," he said.

The child had been with him when he'd cut Pantuff's throat, standing at the foot of the bed while Veale used the blade. He'd made it quick because Pantuff had never done anything to irk him beyond choosing to target the wrong woman. Even that wasn't his fault, because how was Pantuff to know that a cookie tin might contain a soul? In return for killing Pantuff, Veale had hoped the child might leave him in peace. He had no intention of bothering Nate Sawyer's widow again, or didn't think so. Then again, he had to admit he was a changeable man.

Now the child was before him. He had not seen it move. One second it was in the corner, the next so near that he could glimpse the holes where its eyes should have been, and smell the cemetery dirt on it. Softly it closed a hand on his and led him from the room. He walked with it to the woodshed at the back of the property, and there it showed him the length of rope. The rope was tinged with green, but not yet rotten. It would take his weight.

As he formed the noose, Veale recalled words spoken to him as a much younger man: "Son, the only thing that's gonna beat you to the cemetery is the headlights on the hearse." He tried and failed to recall the speaker's name. He could remember the face, lined and world-weary, but that was all. Some lawman, now with the dead. Veale had lived longer than many might have expected, although like most men he had hoped to live longer still.

He retrieved a chair from what had once been a kitchen and positioned it beneath a tree. He tested a branch, found it satisfactory, and tied the rope. As he placed the noose around his neck, the child circled. He thought he could hear it singing. Its form was clearer to him now, less chimerical as his state drew nearer to its own, and he could see the girl it once had been. In his final moments he thought his eyes were deceiving him, because the shade of another child appeared behind the first, this one blond where the other was dark, her face a ruin of blood. The circling ceased, and the two children stood hand in hand, the forest growing still around them as though at their bidding. He wondered what was waiting for him on the other side. He prayed it would not be them.

Gilman Veale kicked the chair and set about the inevitable business of dying.

ACKNOWLEDGMENTS

The Sisters Strange was originally conceived and written during the first COVID-19 lockdown, early in 2020. I wanted to give readers something to divert them, and the idea of offering a novella in short daily chapters that could be read easily on a phone or computer screen appealed. When I began the story I had only the title, and a vague notion that the plot might involve an old rune or symbol. The book was then written in weekly sections, with little or no revision, since the text had to be sent to four translators to be rendered into Spanish, French, Greek, and Bulgarian. Actually, working from start to finish without revision is how I usually produce a first draft, but it's one thing writing that way in private, and another exposing the draft, with all its flaws, to a reading public. With *The Sisters Strange*, I had to live with whatever decisions I made, however problematic they might become later in the story. Still, it seemed to work, and at the very least distracted readers from the pandemic on their doorstep, or even inside their own homes.

But when it came to revising *The Sisters Strange* for this book, it rapidly became clear that what might have worked, within limits, on a screen in short 600-to-800-word chunks did not translate comfortably to a printed format. I also wanted to take the opportunity to expand the story, and explore avenues denied me because of the manner of its original publication, like glimpsing an interesting trail in the rearview mirror and deciding, *What the heck, I'll turn back and take a look up there, see what I might find.* Thus it is that *The Sisters Strange* is now twice its original length, and has become a short novel rather than a novella. Nevertheless, this is an opportunity to thank all those who helped bring it to life back in 2020, especially my older son, Cameron

Ridyard, who designed the website for the story and ensured that a new chapter appeared in five different languages, five days a week, for more than two months. Sue Fletcher, Emily Bestler, Ana Estevan de Hériz, and Frédérique Polet—respectively my British, American, Spanish, and French editors—all worked on the original text, as did Eva Monteil-het, who supervised the French translation by Nadia Gabriel. My friend Stefano Bortolussi, who has translated many of my novels into Italian, looked after that version of the story; Cristina Rizopoulou, who was also familiar with my work from previous translations, took care of the Greek iteration, and Haris Nikolakakis and the nice folks at Harlenic/BELL facilitated additional publication through their website. Finally, Irina Manusheva, another longtime translator of my books, shepherded the Bulgarian version, and was supported by Prozorets, my Bulgar-ian publishers, who also made the novella available through their own social media. Particular thanks go to Liuboslava Rousseva, Aneta Pan-teleeva, Anna Georgieva, and Vanya Zvezdarova. Plaudits, too, to all the staff and publicists who helped bring the novella to the attention of readers, including Rebecca Mundy at Hodder & Stoughton; David Brown and Gena Lanzi at Atria; Delia Louzán Fariña at Tusquets; Sophie Thiebaut at Les Presses de la Cité; and Rosa Vito and Noemi Proietti at Fanucci. The appearance of *The Sisters Strange* in revised form is a welcome opportunity to acknowledge again their support for the endeavor. The information on dice came primarily from *Dice: Deception, Fate & Rotten Luck* (Quantuck Lane Press, 2003) by Ricky Jay and Rosamond Purcell.

The Furies was a different, perhaps simpler, proposition, but I want to thank Gordon Walsh for casting an eye over it prior to publication, and being willing to revisit those difficult early days of the pandemic.

At Atria/Emily Bestler Books I remain in the safe hands of my editor, Emily Bestler, assisted by Lara Jones, Gena Lanzi, David Brown, Raaga Rajagopala, and many, many more. I'm grateful to you all. Thanks also to everyone at Hodder & Stoughton and Hachette Ireland, particularly Sue Fletcher, Carolyn Mays, Swati Gamble, Rebecca Mundy, Oliver Martin, Alice Morley, Catherine Worsley, Alasdair Oliver, Jim Binchy, Breda Purdue, Elaine Egan, Siobhan Tierney, Ruth Shern, and Dominic Smith and his team. Dominick Montalto and Sarah Wright, meanwhile, have the unenviable task of trying to catch all my errors at copyedit. They do their best, but I'll own any that have crept through, with apologies.

My agent, Darley Anderson, and his staff continue to be rocks of patience, support, and good humor. Clair Lamb maintains a watchful eye on social media, as well as acting as first port of call for booksellers and readers, and provides a sharp pair of eyes when required, as does Cliona O'Neill, while Cameron keeps our website (well, his website, since he designed it) looking spruce. Finally, thanks to Jennie, Cam, and Alistair—and Megan and Alannah—for being you.

John Connolly
March 2022